Hablot Knight Browne, William Harrison Ainsworth

Ovingdean Grange

A tale of the South Downs. Vol. 1

Hablot Knight Browne, William Harrison Ainsworth

Ovingdean Grange
A tale of the South Downs. Vol. 1

ISBN/EAN: 9783337089290

Printed in Europe, USA, Canada, Australia, Japan

Cover: Foto ©Andreas Hilbeck / pixelio.de

More available books at **www.hansebooks.com**

OVINGDEAN GRANGE

A TALE OF THE SOUTH DOWNS

BY

WILLIAM HARRISON AINSWORTH

ILLUSTRATED BY HABLOT K. BROWNE

LONDON
GEORGE ROUTLEDGE & SONS, LIMITED
BROADWAY, LUDGATE HILL

INSCRIBED

TO THE

Rev. ALFRED STEAD,

RECTOR OF OVINGDEAN.

BY ONE OF HIS FLOCK.

CONTENTS.

BOOK I.

JOHN HABERGEON.

BOOK II.

INCREASE MICKLEGIFT.

BOOK VII.

CAPTAIN TATTERSALL OF THE *SWIFTSURE*

BOOK VIII.

CHARLES THE SECOND AT OVINGDEAN GRANGE

BOOK IX.

BRIGHTELMSTONE IN 1651.

ILLUSTRATIONS.

OVINGDEAN GRANGE.

BOOK I.

JOHN HABERGEON.

A VIEW FROM AN OLD BARROW ON THE SOUTH DOWNS.

Fairer spot than this cannot be found amidst the whole range of the South Downs—nor one commanding more delightful views.

Look at it and judge.

It is the rounded summit of a hill; or, to speak with greater precision, the mid-summit of a series of soft bosomy eminences, springing from a hilly ridge, that trends towards the coast, and rises and falls smoothly and gently in its course, like the waves of a slightly agitated sea. The lovely mount is covered with short elastic sward, redolent of thyme and other sweet-smelling herbs, and is crowned by an ancient bowl-shaped British barrow, on the bank of which we will seat ourselves, and look around.

How pleasing is the prospect! how fresh the air that visits us! No breeze so fine and invigorating as that of these Sussex downs; no turf so springy to the foot as their smooth greensward. A flock of larks flies past us, and a cloud of mingled rooks and starlings wheels overhead. Mark yon little T-shaped cuttings on the slope below us—those are the snares set by the shepherds for the delicious wheatear—our English ortolan. The fairies still haunt this spot, and hold their midnight revels upon it, as yon dark-green rings testify. The common folk hereabouts term the good people "Pharisees," and style those emerald circles "hag-tracks:" why, we care not to inquire. Enough for us, the fairies are not altogether gone. A smooth, soft carpet is here spread out for Oberon and Titania and their attendant elves to dance upon by moonlight; and there is no lack of mushrooms to form tables for Puck's banquets.

Own that no hills can be more beautiful than these South Downs. They may want height, boldness, grandeur, sublimity; they possess not forest, rock, torrent, or ravine; but they have gentleness, softness, and other endearing attributes. We will not attempt to delineate the slight but infinite varieties of form and aspect that distinguish one hill from its neighbour; for though a strong family likeness marks them all, each down has an individual character. Regarded in combination with each other, the high ranges form an exquisite picture.

Contemplation of such a scene soothes rather than excites, and inspires only feelings of placid enjoyment. We are called upon for no violent emotion. We are not required to admire Nature in her wildest and most savage aspect. We have a peaceful landscape before us, of a primitive character, and possessing accompaniments of pastoral life. Yonder is the shepherd, with crook and dog, watching his flock browse on the thymy slopes—the unequalled sheep of the South Downs, remember. At our feet lies a well-cultivated valley, with broad patches of turnip and mangel-wurzel on one side, and a large stubble-field on the other, where the ploughman with his yoke of patient oxen is at work. In this valley you may note a farm-shed and a sheepfold, with rows of haystacks and cornstacks at various points, evidencing the fertility of the soil. In front of us is the British Channel. A burst of sunshine illumines the tall white cliffs on the east, and gleams upon the far-off lighthouse. That pharos is on Beachy Head. On the near height overlooking the sea stands a windmill, while a solitary barn forms a landmark on that distant hill. Altogether, a charming picture.

But we have not yet fully examined it.

The beauteous hill, on the brow of which we are seated, has necessarily a valley on either side. On the right, and immediately beneath us, is a pretty little village, nestling amid a grove of trees, above whose tops you may discern the tower of a small, grey old church. With this village we trust to make you more intimately acquainted by-and-by. It is Ovingdean. On the left, and nearer the sea, you may discern another, and considerably larger village than Ovingdean, almost as picturesque as the latter, and possessing a grey, antique church at its northern extremity. This second village is Rottingdean.

Behind and around on every side, save towards the sea, are downs — downs with patches of purple heather or grey gorse clothing their sides—downs with small holts within their coombs, partially cultivated, or perfectly bare—everywhere downs.

Pleasant it is where we sit to watch the clouds chase each other across the valleys, up the hill-side, over the hill-top, then losing them for a while, behold them again on a more distant eminence, producing in their passage exquisite effects of light and shade. Meet emblem those fleeting clouds of our own quick passage to eternity.

Smiling, and sunny, and joy-inspiring are the downs now; but at times they have a graver aspect. At shuddering dawn, or at the midnight hour, they have a solemn and mysterious look, and seem, like the Sphynx, to mutter secrets of the Past. Of most other places in the land the ancient features are changed, disfigured, or wholly obliterated; but the old visage of the Sussex Downs is unaltered. It is the same as when the Celtic Britons held their funeral ceremonies on this green mount; as when the warlike Romans made their camps upon yonder neighbouring hill; as when our Saxon ancestors dwelt in those secluded valleys, and gave names to them which we still retain. What wonder that such ancient hills—ancient, but endowed with perpetual youth—should sometimes discourse of the great people they have known! What wonder when the scene is the same that the shades of the mighty departed should sometimes revisit the theatre of their earthly actions!

Before quitting our seat on this old tumulus, let us hear what delightful Gilbert White has to say about the district: "Though I have now travelled the Sussex Downs upwards of thirty years," writes this charming natural historian, "yet I still investigate that chain of majestic mountains with fresh admiration year by year, and think I see new beauties every time I traverse it. Mr. Ray was so ravished with the prospect from Plumpton Plain near Lewes, that he mentions those scenes in his 'Wisdom of God in the works of Creation' with the utmost satisfaction, and thinks them equal to anything he had seen in the finest parts of Europe. For my own part, I think there is something peculiarly sweet and amusing in the shapely figured aspect of chalk hills in preference to those of stone, which are rugged, broken, abrupt, and shapeless. Perhaps I may be singular in my opinion, and not so happy as to convey to you the same idea; but I never contemplate these mountains without thinking I perceive somewhat analogous to growth in their gentle swellings and smooth fungus-like protuberances, their fluted sides, and regular hollows and slopes, that carry at once the air of vegetative dilatation and expansion. Or, was there ever a time when these immense masses of calcareous matter were thrown into fermentation by some adventitious moisture; were raised and leavened into such shapes by some plastic power; and so made to swell and heave their broad backs into the sky so much above the less animated clay of the wild below?"

With all our admiration of the amiable author of the "Natural History of Selborne," we are not disposed to regard our South Downs in the light of vegetable productions or chemical fermentations; but we leave the solution of the question to the geologist.

And now let us descend to Ovingdean, which lies at our feet.

II.

OVINGDEAN GRANGE IN THE YEAR SIXTEEN HUNDRED AND FIFTY-ONE.

SINCE the year 1651 but slight change has taken place in the general aspect of the sequestered little village of Ovingdean (*Offingas den*, in Saxon), situated in a charming dene, or woody valley, amidst the South Downs, and within a mile of the coast.

During the two centuries that have elapsed since the date assigned to our story, the habitations of this secluded little village, which, notwithstanding its contiguity to the queen of watering-places, Brighton, seems still quite out of the world, have scarcely—with one important exception, namely, the modern mansion known as Ovingdean House—increased in number, or consequence. Indeed, the Grange, which, in the middle of the seventeenth century, was the principal residence of the place, is not only greatly reduced in size, but has entirely lost its original and distinctive character. Still, regarded without reference to the past, Ovingdean Grange, as it now appears, is a fair-proportioned, cheerful-looking domicile, and with its white walls and pleasant garden, full of arbutuses, laurestines, holms, and roses, offers a very favourable specimen of a Sussex farm-house. In one respect, and that by no means an immaterial one, the existing Grange far surpasses its predecessor; namely, in the magnitude and convenient arrangements of its farm-yard, as well as in the number of its barns, cow-houses, and other outbuildings, all of which are upon a scale never dreamed of in the olden time.

But as it is with the ancient house that we have now to do, we must endeavour to give some notion of it.   Even in 1651, Ovingdean Grange was old, having been built in the reign of Henry VIII. Constructed of red brick, chequered with diamonds, formed of other bricks, glazed, and of darker hue, mingled with flints, it seemed destined to endure for ages, and presented a very striking frontage, owing to the bold projections of its bay-windows with their stone posts and lintels, its deep arched portal with a stone escutcheon above it, emblazoned with the arms of the Maunsels, at that time its possessors, its stone quoins and cornices, its carved gables, its high roof, covered with tiles encrusted with orange-tawny mosses and lichens, and its triple clusters of tall and orna-mented chimney-shafts.

Old Ovingdean Grange did not want a rookery.   In a fine grove of elms, occupying part of the valley towards the south, a large colony of these aristocratic birds had taken up their quarters. Nor must we omit to mention that many of the trees, in the upper branches of which the rooks' nests might be seen, had attained a girth and altitude not a little remarkable, considering their proxi-mity to the sea.   It has been already intimated that the ancient farm-yard was neither so extensive nor so well arranged as its suc-cessor, but it possessed one of those famous old circular dovecots, which used to be the pride of a Sussex country-house, and which, before pigeon-matches were introduced, never failed to supply the family table with a savoury pie or a roast.   At the rear of the house was a garden, walled round, and laid out in the old-fashioned style, with parterres and terraces; and beyond it was an orchard full of fruit-trees.   Higher up on the down was a straggling little holt, or thicket, the trees of which, by their stunted growth and distorted shapes, manifested the influence of the sea-breezes.   When we have mentioned a large close, encompassed by a shaw, or fence of low trees, and displaying within its area a few venerable hawthorns, ancient denizens of the downs, we shall have particularised all the domains of old Ovingdean Grange.

The little village of Ovingdean consisted then, as now, of a few neatly-kept cottages, clustered like beehives near the mansion, some three or four in the valley, but the most part amongst the trees on the side of the eastern down. These cottages were tenanted by the bailiff, the husbandmen, shepherds, and other hinds employed at the Grange.

But the most pleasing feature of the place, and one by which it is happily yet distinguished, was the church. Scarce a stone's throw from the Grange, at the foot of a wooded escarpment, on the western side of the dene, and on a green and gentle declivity, stood, and still stands, the reverend little pile. Grey and old was Ovingdean church at the time of our story for its architecture is Norman and Early English, but it is upwards of two centuries older now, and somewhat greyer in consequence, though Time has dealt kindly with it, and has touched it with a hand so loving and tender, that if he has robbed it of aught, he has only added to its beauty. Peace rests upon the antique little fane, and breathes from out its hoary walls. Peace rests upon the grassy mounds and care-fully-tended tombs lying within its quiet precincts. Nothing more hushed, more sequestered, more winningly and unobtrusively beau-tiful, can be conceived than this simple village churchyard. The grey old walls that surround it, and shut it in like a garden, the trees that shade it, and completely shelter the holy edifice on the north, give it a peculiar air of privacy and tranquillity. Subdued by the calming influences of the spot, the heart becomes melted, the thoughts soar heavenward. Truly, a quiet resting-place after the turmoil of life.

Nor will the devotional feelings inspired by a pause within these hallowed precincts be lessened by an entrance into the sacred edi-fice itself; for there, if you love simplicity, you shall find it; there you shall behold a primitive little village church, without orna-ment, yet possessing the richest ornament in the absence of all decorative artifice; lacking not the graces of ecclesiastical architec-ture as displayed in the rounded arches dividing its nave from the chancel, and elsewhere in the structure; there, nothing shall dis-turb your religious train of thought; there, you shall find a rustic congregation, and shall listen to rustic voices chanting the holy hymn; and above all, you shall hear our Church's noble service well and worthily performed, and shall have good ghostly council from a good man's lips.

Though sufficing for the thinly-peopled parish in which it stands, the dimensions of Ovingdean church are modest enough, the nave and chancel, taken together, being little larger than those of many a private chapel. Aisles it has none, though it may once have possessed a south wing, marks of an arch being still discernible on the external wall on this side of the edifice; the roof is open, and crossed and supported by stout beams of oak; and the low square western tower, entered from within, serves the joint purposes of vestiary and belfry. We should prefer the true colour of the stone and timber to whitewash, but the latter, at all events, is clean and cheerful to look upon, and serves to display the many hatchments and marble tablets reared against the walls. Over the screen separating the nave from the chancel may be read these comforting words: "*Come unto me all ye that labour and are heavy laden, and I will give you rest.*" Together with this verse from the Psalms, well suited to the place: "*This shall be my rest for ever: here will I dwell, for I have a delight therein.*"

But though we love the old pile, we must not linger within it too long, but go forth into its quiet churchyard, now basking in sunshine, and visited by the sweet and delicate air of the downs. If there be a gleam of sunshine in the skies, it seems to seek out this favoured spot; while, when the rain descends here, it falls gently as the tears of a mourner. Would you see, ere we pass out by the arched gateway leading to the rectory, two relics of two centuries ago? you may perceive them in yon pair of decayed elder-trees, whose hoar, gnarled, corrugated trunks, and fantastically twisted branches, flung out like huge antlers, have but little vitality about them, and yet are deservedly spared for their age and picturesque appearance.

Where the present cheerful and commodious parsonage-house now stands, stood, in earlier days, a small monastic-looking structure, of higher antiquity even than the Grange; and this time-honoured edifice, all traces of which, except some portions of its garden walls, have disappeared, had served as an abiding-place for many successive pastors of the neighbouring church.

But alas! in the unhappy and distracted times of which we propose to treat, this little manse sheltered no minister of our Church. A woful change had come over it. The good pastor, who for years had dwelt there, honoured and beloved by all who profited by his teaching; who was pious, charitable, tolerant, and irreproachable in conduct; this excellent man, with whom no fault could be found, save that he was a firm and consistent supporter of the established Church of England, and a resolute maintainer of its tenets and of episcopal jurisdiction, was deprived of his benefice, driven from his dwelling, and no longer permitted to exercise his sacred functions within those walls where his voice had so often been heard. The Reverend Ardingly Beard, for so was named this sufferer in a good cause, bore his own crosses without a murmur, but he ceased not to deplore the fallen state of the Church, now become a prey to ravening wolves. When condemned as an obstinate and incurable prelatist and malignant, and dispossessed of his church and living, he had the additional grief and mortification of finding his place occupied by the Reverend Master Increase Micklegift (as the latter chose to style himself, though his real name was Zaccheus Stonegall), an Independent minister, and a zealous expounder of his own doctrines, but whom Mr. Beard regarded as a hypocrite, and highly dangerous to the spiritual welfare of his somewhile flock.

But the deprived clergyman did not retire altogether from the scene of his labours, though prevented from continuing them as heretofore. He obtained an asylum at the Grange, with its owner and his assured and sympathising friend, the Royalist Colonel Wolston Maunsel. For many years a widower, the good pastor had found solace in the companionship and affectionate attentions of the only child left him, his daughter Dulcia. At the time of his suspension from his religious functions, which unhappy event occurred about four years before the date of our story, Dulcia Beard had just reached her fifteenth spring, and though she felt the blow at the moment with as much acuteness as her father, yet with the happy elasticity of youth she speedily shook off its effects, and regained her wonted buoyancy of spirit. In sooth, there was not much to make her regret the change of abode.

Apartments were assigned to her father and herself at the Grange, where they might dwell as retired as they pleased, and in order to remove any sense of dependence on the part of his reverend guest. Colonel Maunsel appointed him to the office of his domestic chaplain. Thus, though forbidden, under the penalty of fine and imprisonment, to preach to his somewhile flock in public, or even to perform the church-service covertly, our good clergyman was enabled to address in private such as were not backsliders or apostates, and prevent them from wavering in the true faith. Greatly beholden, therefore, did the worthy man feel to him who, under Providence, afforded an asylum fraught with so many advantages to himself and his dearly beloved child.

In all respects Dulcia Beard merited her father's love. A gentler, sweeter disposition than hers could not be found; purer and higher principles than she possessed never existed in female bosom. As she grew towards womanhood her personal charms became more fully developed. Soft and delicate in mould, her features expressed in every line the amiability and goodness of her nature. Impossible to doubt the candour of her clear, blue, earnest eyes. Equally impossible to misunderstand the serenity of her marble brow, or the composure of her classic countenance. Calm was her countenance, but not cold; classic were her features in form, but with nothing rigorous in their outline. If her features corresponded with her nature, so did her person correspond with her features. Graceful in the highest degree, her figure was tall, and of exquisite symmetry. Her manner was entirely unsophisticated, and captivating from its very simplicity. The very reverse of a modish gentlewoman was Dulcia Beard, and owed none of her attractions to art. Whether any other image beside that of her father had found a place within that gentle bosom, will be seen as we proceed.

Colonel Wolston Maunsel of Ovingdean Grange has been described as a Royalist, but his description of himself, " that he was a Cavalier to the backbone," would be more correct. Colonel Maunsel hated the rebels and Roundheads and the whole Republican party, civil, military, and religious, as he hated poison; but if he had a special object of aversion it was Noll Cromwell. The execution of Charles deepened the colonel's animosity towards the regicides, and after the direful tragedy of Whitehall, he assumed a mourning habit, vowing never to put it off till the death of the martyred monarch should be fully avenged upon his murderers.

Colonel Maunsel was descended from a good old Sussex family; the branch he belonged to having settled at Ovingdean. Though not brought up to the profession of arms, but rather from habit and position disposed to lead the life of a country squire, our loyal gentleman, on the outbreak of the Civil War, alarmed by the imminence of the crisis, and instigated by his own strong Cavalier feelings, had deemed it incumbent upon him to abandon a home he delighted in, together with a wife whom he passionately loved, and joined the standard of the king. For several years Wolston Maunsel served under Prince Rupert, and shared in the victories as well as in the defeats of that great, though somewhat rash, commander. He fought at the famous battle of Edgehill, where Rupert's matchless cavalry did such signal execution upon the Parliamentarians, at Lansdown Hill, and at Chalgrave Field; was present at the sieges of Bristol and Bolton, at the important but ill-starred battle of Marston Moor, and at Ledbury, after which engagement he obtained from the Prince the command of a regiment of dragoons. Colonel Maunsel's last appearance on the battle-field was at Naseby, where his regiment was completely cut to pieces by Fairfax, and he himself severely wounded and made prisoner. With other captives he was sent by the victorious Parliamentary leaders to the castle of Chester, and detained long enough there to shatter his health. Heavy fines were inflicted upon him, which greatly impoverished his estates, but after nearly a year's confinement he was released, and retired to his residence at Ovingdean, where we have found him.

But other calamities, besides defeat and loss of property, had befallen the unfortunate Cavalier. During the time of his immurement within Chester Castle, his beloved wife, who was not permitted to share her husband's captivity, had died from grief and anxiety. An only son, then just sixteen, was, however, left him. Had the Civil War continued, this high-spirited youth, who inherited all his father's principles of loyalty, and hated the Republicans as heartily as his father, would have followed in the old Cavalier's footsteps; but when Colonel Maunsel was set free, the struggle was well-nigh over, the Royalist party was crushed for the time, and did not rally again for nearly five years, when Charles the Second was crowned at Scone, and entered England at the head of a small army, with the futile hope, as it proved, of conquering his rebellious kingdom.

Then it was that Clavering Maunsel, who by this time had become a remarkably handsome young man of one-and-twenty, and was as eager for the fray as a war-horse stirred by the trumpet, was despatched by the colonel to aid the youthful monarch. If his father had tried to restrain the young Cavalier, the attempt would have been ineffectual; but the loyal old colonel did no such thing. On the contrary, he commanded him to go; gave him his own sword, and bade him use it against the enemies of the king, and the slayers of the king's father. While straining his son to his breast at parting, the gallant old Cavalier declared that he envied him, his sole grief being that he could not accompany him. "But of what use to his Majesty would be a battered old soldier like myself, who can scarce move limb without help?" he cried. "So go, my son, and fight for me in the righteous cause. Strike down those accursed traitors and parricides—slay them, and spare not."

With his son, Colonel Maunsel sent a veteran follower, to whose care he knew the young man could be safely confided; and the measure was very judicious, as the event proved. The faithful attendant to whom Clavering Maunsel was entrusted was an ancient trooper in the king's service, named John Habergeon, who had fought with the colonel in many a rude engagement with the rebels, and had bled with him at Naseby. Though numbering more years than his old master, John Habergeon's strength was by no means on the decline. Hoary was he as an Alp; his gigantic frame was as hard as iron; and few younger men could cope with him in personal encounter. John Habergeon's exterior was by no means prepossessing. His features were harsh, and his manner crabbed and stern. His figure was gaunt and tall; and he stood so stiff and erect that he lost not an inch of his stature. Yet under this rugged exterior there beat a heart tender as a woman's; and follower more faithful and devoted could not be found than trusty John Habergeon.

It was not without some difficulty and danger that Clavering and his companion managed to reach Worcester, in which loyal city the adventurous young king had established his head-quarters. Though the new comer brought him no important levy of horse or foot, but only a single follower, Charles received the young man with great satisfaction, and well aware of his father's high character, misfortunes, and fidelity to the royal cause, at once bestowed upon him the command of a troop of horse under Colonel Wogan.

It is not our purpose to describe the events preceding the disastrous day of Worcester, nor to furnish any details of that fatal engagement, when the hopes of the young monarch and his adherents were utterly destroyed. Having as little sympathy as the Cavaliers themselves with the Republican army and its victorious general, it is no pleasure to us to record their successes. Suffice it then to say, that while preparations were making by Charles and his generals for the coming conflict, Clavering exhibited the utmost ardour and impatience; and when at length the luckless 3rd of September arrived, proved himself by his fiery courage, and perhaps by his rashness, to be his father's son. Some intelligence of his brave doings during the battle had been received at Ovingdean Grange, but what became of him afterwards was not known. His name did not appear amongst the list of the slain; but such lists in those troublous times were ever imperfect. Wogan's regiment, it was known, had suffered severely in covering the king's retreat; and what so probable as that foolhardy and inexperienced Clavering had fallen then. So at least feared his father. So feared another, whose gentle heart was distracted by doubt and anxiety.

Sad presentiments had filled Dulcia's breast when young Maunsel, full of martial ardour and enthusiasm for his cause, had set out

on the expedition. She had accompanied him to the summit of
the down overlooking the neighbouring town of Brightelmstone,
then giving little promise of its future magnitude and importance,
and chiefly noticeable from this point by a cluster of quaint old
houses, with red-tiled roofs and gables, grouped around the ancient
church on the hill, together with a short scattered street, consisting
mostly of cottages and mean habitations, running towards the sea:
—she had accompanied him, we say, to this point, and after a
tearful parting—tearful on her side, at least—had gazed wistfully
after him till he gained the brow of the opposite hill, when he
waved a farewell with the scarf she had embroidered for him, and
disappeared from view.

Had he disappeared for ever ? was the question that occupied
Dulcia, as she returned to the Grange with her attendant, Patty
Whinchat. Very beautiful and very picturesque did the old
house appear, embosomed amidst its trees, and with the old church
adjoining, as viewed from the high ground she was traversing, but
she looked not towards it, for her thoughts were wandering in another direction. Patty, a lively little damsel, and disposed to take
a cheerful view of things, chattered away, and assured her mistress
that Master Clavering would soon be back again, after killing all
the Roundheads; but after a while, receiving neither response nor
other encouragement to talk, she became silent, and tried to shed a
few tears for company.

Often did Dulcia recur to this parting with Clavering, and
never without reviving the sad forebodings which she had then
experienced. These, however, were vague fears, and easily shaken
off. But when she heard of Worcester's disastrous fight—when
rumours of dreadful slaughter of the Royalists reached her—when
day after day passed, and no tidings came of Clavering,—we may
imagine how much she suffered. She dreaded to receive confirma-
tion of her worst fears, and yet this suspense was well-nigh intolerable. By day a pallid image with stony eyes was ever before
her; and at night she beheld the same figure in her dreams,
stretched like a blood-stained corpse upon the battle-plain.

As to Colonel Maunsel, though anxiety as to his son's fate was

CLAVERING SETTING OUT TO JOIN THE KING

p. 16.

naturally uppermost in his bosom, the consideration of what he deemed to be a great national calamity weighed so heavily upon him, as in some degree to absorb his private griefs. The issue of the battle of Worcester he deemed fatal to his country. England was dishonoured; its glory obscured. Right, religion, loyalty, were trampled under foot. Republicanism was clearly in the ascendant: the star of monarchy, which had shone for a moment with its accustomed splendour, had set, he feared, for ever. While deploring the prostrate condition of his own party, now at the mercy of its hated opponents, he felt yet more acutely the terrible jeopardy in which the head of that party was placed. What had become of Charles, after the conflict on which he had staked his fortunes, the colonel could only conjecture. But he felt certain that the royal fugitive had as yet contrived to elude the vigilance of his enemies. Charles's capture would have been too loudly proclaimed not to be quickly known throughout the realm. But it was almost equally certain that the young king was yet within the country, and his retreat might, therefore, at any moment be discovered. A large reward was offered for his capture; and the penalties of high treason, loss of life and forfeiture of estate, were adjudged to such as should harbour him, or aid in his escape. Colonel Maunsel was well aware, from his own feelings, that no personal risk would prevent any loyal subject from assisting his sovereign; but he naturally dreaded lest the reward offered by the council of state might tempt some sordid knave to cause Charles's betrayal. All these considerations sorely perplexed and grieved the old Cavalier's spirit. The burden of his anxiety was almost greater than he could bear, and threatened to bow him to the ground. He began to fear that the messenger who brought him word that his son had been found amongst the slain, would tell him that the king had been captured. Such tidings, doubly calamitous, he was well assured, would prove his own death-blow.

III.

SHOWING WHAT BEFEL CLAVERING MAUNSEL AFTER THE BATTLE OF WORCESTER.

A WEEK had elapsed since the calamitous day at Worcester—a week, as we have shown, of frightful anxiety and suspense to the principal inmates of Ovingdean Grange—but still no tidings came of Clavering Maunsel, or of his faithful follower, John Habergeon. Neither had news, good or bad, been received relative to the fugitive king.

Somewhat late at night, the old colonel was sitting with Mr. Beard and Dulcia in the great hall of the mansion. Supper had been discussed, though a couple of long-necked flasks with tall glasses were still left upon the huge oak table; prayers had been read by the good clergyman; and the little party were conversing sadly together before their separation for the night. Colonel Maunsel ordinarily retired at an earlier hour than this, but he cared not now to seek his chamber, since he found no rest within it.

The hall in which we discover the little party was spacious and lofty, with a moulded ceiling, panels of dark oak, a high carved mantelpiece, deep bay-windows, having stained glass within them, and an elaborately carved doorway corresponding with the mantel-piece, and opening upon a corridor. Several old family portraits, male and female, in the costume of James the First's time, and in

that of Elizabeth, adorned the walls. Mingled with these portraits were trophies formed by pieces of old armour, coats of mail
and shirts of mail, skull-caps, bucklers, and chanfrons, surrounded
by two-handed swords, battle-axes, maces, cross-bows and long
bows; while a buck's head with enormous antlers occupied a con-
spicuous position opposite the fireplace. The night being chilly, a
comfortable wood fire blazed upon the dogs on the hearth, and
diffused a cheerful light around. A few high-backed arm-chairs
of richly carved oak, cushioned with crimson Utrecht velvet, together with an open cupboard, on the shelves of which were displayed several capacious flagons, parcel-gilt goblets, and other
drinking vessels in glass and silver, with a massive salver, gilt like
the goblets, in the midst of them, constituted the furniture of the
room.

There was one portrait, hung apart from the others, that claims
special attention. It was a full-length picture, by no less a
painter than Vandyke, of a young and lovely woman, attired in a
robe of rich white satin, made very low in front, so as to display a
neck of ravishing beauty, and far whiter than the satin, pearl
ornaments upon the stomacher, a pearl necklace around the throat,
pearl earrings, and bracelets of the same gems on the arms. The
features of this charming personage had a somewhat pensive expression that by no means detracted from their loveliness; the
eyes were magnificent, and black as night; the hair of raven hue,
contrasting forcibly with the dazzling whiteness of the skin. The
dark locks were taken back from the centre of the forehead, and
disposed in thick ringlets at the sides of the face, their sole ornament being a spray of green leaves placed on the left of the head.
This portrait, which bore the date 1630, represented Lady Cle-
mence Maunsel, the colonel's wife, and when gazing at her be-
witching lineaments, no one could wonder that he had passionately
loved her, or that he ceased not to deplore her less.

At the time that his wife's portrait was painted, Wolston
Maunsel was scarcely her inferior in point of personal appearance,
and they were noted as the handsomest couple in Sussex. Long
years and much suffering, both of mind and body, had done their

work with him, but he had still a very noble and striking coun‑
tenance. His locks were grizzled, and flowed over his neck and
shoulders in Cavalier fashion; his beard was pointed in the style
familiarised to us by Vandyke. His figure was tall and spare,
but his wounds and after sufferings had stiffened his limbs, afflict‑
ing him with rheumatic pains, which caused him to move with
difficulty, and prevented all active exertion. His features were
finely formed, but very thin, his complexion dark, and his black
overhanging eyebrows and keen grey eyes gave him a stern and
austere expression. His habiliments, we have said, were sable;
his black taffeta doublet and vest were of the graceful fashion of
Charles the First's time; his trunk hose had knots of ribbons at
the knees; black sik hose encased his still shapely legs; and his
shoes were of Spanish leather, high-heeled, and with black roses
on the instep. A wide falling band of lawn, edged with lace, set
off the old Cavalier's handsome physiognomy.

A venerable-looking man was the Reverend Ardingly Beard,
with a bald head and the snowy honours of age upon his chin, for
the clergy of those days wore the beard. Bitter had been his cup,
but it had not soured his heart, as was plain from his benevolence
of expression and kindliness of manner. Resignation to the will
of Heaven was the governing rule of the good man's life, and the
influence of this principle was apparent not only in his conduct,
but in his aspect and demeanour. Patience and humility were
written in legible characters in his countenance. Prohibited by
the enactments in force against the clergy of the Church of Eng‑
land from wearing the cassock, he was compelled to assume the
garb of a civilian. His garments were sombre in colour, like
those of the colonel, but of a coarser fabric. Little more need be
said of the worthy pastor, except that, as his eyesight had begun
to fail him, he was obliged to have recourse to spectacles.

Dulcia Beard has already been described as singularly beautiful,
but sooth to say, if her anxiety should not be speedily relieved,
her beauty will run great risk of being materially impaired. Al‑
ready, her cheeks have lost their bloom, and the lustre of her eyes
is sadly dimmed. Her manner, too, has quite lost its cheerfulness,

and she heaves deep and frequent sighs. Patty Whinchat, her handmaiden, is in despair about her young mistress, and feels certain, unless Master Clavering should come back, and quickly too, that she will break her heart. Patty cannot understand why Mistress Dulcia should be so foolish, seeing that there are other young men in the world quite as handsome as Master Clavering, but there is no use reasoning with her—pine away she undoubtedly will, in spite of all that can be said.

By degrees the conversation, which, as may be supposed, had never been of a lively character, began to flag, until at length it wholly ceased. Fain would Dulcia have withdrawn, but she did not like to disturb Colonel Maunsel, who remained with his face buried in his hands, as if lost in gloomy thought. After a long pause the old gentleman roused himself, as if by a great effort, and for a moment gazed vacantly at his companions.

"I crave pardon," he said, as soon as he had collected his scattered thoughts. "I had forgotten that I was not alone; but you will excuse me. In truth, I can bear this state of suspense no longer, and intend to set forth for Worcester to-morrow, and ascertain, if I can, the fate of my son."

"But consider the risk you will run, my good sir," mildly objected Mr. Beard; "and how unfit you are for such a journey."

"Unfit I am for it, I well know," the colonel rejoined, mournfully; "and like enough the effort may kill me, but I may as well go as tarry here, and die by inches. However, I will take counsel of one who can best guide me in the matter."

"Ay, take counsel of Heaven ere you decide, sir," the clergyman said.

"My counsellor is in heaven," the colonel returned. "Lend me your arm, Dulcia. I would fain arise."

Thus called upon, the young maiden instantly flew to his assistance, gave him his crutch-handled stick, and helped to raise him from his seat. The old Cavalier got up with great difficulty, and his rheumatic pains extorted a groan from him. After a momentary stoppage he moved on in the direction of his wife's portrait, halting opposite to it. Dulcia, who still supported him, watched his proceedings with some surprise, but she made no remark. The colonel gazed wistfully at the portrait, and then, in earnest and supplicating tones, but so low as scarcely to be audible to Dulcia, besought his dear departed wife to give him some sign by which he might know whether his design met with her approval.

Filled with wonder at the singularity of the proceeding, Dulcia began to fear that grief had turned the old colonel's brain; but she had little time for reflection, for scarcely were the words uttered than a noise was heard without in the corridor, and the next moment Patty Whinchat, in a state of the greatest excitement, and followed by an old serving-man wearing the colonel's livery, rushed into the room.

" That is my answer!" Colonel Maunsel almost shrieked. " What is it, woman? Speak!" he vociferated.

" Oh! your honour, John Habergeon is come back," responded Patty, well-nigh out of breath.

" Has he come alone?" the colonel faltered.

" No, your honour, no!" Martin Geere, the old serving-man, cried. " The wench has lost her wits. John has brought Master Clavering with him, but the young gentleman be in a sorry plight —a woful, sorry plight, for sure."

" But he lives! he is safe!" the colonel exclaimed, in a transport of delight. " Where is my boy? Bring him to me—bring him to me, quick."

" He is here, your honour," responded the sonorous voice of John Habergeon from the corridor.

Heavy footsteps resounded from the passage, and in another instant the old trooper appeared, sustaining his young master with his stalwart arm. Leading Clavering to the nearest chair, he deposited him within it, with as much tenderness and solicitude as could be exhibited by a nurse towards a sick man.

On beholding his son, the colonel uttered a cry, and shaking off in his excitement the rigidity of his limbs, and seeking for no support, rushed towards him with a quickness which, under other circumstances, would not have been possible. Dulcia and Mr.

Beard followed, but remained standing at a little distance, unwilling to interrupt the meeting between father and son. In the mean time, several others of the household, male and female, had flocked into the room. These persons, when he had placed his young master in the chair, as before related, John Habergeon took upon him to dismiss.

In good sooth, Clavering Maunsel was in a sorry plight. His apparel was soiled and torn; and the jerkin, over which he had worn a corslet on the field, was stained with blood. His long dark locks were dishevelled and unkempt, as if he had gone bareheaded for days; and such, indeed, was the fact. His lineaments were ghastly pale from loss of blood and other suffering; and his right arm appeared to be broken, for it was bound up, and supported by the very scarf which Dulcia had embroidered for him.

"My boy—my dear boy! how I joy to see thee back again!" the old colonel exclaimed, embracing him, and bending over him with effusion. "I had well-nigh given thee up for lost."

"You must thank John Habergeon for bringing me to you, father," Clavering replied. "Without him, you would never have beheld me more. But why come not Dulcia and her honoured father nigh me? I long to greet them, but am too much exhausted to rise."

Thus summoned, the young maiden was instantly by his side. Clavering extended his uninjured arm towards her, feebly pressing her hand, and fixing a tender look upon her, while she remained gazing upon him with tearful eyes. The good divine next came in for his share of the wounded man's notice.

"I shall die content now that I have seen you all once more," Clavering cried, in a feeble voice, and half closing his eyes, as he sank back in the chair.

"Tut! tut! talk not of dying!" Colonel Maunsel exclaimed. "I tell thee thou shalt live—live and grow hearty again, and shalt carry havoc amongst those canting Roundheads and rebels. I was worse hurt at Naseby than thou art, and should speedily have recovered from my wounds, had I been properly tended, and not lodged in that pestilent castle of Chester, where the prison fever took me and brought me to the gates of death, leaving me ever afterward stiff of joint and lame of limb, so that I can neither mount horse nor bear sword. But thou shalt get well again in less than a month, I warrant thee, Clavering, and be ready once more to fight the king's enemies. Thou hast youth and a sound constitution to back thee, and need'st fear nothing."

"He looks very faint!" Dulcia exclaimed, anxiously. "A cup of wine, methinks, would do him good."

"Well thought of, girl," the colonel cried. "A cup of wine instantly."

"Captain Clavering is suffering more from weakness and want of nourishment than from his wounds," John Habergeon said, filling a goblet with sack, and handing it to Dulcia. "Give it to him, fair mistress," he continued, with a gruff kind of gallantry. "The cup will taste better from your hands than mine;" adding, in a tone calculated only for her ear, "he hath talked of scarce any one else save you since he got his wounds."

Blushing deeply, but taking no notice of this embarrassing whisper, Dulcia gave the goblet to Clavering, who looked at her fixedly as he raised it to his lips.

Just then, the groom of the kitchen, Giles Moppett, accompanied by Martin Geere and Patty Whinchat, entered the hall, bringing materials for a plentiful repast, which they proceeded to place upon the table with all possible expedition. Fortunately the larder happened to be well stocked. The viands were chiefly of a substantial character—so much the better, John Habergeon thought, as he looked on, almost with a wolfish eye, while the dishes were being set upon the board. There was a mountainous roast round of beef, a couple of boiled pullets, little the worse for their previous appearance at the board, a dish of larks, a huge pigeon-pie, and, better than all, the remains of a magnificent roast bustard—bustards were then to be met with on the South Downs. As soon as the arrangements for this impromptu supper were completed, Clavering, upon whom the generous liquor he had swallowed had produced a very beneficial effect, was borne to the table by his father's directions, without moving him from the chair wherein he sat. Giles

Moppett, who acted as carver, then inquired what his young master would be pleased to take; but Clavering refused to touch anything till John Habergeon had been served, and bade Moppett fill a plate with roast beef for the old trooper. John was far too hungry to be bashful, so he sat down, as he was enjoined to do, and speedily cleared his plate, which was promptly replenished by Moppett. The old trooper was no indifferent trencherman in a general way; but just now he seemed to possess an inexhaustible appetite, eating like one half famished. After doing prodigious execution upon the round of beef, he devoured a leg and a wing of the bustard—no trifling feat in itself—only pausing occasionally in his task to empty a flagon of nut-brown ale, poured out for him by the attentive Martin Geere. Finally, he attacked the pigeon-pie, and soon made a great hole in it. His prowess was watched with infinite satisfaction by Colonel Maunsel, who encouraged him to go on, repeatedly ordering Giles Moppett to fill his plate anew. At first, Clavering ate sparingly and slowly, but as he gained strength his appetite increased, and if he could have used both hands, he might, perchance, have rivalled John Habergeon's wondrous performances, for he seemed to have fasted as long as the old trooper. But, notwithstanding his insatiable hunger, the young man took good care to call in Dulcia's aid to cut up his meat for him, which he was certainly entitled to do, seeing that he could not perform the task for himself. A pause, however, in this terrible masticating process having at length arrived, on Clavering's side, at least—for John, it seemed, would never cease—Colonel Maunsel thought he might venture to ask for some particulars of his son's escape after the battle. The first inquiries, however, of the loyal old gentleman were, whether Clavering knew aught of the king?

"I trust his Majesty has escaped his enemies, father," the young man replied; "but I have heard nothing concerning him since I was separated from him, in the manner I will proceed to recount to you. After the rout on that unlucky day, when all went against us, and the king was compelled to retire, I had the honour of forming part of the small escort that attended him, having previously assisted, with my Lord Cleveland and Colonel Wogan, in covering his retreat from the city. We rode off at nightfall in the direction of Stourbridge, his Majesty having decided upon taking refuge at Boscobel House, whither Mr. Charles Giffard, than whom there breathes not a more loyal gentleman, had undertaken to conduct him."

"I know Charles Giffard well," Colonel Maunsel remarked, "and can avouch, from my personal knowledge, that he is as loyal as thou hast described him. I also know Boscobel, and White Ladies, another house belonging to the Giffards, and in either place his Majesty would find a secure retreat. The king could not be in better hands than those of loyal Charles Giffard. But go on, my son; how far didst accompany his Majesty?"

"Within a mile of Stourbridge," Clavering replied; " when we were attacked by a troop of the enemy's horse, and the king was exposed to much peril, running great risk of capture."

"Capture! 'Sdeath! you would none of you have suffered those vile knaves to lay hands on his Majesty's sacred person!" the old colonel exclaimed, his eye blazing fiercely, and his limbs trembling with passion. "Oh! that I had been there, with an arm as strong as that which I boasted before Naseby! What didst thou do, boy?"

"That which you would have done yourself, sir," Clavering re-joined. "I used your sword to some purpose against the crop-eared curs, and made them feel the edge of the weapon. Finding the king beset by the captain of the troop and three or four of his men, who had recognised his Majesty, and were shouting out 'that the Lord of Hosts had delivered Abijam, the son of Rehoboam, into their hands,' and were menacing him with death if he did not yield himself up to them, I fired my pistol at the head of their leader, and throwing myself upon the others, assailed them so furiously, that the king was able to extricate himself from them and get clear off."

"What! thou hast been the happy instrument of saving his Majesty's life—thou, my darling son!" the old Cavalier exclaimed, in tones half broken by the deep emotion which he vainly endea-voured to repress. "By Saint George! thou hast done well, Clavering—thou hast done well. And if thou hadst perished in the act, thou wouldst have died the death which I myself should have most coveted—a death worthy of one of our loyal house."

"But, Heaven be praised, my brave young friend is spared to us!" Mr. Beard ejaculated. "May he be preserved to be a prop to your declining years, sir," he added to the colonel.

"May he be preserved to aid in King Charles's restoration, that is all I pray for!" the old Cavalier exclaimed.

"I cry 'Amen' to that prayer, father," the young man rejoined, fervently.

Hitherto Dulcia had abstained from speech, though her cheek had glowed during Clavering's narration. She now ventured to remark:

"But you have more to tell us of that desperate encounter, have you not? It was there that you received your hurts?"

"You are right, Dulcia," Clavering replied. "His Majesty, whom Heaven preserve! had got off as I have informed you, but I myself was surrounded, and had a sharp conflict with the base knaves, from whom I neither expected to receive quarter, nor would have deigned to accept it, and who, moreover, as you may guess, were mightily enraged at the king's escape. Ere long my right arm was disabled by the blow of a pike, and being thus at the mercy of the murtherous rascals, I should have been despatched outright, if it had not been for John Habergeon——"

"Say not a word about me, captain, I beseech you," the old trooper interrupted, looking up with his mouth full of pigeon-pie.

"I marvelled where John could have been all this while," the colonel observed. "I thought he could not have been far off."

"John was by my side, sir," Clavering rejoined. "By my side, did I say? He was in front—at the rear—on the right—at the left—everywhere warding off blows aimed at me, and doing terrible execution upon the rebels. But even John could not save me from being thrown from my steed, and trampled under foot by the Roundhead troopers, who tried to dash out my brains with their horses' heels. The stoutness of my casque saved me from their malice, and my breastplate protected me from all other harm except some trifling bruises——"

"Call you hurts such as yours trifling, my good young friend?'
the pastor cried. "You must needs have a frame of iron to bear
such injuries, and speak lightly of them."

"'Fore Heaven! Clavering is as tough as his father," the old
colonel remarked, smiling complacently; "and can bear much
knocking about. There is nothing like a close headpiece with
great cheeks, and a stout corslet and cuissarts, if you have the ill
luck to be hurled on the ground and ridden over. Your well-
tempered breastplate stood you in good stead on this occasion, boy."

"It was much dinted, I promise you, father," Clavering replied.
"Howbeit, I escaped with life, though those caitiff troopers declared
they would send me to perdition."

"Heaven open their own eyes and save them from the pit!" the
clergyman ejaculated.

"Nay, such spawn of Satan deserve not your intercession for
them, reverend sir," the old Cavalier exclaimed, impetuously. "I
would despatch such devil's servants to their master without an
instant's scruple. Oh! John, my worthy friend," he added to the
old trooper, who was still quietly pursuing his meal, as if in no wise
concerned in Clavering's relation, "I estimated thee aright. I knew
thou wouldst be serviceable to my son."

"I would not have stirred a foot for those cursed Roundhead
curs, your honour," John Habergeon replied; "but I wanted to
draw them from Captain Clavering as the sole means of saving his
life, so I made pretence of flight, and the rascals galloped after me.
They shot my horse, but I got off scathless."

"Thou art a brave fellow, John," the colonel said.

"Brave, indeed! and trusty as brave!" Clavering cried. "He
rescued me from certain destruction. I was unable to stir from the
spot where I fell, and if those butcherly Roundheads had returned,
or others of their side had come up and found me lying there
and still breathing, they would infallibly have knocked out my
brains."

"Now to look at dear, good John Habergeon, no one would
guess what a warm heart he possesses," Dulcia exclaimed. "I ever
liked him; but I knew not his true worth till now."

"Men must not be judged by their exterior, chil*l*,' Mr. Beard
said. "The sweetest kernel hath sometimes the roughest shell."

"Just as the best blade may be found in an ill scabbard," the
colonel said. "John is somewhat harsh of feature, it must be
owned, but he hath a right honest look. You would never mistake
him for a Puritan."

"I trow not, your honour, if a real Puritan were nigh," the old
trooper replied, with a grin. "But enough, methinks, has been
said about me."

"Not half enough," Clavering rejoined. "I have not told you
a tithe of what John did for me, father. When you know all, you
will comprehend how much gratitude I owe him. He bore me in
his arms from the scene of strife to a place of safety, where he set
my broken arm, and put splints, which he himself quickly prepared
as well as any surgeon could have done, over the fracture, bound
up the limb, dressed my bruises, and, this done, he again carried
me to a barn, where we passed the night, John watching by me all
the while. After some hours' rest I was able to move, and we set
out before daybreak across the country, as near as we could conjecture in the direction of Stratford. We made but slow progress,
for I was very stiff and weak; but John lent me all the aid he
could, cheering me on, and talking to me of home and of those I
loved, when I was half inclined to lie down in despair. As the
day advanced, he procured me some milk and bread, without
which I could no longer have gone on, for I had tasted nothing
since the previous morn—the morn, you will remember, of the
fatal battle. Having partaken of this food, I was enabled to continue my journey, and ere night we had found shelter in a thicket
between Stratford and Long Marston, when John left me for
a while to procure fresh provisions for our support. The faithful
fellow came back, bringing with him meat and a bottle of stout
ale; but though half famished, he would touch nothing himself till
I had eaten and drunk. But I must be brief, for this talking is
too much for me. During the whole of our toilsome journey hither
exposed as we have been to constant hazard from the Republican
troops which are scouring the country in every direction, dreading

almost to show our faces lest we should be set upon by some Roundhead churls, resting now in a wood, now beneath a haystack, but
never under a roof, obtaining food with difficulty, and the little we
got of the coarsest kind,—during all these difficulties and dangers,
my trusty companion, who might easily have provided for his own
safety, kept ever by my side, and tended me, cheered me, watched
over me—nay, actually in two instances saved me from capture
with his good right hand, for I could do nothing in my own
defence—and finally succeeded in bringing me home in safety."

"Blessings upon him for his noble conduct!" the clergyman exclaimed.

"Ay, blessings upon him!" reiterated both the colonel and
Dulcia.

"Well, it is all right now, since I am back again at the dear old
house," Clavering continued. "As to my wounds, I heed them
not. They will soon heal. But the thought of *how* I got them
will last during the rest of my life."

"Thou art a true Maunsel, every inch of thee, Clavering," his
father cried, in approval. "What signifies a limb lost, or a drop
of blood the less in one's veins, if we have done good service to the
royal cause. And thou hast saved the king's life. Think of that
—think of that, Clavering Maunsel."

"I *do* think of it," the young Cavalier replied.

"I crave your honour's leave to propose a toast," John Haber
geon cried, rising.

"Thou hast my full license to do so," Colonel Maunsel rejoined
"Fill thine own glass from that flask of Malvoisie to the brim, and
all of us will follow thine example. Even fair Mistress Dulcia will
not refuse thy pledge."

"Nay, that I will not, in good sooth, colonel," Dulcia cried.

"You will all do me reason, I am sure, when you hear my toast,"
John said. "A health to King Charles, and may God preserve
him from his enemies!"

All arose; the colonel unassisted, for his new-found activity had
not yet deserted him; and Clavering contrived to get up from his
chair. The glasses being filled, the toast was drunk by the whole

company, including even Dulcia, who raised the goblet to her lips. Colonel Maunsel repeated the words pronounced by the loyal old trooper with great fervour and solemnity; adding, "I will put a rider to thy toast, John, and drink to his Majesty's speedy restoration."

While the party was thus occupied, none of them were aware that their proceedings were watched from the bay-window on the left by a sallow-faced, sinister-looking personage, habited in a Geneva cloak and bands, and wearing a tall steeple-crowned hat on his head. We have said that this spy was unobserved by all the party; but his presence did not pass unnoticed by the quick eyes of Patty Whinchat, who entered the hall just as the treasonable toast (for such it would sound in the ears of a Republican) had been drunk.

"Mercy on us!" Patty screamed. "There's a man at the window."

"What say'st thou, wench? A man at the window!" Colonel Maunsel cried. "Go and see, John. I can discern no one."

The old trooper did not require bidding twice, but rushed to the bay-window indicated by Patty. However, he could perceive nothing to justify the girl's alarm, and told the colonel as much.

"What manner of man didst fancy thou sawest, wench?" the colonel cried.

"It was no fancy, your honour; I'm sure I saw him," Patty rejoined. "I saw his hatchet-face, and his cat's-eyes, and his tall, sugar-loaf hat, and his Geneva cloak and bands——"

"Oons! that should be Increase Micklegift, from thy description, wench," the colonel interrupted.

"It *was* Increase Micklegift whom I beheld," Patty replied. "I'll swear to his ugly nose."

"No occasion for swearing, Patty," the clergyman remarked. "We will believe your simple affirmation."

"Go and send some one forth, Moppett," the colonel said to the groom of the kitchen, "to ascertain whether this pestilent rascal be indeed within the garden, or elsewhere lurking about the premises."

"I'll go myself," John Habergeon rejoined; "and if I catch him, I'll treat him as I would a hen-roost plunderer."

"Nay, harm him not," the clergyman cried; "but admonish him."

"Ay, ay, I'll admonish him, your reverence," John Habergeon replied, "—with a cudgel."

This incident caused Colonel Maunsel considerable uneasiness, and somewhat abated his satisfaction at his son's return. Clavering, he well knew, might at any moment be arrested as a traitor to the Commonwealth, for having borne arms for his lawful sovereign, and might even suffer death for a display of loyalty, which the Rump Parliament regarded in the light of high treason. Since Clavering was in this danger, it was necessary that the utmost caution should be observed in regard to him; and though the colonel could rely upon his household to maintain perfect secrecy as to their young master's return, yet if Increase Micklegift had become aware of the fact, concealment would be hopeless. Moreover, Colonel Maunsel felt satisfied, from his knowledge of the Independent minister's character, that he would not hesitate to denounce Clavering.

These considerations, as we have said, greatly alarmed the old Cavalier; but he was somewhat reassured by John Habergeon, who, on his return, after some quarter of an hour's absence, declared that he, with Giles Moppett and Martin Geere, had carefully searched the garden without finding any traces of the supposed spy. But, to make all sure, they had gone up to the old rectory, where the Independent minister had taken up his abode since Mr. Beard's secession, and knocking at the door, had been answered by Increase himself from his chamber window, who bade them be gone about their business, and not disturb him at that unseasonable hour of the night.

This latter piece of information was well calculated to allay the colonel's fears, and he began to agree with John Habergeon, that Patty Whinchat, in spite of her positive assertions to the contrary, must have been mistaken, and could not have beheld the mischievous Independent divine. Deeming, therefore, that further precautionary measures were unneeded for the night—whatever might be requisite on the morrow—he saw his son conducted to his chamber by John Habergeon (Clavering's parting with Dulcia must be left to the fair reader's imagination), and tarried with him for some time, when he himself sought his couch. Long ere this, all the other inmates of Ovingdean Grange had retired to rest, happier than they had been for many days.

BOOK II.

INCREASE MICKLEGIFT.

I.

SHOWING THAT A CHIMNEY MAY SERVE FOR OTHER PURPOSES THAN AS A PASSAGE FOR SMOKE.

DOMICILIARY visits to the residences of country gentlemen noted for their fidelity to the Crown were so frequent at the period, that almost every house belonging to an adherent to the royal cause was provided with a hiding-place, wherein a kinsman, whose proceedings had jeopardised his safety, or a fugitive Cavalier, seeking shelter from the foe, might be secreted until the danger should have passed by.

Ovingdean Grange possessed a retreat of this kind, very skilfully fabricated amidst the brickwork of a large external chimney at the north-east angle of the mansion. No indication of the hiding-place was perceptible from without, even on careful examination. The chimney had nothing unusual in its shape, though of great size ; large chimneys being common enough in old Sussex houses, as may be observed in many still in existence. The lurking-place, as may be supposed, was extremely contracted in its dimensions, and would just hold two persons. Built in juxtaposition with the chimney funnel, it sprang to a height sufficient to enable its occupants to stand upright within it. Light and air were admitted by a narrow loophole, screened from observation by a grotesque stone gargoyle projecting from the roof of the building. Access to the spot was of course obtained from within. In a spacious bed-chamber at the rear of the house, used by Colonel Maunsel himself, there was a large oak chimney-piece, the left jamb of which, carved as a pilaster, turned upon a pivot, and could be instantly set in motion by a spring concealed amidst the foliage of the capital. On opening this secret door an aperture was disclosed large enough to admit a man, and communicating with a narrow passage constructed within the thickness of the walls. A second obstacle, however, was set in the way of the searchers, should they have succeeded in penetrating thus far. Within a couple of yards of the fireplace, the passage was blocked up by what seemed solid masonry; but the impediment, though apparently insurmountable, could easily be removed by touching a second spring. Beyond this, the passage was free, and soon terminated in the small chamber already described.

This hiding-place naturally occurred to Colonel Maunsel, as he lay awake, and painfully ruminating, on the night of his son's return to the Grange. But though the asylum might be a secure one, in case Clavering should be denounced by Increase Micklegift (for the colonel could not wholly shake off the apprehension of this possibility), yet recourse must not be had to it, except at the last extremity, since the occupation for any length of time of such a narrow cell by the young man, in his present wounded and enfeebled state, might be productive of most disastrous consequences. The best thing to be done, it seemed to the colonel, was to bring Clavering to his own room, so that the young man might take instant refuge within the hidden chamber, in case the house should be menaced with a perquisition. Fortunately, none of the household, except trusty John Habergeon, were acquainted with the hiding-place, so that no threats or maltreatment on the part of the searchers could extort from them a revelation of the secret.

All continued tranquil, however, during the night. Worn out with the extraordinary fatigue and privations he had undergone, Clavering slept so soundly, that if the malevolent Independent minister, accompanied by a dozen Roundhead musketeers, had knocked at his door, he would scarce have been aroused. John Habergeon, who occupied a truckle-bed in his young master's room, slept soundly too, but the old trooper had the vigilance of a watch-dog, and would have been up, and on the alert, on the slightest disturbance. A pair of pistols lay within his reach, in case of a surprise.

Long before daybreak, Colonel Maunsel, who had slept but little, as we have stated, arose, and wrapping himself in a dressing-gown, took a taper, which burnt within his chamber, and proceeded to inspect the hiding-place. Both the secret springs acted perfectly, and the cell seemed as dry and comfortable as such a place could well be; indeed, its contiguity to the chimney funnel kept it warm. Still it must be fitted up yet more conveniently for Cla-vering's reception. Fraught with this resolve, and in order that no time might be lost, the colonel repaired at once to his son's room, marvelling within himself, as he went, that he was able to move about in this way without assistance. But strength seemed to have been given him for the perilous conjuncture. John Haber-geon started up as he entered the room, and the first impulse of the old trooper was to seize the pistols lying beside him, but he instantly laid down the weapons on recognising the intruder. Colonel Maunsel desired him, in a low tone, to come with him, and John having huddled on his garments as expeditiously as he could, they quitted the room together, without disturbing the wounded sleeper. Acting under the colonel's directions, John placed a variety of articles within the cell, likely to be required by Clavering, if he should be forced to occupy it; and these arrangements being satis-factorily made, and the secret door restored to its customary position, the old trooper looked at his master, as if awaiting further orders, and receiving none, he observed:

"A plan has just occurred to me for deceiving the enemy, which, with your honour's permission, I would fain put into execu-tion without delay. For my own part, I believe it was a false alarm that we got last night; but I may be wrong, and any way we ought to be cautious where Captain Clavering's liberty and life are concerned. My notion is to make pretence of quitting the house before daybreak, so that if Increase Micklegift, or any other scoundrelly spy like him, should be lurking about the premises—as may be the case, for aught we can tell—he may fancy the captain has taken flight in reality. If your honour thinks well of the scheme, I'll hie to the stables at once, and saddle a couple of horses——"

"Thy stratagem is good," the colonel interrupted; "but I dare not adopt it. My son is too weak to ride forth at this hour."

"I don't intend he should, your honour," John Habergeon rejoined. "I should be loth to disturb the captain from such a slumber as he hath not enjoyed since he quitted Worcester; but there is no occasion for that. Martin Geere shall be the young gentleman's representative, and with one of your honour's cloaks wrapped round him, and one of your honour's hats upon his head, Martin will play the part indifferent well, especially as there won't be light enough to observe him very narrowly. My object is not merely to delude the enemy, but to persuade the household that Captain Clavering is gone. It is safest to keep those talkative women-folk in the dark. I can rely upon old Martin's silence and discretion."

"Ay, I doubt not Martin may be depended upon," the colonel remarked. "But whither will you go? What will you do with the horses?"

"We shan't ride far, your honour," John replied. "I will make clatter enough before the rectory for Increase Micklegift to hear us, and a word or two roared out as we pass will satisfy the rascally preacher it is no other than Captain Clavering whom I have with me. This done, we will gallop off in the direction of Brightelmstone, and when fairly out of hearing we will manage to steal back, unobserved, over the downs."

"A rare plan, i' faith!" Colonel Maunsel exclaimed. "Thou hast a ready wit, John. About it at once, and success attend thee!"

John then departed on his errand, and Colonel Maunsel once more betook himself to his son's chamber.

Clavering was still buried in profound sleep, and while gazing on the young man's pale and toil-worn features, and thinking how necessary rest was to him, the colonel had scarcely the heart to deprive him of it. So he sat down by the couch.

How many anxious thoughts passed through the fond father's breast as he gazed upon his sleeping boy. Clavering was the only being upon whom his affections were centred. To lose him again as soon as found would be fearful indeed. So terrified was the kind-hearted gentleman by the thought of such a disaster, that he knelt down and prayed Heaven to avert it.

Much comforted, he arose and resumed his seat by the bedside. Presently the sleeper's lips moved, as if he were essaying to speak, and his sire, bending towards him, heard him distinctly pronounce the name of Dulcia. Slight as was the circumstance, it confirmed a suspicion which the old Cavalier had begun of late to entertain, that a mutual attachment subsisted between the young folk; and the certitude of the fact was by no means agreeable to him. Extremely partial to Dulcia, entertaining, moreover, a sincere respect and esteem for her worthy father, Colonel Maunsel was yet a very proud man, and never contemplating such a union for his son as might here take place, would infallibly have refused to sanction it.

However, this was not a moment wherein to trouble himself with so light a matter—light, at all events, he deemed it in comparison with the serious considerations before him—so he dismissed the subject from his mind. Indeed, he had little time for reflection. The hour had advanced. Ere long the household would be astir, and it was needful to awaken Clavering, in pursuance of his plan.

The heavy chains of slumber in which the young man was bound did not yield to the colonel's first attempt to break them; neither, on opening his eyes, did Clavering appear to be conscious where he was, nor who was near him. Calling out fiercely that he would never yield with life to a rascally Roundhead, he commanded his father to take his hands from off him; but immediately perceiving his error, he became silent, while the colonel in a few words explained his intentions.

On this Clavering arose, and, attiring himself with his sire's aid, accompanied the latter to his chamber.

II.

WHAT PASSED BETWEEN THE INDEPENDENT MINISTER AND DULCIA IN THE
CHURCHYARD.

It was now peep of day. The summit of the eastern downs
glistened in the early sunbeams, though the nearer slopes still
remained grey and sombre. Thinking that the fresh morning air
would revive him, Colonel Maunsel drew aside the window curtains, and throwing open the casement, looked forth upon the garden. Animate nature was just beginning to feel the quickening influence of the God of Day. The garrulous occupants of the higher
trees made the welkin ring with their cawing as they flew past in
quest of their morning meal; lesser birds twittered amongst the
boughs; the mavis burst from the holm-tree to dispute the first
worm upon the grass-plot with the intrusive starling; pigeons were
circling around the house, or alighting on the roof; lowings of
.xen and other noises resounded from the farm-yard; and the
tinkling of the sheep-bell was heard on the adjacent down, where
might be seen the fleecy company, just released from the fold, in
charge of the shepherd, and looking as grey as the turf on which
they browsed.

At such an hour, and on a spot which ought to have been sacred
from intrusion, the presence of an enemy was as unexpected as unwelcome. Yet as the colonel's eye wandered over the garden, now
resting upon one object, now on another, he fancied he saw a dark

figure pass quickly by an arched opening in an avenue of clipped yew-trees. The noise of stealthy footsteps at the same moment reached his ear, convincing him that he was not deceived. Hastily withdrawing from the window, he took up a position enabling him to command this portion of the garden, while it did not expose him to observation. As he thus watched, a head was protruded from the end of the alley nearest the house, but it was so suddenly withdrawn that he could not tell to whom it belonged.

After waiting for several minutes without perceiving anything further of the owner of the head, the colonel turned to mention the circumstance to his son, and then found that Clavering, overcome by weariness, had thrown himself, dressed as he was, upon the bed, and was once more wrapped in slumber. Not caring to wake him, the brave old gentleman took up his sword and was on the point of descending to the garden, when a tap was heard at the door, and John Habergeon entered the room.

On learning what had occurred, John tarried not a second, but, flying down stairs, made the best of his way to the yew-tree avenue: the colonel looking on all the while from the window. John, however, started no spy from the covert, and only disturbed a pair of blackbirds in his search. Nevertheless, he extended his investigations, as far as he judged prudent, in the direction of the parsonage house, but with an equally fruitless result, and he was obliged to return to his master without any intelligence respecting the intruder. The old Cavalier was much troubled. That some one had been lurking within the garden he felt sure, for he could not doubt the evidence of his senses; and that this person came with no friendly intent was equally manifest. Danger, therefore, was to be apprehended, and must be the more carefully guarded against, inasmuch as its designs were secret.

John then related what he had done. According to his own belief, his stratagem had been perfectly successful. Old Martin Geere having been disguised in the manner arranged, the pair rode slowly up the hill-side by the rectory, and when close to the house, John halted for a moment to vociferate an adieu

to the Independent minister, and was well pleased to hear a
window suddenly opened, and to perceive the reverend gentleman
with a nightcap on his head, look out at them. Rating them
for a couple of drunken malignants, and declaring that Satan was
at their heels, and would assuredly trip them up ere they had proceeded far on their journey, Increase might have favoured them
with a still longer harangue, but that John interrupted him
with a roar of derisive laughter, and pushed on after his companion. John and old Martin then crossed the hill, and, shaping
their course in a northerly direction up the valley as if bound for
Falmer, got round to the Rottingdean road, and so over the down
to the little thicket at the back of the Grange, where Martin dismounted, and John, taking both horses to the stables, called up
the groom and his helpmate, leading them to suppose that their
young master was gone. Not having encountered any one during
the ride, John had persuaded himself that his return to the stables
was unnoticed, until the incident in the garden made him fear that
his supposition might not be altogether correct. He now naturally
enough concluded, that Increase Micklegift, suspecting an attempt
to dupe him, had stolen down to the Grange to satisfy himself of
the truth. If so, he could have learnt little. The wary measures
taken were sufficient to mislead him. Such was the conclusion
arrived at both by the colonel and John. But they agreed, that
the utmost caution must be observed while they were watched by
an enemy so wily as the preacher.

"It vexes me much to think that I cannot send for a surgeon
to attend upon my son," the colonel said. "There is Master
Ingram of Lewes, a man well skilled in his profession, or Ralph
Hoathleigh of Brightelmstone, or even old Isaac Woodruff of
Rottingdean—any one of them would do; but I dare not trust
them. Besides, it would excite suspicion if a surgeon were sent
for."

"No need to send for one, your honour," the old trooper replied.
"The captain's wounds are in a fair way of healing, and his
broken bones have already begun to knit together. He only wants
rest and good nursing to set him up again, and he is sure of the
latter, with me and gentle Mistress Dulcia to attend upon him."

"Dulcia!" the colonel exclaimed, looking at him fixedly. "Why should she come nigh him? Saidst thou not, erewhile, that it would be safest not to let the women-folk into the secret, lest they should blab?"

"Ay, marry did I," John rejoined; "but I did not include Mistress Dulcia amongst the tattlers. Heaven forbid! She is discretion itself, and would never breathe a word to jeopardise the captain."

"Humph!" the colonel ejaculated. "At all events, she shall not nurse my son."

"Then I won't answer for his cure," John answered, gruffly.

"Not so loud, I prithee, John. Thou wilt awake him. By Heaven, he opes his eyes!"

"Then acquaint him with your resolve."

"What is't, my father?" Clavering cried, from the couch.

"His honour the colonel deems it expedient that during your confinement to this chamber, you should be solely under my care, captain; as if you had not had enough of an old trooper's rough nursing, and stood not in need of gentler care."

"If I am to be deprived of Dulcia's society, I will not remain here," Clavering exclaimed, springing from the couch.

"I told your honour how it would be," John cried, chuckling.

"Thou art in league against me, rascal," the colonel ejaculated, shaking his hand at him. "And as to thee, Clavering, thou art a wilful and undutiful boy. A soldier should have a soldier's attendance merely. But since thou art so weak and womanish that none save Dulcia will serve thy turn to watch over thee and tend thee, even be it as thou wilt."

"My father!———"

"Get well as quickly as thou canst, that is all I ask."

"Your honour hath ta'en the best way to ensure that object," John observed.

"Hold thy peace!" the colonel cried. "Within yon closet thou wilt find all thou needest to perfect his cure: unguents of great virtue, sovran balsams, cordials, and an elixir prepared for me by my worthy friend Sir Kenelm Digby, which ought to call back the vital spark if it were on the eve of departure. Use what thou wilt; but mark me! if thy patient gets not well speedily, I'll send for Master Ingram."

"Nay, I shall be myself again in less than a week," Clavering cried. "I am stronger already, and with the prospect of such attendance——"

"Peace, I say!" his father cried. "I have heard reasons enow, and have yielded against my better judgment. Aid me to attire myself," he added to John, "and then I will leave my son master of the room. Thou wilt have to be groom of the chamber, as well as head-nurse, John, for none of the household will come nigh ye, except old Martin Geere. And now, give me my hose and doublet."

At a somewhat later hour in the morning, though still comparatively early, Colonel Maunsel was joined in the library, whither he had repaired on going down stairs, by Mr. Beard and Dulcia, both of whom were under the impression that Clavering was gone; and one of them, at least, was much relieved by finding that such was not the case.

A bell having been rung for prayers, the greater part of the household assembled at the summons, and the clergyman read a portion of the Holy Scriptures to them; after which he knelt down, and the rest following his example, he offered up an extempore prayer for the preservation from all danger of the lord of the mansion and his son. All joined fervently in this supplication, but none more so than Dulcia.

Their devotions ended, the old Cavalier and his guests proceeded to the hall and partook of breakfast. Martin Geere was in attendance at the meal, which was of a substantial character, according to the habits of the period, and the colonel, when he could do so without observation, privily despatched him up-stairs with a supply of eatables for his son. No mystery was made about John Habergeon, since his return was known to the household, and the old trooper could take care of himself in the buttery.

Breakfast over, Dulcia and her father rose to depart, when the colonel, calling the latter to him, said, in a low tone, "Go up-stairs, child, to Clavering. Your society will cheer him, and help to while away the tedious hours of his captivity. You will find him in my chamber with John Habergeon. Be cautious, and, above all, arouse not Patty Whinchat's suspicions."

Dulcia blushingly withdrew, and Colonel Maunsel soon afterwards got up and repaired to the library.

Meanwhile, Dulcia having retired to her own room, was awaiting a favourable opportunity to visit the captive, when she was interrupted by the sudden entrance of Patty.

"Oh! I've seen him—I've seen him!" gasped the handmaiden, who looked pale and terrified.

"Seen whom?" Dulcia exclaimed, thinking naturally of Clavering.

"Why, Increase Micklegift, to be sure, madam. Who else could frighten me so much? I happened to be in the corridor just now, when he came up to me—how he got there I can't tell!—and seizing me rudely by the arm, uttered these words in my ear: 'Bid thy young mistress come to me without delay. I would speak to her on a matter which concerns her nearly. I will tarry for her during the space of one hour, within the churchyard. If she comes not within that time, she will ever hereafter rue her negligence. Convey my message to her at once.' And with this he disappeared. I am sure, from his looks, he has some evil design. You won't go, of course, madam?"

"Yes, I will, Patty," Dulcia replied, after a moment's reflection. "I have no fear of him. I will go at once, and you shall attend me. It may be important to others to ascertain his purpose. Give me my hood, child."

Approving of her young mistress's spirit, Patty made no further remonstrance, and Dulcia having quickly attired herself for the walk, the two young women left the room, crossed the entrance-hall without stoppage, passed out at the front porch, and proceeded towards the church.

As they advanced, they saw the dark figure of the Independent divine within the churchyard. Increase Micklegift had an austere and somewhat ill-favoured countenance, but his features, though large and harsh, were by no means devoid of intelligence. His eyes were dark and restless, and his singularly pale complexion contrasted forcibly with his coal-black hair, which was cropped close as the skin of a mole. He was attired in the garb of a Puritan preacher, and wore the tall sugar-loaf hat which Patty had remarked at the window on the previous night. In age Micklegift might be about thirty, and his person was tall and thin, but extremely muscular. On seeing the two damsels approach, he advanced slowly to meet them, and making a grave salutation to Dulcia, said to Patty, "Tarry by the gate, maiden, until thy mistress shall return to thee."

He then signed to Dulcia to follow him, and walked on in silence until they turned the angle of the church, and drew near the entrance-porch, when he stood still. Patty's inquisitive disposition might have led her to creep stealthily after them, if she had not observed a man suddenly spring over the wall on the north of the churchyard, and make his way cautiously round the tower of the sacred edifice. Patty suppressed the scream that rose to her lips on discovering that this individual was John Habergeon.

Having come to a halt, as related, Micklegift said, in a supplicatory tone, while a flush overspread his pale features, "Hearken unto me, maiden. Ever since I set eyes upon thee, my heart hath yearned towards thee. Thy charms have been a snare unto me, in which I have fallen. Yet though I have burnt with love for thee, I have not ventured to declare my passion, for I have perceived that I am an object of aversion in thy sight."

"Forbear this discourse, sir," Dulcia cried, "or you will drive me away from you instantly."

"Despise me not, but pity me, maiden," implored the preacher. "My love for thee is as a tormenting fire which consumes my very vitals. It disorders my brain, and drives me to the verge of madness. Have compassion upon me! I will be thy slave—anything thou wilt have me be—if thou wilt but love me."

"I will hear no more," Dulcia said, turning to depart.

"You shall hear me out," Micklegift cried, changing his tone to one of menace, and seizing her arm. "Love, like mine, unrequited, makes a man desperate. Another has possession of your heart;

MICKLEGIFT AND DULCIA   p. 48

but he shall not be an obstacle in my path. The malignant Clavering Maunsel is concealed in his father's house. I know it. It is
vain to attempt denial with me. The life of this traitor to the
Commonwealth is in my power. I can denounce him at any
moment, and I *will* denounce him, if you continue inflexible."
After a moment's pause, during which he watched the impression
he had made upon her. he went on: "Not only is Clavering
Maunsel's life in my power, but a word from me will consign your
father to a prison, where he may rot unheeded."

"And have you the heart to act thus against those who have
never offended you, inhuman man? Have some pity for them."

"You have no pity for me, damsel. You care not how much I
suffer. Now hear my fixed determination. Either consent to become my wife, or I will use the means of vengeance placed in
my hands."

"Give me till to-morrow for consideration," Dulcia replied.

"I will grant the time you require, on your solemn promise
that you will neither give warning to Clavering, nor mention aught
that has passed between us to your father, or to any other person."

"I give the promise you exact," she rejoined.

"Enough. To-morrow I shall expect your answer—here, at the
same hour. Till then, farewell!"

Released from his gripe, the terrified damsel instantly made her
escape.

"I am bound by no promise, villain," muttered John Habergeon, who was ensconced behind the angle of the church tower.
and had heard all that had passed, "and I will take means to
defeat thy black design."

III.

A TROUBLESOME day was in store for Colonel Maunsel. He
was in the library, seated in an easy-chair, meditating upon the
"Eikon Basilike," when Martin Geere entered, and, with a per-
turbed countenance, informed him that a state-messenger was without, and desired instant speech with him. The visit boded the
colonel no good, but he ordered the man to be admitted. The
messenger, however, did not wait for permission to present himself, but followed close upon Martin. He was a tall, stern-looking
man, having the appearance of a soldier, and carried a long sword
by his side and a pair of large pistols in his belt. He made no
salutation to the colonel, neither did he attempt to remove his
broad-leaved hat from off his close-cropped head.

"What wouldst thou with me, thou unmannerly fellow?" the
old Cavalier demanded, eyeing him with great displeasure.

"Thou hadst best show some respect to my order, though thou
showest none to me," the man coldly rejoined, taking a parchment
from his girdle. "Be it known to thee, Wolston Maunsel, somewhile colonel in the service of the Man Charles Stuart, that by
virtue of this order from the Council of State, thou art confined
and restricted, on pain of imprisonment, within a limit of five
miles of thine own dwelling.

"How?" the colonel exclaimed. "Confined within a range of five miles!"

"The limit is large enough for a dangerous and plotting malignant like thee," the messenger rejoined. "See thou exceed it not. But I have yet more to declare unto thee. Forasmuch as thy son, Clavering Maunsel——"

"Ha! what of him?" the colonel cried, unable to conceal his agitation.

" — being charged with high treason against the Commonwealth, and a warrant having been issued for his apprehension, in order that he may be brought before a court-martial, in virtue of a commission from his Excellency General Cromwell, this is to give thee notice, that if thou shalt harbour thy said son Clavering, or lend him aid so that he escape, and the ends of justice be thereby defeated, thou thyself, and any of thy house who may act under thee, will incur the penalties of high treason. Thou art warned, and a like warning will be delivered to thy whole house."

So saying, the man strode towards the colonel, laid down the parchment on the table before him, and, turning on his heel, departed.

Colonel Maunsel remained for some time, half stupified, with his gaze fixed upon the warrant. At length he took it up, and after glancing at it, dashed it down with a burst of passion. His wrath, however, gave way to feelings of alarm, when he learnt from old Martin Geere that, prior to his departure, the state-messenger had collected the household together, and informed them that if they aided in concealing their young master, now or hereafter, they would be severely punished.

"But your honour need have no fear," the faithful old fellow said. "They all believe the captain is gone; but if they knew he was hidden in the house, they would endure torture rather than betray him."

At this juncture Mr. Beard entered the library, and learning what had occurred, besought his patron not to be cast down, but to place his reliance upon that Power which had delivered him from so many difficulties and dangers.

"It is my son's safety that concerns me most," the old Cavalier groaned. "So he escape, I care not what becomes of me. But, sdeath!" he cried, breaking out into fresh fury, "I should never have desired to quit my own domain, if the tyrannous Council had not made me a prisoner."

He then paced to and fro within the room for some minutes, exclaiming, with much bitterness, "By Heaven! it is intolerable to be insulted thus in one's own house. O what a land we live in! Everything seems at sixes and sevens. All honourable usages are at an end. Respect for age and station is gone. Fanaticism and hypocrisy usurp the place of religion and virtue, and he is esteemed the godliest man who can dissemble most, and best put on a sancti-monious visage and demeanour. Out on the pestilent knaves who have thus abolished all that was good in the country, and set up all that is bad—a low-born crew who would grind down all to their own base level!"

"Yet there are some good men among them, honoured sir," Mr. Beard observed, "who have been influenced by worthy motives, and by love of their country, in what they have done."

"I marvel to hear you say so, sir," the old Cavalier re-joined. "Were the motives worthy of those bloody butchers who slaughtered their virtuous king? Are their motives worthy who have overthrown our Established Church, and set up the Na-tional Covenant in its stead? Are their motives worthy who per-secute and despoil, outrage and insult in every way all those who have shown loyalty and devotion to their king, and zeal for the country's welfare? Out upon them, I say!"

"I can make every allowance for your warmth, honoured sir, for you have much to move you to indignation," the good clergyman said; "but I would not have you blind to the truth. Faults there have been in high places beyond doubt—grievous faults—else had not those who filled them been cast down. Deeply must the princes and mighty ones of the land have sinned, or the Lord would not have visited them so severely with His displeasure."

"You seem to have caught the general infection, sir," the old Cavalier observed, sarcastically, "and speak as by the mouth of Increase Micklegift."

"I speak according to my conviction, my honoured patron, and I speak the more boldly, because I am well assured that it is only by acknowledgment of our errors, and resolution of amendment for the future, that we can turn aside Heaven's wrath from against us. Such men as Cromwell are instruments of divine displeasure."

"Name him not," cried the colonel, vehemently; "or name him as the arch-hypocrite, the regicide and parricide that he is. But you are right. We must have deeply sinned, or we could not have been yielded to the dominion of such as Cromwell. O England! when will thy days of gloom be over?"

"When her offences are expiated," the clergyman rejoined.

"Merry England men were wont to style thee when I was young," the colonel said, in a mournful tone; "but merry thou art no longer. Melancholy England were nearer the mark; sour England; distracted England; the England of Noll Cromwell and the saints. Heaven defend me from such a ruler, and such saints! Hearty, joyous, laughter-loving England thou art not. Men smile no longer within thy cities. Gaiety is punished as a crime, and places of pleasant resort are forbidden to thy youth. Upon thy broad breast sits the night-hag Puritanism, scaring away thy dreams of happiness, and filling thee with terrors. It is ill with thee, England. Wrong hath become right within thee—loyalty, treason—religion, an offence. Heaven grant thee a speedy deliverance from the wretched thraldom in which thou art placed!"

"I do not despair of England, sir," Mr. Beard remarked.

"Neither do I," the old Cavalier rejoined—"when Noll Cromwell shall be overthrown, and the monarchy restored. But, till that consummation arrives, I am much tempted to exile myself from her shores."

Here Martin Geere presented himself again, and with new terror imprinted upon his countenance.

"What's the matter now?" the colonel exclaimed. "I guess from thy looks that thou bring'st fresh tidings of ill."

"I bring no good news, in sooth," Martin replied. "There are two men without who crave admittance to your honour—crave, did I say?—nay, they insolently demand it. One of them is

Thomas Sunne, the Brightelmstone deputy of the Committee for the Sequestration of Livings. His reverence knows him——"

"Too well," Mr. Beard observed.

"The other I take to be a messenger, for he hath a warrant, and beareth a truncheon of office."

"Ay, and he will use it on thy shoulders, sirrah, if he be kept longer here," exclaimed a peremptory voice without.

And the next moment two personages stepped into the room. The foremost of them, who was he that had spoken, was of middle age, short and stout, and was somewhat showily attired in a blue doublet and scarlet cloak; the latter garment, however, was weather-stained, and had lost much of its original brilliancy. His doublet was embroidered with the badge of the Goldsmiths' Company—a leopard's head and a covered cup. His companion was an elderly man, with a sour, puritanical countenance, clad in sad-coloured raiments, and wearing a steeple-crowned hat. Neither of them uncovered their heads on entering the room.

"Ahem!" cried the foremost of the two, clearing his throat to enable him to speak more emphatically. "It is Wolston Maunsel, I surmise, before whom I stand?"

"Thou art in the presence of Colonel Maunsel, thou saucy knave," the old Cavalier haughtily rejoined. "Who, and what art thou?"

"I am not bound to answer the interrogations of a known malignant like thee. Nevertheless, I will tell thee that my heathenish name was Lawrence Creek, but since I have put off the old man, I am known as Better Late than Never, a saintly designation, and one becoming an elder, like myself. I am an emissary unto thee, O Wolston Maunsel, from the Commissioners of Goldsmiths' Hall, in Foster-lane, London, to whom, as thou knowest, thy forfeiture to the State hath been assigned, to summon thee to appear before the said commissioners within ten days to pay two hundred pounds for thy five-and-twentieth part of the fine which hath been set upon thee."

"My fine hath been fully discharged," the colonel said. "I have already paid the commissioners five thousand pounds."

"That is no concern of mine," the other rejoined. "Thou must appear before them to explain matters."

"A pest upon thee!" the old Cavalier angrily ejaculated. "Thou art enough to drive a man distraught. I cannot stir hence. I have just received an order from the Council prohibiting me, on pain of imprisonment, from going more than five miles from home. Here is the warrant. Read it, and satisfy thyself."

"It is no concern of mine," the emissary replied, declining to look at the warrant. "I shall leave the order with thee. Neglect to obey it at thy peril."

And, as he spoke, he placed a scroll on the table, and drew back a few paces, while the second individual stepped forward.

"My business is with thee, Ardingly Beard," this personage said. "Thou knowest that I have been appointed, together with my colleague, Thomas Geere of Ovingdean, brother to Martin Geere, who still continues in the service of the dangerous malignant, Wolston Maunsel——"

"I am glad my brother Tom hath had the grace not to present himself before his honour," Martin remarked.

"Thomas Geere was once one of my flock," Mr. Beard observed, sadly.

"He hath seen the error of his ways," Sunne rejoined. "But, as I was about to say, thou knowest that he and I have been appointed by the Committee for the Sequestration of Livings to collect, gather, and receive the tithes, rents, and profits of the benefice of the church of Ovingdean, now under sequestration, and to provide for its care. Thou knowest also how we have applied those profits."

"I have some guess," the clergyman observed. "Partly to your own use, partly in payment of Increase Micklegift."

"Wholly in payment of that godly divine," Thomas Sunne rejoined. "Now give heed to what I say unto thee, Ardingly Beard. It is suspected that thou continuest secretly to perform the rites and services of thy suppressed church. Take heed, therefore. If the offence be proved against thee, thou shalt pay with thy body for thy contumacy. A year's imprisonment in Lewes Castle will teach thee submission."

" Heaven grant thee a more Christian spirit, friend," the clergy-man meekly rejoined.

" Friend, quotha! I am no friend of prelatists and covenant-breakers," the other rejoined. " Wilt thou take the National Covenant?"

" Assuredly not," Mr. Beard replied, firmly.

" Begone both of ye!" Colonel Maunsel cried, losing all patience, " and rid my house of your hateful presence."

" You had best lay hands upon us, Wolston Maunsel," the emis-sary from Goldsmiths' Hall cried, in a taunting and insolent tone. " I should like nothing better."

" Nor I," Thomas Sunne added.

" Be patient, I implore of you, honoured sir," the clergyman cried, " and let them go."

" Show them forth, Martin, or I shall do them a mischief," the colonel cried. Whereupon the two men withdrew, muttering threats, however, as they departed.

As soon as he and Mr. Beard were left alone, Colonel Maunsel gave vent to a fresh explosion of rage.

" Perdition seize these Roundhead miscreants!" he exclaimed. " They have set me upon the horns of a dilemma. How am I to fulfil such contradictory orders? Here is one that tells me I must not stir from home: another, commanding me to come to London. If I obey one, I must perforce neglect the other; and, for my own part, I am well disposed to pay respect to neither."

" I scarce know how to counsel you, honoured sir," the clergy-man rejoined. " Truly, it is a most embarrassing position in which you are placed."

" It is more embarrassing than you deem, reverend sir," the colonel returned. " I have not wherewithal to pay the fine imposed upon me, and must borrow the two hundred pounds, at heavy usance, from old Zachary Trangmar, the money-lender of Lewes."

" I am grieved to hear it, sir," Mr. Beard observed.

" These bloodsuckers will never let me rest till they have utterly ruined me," pursued the colonel; " and such, I doubt not, is their intent. Their aim is to cripple all true men. Heaven confound their devices!"

"Amen!" the clergyman ejaculated.

"Well! well! the difficulty must be met, and bravely too," the old Cavalier cried—"no tame yielding, or crying for quarter on the part of Wolston Maunsel. I will fight the good fight, so long as there is breath in my body. I must go forthwith to Lewes—it is almost within my prescribed limits—and see Zachary Trangmar. I shall have to give the extortionate old rascal my bond, for he will not trust to the word of a gentleman."

"I cannot become surety for you, honoured sir," the clergyman observed; "or I would willingly be so."

"No, no," Colonel Maunsel exclaimed, hastily. "The old usurer will be content with my own security. Unluckily, it is not the first transaction I have had with him. If the knaves go on plundering me in this manner, I shall have little, beyond my good name, to leave my son."

"And that will be his fairest inheritance, sir," Mr. Beard observed.

"It is not likely to content him, though," the colonel rejoined, with a half laugh. "However, we must hope for better days, though neither you nor I may live to see them, reverend sir. Meanwhile, we must provide for the present. I will ride to Lewes this morning, and Dulcia shall accompany me. John Habergeon will watch over Clavering, and will know how to act, in case of difficulty. To your charge, good sir, I confide the rest of the house during my brief absence."

Mr. Beard bowed, and the colonel arose, observing, that when he last got on horseback, his rheumatism was so bad, that he thought he should never more be able to mount steed; but he felt quite equal to the effort now. Summoning Martin Geere, he bade him cause a couple of horses to be saddled—one of them for Mistress Dulcia. And seeing the old serving-man stare at the unexpected order, he added, "The day is fine, and tempts me to take an hour's exercise on the downs."

"But your honour hath not ridden for more than two months," old Martin stoutly objected.

"No matter, I mean to ride to-day. See that the horses are got ready forthwith."

"I should not have supposed that your honour would like to leave the house just now," Martin persisted. "How says your reverence? When robbers are abroad, it were well, methinks, that the master stayed at home to guard his treasure."

"My honoured friend has good reason for what he doth," the clergyman replied; "and I trust we shall be able to protect the house and all within it, during his absence."

"Nay, then I have nothing more to urge," the old serving-man rejoined.

"Hark ye, Martin," the colonel cried, arresting him; "bid Eustace Saxby, the falconer, hold himself in readiness to go with us; and tell him to bring with him the young Barbary falcon and the merlin that he hath lately manned and lured, and I will try their flight at a partridge. Use despatch, for I shall set forth presently.

BOOK III.

HAWKING ON THE DOWNS.

I.

THE OSTREGER AND HIS SON.

HORSE, hawk, and man were at the gate, awaiting the colonel's coming forth with Dulcia.

Stately and upright sat the hawks on the falconer's gloved fist, as if conscious of their tufted hoods of crimson and white velvet, their jesses and bewets with bells affixed to them, and their silver-linked varvels, graven with their owner's armorial bearings. Both birds looked in fine condition : plumage glossy and unruffled, legs and talons without speck or blemish. Gallant to behold was the Barbary, or tartaret falcon; not remarkable in point of size, for it was smaller than a tercel-gentle; but specially to be admired for its proud neck, broad breast, fine sails and beams, and long train; and, when unhooded, for its keen-bent beak, with barb feathers beneath the clap, wide nares, and full black eye. Fierce and courageous, also, was the tartaret's companion, the merlin; very nimble of wing, and, like the Barbary falcon, armed with strong singles and pounces.

Eustace Saxby, the falconer (or ostreger, as he preferred to be styled), was as gallant-looking as the hardy birds on his fist. Clad in a doublet of Lincoln-green, with his master's arms embroidered on the shoulder, with his upper hose tied with ribbons at the knee, and his feet protected by stout leather buskins, he carried in his right hand a tall hawking-pole, and was provided with a large hawking-bag, containing coping-irons, knives, scissors, creance, and other implements of his craft ; together with medicines in the shape of mummy-powder, washed aloes, saffron, and casting. Eustace Saxby was a strong, well-built man, in the prime of life, with a hard but honest-looking physiognomy, of the true Sussex cast. No Puritan he. Abhorring a Roundhead as much as his master, Eustace allowed his long locks to flow over his shoulders from beneath his green velvet cap, to manifest his contempt of the crop-eared curs. When younger, our ostreger had been remarkable for activity, and could then walk faster than any man in the county, and keep up in running with a horse at full speed; but having now grown stiffer in the joints, he was forced to cede the palm of fleetness to his son, Ninian.

Close to the ostreger stood his assistant, Barnaby Lashmere, carrying a square wooden frame suspended by broad leather straps from his shoulders. On this frame were perched several other hawks, of various kinds, in hoods and jesses, in readiness for the colonel, in case he might choose to take any of them with him.

Ninian Saxby, who filled the post of under-falconer, was with his father on the present occasion. A very good-looking young fellow of one-and-twenty was Ninian, with a fresh complexion, a merry blue eye, and brown curling hair. His lithe figure and active limbs seemed made for running and vaulting, and he excelled in all manly sports. A rattling tongue had Ninian, as well as a bright eye, and his pleasant talk and winning smiles made him a general favourite with the village damsels, even with those of a Puritanical turn; but his fondness for dancing and other pastimes, gaiety of manner, and light discourse, frequently drew upon him the grave rebukes of the elders. Ninian, however, cared little for such censure. The young falconer was too indiscriminate in his attentions to the damsels generally, and too fickle in his regards, to be assigned to any one in particular; but if he had a preference, it was supposed to be for Patty Whinchat—the pretty handmaiden herself being decidedly of that opinion. Ninian's habiliments resembled those of his father; his green jerkin was vastly becoming to him, while his green velvet cap, with a single heron' plume in it, placed jauntily on his curly head, suited well with the handsome and somewhat saucy features beneath it; giving the wearer quite as much the air of a page as of a falconer. Ninian had a bugle slung at his back by a green cord, a cross-bow over his shoulder, and a case of quarrels with a gaffle for bend-ing the bow at his hip. Moreover, he had two fine spaniels, coupled together, and in leash, in his charge.

Falconers, hawks, dogs, horses, and grooms, formed a picturesque group, viewed in combination with the ancient mansion, near whose porch they were assembled. Amidst the group, old Rupert, Colonel Maunsel's favourite charger, and as noble a piece of anti-quity as the colonel himself, occupied a prominent place. Rupert's best days were long past, it is true—and so, alas! were his master's—but though there were unmistakable marks of age about him, he was a fine animal still. There was fire in his eye, courage in his arching neck, that told of former mettle. Bright bay had been old Rupert's colour, but the hue was now sadly changed, and the flanks were dull, which had once shone like satin. He was furnished with a large easy saddle, having a high pommel, and a troussequin at the hinder bow. A dapple-grey palfrey, with white mane and tail, was destined for Dulcia, and this lively, but well-trained little animal, by his pawing, champing, and snorting, offered a strong contrast to the sedate deportment of the ancient charger.

Notwithstanding his reduced revenue, Colonel Maunsel still managed to keep up a large troop of servants of one kind or other. Born upon the estate, most of the members of the old Cavalier's establishment were so attached to him, that they would never have quitted his service, except upon compulsion. Wages were with them a minor consideration; one and all express-ing their readiness to share their good old master's reverses of for-tune.

With the grooms and falconers awaiting the colonel's coming forth, were gathered several others of the household: to wit, Giles Moppett, with a fat turnspit at his heels; Elias Crundy, the yeoman of the cellar, who had brought out a large black jack filled with stout ale for the falconers; Holney Ticehurst, the upper gardener, and Nut Springett, his man, with two or three hinds from the farm-yard.

The unusual circumstance of the colonel's riding forth to enjoy the pastime of hawking would have sufficed to bring a portion of the household to the gate; but there was another motive for gathering together so many of them on the present occasion, which might easily be detected in the serious expression of their countenances. The state-messenger's warning had struck terror into them all. Not that their fidelity to the colonel and his son was shaken by it; but knowing that Clavering had returned on the previous night, they were very apprehensive for his safety; for though told that the fugitive had left again before daybreak, few of them credited the statement, but felt convinced that he was hidden in the house.

It was on this alarming topic that they were now conversing together.

"Ah, well-a-day! these be sad times indeed!" old Ticehurst observed. "Wheresoever our young master may be, there I hope his enemies will never find him. Hast any news to gi' us, Master Moppett? Thou be'st a scholard like his reverence, Master Beard, and read'st de pappers."

"I have no news likely to yield thee much satisfaction, good Master Ticehurst," Moppett replied. "I have read both the *Perfect Diurnal* and the *Mercurius Politicus*, and they are full of nothing save the Lord General Cromwell's late glorious victory over the Scots king (as they term his most sacred Majesty) at Worcester; telling us how old Noll returned to London, and was met by a procession of the Men of Westminster, and how he made a triumphal entry into the City; how great rejoicings were held, and how the poor Scots prisoners were marched through the streets. Stay! I have one piece of news—and sorry bad news it is!—the brave Earl of Derby, the Earl of Lauderdale, and some other Royalists, who fought at Worcester, have been cap tured in Cheshire, and it is said will all be brought to the block Heaven avert the like fate from our young master!"

"Ay, Heaven avert it from him, and from one higher than him," said Eustace Saxby, in a deep, earnest tone. "Canst give us any tidings of the King, Master Moppett? Hath he escaped the bloodhounds set on his track? 'Tis to be hoped he will be watched over as David was when pursued by Saul."

"There be all sorts of rumours concerning him," Moppett rejoined; "and right glad am I that there be so, for their number will serve to mislead his enemies. Most likely his Majesty be hidden in some ellinge old house in Hampshire, waiting for a vessel to convey him to France. Such is the colonel's opinion."

"And the colonel ought to know, methinks, if any man doth," Elias Crundy observed. "But why don't his Majesty come to the Grange? Our master could soon hire him a fishing-smack at Newhaven or Shoreham to carry him across the Channel."

"That's more easily said than done, Elias," Eustace Saxby rejoined. "No one is allowed to embark at any port along the coast without special license. And as to the Grange being a safe hiding-place, I'm very doubtful about it. Only yesterday, I heard from a Brightelmstone Jug, whom I met at Rottingdean Gap, that a troop of old Noll's terrible Ironsides, under Captain Stelfax, have arrived at Lewes; and that all houses in the neighbourhood, suspected of harbouring fugitive Royalists, are to be strictly searched by 'em—the Grange one of the first."

"Lord presarve us from these ravenous wolves and regicides!" Crundy exclaimed. "That be bad news, indeed! But I hope it ben't true."

"I'm afeardt yo'n find it o'er true, Elias," Nut Springett remarked, shaking his head.

"I've heard John Habergeon speak of Captain Stelfax," Giles Moppett said; "and a bloody and barbarous rebel he must be, from John's account. He goes to work at once with thumbscrew and boot—thumbscrew and boot—d'ye mind that, my masters? If he comes here we shall all be put to the torture."

"And if we be, the truculent Roundhead shall discover nothing," Eustace Saxby cried, resolutely. "Let him do his worst. He will learn what stuff a loyal Sussex yeoman is made of. If any black jack ben't empty, prithee fill up the horn, Elias. I would fain drink a health, which Master Moppett tells me was drunk in the dining-hall last night—soon after young master's return."

"Drink it under thy breath then, Eustace," Moppett observed; "there be spies about, and no saying who may overhear thee."

"In that case, I'll drink confusion to the king's enemies! and may his Majesty soon enjoy his Own again!" the falconer exclaimed aloud, emptying the foaming horn offered him by Crundy.

Ninian Saxby took no part in the foregoing discourse. After quaffing a horn of humming ale with the rest, he began to wind a call upon his bugle that made the walls of the old house echo to the cheerful notes. Perhaps this might have been intended as a signal, for as he sauntered towards the porch, who should issue from it but Patty Whinchat!

"Give you good day, sweetheart," quoth Ninian, gallantly doffing his cap. "How blithe and bonny you do look this morning, fegs! Now for a well-turned phrase to tickle her ears withal," he added to himself. "You look for all the world like a newly-roused tercel-gentle—the tercel is the falcon's mate, Patty, and the falcon is a hawk for a prince—when after mantling, as we falconers term it, she crosseth her wings over her back, and disposeth herself to warble."

"To warble!" the handmaiden exclaimed. "Lawk a mercy! I never yet heard that a hawk doth sing."

"Neither doth she, Patty; but she warbleth, nevertheless—that is to say, she sitteth erect as yon tartaret doth on my father's fist. Dost know what 'coming to the lure' means, Patty? If not, I will teach thee—I will, fegs!"

"Nay, I know well enough," she rejoined, "and I would have you know, in return, that I am not to be lured, like a silly bird, by the call of a cunning falconer, or by the tinkling of silver bells. If you must whistle for some one, let it be at Morefruit Stone's door, and I warrant you his daughter Temperance, Puritan though she be, will come forth quickly. The luring-bells may be tried with Dorcas Thatcher, the milkmaid."

"You are like a raking musket, Patty, that forsaketh her

proper game, and flyeth at daw, or pie, or any other bird that chances to cross her. I, Ninian, am thy quarry—I am, fegs! Thou shalt bind me, and plume me, and truss me, if thou wilt."

"A truce to this nonsense, sirrah," she rejoined. "Be serious for a moment, if you can, and attend to me. There is something strange going on in the house. I can't make it out, for Mistress Dulcia won't admit me into her confidence."

"A word in your ear, Patty," the young falconer said, drawing closer to her. "Is anybody hidden in the house?—you understand, eh?"

Patty did not trust herself to answer otherwise than by an affirmative nod.

"Young master?" Ninian whispered.

Another nod.

"You're quite sure of it?"

Two more nods.

"I thought as much," Ninian muttered. "Then it behoves us all to be upon the watch—it does, fegs!"

"It behoves you to keep a close tongue in your head, sir, and not to blab a secret of such importance to any of the numerous maidens to whom you pay court. However, I *do* want you to keep watch over some one in particular."

"Name him, and it shall be done—it shall, fegs!"

"It is Increase Micklegift. May I trust you, Ninian? Well, then, my young lady met him this morning in the churchyard."

"Met Increase Micklegift! whew! What sort of 'lure' did *he* use, Patty?—the whistle, or the bells, eh?"

"She was scared by him, rather than lured, poor gentle dove!" the handmaiden rejoined.

"Say the word, Patty, and a bolt from my cross-bow shall visit the canting preacher's skull—smash it like an addled egg. It shall, fegs!"

"Killing him won't help Mistress Dulcia. I'll tell you what to do. But hush! they are coming forth. More another time."

So saying, she hastily retreated, while Ninian drew back with equal celerity.

F 2

A moment or two afterwards, the stately figure of Colonel Maunsel appeared at the doorway. The old Cavalier had offered his hand to Dulcia to lead her forth, and was ceremoniously preceded by Martin Geere, and followed by two other serving-men.

But before accompanying them to their horses, and noting the effect produced by the colonel's appearance on his attached retainers, let us see what had taken place within the house since we last left it.

II.

THE PROCLAMATION.

AFTER giving directions to Martin Geere, as before related, Colonel Maunsel, attended by Mr. Beard, sought his son, in order to acquaint him with his meditated ride to Lewes. Clavering's disappointment will be readily conceived, on hearing that, in consequence of this arrangement, he should be deprived of Dulcia's society, on which he had fondly calculated. However, he did not venture to remonstrate, but accepted, with the best grace he could, Mr. Beard's offer to remain with him during the colonel's compulsory absence.

At this juncture, John Habergeon returned to his post, which he had temporarily quitted, as the reader is aware; and the colonel briefly explained his plans to him. The old trooper made no objection, but informed his master that he had ascertained, beyond a doubt, that Increase Micklegift had discovered that Captain Clavering was concealed in the house. John did not deem it needful to state how he had obtained this information, neither did he declare what he meant to do; but he appeared so sanguine as to his ability to baffle the enemy's machinations, that he allayed the fears which his intelligence was calculated to excite.

As the principal bedroom in the house, the colonel's chamber was of considerable size,—it was, in fact, a double room, for there was an inner apartment, which did not communicate with the

gallery, and the entrance to which could be screened by a thick
arras curtain. Wainscoted with lustrous old black oak, and hung
with faded tapestry, the larger room had an extremely sombre air.
In it were one or two closets, and it was furnished with a large oak
armoire, half a dozen high-backed chairs, and a great elbow-chair,
always used by the colonel himself, and placed near a massive oak
table, on which were writing materials and a few books. In the
inner chamber stood the bedstead, a very antique piece of furniture, with lofty tester, carved posts, and heavy hangings.

His conference with John Habergeon finished, the colonel repaired to the inner room. Opposite the bed stood a large oak
coffer, banded with iron. Unlocking this chest, after rum-
maging for a short space amongst its contents, he found the deed
he was looking for, secured it about his person, and then summoning John to his aid, proceeded to equip himself for the ride; putting on a dark riding-dress, with boots having immense funnel
tops, and large spurs.

Mr. Beard, meantime, had gone down stairs to look after his
daughter, and returned with her, just as the colonel's preparations
were completed.

A green velvet robe, with long skirts, ornamented with gold lace
in front, and a feathered hat, constituted Dulcia's riding apparel;
and very well it became her. The young damsel had been the
colonel's constant companion so long as he was able to take horse
exercise, and he had bestowed this somewhat showy dress upon
her in order to evince his contempt of the primness and simplicity
affected by the Puritans.

Very little time was allowed the young folk for conversation;
but even in that brief interval, Clavering could perceive from
Dulcia's manner that her mind was troubled. To a candid nature
like hers it was very painful to have a secret from her father ; and
equally distressing was it to her to think that Clavering should be
menaced by a danger of the existence of which she could not warn
him.

Aware of the cause of her anxiety, John Habergeon sought an
early opportunity of relieving it, and while the colonel was talking

apart with Mr. Beard, the old trooper approached her, and whispered, " Be not uneasy, my dear young lady. I overheard what
passed in the churchyard. No harm shall befal his reverence or
Captain Clavering. Trust to me."

These words produced an instantaneous change in Dulcia's spirits,
and the few minutes more allowed to the young people ere the
colonel went down stairs, were far more agreeably spent than those
which had preceded them.

Every head was uncovered as the colonel and his fair companion issued forth, and old Rupert, recognising his master's
voice and footstep, pricked his ears, and neighed a welcome.
Raising his black Spanish hat, looped at the side, and ornamented
with a sable ostrich plume, in return for the salutations of his de-
pendents, the old Cavalier paused for a moment to look round,
still retaining Dulcia's hand within his own. Though he appeared
thin and careworn, all his retainers were struck by his unwonted activity, for he did not seem to need the support of his
crutch-handled stick, or even of Dulcia's arm.

After exchanging a few words with Eustace Saxby, who advanced to receive his instructions, the colonel assisted Dulcia to
her saddle, and then prepared to mount Rupert. On being
brought up to his master, the old charger manifested his delight
by whinnying softly, and thrust his nose into the colonel's hands,
as the latter patted him kindly. The moment was now come
when the old Cavalier's new-born activity was to be more sharply
tested than it had hitherto been. When he placed his foot in
the stirrup and attempted to mount, the effort wrung a groan
from him, and it required the strong arm of the groom to lift
him upon Rupert's back.

Hawking not being the real business that the colonel had in
hand, he dispensed with the attendance of Barnaby Lashmere
and the supplementary hawks, contenting himself with the birds
which the ostreger had upon his fist.

The party then set forth in gallant style, but had scarcely issued
from the gate, when they came to a sudden halt.

On gaining the road, it was noticed for the first time by all, that a board had been hung against the trunk of a large tree which grew by the gate. On this board, evidently designed for the purpose, was pasted a Proclamation, from the Council of State, for the Discovery and Apprehension of Charles Stuart, his Adherents and Abettors. A Reward of 1000*l.* was offered to whomsoever should apprehend the said Charles Stuart: while penalties of High Treason were menaced against all who should harbour him, or aid him to escape. Proportionate rewards were offered for the apprehension of Charles Stuart's adherents, with penalties of fine and imprisonment for concealing them, or lending them assistance. Strict commands were given, in conclusion, to all officers of Port Towns, and others in authority, to permit no person to pass beyond Sea without special license.

After perusing the proclamation, the colonel demanded, in a furious voice, who had dared to put it up?

An answer came from an unexpected quarter. Some half-dozen individuals, who had been standing behind another large tree at a short distance from the first, now came forward, and one of them detaching himself from the rest, marched towards the colonel. It was the state-messenger, with whom the old Cavalier had parleyed that morning.

"Thou askest by whom that proclamation touching the apprehension of the Man Charles Stuart hath been set up," the messenger said. "Know, Wolston Maunsel, that it was I, Nehemiah Lift-up-hand, who placed it on the tree growing at thy gate. I did so at the bidding of Hezron Stelfax, Captain of the Lord-General Cromwell's own chosen troop of Ironsides; the said valiant and God-fearing captain being now at Lewes."

"Pluck it down, some of ye, and hew it in pieces," the colonel ejaculated, wrathfully.

"Let any man remove it on peril of his life," Nehemiah cried, taking a pistol from his belt. "I have placed the mandate before thy dwelling, thou son of Belial, and there it shall remain."

As the words were uttered, the persons by whom the messenger was attended came up, and proved to be the emissary from Gold-smiths' Hall, Thomas Sunne, Thomas Geere, and Increase Micklegift. The Independent minister, however, kept a little in the rear of the others.

"Do as I bid ye! On your fealty to me—on your allegiance to the king—I charge you pluck down that proclamation," the colonel vociferated.

But no one stirred.

"Thy servants owe no allegiance to the son of the man who caused Israel to sin," Nehemiah rejoined, "and who provoked the Lord God of Israel to anger by his vanities. Even as Elah, the son of Baasha, was slain by Zimri, captain of the chariots, so shall Charles, the son of Charles, perish by the hand of the great captain of our new Israel."

"Take heed lest an Omri arise to depose thy murderous and rebellious leader," the colonel retorted, carried away by passion, "and cause him to burn the king's house over him, so that he perish by fire, like Zimri. Since none of you will pluck down that insolent placard, I will do so myself."

Ere he could execute his rash purpose, however, the twang of a bow was heard, a quarrel whistled past, and plunged deeply into the bark of the tree, severing the cord by which the board was hung to a small branch. Whereupon, the proclamation instantly dropped to the ground.

A loud burst of laughter from his companions followed this proof of Ninian's skill in the management of the cross-bow. But the young falconer took instantly to his heels; probably thereby escaping the vengeance of Nehemiah, who, on discovering the author of the mischief, discharged his pistol at him, but without effect.

The report of the pistol, echoing loudly through the valley, brought several other persons to the scene of action. Menacing cries arose at the same time from the colonel's attendants, amongst whom were Eustace Saxby, Martin Geere, Giles Moppett, old Ticehurst, Elias Crundy, and the rest of our acquaintances, who had accompanied their master to the gate. But the most formidable demonstration was made by Ninian, who having fled to the farmyard, presently returned at the head of a posse of rustics, armed with flails, pitchforks, and bills. These sturdy fellows, as they rushed up, surrounded Colonel Maunsel and Dulcia, like a body-guard, uttering fearful threats against the Roundheads.

On the other hand, Nehemiah and his party had been materially reinforced, and maintained their ground resolutely. No sooner was the pistol fired by the state messenger, than, apprehensive of mischief, Thomas Geere hurried off to all such cottages as were tenanted by Puritans, and in a very short space of time collected together some dozen or fourteen hinds, armed much in the same manner as Ninian's companions. Chief amongst these upholders of the authority of the Rump Parliament was Morefruit Stone, a fanatic of such a morose-looking and ill-favoured aspect, that if his daughter Temperance had borne any resemblance to him, it is not likely she would ever have caused Patty Whinchat a moment's jealous uneasiness.

A conflict seemed imminent; and if it took place, the passions of the men on both sides being fully roused, there could be no doubt that the consequences would be disastrous. It was this feeling that prevented the colonel from allowing his men to make an attack upon their opponents.

Taking up a position by the side of his father, Ninian began deliberately to bend his cross-bow with the gaffle, muttering to himself, as he did so,

"'Twere a pity to lose a chance like this. If I happen to hit yon psalm-singing rook, 'twill be a good riddance, and little harm done, fegs!"

Unconscious of his danger, the Independent divine seemed anxiously bent upon preventing a collision between the opposing parties. Addressing himself to the Puritanical cottagers, over whom, as their minister, he naturally exercised great control, and specially to Morefruit Stone, as an elder, he enjoined them not to strike a blow unless they themselves were stricken; and his pacific efforts were seconded by Thomas Sunne, who seemed to labour under great alarm. Having succeeded in keeping the members of his flock quiet, Micklegift next addressed himself to Nehemiah, who boldly confronted the colonel and his clamorous attendants. The state-messenger had not budged an inch, but having drawn a second pistol from his belt, held it in readiness.

"Put up thy weapon, Nehemiah," Micklegift said to him, "and cut not off any of these malignants in their sin. Leave them time for repentance and amendment. Perchance, they may yet be gathered into the fold."

"How sayst thou?" Nehemiah exclaimed. "Wouldst have me allow the proclamation of the Parliament, whose officer I am, to be cast down and trampled under foot? Wouldst have me tamely stand by, and hear his Excellency the Lord-General Cromwell insulted by yon contumacious malignant? As spake Joshua the son of Nun,—'O Lord, what shall I say, when Israel turneth their backs before their enemies?'—what shall I say unto the captain of our second Joshua when his mandates have been set at nought. Interpose not between me and these men of Ai."

"I say unto thee again, put up thy weapon, Nehemiah," the Independent minister rejoined; "for if thou take the life of this man, or the life of any of his followers, thou shalt not be justified. Make not of this peaceful dene a second Valley of Achor."

Then seeing Colonel Maunsel draw his sword, as if about to lead his men to the attack, he stepped fearlessly towards him, and taking hold of his bridle, besought him to desist.

"Who art thou who wouldst stay me?" Colonel Maunsel cried, feigning not to recognise him.

"Thy friend, if thou wilt let me be so," Micklegift rejoined, in a pacific tone, "who would fain save thee from the peril into which thou art about to rush. Have respect, I pray thee, for lawful and constituted authority. Join thy entreaties to mine, damsel," he added to Dulcia, seeing that the colonel paid little heed to him, "and prevail upon this hot-headed gentleman not to bring certain destruction upon himself and others."

There was a certain significance in Micklegift's tone that, even in that moment, did not escape Dulcia, and she at once comprehended the jeopardy in which the infuriated old Cavalier's rash

ness might place Clavering and her father. She therefore implored the colonel not to engage in actual strife with the Parliamentary officer and his supporters.

"I shall not come to blows with them till you are out of harm's
way, rest assured, girl," the old Cavalier rejoined.

"Disperse your followers, Colonel Maunsel," Micklegift continued, in a low tone, "and I will answer for it that the matter
shall be amicably adjusted. Believe me, I counsel for the best."

"Indeed he does," Dulcia cried. "In this instance, at all
events," she added.

"What! dost thou, too, side with Puritans and rebels, girl?"
the colonel cried. "Well, I own I have been over hasty," he
continued, returning his sword to the scabbard; "yet the knave
gave me great provocation." Then turning to his followers, he
said, "I thank you, good fellows, for this display of your attachment, but I will not put it to further proof. Return to your occu-
pations, all of you—except Eustace Saxby."

Upon this, the throng around him moved off, though reluctantly,
and with very dissatisfied looks; many of them turning round as
they went to shake their fists at the Roundheads, or make other
gestures of defiance. Observing Ninian linger behind, the colonel
motioned him to depart.

"Must I go too, your honour?" the young falconer asked.

"Of a certainty," the old Cavalier answered. "Yon pestilent
varlet will be sure to take exception to thee."

"Here's wishing your honour and Mistress Dulcia a pleasant
morning's pastime, then," Ninian said, doffing his cap, "though it
hath begun badly, fegs! Take the spaniels, father. I'll go round
by the shaw," he whispered, "and join you by the nearest burgh
on the downs. The rook hath 'scaped me now," he muttered,
eyeing Micklegift askance, as he went away; "but though I have
missed this chance, I may find another."

Meanwhile, at the exhortation of Micklegift, Morefruit Stone
and the rest of the sanctimonious flock had likewise returned to
their labour

"Peace is restored," Micklegift said to the colonel. "Proceed on thy way."

"Hold!" Nehemiah exclaimed. "I will not shut mine ears to the voice of a Minister of the Word, and since thou desirest peace, peace there shall be. Yet ere I suffer this dangerous malignant to pass, I must know his errand. He is placed under restraint by the Council, and may not go beyond a limit of five miles."

"You hear what the man in authority saith," Micklegift cried, addressing the colonel. "Satisfy him, I pray you."

"My errand is apparent," the old Cavalier rejoined, chafing at the interruption. "I am not as yet a prisoner in my own house, and am about to enjoy the pastime of hawking upon yonder downs."

"So thou sayest," Nehemiah rejoined; "but I have been too often deluded by those of thy dissembling party to trust thee without some pledge of thy sincerity."

"Ha! dost dare to doubt me, fellow?" the colonel cried.

"Hinder him not," Micklegift interposed. "I will be his surety."

"Thou!" Nehemiah exclaimed, in astonishment, while the colonel himself looked equally surprised.

"Even I, one of the elect," the minister replied. "Let him pass freely. These worthy persons," he added, in a lower tone to the colonel, glancing at the same time at Dulcia, "tarry with me till to-morrow, and much vexation and trouble may be spared thee by discreet behaviour towards them."

To this speech the colonel vouchsafed no reply, but rode slowly past Nehemiah and the emissary from Goldsmiths' Hall, who stood beside him, followed by the elder Saxby with the hawks and spaniels.

As Dulcia went by, the Independent minister drew near her, and regarding her fixedly, said in a low tone, "I shall expect thy answer to-morrow, damsel."

III

THE TARTARET AND THE HERON.

AFTER this somewhat inauspicious commencement of his ride, Colonel Maunsel, with Dulcia and Eustace Saxby, turned off on the right, and mounting a steep road cut in the chalk, which skirted the garden-wall, soon gained the charming down at the rear of the mansion.

The day was delightful. A pleasant breeze, fresh but not too strong, and redolent of the sea, came from the south-west. Fleecy clouds swept rapidly overhead, their shadows flitting across the downs in the direction which the party were about to take. So invigorating was the breeze—so beautiful the prospect—so calm and gentle the aspect of all nature—that the colonel, though worn-out by long watching, fatigue of body, and great mental anxiety —exasperated, moreover, by the insults he had recently endured —soon experienced the kindly influence of the scene, felt his chest dilate, and his spirits revive.

At no point, as we have elsewhere remarked, are the downs more beautiful than here. Our old Cavalier had a great love for the eminence on which he now found himself. In moments of impatience he talked of exiling himself from the rebellious land of his birth, but he would have been miserable if he had carried his threat into execution. His severe rheumatic attacks having con-fined him of late altogether to the house and garden, summer had gone by, and he had not once visited his favourite downs. It was, therefore, with redoubled delight that he found himself, after so long an absence, once more upon their breezy heights. He seemed as if he would never tire with gazing at the prospect around him. Familiar as it was, if he had looked upon it for the first time it could not have charmed him more.

Crossing the brow of the hill, the party reached the brim of a steep escarpment dipping into a beautifully hollowed combe; and here the colonel came to a momentary halt. The sides of this hollow, smooth as if scooped out by art, were covered with a carpet of the richest turf. Here and there, a little rounded prominence, or gentle depression, heightened their charm, as a mole or a dimple may lend piquancy to the cheek of beauty. A delightful air of solitude reigned over this fairy dell, which well deserves its present designation of the Happy Valley. On the right of the combe, near a circular excavation filled with water for sheep, grew a grove of trees of considerable size, with a thicket beyond them. The sides of the down, which hemmed in the valley on the opposite side, were by no means so steep as those of the escarpment, and had a warm brown tint, being clothed with gorse and heather. Through the midst of the combe wound a road leading from Rottingdean to Lewes, and looking over the shoulder of the hill on the right, could be discerned the old church and clustered houses of the former place.

While contemplating this beautiful combe, the colonel fell into a reverie, which Dulcia did not care to disturb, and Eustace Saxby remained at a little distance behind them. The silence, therefore, was unbroken, until a blithe voice was heard singing:

> "In my conceit, no pleasure like to hawking there can be:
> The tongue it lures, the legs they leap, the eye beholds the glee;
> No idle thought can harbour well within the falconer's brain,
> For though his sports right pleasant be, yet are they mixed with pain.
> He lures, he leaps, he calls, he cries, he joys, he waxeth sad,
> And frames his mood, according as his hawk doth ill or bad."

"Ah! art there, Ninian?" the colonel exclaimed, as, recognising the voice of the singer, he looked back and perceived the

young falconer descending the slope towards them. " I ought to
chide thee for disobeying orders. But i' faith! I am not sorry thou
hast come after us."

Ninian, who had disencumbered himself of his cross-bow, and
brought a hawking-pole with him instead, laughed cheerily, and
went on with his song:

> " At cockpit some their pleasures place to wager health away,
>   Where falconers only force the fields to hear the spaniels bay.
>   What greater glee can man desire, than by his cunning skill,
>   So to reclaim a haggard hawk, as she the fowl shall kill;
>   To make and man her in such sort, as tossing out a train,
>   Or but the lure, when she's at large, to whoop her back again ?"

" Well sung, i' faith, lad!" exclaimed the colonel, as Ninian
drew near him. " There is good sense in thy ballad."

" It is written by old Geordie Turbervile," Ninian replied.
" There is more of it, if your honour and Mistress Dulcia have
patience to listen."   And he struck up again:

> " When hawks are hurt and bruis'd by rash encounter in the skies,
>   What better skill than for their harms a powder to devise,
>   To dry the blood within the bulk, and make the mummy so
>   As no physician greater art on patients can bestow ?
>   To cut her hoods, to shape her jess, her tyrets, and her line,
>   With bells and bewets, varvels eke, to make the falcon fine,
>   Believe me is no common skill, nor every day devise,
>   But meet for civil, courtly men that are reputed wise."

" A good song, and well trolled," cried the colonel. " But let
us set forward."

Taking their way over several gentle undulations, covered with
the softest sward, and still keeping on the uplands, the party, ere
long, approached a large barn, in front of which was a stubble-
field, and here, as a covey of partridges was pretty sure to be
found, the spaniels were uncoupled, and set free by Ninian, while
the colonel took the merlin from the elder Saxby, and began to un-
strike her hood.

After ranging for a while within the new-shorn field, bounding
from ridge to ridge, and leaving scarce an inch of ground untried,

the dogs became suddenly motionless, and Eustace Saxby, who, with his son, had followed them cautiously, now gave a sign to his master, by raising his hand, that the partridges were found.

The colonel then advanced, and when within a short distance of the falconers, unhooded the merlin, and cast her from his fist, crying out, "Hey, gar! gar!" No sooner was the merlin upon the wing, than, urged by Eustace, the spaniels rushed in and sprung the partridges. After them darted the hawk, while the terrified birds, instantly perceiving their danger, strove to escape by rapid flight—vainly strove, as it turned out, for with marvellous quickness two of their number were stricken to the ground by the merlin, and almost as quickly retrieved by the spaniels, who, guided and incited by the cries of the falconers, followed the flight of the hawk.

At this moment, and while the partridges, scattered in their terror, were still upon the wing, the Barbary falcon, which had been committed to Dulcia, was unhooded by her and cast off, and with inconceivable swiftness joined her companion in the chase. All was now animation and excitement, the falconers shouting and encouraging dogs and hawks, and loudly applauding every successful stroke of the latter, the colonel riding after them shouting likewise, and closely attended by Dulcia.

Being very fleet of wing and keen of beak, the tartaret did terrible execution. Such of the scared and bewildered partridges as escaped from the merlin fell beneath his griping talons, and almost in as brief space as we have taken to recount the occurrence, was the whole covey struck to the ground, and retrieved by the spaniels. The hawks were then lured back by the falconers, and bountifully rewarded for their pains by gorges of the prey—the elder Saxby making for them what is called the Italian *soppa*. The partridges having been counted, and tied together by Ninian, were given by him to a shepherd lad, who had joined them, to convey to the Grange.

So excited had Colonel Maunsel been by the pastime, that for the moment he quite forgot his troubles, and it was with improved spirits that he once more set forward on his way; shaping his

course in a north-easterly direction over the downs, chatting plea·
santly with Dulcia as he went, and now and then addressing a
word to the falconers, who kept close beside him. He resisted,
however, all their attempts to induce him to flee the hawks again;
declining to enter a holt, wherein Ninian told him there was a
nye of pheasants; and paying no attention to Eustace, when the
latter pointed out a reedy pond in a hollow, where he would be
sure to find wild-fowl—a spring of teals, or a covert of coots.
Neither would he permit a cast of the merlin at what the young
falconer styled a " congregation" of starlings.

Proceeding in this way at an easy pace—now descending
into a broad valley—now mounting another heather-clad down—
anon passing over an elevated platform covered with fine green
turf, on which he encountered a large square encampment, the
colonel reached the summit of Kingston Hill, where a magnificent
view burst upon him. Almost at his feet, as it seemed—though,
in reality, three or four miles off—lay the ancient and picturesque
town of Lewes.

A very striking object is Lewes, as viewed from this lofty
eminence; but, striking as it is, it constitutes only a small portion
of the vast and extraordinary picture presented to the looker-on—
a picture so vast, indeed, that it cannot be taken in at a glance, but
must be regarded from the right, and from the left. Surrounded
by an amphitheatre of lofty hills, and planted upon a protruded
town, rising amid the Levels, the old town occupies a singularly
commanding position. In the midst of it, reared upon a high
mound, so as to dominate the surrounding structures, stands its
proud Norman castle, with its grey gateway, ivied towers, and keep.
Many churches and venerable edifices are there in the quaint old
town—many large gardens and fine trees—and most noticeable of
all, the picturesque ruins of its reverend priory.

Beneath Kingston Hill lie the broad Lewes Levels, a large alluvial plain, through which the narrow and meandering Ouse flows
towards the sea, to find an embouchure at Newhaven. At the
southern extremity of the valley is Newhaven itself, with the bold
promontory called the Castle Hill overlooking its harbour. Oppo

HAWKING ON THE DOWNS

p. 83

site, on the eastern side of the wide plain, is the majestic Mount Caburn, the southern point of the Cliffe range of hills, Firle Beacon, and Malling Hill, with its sheer white cliff, at the back of Lewes. Towards the north-east the eye ranges over a vast woody tract, comprising a great portion of the Weald of Sussex, but known in the days of Roman subjugation as the Anderida Sylva, in the days of the Saxons as the Andredswald, and during the Heptarchy as the Royal Chase. Inward, the view extends as far as Crowborough and the Reigate Hills—a range of nigh forty miles. To the west of Lewes, and commanding the Weald, is the monarch of the South Downs, Mount Harry, so designated after the famous battle fought upon its sides wherein Harry the Third was worsted by Simon de Montfort and the Barons.

While the colonel gazed delightedly upon this immense panorama, Ninian, whose quick eye was sweeping the horizon in search of some bird upon which to exercise the prowess of the Barbary falcon, perceived a heron, probably from the heronry in Angmering Park, sailing slowly towards them, in the direction of the marshy flats near Newhaven, and he instantly called his master's attention to the stately bird. The old Cavalier hesitated for a moment, thinking the tartaret too small to make a flight at a heron, but being assured on this score by Eustace, he assented. When the heron, who came slowly on, with wide wings expanded, and long neck and bill stretched out, had drawn sufficiently near, as the colonel judged, he took off the tartaret's hood, and dismissed her, shouting out, as before, " Hey, gar! gar!" while the falconers also encouraged her by their cries.

Startled by these noises, and at the same moment perceiving her enemy, the heron instantly quickened her flight. Swift as an arrow from a bow, the brave little tartaret climbed towards her quarry. It was a fine sight to watch her mount, and strive to overtop the heron, who now, fully comprehending her danger, soared upwards likewise, till well-nigh lost to view.

Both birds now looked like specks as their movements were watched by the group below. Ninian, who had the quickest and best eye of the party, and who had never lost sight of the birds, told them at last, with great exultation, that the tartaret had made her mountée, and got above the heron. On hearing this, the colonel uttered an exclamation of delight, as did the elder Saxby. Hoping to avoid the hawk's fatal stoop, the heron now descended as rapidly as she had previously soared aloft— the tartaret coming after her with equal quickness.

The crisis of the struggle was now at hand, as the watchers well knew, and they looked on with increased anxiety. All at once the heron turned over on her back, with her long, sharp beak pointed upwards, like a lance, to impale her foe.

At this moment the tartaret made her stoop, and dropped like a stone upon her quarry, seizing her and binding her. Both birds then fell together, and reached the ground at the foot of the precipitous descent, down which Ninian ran with great swiftness, hoping to be in time to rescue the hawk. But ere he got up all was over with the brave little tartaret. The heron's bill had transfixed her when she made her stoop, and the gallant bird was dead ere touching the ground.

The hawk and her quarry were lying together. The heron was still alive, but grievously wounded, and Ninian at once de-spatched her.

IV.

CAPTAIN STELFAX.

" ALACK! alack! my pretty tartaret, thou art beyond the aid of mummy-powder," Ninian exclaimed, as having liberated the yet warm body of the falcon from the cruel bill of its adversary, he was smoothing the blood-stained mails on its breast. " A lusty, roystering hawk thou wert, and sore grieved am I to lose thee!"

He might have gone on bemoaning his favourite for some while longer, had not the trampling of horses suddenly roused him. Looking in the direction whence the sound proceeded, he perceived a small body of troopers advancing towards him at a rapid trot along the road leading from the adjacent village of Kingston to Iford and Rodmill. He knew that these men must belong to the Parliamentary army, for since the rout at Worcester not a dozen Royalist soldiers, horse or foot, could have been got together. The little band numbered twenty men, and with them was an officer. Having heard from his father that a detachment of Cromwell's Ironsides had just arrived at Lewes, Ninian rightly divined that these men must belong to that invincible troop. Their leader, in fact, was no other than the dreaded Captain Stelfax.

Not liking to hurry off, the young falconer judged it best to remain where he was until the troop should pass by. They were now within bow-shot of him, and he could discern that they were all powerful-looking men, well-mounted, well-accoutred, and apparently well-deserving the hardy name they had acquired. Their doublets and saddle-cloths were of scarlet, the original bright hue of which had suffered from exposure to weather, and service in the field; but their steel breastplates, tassets, and head-pieces, were highly polished, and gleamed brightly in the sunshine. Each trooper had bandoleers over his shoulder, with powder-flask and bullet-bag attached to the broad leathern belt; and bore a long sword at his side, and a carabine slung from his shoulder.

There was no marked distinction between the leader of the troop and those under his command, except that the helmet and corslet of the latter were filigrained, and in lieu of bandoleers he had a crimson sash fringed with gold across his shoulder. At his side he carried a long Toledo sword. Captain Stelfax was a man of middle size, heavily built, square set, and very muscular, and endowed with such prodigious strength of arm, that, like a knight of old, he could cleave a foeman to the chine. Captain Stelfax was not thought to be so rigorous an ascetic as the elders of his troop might have desired, but being a thoroughly brave soldier, and of tried fidelity to the cause, his failings were regarded with a lenient eye. Though ferocious in the field, and merciless, it was said, in his treatment of those who came within his grasp, his expression, on the whole, was good humoured, and his features handsome, though rather coarse. His hair was cropped short, but he wore a bushy red beard, the glowing hue of which put to shame the tarnished splendour of his scarlet doublet. A weighty man, like this captain of Ironsides, required a strong horse to carry him, and he rode a great sorrel charger, who seemed quite equal to his burden.

Captain Stelfax, it presently appeared, had descried the party on Kingston Hill, and, curious to know who they were, on coming near Ninian, halted his men, and shouted to the young falconer to come to him. Ninian did not dare to disobey, and though he would much rather have taken to his heels, he affected great alacrity in complying with the summons. Captain Stelfax put a few interrogatories to him in a brief authoritative tone, and appeared satisfied with the replies he received; but as soon as he ascertained that it was Colonel Maunsel who was on the heights, he turned to one of the troopers nearest him, whom he addressed as Sergeant Hadadezer Delves, and, pointing out the party stationed on the hill, bade him bring them down to him.

Sergeant Delves executed his commission with great promptitude. Notwithstanding the precipitous nature of the ascent, he very soon gained the summit of the hill, and presenting himself before Colonel Maunsel, delivered his leader's message to him. Knowing that refusal was impossible, the old Cavalier expressed his readiness to accompany the sergeant—the more so, he said, as he was actually intending to proceed in that direction—and only stipulated that he and the young lady might be allowed to descend at a point where the declivity was less abrupt. To this the sergeant made no objection, and a bridle-road being indicated by Eustace Saxby, the whole party soon afterwards reached the valley without misadventure.

Captain Stelfax made no advance to meet the colonel, but remained lolling back listlessly in his saddle, with his left hand on the hinder bow, while the greater part of his men having lighted their pipes, puffed away at them vigorously. On approaching the Roundhead troop, Colonel Maunsel haughtily demanded of the officer wherefore he had been sent for?

Without changing his position, or making him any reply, the captain of the Ironsides regarded him insolently for a moment, and then casting his eye upon Dulcia, appeared much struck with her charms. He did not care to conceal his admiration, but gazed at her with much boldness.

"Is this comely damsel your daughter, Colonel Maunsel?" he inquired.

Offended by the question, as well as by the other's deportment, the old Cavalier felt disinclined to answer. Putting a constraint upon himself, however, he rejoined coldly, "She is the daughter of the Rector of Ovingdean, who has been deprived of his benefice, and who resides with me."

"Ardingly Beard, is he not named?" the other rejoined. "I have him upon my list of suspected. And his daughter is called Dulcia. I like not the name. It is heathenish, and beseemeth not one so richly endowed with good gifts. Nay, avert not your face from me, damsel. A rough soldier's talk need not offend you. Perchance you have heard of Hezron Stelfax, captain of the Lord General's chosen troop of Ironsides? I am he."

"Ask me not, then, what I have heard of you, sir," Dulcia replied, sharply, "or I may be forced to utter that which will not sound pleasing in your ear."

"You can say naught that will be displeasing to me, I am well assured," he rejoined. "But what have you heard of me? Speak out, and fear not."

"I have heard that your whole troop are cruel and bloodthirsty," she replied; "and that you are the cruelest among them."

"Ho! ho!" Stelfax laughed. "Cavaliers' tales, believe me. I am cruel only to my foes—bloodthirsty only in the field. And so is every soldier, malignant as well as Parliamentarian. But since you reside with Colonel Maunsel, damsel, you must have known his son, Clavering?"

Dulcia made no reply, but her cheek burnt hotly.

"What of him?" demanded the colonel, who had with difficulty controlled his anger during this discourse.

"Have you not heard?" the other said, looking at him steadfastly.

"Heard what?" the colonel cried.

"Your son fought at Worcester," Stelfax rejoined; "on that great day when the Lord of Hosts so wonderfully manifested his power, covering our heads in the conflict, and enabling us utterly to overthrow our enemies. Praise and glory to His holy name for the great success given us. 'Thou didst march through the land in indignation. Thou didst thrash the heathen in anger. Thou wentest forth for the salvation of thy people; thou woundedst the head out of the house of the wicked.'"

"It is not your intention, I presume, Captain Stelfax, to hold forth to me like a preacher at a conventicle," the old Cavalier observed, contemptuously. "What have you to tell me concerning my son?"

"I do not desire to give you needless pain, colonel," Stelfax rejoined. "But it is plain you have not received intelligence of your son's fate. Learn, then, that he was amongst the slain at Worcester."

"My son amongst the slain!" the colonel exclaimed.

"His body was found, recognised, and buried on the field of battle," Stelfax returned. "But you need not repine. Many an adherent of the Man Charles Stuart suffered greater loss on that day—glorious to us, if disastrous to your cause. Neither need you grieve, fair damsel, for this poor youth," he added to Dulcia. "A better man may be found to supply his place."

"Were he lost, his place could never be supplied to me!" Dulcia murmured.

"Colonel Maunsel," Stelfax now said to the old Cavalier, "I sent for you to give you a warning. You are known to be ill-affected towards the Commonwealth——"

"I am known for my loyalty to my king, whom Heaven pre-serve!" the colonel cried.

"Take heed you give not Charles Stuart shelter. Take heed you aid him not so that he escape beyond sea," Stelfax said, sternly, "or you will find little mercy from your judges."

"I expect none," the colonel rejoined—"neither mercy nor justice. Have you done, sir?"

"For the present—yes," Stelfax rejoined. "Yet hold! It is part of my duty, Colonel Maunsel, to make a strict inquisition of your house—Ovingdean Grange, I think 'tis called—to ascertain whether any fugitive malignant be concealed within it. Should you find me there on your return, you need not feel surprised. And now, my men, forward!—Farewell, sweet Dulcia! We shall soon meet again." So saying, he departed with his troop towards Iford.

Colonel Maunsel rode on in silence and great anxiety towards Kingston, until the Parliamentary leader and his men had disappeared from view. He then said to the younger Saxby, "Thou art swift of foot, Ninian. Dost think that thou canst reach the Grange before yon redcoats?"

"Ay, marry can I," the young falconer rejoined.

"Off with thee, then," the colonel cried. "On the instant of thine arrival, seek out John Habergeon—thou wilt find him in my chamber—and acquaint him with the intended visit of this rebel captain. Say to him—and say to the whole house—that my son is reputed to have been slain at Worcester—dost understand?"

"Perfectly, your honour," Ninian replied. And mounting Kingston Hill with the lightness and swiftness of a deer, he ran across the summit, and then dashed down on the further side of the eminence.

Meanwhile, Colonel Maunsel and Dulcia, attended by Eustace Saxby, rode on towards Lewes.

BOOK IV.

THE SEARCH BY THE IRONSIDES.

I.

THE PRIORY RUINS.

APPROACHING Lewes by the picturesque suburb of Southover, the little party halted near the ruins of the once magnificent priory of Saint Pancrace.

Here, quitting the road, the colonel and Dulcia, followed by the ostreger, with the merlin on his fist and the spaniels at his heels, entered a smooth, green area, of several acres in extent, surrounded by crumbling walls and arches, partly overgrown by ivy and brambles, and giving some slight evidence of the vast dimensions of the majestic pile formerly occupying the spot.

The Priory of Lewes, the first of the Cluniac order in England, was founded in the latter part of the eleventh century by William de Warenne and Gundreda his wife, daughter of the Conqueror, and was ruthlessly destroyed at the period of the Reformation by command of Thomas Lord Cromwell. The size and splendour of the conventual church—a portion only of the monastery—may be estimated by the report of Cromwell's commissioner, John Portmarus—a name to be held in abhorrence by the antiquary—who thus wrote to his employer in 1538 : " I advertised your lordship of the length and greatness of this church, how we had begun to pull the whole down to the ground, and what manner and fashion we used in pulling it down. I told your lordship of a vault on the right side of the high altar, that was borne with four pillars, having about it five chapels, which be compassed in with the walls, 70 steps of length, that is feet 210. Now we are plucking down a higher vault borne up by four thick and gross pillars, 14 foot from side to side, about in circumference 45 feet."

From the measurement furnished by this Vandal, we learn that the circumference of the conventual church was 1558 feet; the thickness of the steeple walls 10 feet, and the height of the steeple above the roof of the stately fabric, which was near 100 feet high, 90 feet. Of these ponderous pillars, storied windows, vaulted chapels, embowed roof, high altar, steeple, cloisters, and proud monuments, all are gone. Even the bones of the illustrious founders of the hallowed pile have been disinterred, and conveyed to another resting-place !

Out of the disjointed fragments left—here a range of thick walls with gaping apertures—there a solitary, misshapen piece of grey masonry—further on a yawning pit—it is scarcely possible for the eye of fancy to reconstruct the magnificent edifice. The knave Portmarus did his work effectually, and the only regret is, that he did not obtain the same reward for his services from Cromwell which the latter obtained from *his* master.

But though nothing but a few venerable walls told of the former magnitude and grandeur of the ancient priory and its church, still those ruins were picturesque and beautiful. A clear rill flowed through the spacious court, washing the base of the ivy-grown fragments, and into this rill the dogs instantly plunged to drink and bathe. A herd of goats wandered amidst the broken walls, nibbling the rich pasture afforded by the turf.

Within a bow-shot of the priory, on the south-west, stood a very singular structure, which has now totally disappeared. This was an immense pigeon-house, built of brick, in the form of a cross, with a tower in the centre. The structure was as large as many a church—much larger, indeed, than our diminutive church of Ovingdean—and its proportions will be readily conceived when we mention that it contained upwards of three thousand holes for pigeons, constructed of hewn chalk-stone. Around this gigantic dove-house clouds of pigeons circled; and when by accident the whole flock arose together, the air was almost darkened, while the flapping of wings was prodigious.

Hard by the priory ruins on the east, and overlooking them, stood that remarkable mound, the construction of which has been attributed to one of the Earls of Dorset; though the hillock was probably, as has been conjectured, thrown up in monkish times, and designed for a Calvary. Undoubtedly, no better position whereon to rear cross or chapel could be found than is afforded by this artificial eminence. The large but shallow excavation at its foot— jocosely designated the Dripping-Pan—shows whence the soil was taken to compose the mound.

Colonel Maunsel's sole purpose in seeking this retired spot being to leave Dulcia within it during his visit to Zachary Trangmar, he presently dismounted, and consigning old Rupert to the charge of the ostreger, and promising speedy return, he went his way.

Amid a scene so beautiful, and on a day so bright and sunny, with so many objects of great and peculiar interest around her— the ruins of the antique priory, with its historical associations —the gigantic dove-house, with its myriad occupants, in itself a never-wearying spectacle—the neighbouring mound—the old and picturesque town of Lewes, with its quaint, climbing houses and its towering castle—the noble amphitheatre of downs encircling her, and now glowing radiantly in the sunshine,—with this picture before her, Dulcia might have been glad to be left to its contemplation for a while, had her mind been at ease. But, alas! ever since the interview with the terrible captain of Ironsides new fears had beset her, and full of anxiety for Clavering and her father, she found it impossible to enjoy the various objects of attraction displayed before her.

After gazing listlessly around, scarcely noticing the cloud of doves hovering overhead, or alighting on the ruins, and which specially attracted the attention of Eustace Saxby, making him long to try the merlin at such a wonderful "flight," Dulcia fixed her eyes on the little rill flowing at her feet, and pensively awaited the colonel's return.

II.

MOCK-BEGGAR HALL AND ITS INMATE.

THE pleasant suburb of Southover, now constituting an important portion of Lewes itself, consisted, at the time of which we write, of a few scattered houses, some of which skirted the road leading past the church dedicated to Saint John the Baptist, where now rest the bones of William de Warenne and Gundreda; while others were built on the south side of the gently sloping and well-wooded hill. A clear brook flowing through a charming valley separated the suburb from the parent town. Towards this valley our old Cavalier now wended his way. Traversing a road shaded by noble trees, and crossing a little bridge over the brook, he presently reached the porch of an ancient mansion.

Though ancient, the house was in excellent preservation; the hard grey Caen stone of which it was constructed looking as fresh as if it had only just left the mason's chisel, and promising to resist the destructive action of the weather for centuries to come. On either side of the porch—to approach which a couple of steps leading into a small court had to be descended—was a far-projecting wing, furnished with bay mullioned windows. The wings had gable roofs, and on the northerly side of the habitation there was a massive stone chimney of very ornamental construction. A tolerably extensive garden was attached to the house; laid out in the old-fashioned style, planted with yew-trees and evergreens, possessing good walls for fruit, and watered by the brook that flowed through the valley.

Hospitality on a profuse scale might have been anticipated from such a goodly exterior as was presented by Mock-Beggar Hall—for so was the house designated, perhaps in derision—but slight hospitality was practised within it. The door did not stand wide open so as to admit a view into a spacious hall, thronged with serving-men. On the contrary, it was closely barred. No smoke issuing from the massive stone chimney told of preparations for good cheer. Most of the chambers were dismantled, while the few that were still occupied were meagrely furnished. In the kitchen, where many a noble sirloin and fatted haunch had erstwhile been roasted, little cooking now went on. The house looked starved. In it dwelt a hard, griping usurer and miser.

Old Zachary Trangmar had known how to profit by the troublous times in which he lived. When men are driven to extremity, money must be had at any rate of usance, or at any sacrifice, and the desperate circumstances of most of the adherents of the royal cause had been the old usurer's gain. A loan under such circumstances had put him in possession of Mock-Beggar Hall—heretofore known as the Priory House. He had sold its handsome furniture and fine pictures, and meant to sell the house itself, as soon as a favourable opportunity for doing so should offer. Meantime, he occupied it himself. Old Zachary's establishment consisted of three persons only, an aged domestic and his wife, who having lived with him for many years, were accustomed to his thrifty and penurious habits, and a stout porter, Skrow Antram by name, whom he thought it necessary to maintain as a protection against robbers.

Colonel Maunsel knocked at the door of Mock-Beggar Hall, and presently afterwards a little grated wicket was opened, and a surly, ill-favoured countenance appeared at it. After scrutinising the colonel for a moment, Skrow Antram, for it was he, grunted out a word of recognition, shut-to the wicket, and departed, as was evident by his retreating footsteps, to consult his master. Ere long, he returned and unbarred the door. Thus displayed to view, Skrow Antram proved to be a powerfully built man, of middle age, and dark, sinister aspect, who, it would seem, could scarcely have been hired on the strength of his honest looks. He wore a leathern doublet with pewter buttons, with petticoat breeches of green serge tied at the knee. Making a clownish obeisance to the colonel, Skrow forthwith proceeded to usher him into his master's presence.

Old Zachary Trangmar occupied a room on the ground floor, looking into the garden. It had once been a library, but books and book-shelves were gone; and the sole piece of furniture placed against the bare walls was a large dingy oak press. The old usurer was seated at a table covered with deeds and papers. Within reach of his hand was a pair of small scales, nicely adjusted for weighing gold. Further on lay a pile of account-books with sheepskin backs. Close behind the money-lender, on the floor, was a large chest, bound with iron hoops.

Though between seventy and eighty, old Zachary was as quick of intellect as ever, and keen were the glances which he cast from beneath his grey overhanging eyebrows at the colonel, on the entrance of the latter. Old Zachary wore a black velvet doublet, much frayed, and over it a loose murrey-coloured robe, which, like the doublet, had seen better days. A black silk skull-cap protected his bald head. His shrunk shanks were encased in nether-hose of lambswool, and his feet thrust into a pair of pantoufles. His features were sharp and pinched, his frame excessively thin, and his skin as yellow as the parchment of deeds lying beside him.

Silently saluting his visitor, old Zachary motioned him to a seat. Colonel Maunsel bowed gravely and somewhat haughtily, and took the chair, but uttered not a word till Skrow Antram had retired.

The usurer then looked at him with a shrewd smile.

"The old business, I presume, colonel? More money—ha! Nothing else would bring you to Mock-Beggar Hall, as fools call my dwelling. You couldn't have come at a worse time. All going out—not a doit coming in. As I hope to be saved, I haven't received a noble for this fortnight past!"

"What of that, thou avaricious rascal?' cried the colonel.

"Thy strong-boxes are replete with rose-rials, broad pieces, and angels. I know it well, man—so attempt not to plead poverty with me."

"Heaven forfend that I should plead poverty!" Zachary returned. "I meant not that. Money enough is owing to me in all conscience; and if I only get my dues I shall account myself rich. But ready money is what I lack. You are mistaken if you suppose my chests are full, colonel. They have been well-nigh emptied by you and your brother Cavaliers, and my goodly jacobuses and caroluses, my rose-rials and spur-rials, my angels and double crowns, have been turned into musty parchments."

"So much the better for thee, thou insatiate extortioner. Here is another parchment to add to thy stock."

Whereupon, the colonel took the deed from out his doublet.

"I thought as much," the old usurer exclaimed, affecting to groan, though his eye twinkled with covetous satisfaction. "Give it me, and let me look at it," he added, clutching at the deed like a vulture. "I see! I see! this relates to your farm at Piddinghoe, which brings you in a hundred nobles, or about thirty-eight pounds a year? What sum do you want, colonel?"

"Two hundred pounds to pay my fine to the state—I must have it at once, thou old skinflint."

"You are very peremptory, colonel; but suppose I cannot lend it you?"

"Then I must obtain the money elsewhere, or the commissioners must seize upon the farm and satisfy themselves. I warrant me they will be content."

"Nay, that were a pity indeed—and rather than the unconscionable rascals should get it, I will find the two hundred pounds; even though I should inconvenience myself. But I must have a bond, colonel."

"Agreed," the old Cavalier rejoined. "I know thy mode of proceeding too well to dispute that point with thee."

"And the rate of usance as before?" Zachary cried, quickly.

"The rate of usance as before, thirty per cent.—agreed!" the

colonel rejoined, with a sigh. "'Tis too much! But I cannot help
myself, and must submit to thy extortion."

"Nay, but consider the risks I incur, colonel," the old usurer
rejoined—"consider the disturbed state of affairs. If we lived
under a stable government—under a Monarchy—it might be
different—but under a Republic——"

"Tut! tut! all knaves prosper under the Republic,—to the ruin
of honest men," the old Cavalier rejoined.

"Ha! ha! you will ever have a gibe at the Roundheads, colonel.
And I marvel not at it, for they have used you and your party
scurvily. My own sympathies," he added, in a lower tone, "are
for the royal cause—but I dare not manifest them. 'Twould be
my ruin."

"Miserable hypocrite!" exclaimed the colonel.

"You disbelieve me. But I will give you proof of my sincerity. I have the lives of many a Cavalier of consequence in
my power—but they are safe with me. And so is their royal
Master, whose present retreat I could—if I chose—point out."

"Mark me, Master Trangmar," the colonel rejoined, sternly.
"If the exalted personage to whom thou hast just alluded should
be betrayed by thy instrumentality, it shall profit thee little.
Nothing shall save thee from the sword of the avenger."

"I would not betray him for all the wealth of the Commonwealth," the old usurer hastily rejoined. "It was to prove my
loyalty that I unlocked my breast to you, knowing you might be
safely confided in."

"Since you have said thus much, you must say yet more, and
inform me where the royal fugitive now hides his head."

"Not so, colonel," Zachary rejoined. "I can keep a secret as
well as yourself."

"As you please, sir; but you must allow me to put my own construction on your silence. Let us conclude our business."

"Readily, colonel," the usurer returned.

Upon which he unlocked the chest standing near him, and
taking out a leather bag, placed it upon the table. Just as he had
untied this bag, and was pouring forth its glittering contents, the

MOCK-BEGGAR HALL.

p. 101

door was suddenly opened by Skrow Antram, who entered, followed by a tall man. Almost involuntarily, the old usurer spread his skinny hands over the heap of gold, sharply rebuking Skrow for coming in unsummoned, and glancing suspiciously at the person by whom he was accompanied. The latter, though wearing a plain riding-dress of the precise Puritan cut, and mud-bespattered boots, together with a tall steeple-crowned hat and long cloak totally destitute of velvet and lace, had nevertheless a certain air of distinction, combined with great dignity of deportment, and might be described as looking like a Cavalier in the guise of a Roundhead. He was of middle age—perhaps a little past it—but appeared full of vigour. His features were handsome, and rather haughty in expression; his locks were clipped short, in puritanical fashion.

The moment Colonel Maunsel cast eyes upon the stranger he knew him to be Lord Wilmot, the devoted attendant of the fugitive king; while on his part the nobleman, recognising a friend, signed to the other not to betray any knowledge of him.

"How dared you admit this gentleman, Skrow? Hath he bribed you to let him in, eh?" the old usurer cried, with so angry a look at the porter, that the latter beat a hasty retreat. "What seek you, sir?" Zachary added to the new comer. "What business have you with me?"

"Read that letter from Colonel George Gunter, of Racton, and you will see," was Lord Wilmot's reply. "He has urgent and immediate need of five hundred pounds, and has despatched me for it."

"You have come on a fool's errand, sir," old Zachary rejoined, sharply. "Colonel Gunter has had more money of mine than I shall ever see back again. I won't lend him another noble."

"Read the letter before you give an answer," Lord Wilmot cried, authoritatively.

While old Zachary glanced over the missive, signs like those of freemasonry passed between the nobleman and Colonel Maunsel, from which the latter understood for what purpose the money was wanted. In another moment the old usurer threw down the letter.

"I won't lend the money," he cried, in an inflexible tone. " You may go back to Colonel Gunter and tell him so."

"Dost thou not perceive that he promises to pay thee back double the amount in two months?" Lord Wilmot exclaimed. " Is not that enough, thou old extortioner?"

" Ay, but he offers me no security. He *can* offer none; since I hold the title-deeds of his whole estate in yonder press."

" But I must have the money, I tell thee. Much depends upon it," Lord Wilmot exclaimed.

"If the kingdom depended upon it, you should not have it from me—without security," the old usurer rejoined.

"I will be thy security," Master Trangmar," Colonel Maunsel interposed. "This gentleman, I am well assured, is a person of honour. Give him the two hundred pounds you intended for me. Add other three hundred. Thou shalt have my bond, and further security on another farm of mine at Bevingdean."

" You are a true friend to the good cause, sir," cried Lord Wilmot.

" Ah! I begin to see what it all means now," the old usurer exclaimed, rubbing his skinny hands. " Well, sir, whoever you may be, and I have an inkling that I have seen your face before, you shall have the money. Nay, I will go further. Colonel Maunsel's generosity shall not be taxed so far as to deprive him of the two hundred pounds which he requires for his own use. He shall have that amount, without reference to the loan to your master—I crave your pardon—to Colonel Gunter." As he spoke, he again unlocked the coffer, and took out five bags. "Each of these bags," he continued, "contains a hundred pounds in gold. Can you carry them ?"

"I will make shift to do so," Lord Wilmot rejoined, bestowing them hastily about his person. " My friend is much beholden to you, Master Trangmar. Colonel Maunsel," he added, in a low tone, to the old Cavalier, " you have rendered his Majesty a signal service, and I thank you heartily in his name."

" Enough, my lord," the other replied. " Farewell! Heaven speed you !"

" Soh ! there is a visitor who has cost you a good round sum,
colonel," Zachary remarked, drily, as Lord Wilmot departed.

" The visit will cost me nothing," the other returned, coldly.
" The money will be certainly repaid."

" Be not too sure of that," the usurer said. " One can be certain of nothing now-a-days. However, I can pretty well tell
how it will be employed; and I sincerely hope it may lead to the
desired result."

" I heartily hope it may—for whatever purpose it is designed.
And now let us complete our transaction, Master Trangmar. I am
somewhat pressed for time."

" I will only detain you while I draw out a memorandum for
your signature, colonel. My scrivener, Thopas Tipnoke, shall wait
upon you at Ovingdean Grange with the bond—it will be an *obli-
gatio simplex,* as Tipnoke would style it—and he can receive from
you the title-deeds of your farm at Bevingdean, which you propose
to deposit with me. That is understood, and agreed, eh? Will
you please to count this gold"—thrusting the heap towards him—
"and see that you have your just amount."

A few more minutes sufficed to bring the transaction to an end.
Colonel Maunsel signed the document prepared by the crafty
usurer, who was as great an adept in such matters as his scrivener, Tipnoke, and received, in exchange, the two hundred
golden caroluses. The usurer attended him to the door, and, just
as he was about to depart, said to him, " Let me give you one
piece of counsel before you go, Colonel Maunsel. A rigorous
search is about to be made of all houses in this part of the
county suspected of harbouring fugitive Royalists, and as you
are accounted—be not offended, I pray you—one of the most
obnoxious malignants hereabouts, Ovingdean Grange hath the
foremost place on the list. I ask you not whether you have
any one hidden within your house? If it be so, be warned by
what I tell you, and if you value your friend's life and your own
safety, let him depart without delay. The search will be made by
an officer of the Lord General's own troop of Ironsides, Captain
Stelfax, who hath lately come to Lewes—a merciless man, with

the powers of a provost-marshal—and if he should find an unfortunate Royalist, he would think no more of shooting him than of stringing up a deserter. Excuse me, colonel. I have thought it my duty to warn you."

"I thank you, good Master Trangmar," the old Cavalier replied, striving to conceal his uneasiness. "I will take all needful precaution. I met this Captain Stelfax on my way hither, and he threatened me with a domiciliary visit."

"A pest upon him!" ejaculated the old usurer. "His visits are like witches' curses—they kill. Fare you well, colonel. These are sad times. When good men part, now-a-days, they know not how, or when, they may meet again. Heaven grant his Majesty a speedy restoration!—and should we live to see that blessed day, you will not fail to tell him, I trust, who lent the five hundred pounds."

"Nor to mention the rate of interest exacted for the loan," rejoined the colonel, unable to repress a smile. "Well, so thou wilt treat any pestilent Puritan in the same fashion, I care not."

"Trust me, I will sweat him properly if I get such an one into my clutches," old Zachary replied, with a chuckle.

Upon this, Colonel Maunsel quitted Mock-Beggar Hall.

On returning to the priory ruins he found Dulcia and the ostreger where he had left them. With Saxby's aid, he got once more into the saddle, and the party then started for Kingston, whence they mounted the steep hill at the foot of which the little village is nestled, and so shaped their course across the downs towards Ovingdean Grange.

But we must hie thither before them.

III.

HOW NINIAN DELIVERED HIS MESSAGE.

If Ninian had been mounted upon a swift steed he could not have reached the Grange more quickly than he contrived to do by the use of his own active limbs.

Not deeming it necessary to inquire whether Captain Stelfax and his troopers had made their appearance, for he felt certain he had beaten them, the young falconer's first business on entering the house was to seek out John Habergeon. As luck would have it, he found him in the buttery, discussing a jug of ale and a mouthful of bread and cheese—"bren cheese," the old trooper would have termed it in his Sussex vernacular—with Giles Moppett and old Martin Geere, and instantly delivered the colonel's message to him, taking care to add that the leader of the Ironsides entertained the belief that Captain Clavering had been slain at Worcester.

"The latter part of thy news is better than thy first, lad," John cried, swallowing down a huge mouthful, and springing to his feet. "Go all of ye, and spread the intelligence amongst the rest of the servants. Take care they are all of one story, d'ye mind? They will be sharply questioned by this cursed Roundhead officer—I know him well by report. Keep out of sight, Ninian, should the Ironsides come hither before the colonel returns, or they will understand that thou hast been sent on to give the alarm."

John then hurried up-stairs, and acquainting Clavering with the message which had just been brought by Ninian, told him he must take instant refuge within the hiding-place, and remain there till the danger was passed. Scared by the imminence of the peril, and apprehensive of discovery, Mr. Beard counselled flight; but John scouted the idea.

"Where is the captain to fly to?" the old trooper cried. "Were he to venture forth, those lynx-eyed Ironsides would be likely enough to capture him. And then that rascally Micklegift is playing the spy upon all our movements."

"Ay, there is another risk! How are we to guard against that?" Clavering exclaimed. "You say Micklegift is aware of my return, and knows I am concealed in the house. Will he not betray me to Stelfax?"

"No. His lips are sealed till to-morrow," the old trooper rejoined. "Ask me not why? I had rather not explain."

"You have good reason for what you assert, no doubt, John," Mr. Beard remarked; "though such tender consideration for us seems wholly inconsistent with Micklegift's character."

"It is perfectly consistent with his character, as your reverence would admit, if you knew all," John replied. "But the Ironsides may be upon us at any moment—don't suppose they will give us notice of their approach. In with you, captain," he continued, touching the secret spring in the mantelpiece, and disclosing the entrance to the place of concealment. "You have all you require, and are provisioned for a week. Don't be disheartened, if we should be unable to communicate with you for some time; and let no summons—no alarm—induce you to come forth. Mind that."

"I will obey your directions implicitly, John," the young man said. "Yet my mind misgives me, and I enter this retreat with reluctance."

"Have a good heart, sir," John cried, cheerily. "All will turn out well."

"Heaven grant it!" Mr. Beard ejaculated, fervently. "Place

yourself under the care of Providence, my son; and my prayers shall also be offered for your safety."

Upon this, Clavering passed through the aperture, and the next moment the pillar was returned to its place.

It was time. Scarcely had Clavering made good his retreat, when the blast of a trumpet was heard outside the house, proclaiming the arrival of the Ironsides.

IV.

IN WHAT MANNER THE CAPTAIN OF THE IRONSIDES EMPLOYED HIS TIME AT THE GRANGE.

AT this fearful summons, old Martin Geere, Giles Moppett, and some others rushed to the door, and, to their great dismay, found the house invested by a troop of armed men, who, having ridden through the gateway, were now drawn up before the porch.

"What ho, fellow!" cried their red-bearded leader, addressing Martin. "We are come to pay thy master a visit, as thou seest."

"You and your men are right welcome, worshipful captain, and my master, I am sure, will feel greatly honoured," old Martin rejoined; "but he is from home at the moment, hawking on the downs."

"He is at Lewes, thou shouldst say, for I left him riding thither scarce an hour ago with the Episcopalian divine's comely daughter," Stelfax rejoined. "As to welcome, we should have little enough, I warrant me, either from thee or from thy master, if we could not enforce it. But my men are hungry, and would eat; thirsty, and would drink——"

"They shall have the best the house affords, worshipful captain," old Martin hastened to say.

"They ever *do* have of the best when they pay a malignant a visit," rejoined Stelfax, laughing. "Your substance hath been delivered into our hands, and wherefore should we hesitate to take it?

I shall tarry here until thy master returns, for I have to interrogate him."

Giving the word to his men to dismount, Stelfax next directed two of them to stand at the door, and suffer no one to go forth. Every other outlet from the house was to be similarly watched: the guard to be relieved every half-hour, so that no man might be deprived of his share of the creature comforts to be found within. Sergeant Delves was instructed to take the horses to the stables, see them foddered, and then rejoin his leader.

All these orders given, Captain Stelfax sprang from his saddle, and, marching into the entrance-hall, made the whole place resound with his clattering sword and heavy boots. Old Martin Geere and the others kept at a respectful distance, anxiously watching him.

On reaching the middle of the hall, the formidable leader stood still, as if uncertain in which direction he should first bend his steps.

" Will it please you to enter the banqueting-room, or the library, worshipful captain?" Martin Geere inquired.

" I shall enter every room in the house in turn," Stelfax rejoined; " but I care not if I begin with the banqueting-room."

" A small collation shall be served there in a moment, captain," said Giles Moppett.

" Mayhap, your worship may like a cup of Bordeaux, or of Gascoigne wine?" insinuated Elias Crundy.

" Bring a flask of the best wine thou hast in thy cellar, fellow," returned Stelfax; " and broach a cask of thy stoutest ale for my men—unless they prefer wine, in which case thou wilt give it them."

" They shall have whatsoever they ask for, of that your worship may rest assured," Elias said.

" Or your own skins will suffer for it, I promise thee," Stelfax rejoined. " It seems, then, that you have not heard that the rebellious malignant, your young master, was slain at Worcester?"

" Alack! worshipful captain, we have heard the sad tidings," answered Martin Geere, in a doleful tone; " but we have not ventured to tell the colonel. Poor gentleman! the news will break his heart."

"Tut! thou art mistaken," Stelfax cried. "I told him of the occurrence myself, and he seemed more surprised than grieved. But who brought you the news?"

"An old trooper of King Charles's time, John Habergeon, captain."

"Where is the knave? Bring him before me."

So saying, he marched into the banqueting-hall, and flung himself into the arm-chair usually occupied by the colonel. In hopes of mollifying the formidable intruder, Giles Moppett and Elias Crundy both bestirred themselves, and speedily set wine and eatables before him. But this did not pacify the captain, for he roared out, "Why comes not the rogue Habergeon to me? Must I go fetch him?"

"I am here, captain," John responded, entering the banqueting-room. "What would you with me?"

Close behind the old trooper came Sergeant Delves, who had just returned from the stables. Stelfax looked sternly at John, who stood bolt upright before him, never moving a muscle.

"Thou shouldst have been a soldier of the Commonwealth, fellow," observed the Roundhead captain, approvingly—"thou hast the look of an Ironside."

"I am sorry to hear it," John replied. "Your honour might not deem it a compliment were I to say that you are too well-looking for a Puritan, and have more the air of a roystering Cavalier."

"Go to, knave, and liken me not to a profane follower of Jehoram," cried Stelfax, not altogether displeased. "Take heed that thou answerest me truthfully. Thou art newly returned from that battle-field whereat the Young Man, Charles Stuart, was utterly routed, and where our great general, like Pekah, the son of Remaliah, slew many thousands of men of valour in one day because they had forsaken the Lord God of their fathers. Didst thou bear arms in the service of Ahaz?"

"I followed my young master——"

"Who paid the penalty of his rebellious folly with his life—I know it. But I demand of thee if thou wert actually engaged in the strife?"

" I tried to rescue my young master when he was stricken from his horse."

" And thy efforts were futile. He was justly slain, forasmuch as he hearkened not unto the words of Necho, but came to fight in the valley of Megiddo. However, I blame not thy fidelity, and it is well for thee that we take not account of the units of the host, but only of the captains. Thou owest thy safety to thine insignificance. But if thou art ever again caught in arms against the Commonwealth, a rope's end will be thy quittance. Had thy young master been living, I might have spared him the ceremony of a court-martial, my power being absolute."

" It is well for him that he is out of your honour's reach," returned John.

" Therein thou sayest truly, fellow," Stelfax rejoined, with a laugh. " Well, I have done with thee for the nonce. I will question thee further when the profane malignant, thy old master, returns from his ride. Meantime, thou art a prisoner."

" A prisoner !" John Habergeon exclaimed.

" Ay, all within the house are prisoners during my tarrying here. None may stir forth on peril of life."

At this juncture, Mr. Beard and Increase Micklegift entered the room. Having witnessed the arrival of the troopers from the parsonage-house, the Independent minister had come over to watch their proceedings. John Habergeon having informed the Roundhead captain who the new-comers were, the latter prayed them to be seated, and addressed himself to the ejected clergyman.

" Your daughter is a comely damsel, Master Beard," he said— " a very comely damsel. I met her a short while ago, on the other side of the downs, in Colonel Maunsel's company."

" She went out to ride with my honoured patron," Mr. Beard replied.

" You have been told, I doubt not, of the death of your patron's son—the young malignant, Clavering Maunsel?" pursued Stelfax.

" I have been told of it," Mr. Beard replied, casting down his eyes, for it was painful to him to equivocate.

" What is this I hear?" Micklegift exclaimed, in surprise.

"The young man was slain at Worcester," Stelfax remarked, in an indifferent tone.

"That cannot be!" the Independent minister cried.

"Wherefore can it not be, I prithee?" Stelfax retorted. "I say unto thee again, the young man is dead and buried."

"Thou thinkest so?" said Micklegift.

"Nay, I am certain of it," the other rejoined. "There is small chance of his rendering further service to the Young Man, Charles Stuart. But I was speaking of your daughter, sir," he added to Mr. Beard. "She deserves a good husband. Have you ever thought of giving her away in marriage?"

"I have not," the clergyman replied. "She is yet of tender age, and I look to her as the prop of my declining years—should I be spared."

"But you know not what may befal you," Stelfax rejoined. "A wise man will provide against the evil day."

"Your counsel is good, valiant captain," Micklegift remarked. "And Master Beard will do well to commit his daughter to the care of some godly and discreet man, who will be as a safeguard to her."

"Like thyself," John Habergeon muttered.

"Nay, were I Master Beard," cried Stelfax, "I would rather give her to some man with a strong hand, who having carved his way with the sword, will maintain what he hath won with the same weapon."

"What! is this Roundhead captain too a suitor?" John Habergeon muttered. "We shall have the pair at daggers drawn ere long."

"This man is my rival," Micklegift mentally ejaculated; his pale features flushing angrily. "I must thwart his designs."

"I like not this Independent minister," Stelfax muttered to himself. "He is not a true man. I must keep an eye upon him. Well, Master Beard," he added, aloud, to the clergyman—"are you disposed to follow my recommendation, and bestow fair Mistress Dulcia upon a man of might and valour?"

"Or on a man of wisdom and godliness?" Micklegift said.

"His reverence must be hard put to it to answer them," John muttered, with a laugh.

"I shall leave the choice to my daughter," the clergyman replied, gravely; "and until she consults me on the subject, I shall give no thought to it."

A seasonable relief was unexpectedly offered to Mr. Beard at this juncture. A great disturbance was heard in the corridor, and the next moment two troopers entered, dragging in Ninian, with his hands bound behind his back with a leathern thong, and followed by Patty Whinchat, sobbing loudly.

"How now, Besadaiah Eavestaff, and thou, Tola Fell," Stelfax cried, addressing the troopers, "what hath this varlet done, that ye bring him thus bounden before me?"

"He hath assaulted our comrade, Helpless Henly, and smitten him on the head with a bill-staff," Besadaiah replied.

"Is Helpless Henly much hurt?" Stelfax demanded.

"Nay, I cannot avouch that," Besadaiah replied. "Luckily, he hath a thick skull. But the blow was delivered with right good will, and felled him to the ground."

"What caused the attack?" sternly demanded Stelfax.

"I was the unlucky cause of it, an please you, worshipful captain," sobbed Patty. "The soldier wanted to kiss me whether I would or not; so I cried out, and Ninian came to my assistance, and —and—that was all."

"No, not quite all, my pretty damsel," Stelfax said. "What place dost thou fill in the establishment?"

"That of handmaiden to Mistress Dulcia, an please you, worshipful captain," Patty rejoined.

"Mistress Dulcia is well served, I warrant her," Stelfax remarked, with a smile. "Take the varlet forth," he added to the troopers, "and belabour him soundly with your scabbards for ten minutes."

"Oh, spare him!—spare him!" Patty implored, throwing herself on her knees before the captain.

"Get up, Patty," Ninian cried, "and don't ask pity of him. I would sooner die than do so."

"This fellow is thy sweetheart—as the phrase goes with you profane folk—is he not?" cried Stelfax.

"He is, an please you, captain. Spare him! spare him! I am in fault, not he!"

"Well, thou hast won him grace," Stelfax replied, chucking her under the chin. "I marvel not that Helpless Henly was tempted by those cherry lips. Beshrew me, but thou art a pretty lass— almost as comely as thy mistress."

"That is ever the way with the captain," grumbled Eavestaff. "Like Samson the Nazarite, the son of Manoah, any wanton Delilah can prevail over him. Shall we unloose the varlet's bonds?"

"Yea, verily," Stelfax replied. "Yet stay!" he continued, looking hard at Ninian. "This must be the knave whom I encountered with the malignant colonel at the foot of Kingston Hill. There must have been a strong motive for his expeditious return. I will soon find it out," he muttered to himself. "Render an account of thyself, fellow. Why wert thou sent on by thy master?"

"To see all made ready for you, captain," Ninian answered, promptly.

"I have no doubt of it," Stelfax remarked, drily. "And thou hast done thy best to carry out the order. Wert thou to get thy deserts, thou shouldst have double the number of stripes I just now ordered thee; but thou art free. Thou owest thy liberation to this pretty damsel. Let him not out of your sight," he added to the troopers, as they undid the thong.

With a covert glance at Ninian, which seemed to say "Forget not what I have just done for you!" Patty Whinchat hastily disappeared.

Filling a large silver flagon, holding well-nigh a quart, with Bordeaux, Stelfax emptied it without drawing breath; pronounced the wine good; and then, getting up, expressed his intention of forthwith searching the house. He ordered John Habergeon and Ninian to attend him, but made no objection to the company of Mr. Beard and Micklegift, who proffered to go with him. Sergeant Delves and the two troopers brought up the rear. Old Martin Geere joined the party in the hall, and on seeing him, Stelfax cried out,

"Go fetch thy keys quickly, thou Pharaoh's butler. I will have every room and every closet—ay, and every secret place— opened unto me."

"There are no secret places that I wot of, worshipful captain," old Martin replied.

"Thou liest!" Stelfax exclaimed, fiercely; "and I will make thee show them to me, or thou shalt have the thumbscrew."

While old Martin, in a state of great trepidation, hurried off to obey the terrible captain's behest, the latter marched into the library, and glanced around it, making contemptuous observations on many of the objects that met his view. He had just finished his scrutiny when Martin came back with a large bunch of keys.

"I will begin with the ground floor," Stelfax said. "Conduct me to the kitchen and cellars."

The old serving-man bowed and led the way to the back part of the house, Stelfax and the others following him, with the exception of Mr. Beard and the Independent minister, who stayed in the entrance-hall. As Stelfax passed the buttery, he perceived half a dozen troopers seated at a table, with well-laden trenchers and large mugs before them. Amongst them was a great brawny-looking fellow, with his head tied up with a napkin, through which the blood had oozed. This was Helpless Henly. To judge from the expeditious manner in which Henly was clearing his trencher, he was not much worse for his broken pate. On seeing Ninian, the injured Ironside sprang to his feet, and drawing his tuck from its scabbard, would have spitted him as completely as the jack heron had recently transfixed the poor tartaret, but for the interference of his captain, who ordered the fellow to sit down again—a command which he obeyed with ill-concealed discontent, and muttered threatenings at Ninian.

The next visit was paid to the kitchen, where other troopers were discovered, similarly employed to those in the buttery. A brace of them, having satisfied their appetites, were seated near the fire, smoking their pipes, and watching the merry movements of the active little turnspit in his box. Stelfax tarried no longer in the kitchen than allowed him time to number the household, and put a few questions to them.

Next came the cellar. A short flight of steps conducted the searchers into an extensive range of vaults with strong stone walls

and arches calculated to sustain the weight of the superincumbent
structure. Nothing, however, could be discovered within these
subterranean chambers more dangerous than certain hogsheads
of ale placed within the arched recesses. Nor, when the wine
cellars were unlocked, was anything to be discovered except a
goodly supply of long-necked, cobwebbed flasks quietly reposing
in their bins. These bottles offered too strong a temptation to
the troopers to be resisted. Each of them, including Sergeant
Delves, took toll from the bins, carrying off a plentiful supply for
themselves and their comrades. No notice of the spoliation was
taken by their leader.

The cellar doors being locked, the searchers returned to the buttery, where the wine was put aside by the purloiners for future con-
sumption, and this precaution taken, the Roundhead captain intimated his intention of visiting the upper rooms. Upon which, they
repaired to the entrance-hall, where they found Mr. Beard and
Micklegift, and after examining several other apartments on this
floor, the whole party went up-stairs.

Every room in the upper story, large and small—with one exception—was carefully searched; every closet unlocked; every
place, likely, or unlikely, to conceal a fugitive, inspected. The
apartments allotted to Mr. Beard and his daughter underwent the
same rigorous scrutiny; even Dulcia's sleeping-chamber was not respected. In this latter apartment Patty Whinchat had sought refuge,
hoping to escape further molestation, and she was greatly alarmed
when Stelfax and the Ironsides burst upon her retreat. The Roundhead captain, however, sought to reassure her, and thrusting out his
followers, claimed a kiss as the reward of his liberation of Ninian.
Of course, Patty could not refuse the request. Neither did she
exhibit quite so much disinclination to the red-bearded captain's
salute, as she appeared to have done in the case of Helpless Henly.

Colonel Maunsel's chamber was reserved to the last. Refusal to
admit the searchers within it would have instantly awakened suspicion, so old Martin had no alternative but to open it for them.

On entering the room, Stelfax uttered an exclamation which filled
John Habergeon with misgiving. But the trusty old fellow took

heart when the searchers marched into the inner room, and proceeded to its careful examination. The hangings were pulled aside;
the old oak armoire was opened; the closets peered into—but nothing
was found.

John began to hope that the danger was over. But all his fears
revived when Stelfax, throwing himself into the colonel's elbow-
chair, and fixing his eyes upon the great mantelpiece, exclaimed
in a loud voice to Sergeant Delves,

"Bring hither hammer, hatchet, lever, chisel, and auger. I have
work for you to do."

V.

SHOWING HOW INCREASE MICKLEGIFT DID A GOOD TURN TO CLAVERING.

As this terrible order was issued, and the sergeant and the two troopers went forth to execute it, anxious looks were furtively exchanged by the Royalists, who now gave up Clavering for lost. These glances did not escape Stelfax, though he feigned not to perceive them, but smiled to himself. For one moment it occurred to John Habergeon to make an attack upon the Roundhead captain, and by the sacrifice of his own life possibly ensure Clavering's escape. But he was deterred by Mr. Beard, who, reading his desperate purpose in his looks, laid his hand upon his arm, and besought him in a low tone to forbear.

Secretly enjoying the consternation he had occasioned, Stelfax now arose from the chair, and marched to the window as if to look out at the garden, but really to indulge in a quiet laugh.

"If we could only get him out of the room for one minute, before the others return, Captain Clavering might be saved," John Habergeon whispered.

"I see not how that can be accomplished," groaned Mr. Beard. "The poor young man is lost. What will his unhappy father say when he returns?"

"I cannot bear to think of it," John returned, with a look of anguish. "Cost what it may, an effort must be made to save him."

"I may help you in this extremity," said Micklegift, in a low tone to John. "You will not forget the service?"

"Never," John returned, emphatically—"never! But what you do must be done quickly."

"Not a moment shall be lost on my part," Micklegift rejoined. And he moved towards the Roundhead leader.

"Methinks you did not sufficiently examine yon further closet, captain," Micklegift observed. "In my opinion it hath a false back."

"You must have quicker eyes than I have, to have made that discovery, Master Preacher," Stelfax cried, falling at once into the snare. "However, I will go see."

"I will show you what I mean," said the Independent divine, preceding him to the closet.

As he entered the recess with Stelfax, the Independent divine cast a significant look at John, the import of which the latter at once comprehended.

"Thou art lighter of foot than I, Ninian," he said to the young falconer. "Fly to yon closet!—the key is luckily in the door—lock them in!—quick!"

Ninian needed no second bidding. Stealing swiftly and noiselessly to the closet-door, he clapped it to suddenly, and locked it, almost before Captain Stelfax, who was at the further end of the deep recess, could turn round.

Infuriated at the successful trick played upon him, the Roundhead leader dashed himself with all his force against the door; but it was of solid oak, and resisted his efforts. He then roared out to the Royalists to set him instantly free, threatening them with his direst vengeance if they refused; but so far from attending to him, Ninian very coolly took the key out of the lock, saying, with a laugh, "If you wait till I let you loose, captain, you will wait long enough."

Meantime, John Habergeon had not been idle. So soon as Stelfax was secured, he rushed to the mantelpiece, touched the secret spring, and putting his head into the aperture, called to Clavering to come forth without an instant's delay.

The young man at once obeyed the summons. The noise made by the searchers had reached him in his retreat, and guessing the cause, he prepared to stand upon his defence, resolved not to surrender with life. Happily, his resolution was not put to the test.

In a few words John Habergeon explained to him what had occurred. But though he was free, escape might be rendered impracticable by the return of the troopers. What was to be done next? To get out of the house seemed almost impossible. Every outlet, as John knew, was guarded. Still, something must be done—and quickly. No mercy was now to be expected from the maddened Roundhead leader, who was hammering and hacking at the door with his sword, and making a terrific disturbance.

John's brain was usually fertile in expedients, but he was at his wits' end now, when Ninian, coming up to them, recalled his energies.

"Why do you loiter?" the young falconer cried, impatiently. "Those cursed troopers will be back in a moment, and Captain Clavering will be caught."

"But all the doors are guarded!" John cried.

"Except the door of this room, and that will serve our turn," Ninian answered, with a laugh. "Come with me, and I will show you how to get out of the house, in spite of them."

"Have with you then," cried Clavering. "Will you not come with us, sir?" he added to Mr. Beard.

"No, my dear son," the clergyman said. "Do you seek safety in flight; I will abide here."

"You had better come, reverend sir," John cried. "Yon savage Roundhead is no respecter of persons, and will show little consideration for your holy calling."

"I will withstand his malice," Mr. Beard answered, resignedly. "Do not concern yourselves about me. Go!—and Heaven guard you!"

"Quick! quick! or you will be too late!" cried Ninian, who had partly opened the door. "Methinks I hear them coming."

"Make sure that we may venture forth," cried Clavering.

Ninian stepped out into the gallery, and reported that no one was there, but that he could hear the voices of the troopers in the hall below. On this assurance, Clavering and John Habergeon instantly went forth, closing the door after them.

Left alone, the good clergyman sat down, and strove to prepare himself for the scene which he expected to ensue. All the time, Stelfax continued battering at the closet door, and vociferating loudly.

Ere long, Sergeant Delves and the two troopers entered the room, bearing the implements for breaking open the mantelpiece. They were surprised on seeing only Mr. Beard, and at a loss to account for their leader's disappearance, for Stelfax had momentarily ceased his clamour—probably from exhaustion. However, he presently renewed it, and with greater fury than ever, and then Sergeant Delves, beginning to comprehend what had occurred, rushed up to the clergyman, and, seizing his shoulder, shook him violently, exclaiming,

"What! thou perfidious and dissembling Episcopalian, hast thou entrapped our leader, a mighty man of valour like Amasiah, the captain of Jehoshaphat, and fastened him within yon closet? Give me the key thereof instantly, or I will smite thee with the edge of the sword, even as the false priests of Baal were put to death by the soldiers of Jehu."

"To do me injury will advance thee little, friend," replied Mr. Beard, firmly. "I have not the key. Thou wert better liberate thy captain thyself. Thou hast the means of doing so."

Apparently, the sergeant thought the advice good, for he called out to Captain Stelfax that assistance was at hand, which had the effect of tranquillising him. Delves next directed his men to burst open the door—a task which they easily accomplished.

Thus liberated, the Roundhead captain strode forth, sword in hand, and foaming with rage, followed by Micklegift, who maintained the most perfect composure.

"'Tis as I expected!" Stelfax cried, looking around, and seeing only Mr. Beard ; "the treacherous rogues have fled. But they hall not escape me. They cannot have quitted the house."

"Impossible, captain," Sergeant Delves rejoined. "Every issue is guarded."

"We will have them, alive or dead!" cried Stelfax. "Get thee down stairs quickly, Delves, and give the alarm to thy comrades. Bid them be on the alert. If any one attempts to escape, let nim be shot down. Bring up half a dozen men with you. We will search the house from top to bottom but we will find them. Some one must have been concealed within this chamber—perchance the Young Man, Charles Stuart, himself."

"Ha! say you so, captain?" Delves exclaimed "That were a prize indeed!"

"Nay, 'tis mere conjecture," Stelfax rejoined, somewhat hastily "Yet 'tis certain some one has been hidden here. Away with thee down stairs, and leave me to question this Episcopalian preacher."

And as Delves departed, the Roundhead captain marched up to Mr. Beard, and shaking him as roughly as the sergeant had done, fiercely demanded who had been concealed in the room.

"I will answer no questions," Mr. Beard replied, meekly but firmly; "so you may spare yourself the trouble of interrogating me."

"I will find a way of making thee speak, thou perverse and purblind zealot," Stelfax roared. "Think not I will show thee mercy because of thy comely daughter. Thou shalt undergo the torture. My men shall put jagged rings upon thy thumbs that shall pierce deeply into the flesh. Thy legs shall be thrust into an iron boot that shall crush bone and marrow, and make thee lame for life."

"All this you may do, and more, as your savage nature may suggest," the clergyman said, firmly; "yet shall you not force me speak."

"We shall see presently," Stelfax cried. "I ask thee again, who has been concealed in this room?—the Young Man, Charles Stuart, eh?"

Mr. Beard made no reply.

"Put on the thumbscrew, Tola," Stelfax said. "I will waste no more time with him."

"Hold, captain," Micklegift interposed. "I will not permit this worthy man to be tortured."

"Thou wilt not permit it! ho! ho!" Stelfax exclaimed, in a jeering tone. "In what way wilt thou prevent it? Withdraw, if thou carest not to see my order executed."

"No, I will not withdraw. I protest against thy cruel order," Micklegift cried, resolutely. "I lift up my voice against it, and if thou harmest this good man, thou and thy men will repent it."

"I have heard enough," cried Stelfax, fiercely. "Thrust him from the room, and obey my order."

"I will resist them—yea, I will resist them with force," said Micklegift.

The troopers hesitated, not liking to lay hands upon the Independent minister.

At this moment the door opened, and Colonel Maunsel and Dulcia entered the room. The old Cavalier looked pale as death, and greatly agitated. He cast an anxious look around, as if apprehensive that his son's retreat had been discovered. Dulcia was equally alarmed.

"My father! my father!" she shrieked, flying towards the poor clergyman.

BOOK V.

FOX AND WOLF.

§

HOW CLAVERING CAME DOWN THE CHIMNEY; AND HOW MICKLEGIFT LENT HIM
AID FOR THE SECOND TIME.

ILL news travels quickly. Colonel Maunsel was warned of the
danger awaiting him, long before he reached the Grange. Some
half-dozen loyal villagers mounting the down at the rear of the
mansion, stationed themselves near the old barrow, and as soon as
they descried the little party descending the gorse-coloured slopes
of the furthest hill on the north-west, they ran to meet the colonel,
and gave him the alarming intelligence that his habitation was
in the hands of the Ironsides, every door guarded, and no one
allowed to come forth. The faithful rustics, of course, were unable to
state what had taken place inside the house, or what discoveries had
been made, but enough was related to fill the colonel with deepest
disquietude:—the only relief to his anxiety being afforded by the
certitude which he likewise derived from his informants that
Ninian had reached the Grange before the enemy.

On approaching Ovingdean, the loyal rustics took leave of the
old Cavalier and Dulcia, who proceeded to the mansion. Dismounting at the porch, and giving their horses to Eustace Saxby, they
both went in, no hindrance being offered by the sentinels posted
at the door.

Old Martin Geere met them in the entrance-hall—his wobegone
looks announcing disaster. The old serving-man, we may remark,

dreading lest he should betray himself by some indiscreet observation, had quitted the colonel's chamber before Stelfax was entrapped by the agency of Micklegift, and consequently he could
give no account of that occurrence, or what had followed it; but
he knew enough to heighten his master's and Dulcia's alarm,
and fearing the worst—the worst with them being the discovery
of Clavering's hiding-place—they hurried up-stairs, entering the
room, as previously narrated, at the moment when Increase Micklegift interposed to prevent Mr. Beard from undergoing the torture.

Their entrance operated as a check upon the threatened violence.
At the sight of Dulcia, Stelfax, by a sudden effort, constrained his
wrath; while the two troopers involuntarily drew back as the
shrieking maiden rushed up to Mr. Beard, and flung her arms
around his neck.

"What would these barbarous men do to you, my father?"
she asked.

"They would torture him," Micklegift replied, answering for
Mr. Beard, whose agitation almost deprived him of the power of
utterance.

"Torture an unoffending clergyman—an old man—impossible!"
cried Dulcia, in an agonised voice. "Cruel as they are, they cannot mean it. They must have some respect for religion—some
reverence for grey hairs."

"Alas! they have none, my child," Mr. Beard observed. "Neither my age nor my sacred calling would have protected me from
outrage, but for this good man's interposition." And, as he spoke,
he cast a grateful look at Micklegift.

"Is this so?" cried Dulcia to Stelfax. "Do you still hold to
your savage purpose?"

"Nay, I meant but to work upon thy father's fears, damsel,
and so extort a confession from him," the Ironside captain replied. "I did not design to proceed to extremities with him."

"Heaven alone can read our secret thoughts," observed Micklegift, in a tone of incredulity. "But thy part was so well played,
that at least it imposed upon me."

Stelfax bent his brows, but took no other notice of the observation.

Colonel Maunsel had not hitherto spoken, but had looked on in the utmost anxiety, being ignorant, of course, of his son's evasion. He now addressed himself to Stelfax, in the hope of eliciting some information from him.

"You spoke of confession, sir," he said to the Roundhead leader. "What hath Mr. Beard to reveal?"

"You shall learn presently, Colonel Maunsel," the other rejoined, sternly.

"Nay, he shall learn at once," Micklegift interposed. "The valiant captain hath been locked in yonder closet, and waxing wroth at his confinement, he visited his anger on Master Beard's head, charging the unoffending old man with aiding a fugitive to escape."

"How know'st thou Master Beard is unoffending?" Stelfax cried. "Thou wert shut up with me in the closet, and couldst not tell what took place."

"Ha!" the old Cavalier exclaimed, a sudden light breaking upon him.

"The valiant captain seems to suspect that a proscribed malignant hath been concealed within this room," Micklegift continued, with a significant look at Colonel Maunsel.

"I am certain of it," the Roundhead leader returned; "and 1 begin to suspect it was by thy instrumentality, master preacher, that he hath escaped."

"How could that be, seeing I was with thee in the closet?" Micklegift rejoined.

"It might easily be—since it was by thy device that I was led into the snare. Bitterly shalt thou rue it, if I find thee leagued with the Amalekites."

"Let it be proven that I am leagued with them," Micklegift rejoined, "and I will abide any punishment thou mayst choose to inflict upon me."

"Proof that thou art in concert with the enemies of the Commonwealth may appear hereafter," Stelfax retorted. "Meantime, I have a question to put to you, Colonel Maunsel, whereunto I demand a distinct answer. Hath Amon, the son of Manasseh, whose provocations kindled the wrath of the Lord God against Judah—hath Amon, I say, taken refuge in thy house?"

"I will not feign to misunderstand you," the old Cavalier rejoined. "But were it as you suspect, think you I would betray him?"

"You prevaricate, and convert my doubts into certainties," cried Stelfax. "The Young Man hath been here—nay, is here still—for he cannot have eluded the vigilance of the sentinels. Are you aware, Colonel Maunsel, that a Proclamation was posted this morning at your gate, to the effect that whosoever shall harbour Charles Stuart shall be held guilty of high treason? Did you read that Proclamation?"

"I did, and would have trampled it beneath my feet."

"The punishment of high treason is death, colonel—death on the scaffold! Forget not that," Stelfax said.

"I shall but die as my Master died, if I so perish," the old Cavalier rejoined.

Just then, Sergeant Delves entered the room, and the half-opened door afforded a glimpse of several other troopers standing without in the gallery.

"The men await your orders, captain," said the sergeant, advancing towards his leader.

"It is well," Stelfax answered. "Before I proceed to the search Colonel Maunsel, it is right you should know that two of your retainers, John Habergeon and Ninian Saxby by name, have aided and abetted in this attempted escape of a concealed traitor and enemy to the Commonwealth. If they fall into my hands I shall show them little grace."

"Heaven grant them a deliverance!" murmured the colonel.

"And now," continued Stelfax, "I must see the hiding-place within yon chimney. Will you show me the entrance to it voluntarily, or must my men break down the mantelpiece? See it I will."

Colonel Maunsel hesitated, uncertain how to act.

"Advance, men—to your task!" Stelfax said.

"Hold!" the colonel exclaimed. And stepping towards the hearth, he touched the secret spring, and the pillar flew back.

"An ingenious contrivance, truly," cried Stelfax, with a laugh; "but you must have a better device than this to delude me. Give me thy pistol, sergeant," he continued, taking the weapon from Delves. "I will go in myself. Guard thou the entrance. I will not be entrapped a second time." So saying, he stepped into the recess, while Delves planted himself outside it.

Nothing was said during the brief absence of the Ironside leader. Colonel Maunsel, though almost confident of his son's escape, was not wholly free from uneasiness, while Dulcia glanced anxiously and inquiringly at her father, who strove to reassure her with his looks.

In another moment, Stelfax came forth again.

"The bird has flown," he said, "but the nest is yet warm. He cannot be far off."

"The fugitives cannot have left the house, captain—of that I am certain," Delves remarked. "No one has come down stairs."

"We shall discover them, I doubt not," Stelfax rejoined. "Visit yon inner chamber once more, and then we will search elsewhere."

The sergeant did as directed, and made a rigorous but unsuccessful investigation of the apartment.

"I did not expect any one would be found there," Stelfax said; "but nothing must be neglected. You, Colonel Maunsel, and all of you," he continued, "will remain prisoners for the present within this chamber—with the exception of Master Increase Micklegift, who is at liberty to depart."

"Nay, I will tarry where I am," the Independent minister rejoined.

For a moment, Stelfax seemed disposed to insist upon his departure, but, changing his mind, he exclaimed, "Tarry here if thou wilt. Sentinels will be placed at the door, and will suffer no one to go forth."

Upon this, he quitted the room with Delves, and the door was closed upon the prisoners. As soon as this was done, Micklegift approached the old Cavalier, and said to him, "Not altogether unjustly did yon man of wrath tax me with leaguing with your party. Your son owes his safety to me. But for my timely aid he would be now in the hands of his enemies, and you are aware how he would have been dealt with."

"It is quite true, worthy sir," Mr. Beard subjoined. "Good Master Micklegift must be regarded as your son's preserver, as he has since been my defender from violence."

"I thank you from my heart, sir," the colonel said, warmly. "I have been much mistaken in you."

"Thank the worthy man, my child," Mr. Beard said to Dulcia. "We are all greatly beholden to him."

"He has my thanks," Dulcia replied, unable to overcome her strong aversion to Micklegift; "and I trust he has been influenced by good motives in what he has done."

"Why should you mistrust him, my child?" her father remarked, somewhat severely.

"Ay, wherefore shouldst thou doubt me, maiden?" Micklegift said, in a half-reproachful tone. And bending his head towards her, he whispered, "This have I done for thy sake—and I will do yet more, if thou dost desire it."

Dulcia made no reply, but cast her eyes upon the ground.

"Take comfort, worthy sir, I entreat you," Mr. Beard said, noticing that the colonel seemed still a prey to keen anxiety. "All may yet be well."

"Not till I am assured of my son's safety shall I feel relief," the old Cavalier rejoined. "Little has yet been gained. 'Tis a mere escape from one room to another. Flight from the house, guarded as it is, is next to impossible, and I know not where concealment can be found within doors."

"Concealment will not be attempted, I apprehend, sir," Mr. Beard remarked. "Ninian seemed confident of getting out of the house secretly."

"Did he so?" cried the colonel. "Then I have better hopes. Some plan may have occurred to him which does not occur to me. Hist!—did you not hear a noise?"

"Only the trampling of heavy feet as the Roundhead soldiers move from chamber to chamber," Mr. Beard replied. "Pray Heaven your son escape them!'

"Heaven, in its mercy, shield him!" Dulcia cried.

"The noise grows louder!" exclaimed the colonel. "A struggle seems to be taking place in the room overhead."

Unable to repress an ejaculation of terror, Dulcia fell upon her knees, and prayed audibly.

"Methinks the sound comes from the chimney!" Micklegift cried.

"From the chimney!" the colonel exclaimed, advancing towards the fireplace, followed by the Independent minister. "You are right. Some one is coming down," he added, stooping to look up the chimney-funnel. "Who is there?"

"A friend," replied the voice of Ninian. "Is the coast clear? May we come down?"

"Powers of mercy!" the old Cavalier ejaculated. "Can it be? Is my son there?"

"It is the colonel who speaks," Ninian said, evidently addressing some one above him. "Yes, yes, the captain is here. Is all safe below?"

"It is—yet stay! those ruthless Ironsides may return!" the old Cavalier cried.

But before the latter part of his exclamation could be uttered, Ninian dropped lightly on the hearth.

A glance satisfied the young falconer that all was secure. He turned, therefore, and calling up the funnel, "You may come down, captain," assisted another individual to descend, and in a trice Clavering stood before his father.

"My son! my dear son!" exclaimed the colonel, transported with delight at beholding him.

Scarcely had Clavering and Ninian quitted the hearth than John Habergeon landed in safety, and stepped out into the room.

By this time Clavering and Dulcia were together—the latter weeping with delight on the young man's shoulder.

"The enemy are searching the house for you," Dulcia cried. "How did you manage to escape them?"

"Hush!—not so loud," Micklegift said, stepping softly towards the door; "you will be overheard by the sentinels."

"We put ourselves under the guidance of Ninian," Clavering said, in reply to Dulcia's inquiry, "and by his aid got upon the roof, and so reached this chimney, which he declared had holdings withinside for the feet by which we could descend. It turned out as he stated; but the descent would have been impracticable on my part, helpless as I am, but for John Habergeon's support. We meant to lurk within the chimney till the search should be over, when Ninian heard my father's voice—and so here we are."

"But here you must not remain," said the colonel. "The baffled Ironsides may return at any moment. What is to be done?"

"Can we not conceal ourselves behind the hangings in the inner room?" cried Clavering. "One of us might take refuge in the armoire."

"No, no! that would be too dangerous!" John Habergeon exclaimed. "Could we but reach the garden!——That window is a good height from the ground, it is true, but I could drop from it and break no bones—and so could Ninian—but the fall wouldn't suit Captain Clavering's injured arm."

"Think not of me, John," the young Cavalier cried, resolutely. "I am ready to make the attempt."

"It would be useless," Ninian said, cautiously approaching the window and looking forth; "there is a red-coat, with a musket on his shoulder, on guard below."

"Pest on him!" John ejaculated. "We must e'en climb the chimney again."

"So it seems," cried Clavering.

"Be ruled by me, and enter the hiding-place in which you originally took refuge," said Micklegift, advancing towards them. "The captain of the Ironsides has already searched it, and will not, in all likelihood, visit it again."

"The worthy man speaks the truth!" Colonel Maunsel exclaimed. "'Tis the safest place to be found. We are beholden to you for the suggestion, good Master Micklegift. Enter the recess, my son."

" Do not go there," Dulcia cried, detaining Clavering. " I distrust this man. He will betray you."

" Since you doubt me, damsel," said Micklegift, "let the youth
stay here, and be the consequences on your head. He will not
have to tarry long, for methinks I hear the footsteps of his foe
without."

" Why do you keep him back, Dulcia?" the colonel cried, impatiently. " Worthy Master Micklegift is perfectly right, and I owe
him a large debt of gratitude for twice saving my son."

" Spare your thanks, Colonel Maunsel, till the danger be past,"
the Independent minister rejoined. " Seek the refuge I have
pointed out to you, young man—or stay and brave your fate. But
hesitate not. In another moment you will have no choice left."

" I was wrong !—go !—go !" cried Dulcia to Clavering, who
still looked irresolute.

At her entreaty he moved towards the hiding-place, the entrance
to which had already been thrown open by Ninian, who had gone
in. John Habergeon stood outside on the hearth.

" Come! come! captain," the old trooper cried, impatiently.
" One would think you were desirous of being captured. In with
you !"

Upon this, Clavering entered the recess, and John quickly
following him, the pillar swung back to its customary position.

II.

HOW MICKLEGIFT WAS IGNOMINIOUSLY EXPELLED FROM THE GRANGE.

SCARCELY had all been made secure, when the chamber-door suddenly opened, and a sentinel entering, cast a sharp inquisitive look around.

"Methought I heard a noise," he observed.

"Thou didst hear my voice in exhortation, friend," Micklegift said. "Remain here, and I will hold forth to thee."

"Nay, my post is without," the trooper rejoined. And thinking all was right, he went forth, closing the door after him.

For some time no other interruption occurred. Micklegift became somewhat assiduous in his attentions to Dulcia, and she, knowing that Clavering's life was in his hands, did not venture to manifest the repugnance she felt towards him. Not for an instant, however, did she stir from her father's side. Mr. Beard took little part in the conversation, and, indeed, scarcely noted what was said. Colonel Maunsel withdrew into the inner room, and sinking into a chair, gave way to painful reflection.

Thus more than an hour passed, and still Stelfax returned not. Thrice during the interval—long it seemed to the expectants —had a sentinel entered the room. Although the imprisoned Royalists knew that the search would prove ineffectual, intense anxiety was felt by them as to how the Roundhead leader would bear his disappointment. In his anger he might resort to measures of increased severity. The savage character of the man warranted such a conclusion.

At length, the sound of heavy footsteps were heard within the gallery, followed by the grounding of arms, and the stern voice of the captain of the Ironsides could be distinguished, as he questioned the sentinels. Presently afterwards he entered the room. Rage and disappointment were written in his features, and he glanced fiercely at the group before him.

"Where is Colonel Maunsel?" he demanded, in a harsh voice.

"I am here," the old Cavalier answered, rising from his seat, and advancing towards him.

"It may not, perchance, surprise you, Colonel Maunsel, to be told that my search—strict though it has been—has proved fruitless," pursued the Ironside captain; "but though foiled for the moment, I am not to be beaten, as you will find to your cost. Three persons have escaped me—two of your own retainers, and a third person, hidden within this room, whose flight has been traitorously abetted. Now, mark me, colonel. I know you to be proud and stiff-necked, like all your rebellious party; but regard for self may sway you. The three persons I have alluded to are still in your house. Produce them, and you will save me some trouble and yourself vexation. Refuse, and I shall take other three persons in their stead, to be dealt with as the authorities may see fit. You yourself, colonel, will be one of my prisoners." And he slightly paused to note the effect of his words upon the old Cavalier.

"Proceed, sir," said the other, firmly.

"The second person I shall take will be Master Beard," pursued Stelfax, speaking with great deliberation. "The third will be his daughter."

"His daughter!" exclaimed the colonel, starting. "You dare not do it. On what pretence would you make her a prisoner?"

"I render an account of my actions to those only who have the right to question me, colonel," rejoined Stelfax, "and such is not your case. It will be painful to act thus harshly, I admit; but you enforce severity upon me. Deliver up the three men to me, and I depart at once, without offering you further molestation."

"I cannot do so," groaned the colonel—"I would not, if I could."

"Ay, there the truth came out," Stelfax retorted, with a bitter laugh. "That you *can* produce them if you will, I wot full well. It grieves me to the soul to deal harshly with this comely and delicate damsel. That I am forced to do so is owing to perverseness on your part—not to want of humanity on mine."

"Affect not to feel for me, I pray you, sir," cried Dulcia. "Your pity is unneeded and unsolicited. If Colonel Maunsel and my father are made prisoners, I desire to go with them."

"Make yourself easy, my child," Mr. Beard said., "This man will not venture to stretch his authority so far. He cannot mean to do as he avouches."

"Not mean it!" Stelfax echoed, in a jeering tone; "you will see anon whether I mean what I say or not, Master Beard."

"At least give ear unto me," said Micklegift, advancing towards him.

"Peace! I will not listen to thee," cried Stelfax, roughly.

"Yet have I something to say unto thee to which thou wilt willingly attend," said Micklegift, in no wise abashed by the other's rudeness. "It is not meet that this damsel should be made thy captive."

"Intercede not for me, I entreat you, sir?" cried Dulcia, fearing that he meditated treachery. "If my life is to be sacrificed, I will give it cheerfully."

"Nay, your life is not endangered, maiden," said Stelfax; "merely your liberty—for the which, I repeat, you have to thank Colonel Maunsel."

"I say unto thee again, captain, the damsel's liberty must not, and shall not be constrained," said Micklegift.

"Hold thy peace, I say! thou froward fellow," cried Stelfax. "The damsel herself desires not thy mediation."

"Indeed I do not," implored Dulcia. "Beseech you, good sir, let the matter be," she added to Micklegift.

"Thou hearest what she says," cried Stelfax. "Trouble me no further."

"I will not let the matter be," exclaimed Micklegift. "I tell

MICKLEGIFT HAS HIS MOUTH STOPPED

thee, for the third time, thou shalt not take the damsel. Even if she would go freely with thee, she shall not do it."

"This passeth all endurance," roared Stelfax, stamping his foot with rage. "What ho! guard!" he shouted. And half a dozen troopers instantly answering the summons, he continued, "Seize this pestilent fellow who hath dared to wag his evil tongue against me, and disputeth my authority. Thrust a kerchief into his mouth to stop his mischievous clamour. Cast him from the house—and suffer him not, on any pretence, to enter it again."

The Ironside leader's injunctions were instantly obeyed. Micklegift's arms were seized and pinioned behind his back, while a cloth thrust into his mouth prevented his utterance. In this guise, and exposed to further ill-usage as he was forced out of the room and hurried down stairs, he was kicked out of the house, amidst the jeers of the troopers, and of such of the household as witnessed his ignominious expulsion.

III.

HOW THE CAPTAIN OF THE IRONSIDES TOOK POSSESSION OF THE COLONEL'S CHAMBER.

No one among the Royalists, except good Mr. Beard, regretted the summary dismissal of the Independent minister. Dulcia, indeed, regarded his ejection as a most fortunate deliverance, being convinced that he was about to betray Clavering, when his design was frustrated by the Roundhead leader's unwillingness to listen to him.

Captain Stelfax's secret object, however, was to get rid of one whom he looked upon as a troublesome rival. Having accomplished his purpose, he withdrew to the further end of the room, where he held a long consultation with Delves. The old Cavalier, who watched them narrowly, was at no loss to understand from the captain's gestures that he was discussing the possibility of the fugitives still being concealed within the chamber; and it was with no little alarm that at one moment he perceived the glances of both the Ironsides directed towards the mantelpiece. But his alarm was dispelled as quickly as it arose. Stelfax shook his head as if to intimate that no one could have found refuge there.

His conference ended, the captain of the Ironsides marched up to the old Cavalier, and said, "I have resolved upon remaining here till to-morrow, Colonel Maunsel, and if by that time the three persons I have demanded from you be not delivered up to

me, I shall be compelled to execute my threat in respect to yourself, Master Beard, and his daughter. If you are put to inconvenience in finding accommodation and provisions for my men, you
must not blame me."

"I am in your power, sir, and must perforce submit," the colonel
replied. "What is your further pleasure?"

"Humph!" exclaimed Stelfax. "I have no particular orders to
give. My men must be well fed, and well lodged—but they will
see to those matters themselves—and it will be best to content them.
As to myself, I shall merely require this room for my occupation."

"This room!" the colonel exclaimed, visibly embarrassed.
"Will none other serve your turn? This is my own sleeping-
chamber."

"You must resign it to me for to-night, colonel," Stelfax rejoined; noticing, with secret satisfaction, the other's dismay. "I
have taken a fancy to it, and cannot study your convenience."

"So it seems, sir," said the old Cavalier, feeling that remonstrance
would be useless, and perhaps dangerous. "You will not object,
at least, to my making some little arrangements within the chamber, and removing a few trifling articles before you take possession
of it."

"Assuredly not," Stelfax replied. "Remove what you please,
colonel. But what you do must be done in my presence, or in the
presence of Sergeant Delves."

"I find I am indeed a prisoner," sighed the colonel, "since my
every movement must needs be watched."

"Recollect that you yourself render this rigour necessary," Stelfax rejoined; "and thank me that I deal not more harshly with
you. For you, fair damsel," he added to Dulcia, "you are at liberty
to retire to your own apartment, if you are so minded. But forget
not that you are a prisoner to the house; and if summoned to my
presence, fail not in prompt attendance. Master Beard, you can
go with your daughter—on the same conditions."

Not venturing to remain after this dismissal, Dulcia and her
father reluctantly, and full of misgiving, withdrew.

Colonel Maunsel hoped that he might have been left alone

within the chamber for a few minutes, and so snatch an opportunity of communicating with those within the hiding-place; but
this being denied him, he would fain have tarried within the
room. But here again his wishes were defeated, for Stelfax soon
afterwards signified to him, in a tone that left no alternative but
compliance, that he might retire. The only favour he could
obtain was permission to send Martin Geere for such articles as he
might require for the night. This accorded, he withdrew.

It was not without considerable trepidation that old Martin
executed his master's orders; and, on returning to the library,
whither the colonel had repaired, the old serving-man reported
that Stelfax had caused a great wood fire to be lighted, before
which he was comfortably seated—a piece of intelligence which
did not tend to mitigate the old Cavalier's anxiety, since it de-
creased the chances of his son's escape.

Deeply did Colonel Maunsel now regret that he was deprived
of the assistance of John Habergeon, whose shrewdness might
have helped him at this fearful emergency. But John was a
prisoner as well as Clavering; and as to poor old Martin Geere,
he was so bewildered as to be utterly incapable of lending efficient
assistance. Resignation, therefore, was all that was left to the old
Cavalier. He tried to calm himself, but in vain. Suspense and
anxiety quite overmastered him, and reduced him at last to a state
of almost stupor.

If the colonel was plunged into the depths of gloom and de-
spondency, Dulcia and her father were scarcely less miserable. In
vain the good clergyman sought to console his daughter. His
arguments fell upon deaf ears. The poor damsel's faculties were be-
numbed by terror, and for some time she scarcely gave a token of
consciousness—all the efforts of her father and Patty Whinchat
failing to rouse her.

And now to glance at the Ironsides. As may be supposed, the
troopers were by no means displeased by the information that they
were to pass the night at the Grange. Like true soldiers, they
knew right well when they were in good quarters, and were in no
hurry to depart. The supplies of the larder and the buttery, not-

withstanding the large demands made upon them, were by no means exhausted; and if this stock of provisions should fail, there were sides of bacon, hams, and cheeses in reserve within the store-room —while poultry and pigeons in any quantity could be had from the farm-yard. Ale and wine were unstinted. Yet with all this indulgence there was no relaxation of discipline. The sentinels were changed every hour, and constant and strict watch was kept at all the points of the house.

It being the object of the household to keep their unwelcome guests in good humour, everything was done to promote this object. Accordingly, Giles Moppett, Elias Crundy, with the cook and the scullion-wenches, were unremitting in their efforts to please the red-coats, whom Moppett privately declared to be as ravenous as wolves, and as thirsty as camels. On their part, the Ironsides did not give way to any great licence, and took care not to drink to excess, but they smoked incessantly, and made the whole house reek like a tavern with the fumes of tobacco. They went about where they listed, without displaying much respect for the persons they encountered. Thus, three or four of them, smoking of course, entered the library where the unhappy colonel was seated, and, regardless of his looks of anger and disgust, continued to puff away at their pipes as they leisurely examined the portraits on the walls, or other objects that attracted their attention, passing unseemly comments upon them. One of them—it was Helpless Henly —taking up the " Eikon Bisliké," tore the book asunder in a rage, and flung the fragments into the fire. Besadaiah Eavestaff and Tola Fell intruded themselves in the same way upon Mr. Beard, and one of them being a Fifth Monarchy Man, and the other a Muggletonian, they sat down, and sought to enter into a controversy with him. Doubtless, Dulcia, who withdrew with Patty, on the appearance of the two troopers, into an inner apartment, would have been subjected to like annoyance, but that Captain Stelfax had given express orders that her privacy should be respected.

As to the Ironside leader himself, he remained for more than two hours in the colonel's chamber, where, as we have already stated, he caused a wood fire to be lighted, and where subsequently a copious repast was served him, of which he partook. His meal ended, it occurred to him to make an external examination of the house; but, on going forth, he did not allow the room to remain untenanted, leaving Sergeant Delves and three troopers within it, and giving them strict orders on no account to go forth, even for a moment, until his return.

IV.

OF THE MESSAGE SENT BY MICKLEGIFT TO STELFAX; AND OF THE PLAN FOR
ENSNARING THE FUGITIVES DEVISED BY THE LATTER.

ALL the sentinels were at their posts as Stelfax went his rounds, and nothing to excite suspicion had occurred. He next visited the stables, and, as matter of precaution, directed that his own charger, and half a dozen troopers' horses, should be kept saddled and bridled. This done, he proceeded to the garden, in order to study the architecture of the back part of the mansion. The massive chimney in which the lurking-hole was contrived stood on this side of the building, and projected far from the wall, rising from its base in gradations like those of a buttress. Stelfax easily made out the position of the hiding-place, but could detect no other recess of the kind. He was in the act of measuring the projection of the chimney, when Helpless Henly brought word that two persons were at the outer gate, desiring speech with him. On inquiry, these individuals proved to be Nehemiah Lift-up-hand and Lawrence Creek. Stelfax consenting to see them, Henly departed, and presently returned with the two men. Very grave salutations passed between the Ironside leader and his visitors.

"We have come to thee, valiant captain," premised Nehemiah who acted as spokesman, "on behalf of the godly Master Increase Micklegift, to remonstrate with thee on thy behaviour towards

him, and to see if thou wilt make him some amends for the maltreatment he hath received."

"Ye will lose your labour, good sirs," Stelfax rejoined, sternly.
"I will make Master Increase Micklegift no amends. I have
driven him from the house, and forbidden him to return to it."

"This we know, captain," said Nehemiah, "and we grieve that
thou shouldst have so far stretched thy authority against the good
man. He meant thee well, and in his humility and Christian
charity is willing to overlook the dishonourable treatment he hath
experienced, and to be reconciled unto thee."

"I rejoice to hear it," Stelfax rejoined.   "Is this the sum of his
message to me?"

"No, captain," said Nehemiah. "The good man wishes to
be allowed to confer with thee."

"A mere pretence to obtain admission to the house," thought
Stelfax. "He desires to confer with me, thou sayest?" he added
aloud. "On what matter?"

"Nay, I am not in his confidence, valiant captain," Nehemiah
replied; "but I know that his business is of moment."

"Ere I make a reply, I would put a question to thee in my turn,
good master messenger. Said he aught to thee concerning the
daughter of the Episcopalian divine, Master Beard?"

"Yea, verily, he told me thou hadst threatened to take her away
as thy captive," Nehemiah answered. "But he added, that he
felt assured thou wouldst not carry thy menace into effect, inasmuch as he could show thee cogent reasons against it."

"And what, I prithee, were those weighty reasons of his, good
master messenger? Did he mention them?"

"He hinted, as the phrase is, that he had an offer to make to
thee, provided thou wouldst engage to leave the damsel unmo-
lested."

"I knew it!" exclaimed Stelfax. "Take back my answer, good
master messenger, and say unto Micklegift that I reject his proposal, whatsoever it may be. I will have nought to do with him.
He is faithless and perverse, and in league with the Amalekites, and
if he presents himself again within this dwelling while I am here, I

will cause him to be driven forth with blows and fustigation. Say this to him, without circumlocution."

" Since thou thinkest thus unjustly of the worthy man, captain, nothing more can be said," Nehemiah rejoined. " I scarcely like to add what he desired us to declare unto thee in case a deaf ear should be turned to his remonstrances."

" Forbear not out of consideration to me, I prithee, good master messenger," Stelfax rejoined. " Speak out, and fear not."

" Thus, then, spake he, captain," Nehemiah rejoined, boldly. " He offers you friendship and aid; but if you reject them, you may count upon his enmity."

" I laugh at his threats, good master messenger," Stelfax rejoined. " Go tell him so, and rid me of your presence."

" We grieve that our mission to thee has failed," said Lawrence Creek. " Fear not our troubling thee again, for we are both about to depart, on the instant, from this village of Ovingdean. Fare thee well, captain. Peradventure, thou mayst regret thou didst not listen to the peacemakers."

With this the two men departed; while the Ironside leader, turning impatiently on his heel, strode off in a different direction across the grass-plot.

" A pertinacious and malicious knave this Micklegift!" ejaculated Stelfax, as he continued angrily to pace the sward, " and doubtless he will do me an ill turn if he can; but I despise him. The pitiful varlet hath the presumption to aspire to the hand of the lovely Dulcia; but even if she would listen to his suit—which is most unlikely—he shall never have her. No; she shall be mine. Of that I am resolved. No damsel hath ever pleased me so much. She seems to scorn me, but I will find means to bend her stubborn spirit. Ah! I have it!" he exclaimed, his eye kindling, as a plan suddenly flashed across him. " She shall help me to discover those I seek. They are in that room, I am certain."

No sooner was the plan formed than it was acted upon. Re-entering the house, he went up-stairs to the old Cavalier's chamber, and ordered Delves to summon Colonel Maunsel, with Mr. Beard and Dulcia, to his presence.

In a few minutes the three persons thus sent for made their appearance, preceded by the sergeant, and guarded by half a dozen troopers, armed with carabines, among whom were Besadaiah, Tola, and Helpless Henly. The lynx-eyed captain of the Ironsides watched the Royalists closely on their entrance, and detected certain glances from which he drew tolerably correct inferences.

"I shall have the fugitives now," he thought.

Clothing his countenance with its most awful frowns, Stelfax strode up to the little group, and said, in a threatening voice, "I have sent for you, Colonel Maunsel, to put an end to this business. I perceive that I have been trifled with, and am therefore resolved to pursue a different course. I ask you, for the last time, will you deliver up these fugitives to me?"

"I have but one answer to give to the question," the old Cavalier said, "and that is a refusal."

"And you likewise persist in refusing to disclose their hiding-place, eh, Master Beard?" pursued Stelfax.

"I do," the clergyman answered, firmly.

"My final appeal must be made to you, damsel," the Ironside captain went on; "and I would fain hope that you may spare me from a painful task which stern duty imposes. By enabling me to secure these fugitives—who can be nothing to you—nothing in comparison, I mean—you will save Colonel Maunsel and your father from the torture."

"From torture!" ejaculated Dulcia, in affright.

"Heed not what this crafty and cruel man says to you, Dulcia," cried the colonel, "and let not a word escape your lips that may imperil those whose lives hang on your firmness. He dares not put his threat in execution."

"Dares not!" exclaimed Stelfax. "Look you, Colonel Maunsel, I have already been told in this very room that I dare not execute my threats, but the time is come when you will find out your error. My warrant is not from the Parliament, or even from the Council, but from the Lord General himself, and I am empowered by it to deal with refractory malignants as I see fit—as I see fit, colonel— there is some latitude in that phrase, methinks! If I think fit to shoot you in your own court-yard, or to hang you at your own gate, I can do it, and my warrant will bear me out."

"I doubt not that the murderer of his most sacred Majesty will absolve his followers from any crime, however foul," rejoined the colonel.

"That taunt may cost you your life, sir," Stelfax rejoined. "But it is to you, damsel, and not to this imprudent man, that I address myself," he added to Dulcia. "Must I send forth Colonel Maunsel and your father to endure the torture?"

"Oh! no—no—no! I implore you to spare them!" she cried, falling on her knees before him.

"I must shut my heart to your entreaties, damsel," Stelfax said. "Speak! and I show pity—not otherwise!"

"Be firm, Dulcia," Colonel Maunsel exclaimed. And a like injunction was laid upon her by her father.

"You cannot have the heart to carry out your threat?" Dulcia said, rising to her feet.

"There is only one way to move me," he said, in a low voice, and catching her arm. "Be mine!'

"Yours!" she exclaimed, regarding him with mixed disgust and terror, and almost doubting whether she had heard aright. "Yours! Never!"

"Reflect!" he said, under his breath. "I love you to desperation. Be mine, and they are safe. Nay, I will depart without further search."

"Oh! merciful Heaven! what have I done to deserve this trial?" Dulcia ejaculated. "Tempt me not," she added.

"Say the word, and it is done, according to my promise!" Stelfax whispered, thinking he had prevailed.

"I cannot say it," she rejoined, in a tone of anguish. "Whatever may happen, I can never be yours. I would die a hundred deaths first."

"Enough, proud damsel!" he exclaimed. "You shall find what it is to brave my displeasure. Sergeant Delves," he continued, in an inflexible tone, "take these two malignants to some lower chamber suitable for the purpose. Let both undergo the torture of the boot, unless the first to endure the pain shall reveal where the fugitives are hidden.　Begin with Colonel Maunsel."

"Oh! no, for pity's sake, spare them!" cried Dulcia, again falling on her knees before him.

"Arise, Dulcia, I command you," Colonel Maunsel cried. "Come, sir," he added to Mr. Beard, "the base rebels and regicides shall find how little power hath torture over a loyal English gentleman, ever prepared to die for his king; and upon a clergyman of England's true Church, whose life has been spent in his Maker's service　They shall not wring a groan from me."

"Nor from me," Mr. Beard said, with equal firmness.

"Away with them, and put their boasted resolution to the proof!" cried Stelfax, forcibly disengaging himself from Dulcia.

Overcome by terror, the distracted damsel uttered a scream that made the whole chamber ring with its piercing sound.　Full of the deepest commiseration, her father and Colonel Maunsel, who were moving on towards the door under charge of Delves and the troopers, turned to look at her; but their attention was instantly diverted to another object.　That cry of agony had summoned other actors to the scene.　Scarcely had it ceased, when the pillar masking the secret entrance to the hiding-place flew back, and Clavering Maunsel stepped forth.　He was quickly followed by John Habergeon and Ninian.

"Ho! ho!" Stelfax exclaimed, with an exulting laugh.　"Here are the men I want."

On sight of Clavering, Dulcia started to her feet, and flew towards him, while he, yielding to irrepressible emotion, and seemingly insensible to the peril in which he stood, pressed her to his bosom.

Meanwhile, Stelfax regarded the young man narrowly.

"This is not Charles Stuart!" he exclaimed.　"Who art thou?" he demanded.

"I have no longer any motive for concealment," the other answered.　"I am Clavering Maunsel."

"Clavering Maunsel!" echoed the Roundhead leader, in surprise. "Then the report that thou wert slain at Worcester was false?"

"It was false, since you behold me here," was the answer.

"Imprudent boy!" the colonel exclaimed, in accents of mingled grief and reproach. "Thou hast doomed thyself to destruction."

"Alas! alas! I am to blame!" Dulcia exclaimed. "I have been the means of betraying him."

"Ay, that is quite certain," Stelfax remarked, with a bitter laugh.

"Not so! not so!" cried Clavering to Dulcia. "From yon hiding-place I overheard what was passing here; and think you I would have allowed my father and your father to undergo the torture on my account? I only waited till the last moment, in the hope that this dastardly villain would not execute his threat."

"Learn, then, that my order would *not* have been executed," Stelfax replied, with a derisive laugh. "'Twas but a device to lure thee from thy secure retreat, and it has succeeded. Ho! ho!"

"Alas! unhappy boy, why did you come forth?" groaned the old Cavalier. "Your retreat, you see, was not suspected."

"No, in good sooth it was not," Stelfax said. "Having myself searched the burrow and found it empty, I did not suppose it would be again occupied; nor can I conceive how the young man and his companions found access to it, unless they came down the chimney. Ah, I have hit upon the way taken, I find!" he exclaimed, perceiving a smile cross Ninian's countenance. "Possibly, if you had remained quiet, you might have got off," he added to Clavering; "but it is too late to think of that now."

"It is not too late to sell our lives dearly," the young Cavalier cried, brandishing his sword with the only arm capable of wielding the weapon. "You, John, will stand by me—and you also Ninian?"

"To the last!" they both responded.

"Oh! that I had my trusty sword in my grasp!" added John Habergeon. "I would quickly cut a way through them."

"Give fire if they stir!" Stelfax shouted to the troopers.

And the carabines of the Ironsides were levelled at the young Cavalier and his companions.

"I am the cause of your destruction. It is meet I should die with you," cried Dulcia, still clinging to Clavering.

"Hold!" thundered Stelfax to his followers. "That damsel must not be injured. Upon them, and disarm the young man!"

"It is needless," cried Clavering, throwing down his sword. "I yield myself a prisoner."

"'Sdeath! captain, wherefore did you yield?" John Habergeon grumbled. "Why not let us fight it out? We can but die once."

"And never better than now," added Ninian.

"It is useless to struggle against destiny," Clavering cried.

"Ay, it is quite evident that Providence—or, as you profanely say, Destiny—is against you and your party," Stelfax observed. "The Lord has declared himself on the side of those who observe his commandments. Remove these men!" he added to Delves.

At the word, the troopers surrounded the prisoners, none of whom offered any resistance, though both John Habergeon and Ninian eyed their captors fiercely. Dulcia, however, still clung despairingly to Clavering, while Delves sought, though with much forbearance, to remove her.

"Farewell, Dulcia!" Clavering cried, straining her to his heart. "This is my last embrace. We shall meet no more on earth."

"Must we part thus!" she exclaimed, distractedly. "May I not go with you?"

"Your presence would only distract his thoughts from preparation for the death he will speedily have to encounter, damsel," the captain of the Ironsides remarked. "His life is justly forfeited for treason and rebellion against the Commonwealth, and it were idle to hold out any hope of mercy. Assuredly, none will be shown him. Better for himself he had died, as I deemed he had, at Worcester."

"Better, indeed!" echoed Clavering, mournfully.

"There must be an end of this leave-taking, damsel," Stelfax cried, with fierce impatience. "Bid him farewell, and for ever!"

Dulcia made an effort to speak, but the words expired upon her lips, and she fell, insensible, into Clavering's arms.

"Give her to me, and move on," cried Stelfax, advancing to take the fainting maiden from him.

"Off!—touch her not!" cried Clavering. "Here. sir, take her," he added to Mr. Beard, who came up at the moment.

Sad was it to see the inanimate girl consigned to her father—sad to behold Mr. Beard's agonised countenance—sadder yet to mark Clavering's look of utter despair as he so relinquished her.

Colonel Maunsel appeared as if thunderstricken—almost unconscious of what was passing around him. He had sunk, in a heavy, despairing, listless state, into a chair; and it was only when the prisoners were being led forth by the guard that he roused himself.

"Farewell, my dear father," said Clavering, pausing, and regarding him piteously.

"What say'st thou, my son?" the old Cavalier rejoined, passing his hands over his eyes to clear his vision. "Where goest thou?"

"To my last fight," Clavering replied, "where I trust I shall comport myself as courageously and as well as our martyred king did upon the scaffold."

"What! are they taking thee to execution?" cried his father, the dreadful truth rushing suddenly upon him.

"Not to present execution, as I judge, sir," Clavering answered. "I would it were so, for I am a-wearied of life. But you know what mercy is to be expected from these regicides. Give me your blessing ere I go forth," he added, bending the knee to him.

"You have it, my son!" exclaimed the old Cavalier, extending his arms over his head. "May the Father of Heaven, who supported our blessed king in his last hour, support thee in thine!"

"Delay no longer, sergeant," cried Stelfax, wishful to interrupt the scene. "Remove the prisoners, and wait my further orders in the hall of entrance."

Upon this, Clavering arose, and tearing himself from his father's embrace, moved on.

"Farewell, your honour," said John Habergeon, halting a moment by his old master. "Give yourself no concern about me. I shall die a dog's death at the hands of these cursed rebels—but what matters it? I have ever been a loyal subject to my king, and a faithful servant to the best of masters, and that will be my consolation at my last hour. May I take your hand at parting?"

"Farewell, my faithful servant," the old Cavalier replied, warmly grasping John's rugged hand; "we shall not be long separated."

"It were but mockery to wish your honour long continuance in a world like this, where only roguery prospers—you were better out of it," John said. "So, I hope we may soon meet in a place where rebels and regicides will never enter."

"Amen!" the colonel responded; "farewell, John! And farewell to thee, too, my poor fellow!" he added to Ninian, as the latter came up. "'Tis a pity thou shouldst be cut off thus early. But they may spare thee on the score of thy youth."

"I will not ask grace at their hands on that plea—or any other," Ninian replied, resolutely. "Trust me, I will not discredit your honour's house. My last cry shall be, ' Confusion to old Noll, and long life and a speedy Restoration to the lawful ruler of this realm, his most sacred Majesty King Charles the Second!'"

"Gag him, if he dares give utterance to further treason," roared Stelfax, furiously. "Away with them at once, sergeant! Wherefore dost thou suffer them to abuse my patience thus?"

Upon this, Delves put the men in motion, and conducted the prisoners down the principal staircase to the entrance-hall, where Stelfax soon afterwards joined him.

V.

HOW THE CAPTAIN OF THE IRONSIDES INSPECTED THE VILLAGE CHURCH, AND MADE ANOTHER CAPTURE.

GREAT was the consternation throughout the Grange when it became known that Clavering Maunsel and the two others were captured. All the serving-men flocked towards the entrance-hall to satisfy themselves of the truth of the report, and the sad spectacle they there beheld left them no doubt of its correctness.

In the midst of a circle of troopers, carabines in hand, stood the three prisoners; unbound, but deprived of all means of resistance. Clavering looked much depressed, but the other two cast defiant glances at the guard.

Near approach to the prisoners being interdicted, the passage leading to the kitchen and buttery, which opened upon the entrance-hall, was thronged with anxious spectators. Here old Martin Geere, Giles Moppett, Elias Crundy, and others, were stationed, conferring amongst themselves in whispers, and timorously looking on. They had been told by Besadaiah Eavestaff, who was posted at the upper end of the passage, that the prisoners would be taken to Lewes and lodged within the castle, out this was all they could learn.

The information, however, was not strictly correct. The captain of the Ironsides had no intention of departing immediately, having made up his mind to pass the night at the Grange. The

capture of the fugitives did not occasion any change in his plans.
A brief consultation with Delves as to the best means of disposing
of the prisoners until the morrow, led the sergeant to suggest
the village church as a temporary stronghold—churches, in those
days, being not unfrequently used for such purposes, and even as
stables. Stelfax thought the suggestion good, but in order to satisfy
himself of its feasibility, he went forth with Delves to inspect
the sacred structure.

The little church, it will be remembered, was but a short distance from the Grange, standing on the slope of the opposite
down, and the two Ironsides soon reached it. On entering the
porch, the door proved to be locked, whereupon Stelfax despatched
the sergeant to the adjacent rectory for the key. While Delves
departed on the errand, his leader strolled about the churchyard,
examining the venerable structure from different points of view—
not with any feelings of reverence for its sacred character, or admiration of its architectural beauty, but merely with a view to its
adaptation to the purpose of a temporary stronghold. All was
still around. The evening was serene and beautiful. The sun
had sunk below the western hill; and the low square tower of the
church was darkly defined against the glowing sky. The only object
not in harmony with the peaceful scene was the formidable figure
of the Ironside in his martial accoutrements.

Stelfax's examination of the sacred fabric was quite satisfactory
to him. The tower at the west end of the structure appeared to
offer all he could desire in the way of security. It had no outlet
to the churchyard; its windows were only three in number, placed
at a considerable height from the ground, acutely pointed, and so
narrow as to preclude all chance of escape by their means. If the
interior of the tower corresponded with its outward appearance, it
would suit the captain's requirements admirably.

Proceeding to the parsonage-house, Delves opened the door
without troubling himself to knock at it, sought out Micklegift,
and, on finding him, authoritatively demanded the key of the
church. The Independent minister energetically refused to deliver it up, and hastily rising, strove to snatch it from a nail in the

wall, against which it hung. But the sergeant was too quick for him, and possessing himself of the prize, departed with it.

Delves then joined his leader, while Micklegift, sorely annoyed at the occurrence, flew to his garden, which was only divided from the churchyard by a wall, and soon managed to obtain a position whence, without betraying himself, he could command their proceedings, and overhear their discourse—so long, at least, as they remained outside the church. From the few words which passed between them previous to their entering the sacred edifice, he ascertained their design, and resolved to thwart it.

" So, this irreverend and unscrupulous soldier of the Republic," thus ran his meditations, " whose doings put to shame and tarnish the actions of his mighty general, Cromwell—this base officer having had the good fortune to capture the young fugitive malignant and his followers, purposes to bestow his prisoners for the night in my church, as in a stronghold or place of duresse. It is well! Not for any love that I bear Clavering Maunsel—for, regarding him as a rival, I cannot but hold him in aversion; not for any desire I have to serve the Royalist cause, for I am strongly and conscientiously opposed to it; but because of the hatred I bear to this detested Stelfax, and because of the dishonourable treatment he hath shown me, will I confound his devices, and deliver these captives from his hands. Yea, I will set my wits to work to accomplish their liberation, and I doubt not of success."

While the Independent minister was forming this vindictive resolve, Stelfax and his companion had gained an entrance to the church, and the Roundhead leader found, on inspecting the interior of the tower, that the opinion he had formed of its security and fitness was fully justified. " If the place had been built for us," he remarked to Sergeant Delves, as they stepped into the chamber, " it could not have been better contrived."

The interior of the church tower formed a small square chamber, very lofty in proportion to its height:—the room, as we have heretofore stated, being used, at the present day, as a vestiary. Above was a little belfry, which could only be entered by a trap-door in the ceiling; but, as a tolerably long ladder was required to reach this trap-door, and no ladder was at hand, little danger was to be apprehended in that direction. The walls were of solid masonry, coated with plaster and whitewashed. Internally, the tower was some feet lower than the ground outside it, so that the windows were elevated in like proportion from the floor, and far out of the reach of the tallest man. We have already shown that they were too narrow to allow even a slightly-built person to pass through them. The chamber was entirely empty. The sole entrance to the tower was from the body of the church; the door being of stout oak, studded with flat-headed nails, and fitted into a pointed arch.

Having completed their survey, Stelfax and the sergeant quitted the sacred fabric, locking the door as they went forth, and taking the key with them. As they passed through the church-yard, the Ironside leader made some observations upon the strength and security of the tower, and its suitableness for their present purpose, wholly unconscious that his observations reached the ears of Micklegift.

Issuing from the little gate of the churchyard, the Ironsides were about to descend the green slope leading to the valley, when, to their surprise, they perceived a couple of horsemen dash suddenly down the steepest part of the escarpment on their left—the same hill-side, in fact, only at a more abrupt declivity, on which the church it-self was built. The horsemen were not more than a hundred yards off on first coming into sight, but while they themselves were fully visible to the Ironsides, the latter were screened from view by an intervening hedge, and a cluster of overhanging trees. Both horse-men were remarkably well mounted, and appeared to be making for the Grange. Stelfax and his companion stood still to watch their course. Something there was in the appearance of the horse-men that led both lookers-on to the conclusion that they were fugitive Cavaliers; and the curiosity of the Ironsides was greatly excited to learn who they were, and what could have brought them to the Grange, at a moment of such peril to themselves. Mean-while, the supposed Royalists, totally unconscious of danger, galloped on, and were now almost at the gates of the mansion.

"If yon madmen be malignants, as I take them to be," cried Stelfax, with a laugh, "they will fall headlong into the lion's den. To the house, sergeant, and let us assist in their capture!"

So saying, he drew his sword, and closely attended by Delves, who likewise plucked forth his blade, he ran down the slope, and made for the house-gates with all possible despatch.

Another instant confirmed the suspicions which both Ironsides had entertained, that the horsemen were Royalists. Scarcely had the twain entered the gates, through which they rode with insensate haste and utter recklessness of consequences, than they were challenged by the sentinels posted within the court. At once comprehending the peril in which their inadvertence had placed them, the reckless horsemen endeavoured to back out. Seeing this, one of the troopers rushed towards the gates, in order to close them, and cut off their retreat, while the other, presenting his carabine, threatened to fire if they moved. Nothing daunted, however, the Cavalier against whom the musket was levelled, and who was but a short distance from the sentinel, having managed to draw his sword, struck the weapon from the man's grasp. The carabine went off as it fell, but did no mischief.

All this was the work of a minute, and so rapidly had the horsemen turned, that the one next the gates passed through them before the trooper could swing round the heavy iron frames to prevent his exit; while even the hinder Cavalier would have made good his retreat, if Stelfax and the sergeant had not come up at the juncture. Springing at the foremost horseman, Delves made an effort to arrest him, but the Cavalier, plunging spurs into his steed, dashed against him with such force as to hurl him to the ground; in which position the sergeant discharged his pistol at the fugitive, but without effect.

Less lucky than his companion, who thus got off uninjured, the second Cavalier had to encounter Stelfax, who rushed up to him without hesitation, and, seizing his bridle, bade him surrender. The Cavalier replied by a desperate cut at the Ironside leader's head, which might have cleared the way for him if it had taken effect; but Stelfax warded off the blow, and, catching hold of his

antagonist, dragged him by sheer force of arm from his horse.
The contest, though taking some time to narrate, had been, in
reality, so brief, that no one else could take part in it; though
several troopers rushed towards the scene of strife.

The luckless Cavalier who had thus been captured by the
stalwart Ironside leader, was tall and well proportioned. His attire
was sad-coloured, and of Puritan plainness, and his locks cropped
close to his head. Nevertheless, his looks and deportment did not
agree with these symbols of Puritanism. He was a man of middle
age, but of undiminished energies, as his hardy opponent had discovered.

While holding the discomfited Cavalier in his iron grasp, Stelfax
scanned his features for a short space ; and then shouted to Delves,
who by this time had regained his legs, demanding, "Tell me—
whom dost thou hold this malignant to be?"

"It is not Charles Stuart," the sergeant replied, surveying the
captive.

"Charles Stuart!—tush! This man is of middle age. Look
again, and carefully. Hast thou beheld that face before?"

"Yea, verily have I, and at Worcester," the sergeant answered.
"It is the face of one who, at that conflict, commanded the left
wing of the army of Abijam, the son of Rehoboam. It is the
Lord Wilmot."

"Thou art right," Stelfax exclaimed. "It *is* the Lord Wilmot.
Of a truth, this is an important capture—next to that of the Young
Man himself, the most important that could have been effected, and
the one that will give the greatest satisfaction to the Lord General.
But though we have taken a commander of a division, the leader of
the whole army may have escaped us. Peradventure, it was Abijam
himself who hath just fled. Didst thou note the features and person of the man whom thou didst vainly essay to capture?"

"I looked upon him as he charged me," Delves replied; "and
methought he was younger and more active than this man, and of
a swarthy complexion——"

"'Tis he!—'tis Charles Stuart in person! I am well assured of
it," Stelfax cried out in great excitement. "Sound boot and saddle!

I will pursue instantly. I will scour the country round but I will have him."

"You are deceived, sir," said Lord Wilmot, who had not hitherto uttered a syllable. "It is not the king who hath just ridden off. His Majesty is safe across the Channel."

"I will not take your word on that point, my lord," the Ironside leader rejoined. "What ho!" he vociferated at the top of his stentorian voice. "My horse without a moment's delay—'tis well I kept him ready for instant service—three men to go with me. The rest shall remain here to guard the prisoners till my return. The fugitive is yet in sight; but I shall lose him if ye delay—quick, knaves, quick! Ha! he has gained the top of the hill—he disappears—he will escape me if ye loiter!"

"Heaven be praised!" Lord Wilmot exclaimed, with irrepressible emotion.

"Give praises to Heaven if I fail to take your young monarch, my lord, but not before. Here comes my horse," cried Stelfax, vaulting into the saddle. "Lead our noble captive into the house, sergeant. Let his person be searched carefully, and then put him with the other prisoners. If I return not speedily, remove them all to the church tower, and keep strict watch over them. And hark ye, sergeant, if rescue be attempted, spare not, but smite."

"Fear nothing, captain," Delves replied. "I will make a terrible example of all such as oppose our authority."

Three mounted troopers having by this time joined their leader, the little party struck spurs into their horses, and galloped along the valley, and then up the steep escarpment on the left, pursuing the course taken by the fugitive; while Lord Wilmot was led into the house by Delves and the other Ironsides.

BOOK VI.

THE DEVIL'S DYKE.

I.

SHOWING HOW NINIAN ESCAPED; AND HOW THE OTHER PRISONERS WERE TAKEN
TO THE CHURCH TOWER.

A CONFLICT, such as we described in the last chapter, between
Cavalier and Roundhead, where the odds were so greatly against
the . former, could not fail to excite vividly the feelings of staunch
partisans of the royal cause like Clavering and John Habergeon.
But the person among the prisoners who profited by the confusion
incident to the capture of Lord Wilmot and the flight of his
companion was Ninian Saxby. While the attention of the guard
was attracted to what was going on outside, the young falconer
slipped suddenly between two of the soldiers, and, almost at a
bound, reached the entrance to the passage leading to the buttery.

This passage was thronged with various members of the household, and amongst them was Ninian's own father, who beheld with
the utmost anxiety the daring attempt of his son. At the head of
the passage Besadaiah Eavestaff was posted, carabine in hand. But
he failed to impede the young falconer's flight. Before he could
level his gun, his arms were seized by those behind him, and Ninian
was enabled to pass by. No sooner was he gone than the passage
was blocked up, and it could not be cleared till pursuit was useless.
Fortunately for Ninian, the patrol at the rear of the mansion had
just been removed, so there was no further hindrance to his retreat.

On being informed of the young falconer's escape, which he

learnt as he entered the hall with Lord Wilmot and the guard, Sergeant Delves was greatly enraged, and sharply reprimanding the troopers, especially Besadaiah Eavestaff, for neglect of duty, threatened to make a severe example of such of the household as had aided Ninian's flight. The principal offender, and the person who had seized Besadaiah from behind, turned out, upon inquiry, to be the fugitive's own father; but he, too, had disappeared. Delves was therefore obliged to content himself with clearing the passage from all intruders, which he did in a very summary manner. No great pains were taken to recapture Ninian. Though vexed at the occurrence, as knowing it would irritate Stelfax when it came to his knowledge, the sergeant did not like to diminish the guard by sending men to scour the country in quest of an escaped prisoner of little consequence, thereby endangering the security of his more important captives, Lord Wilmot and Clavering Maunsel.

Stelfax's orders in regard to Lord Wilmot were strictly obeyed. The Royalist nobleman was searched; but no letters or papers referring to the fugitive monarch, or calculated to give the slightest clue to his retreat, were discovered. Lord Wilmot smiled contemptuously as Delves scrutinised the tablets and pocket-book handed to him by the searchers. The memoranda contained in these little books were written in a cypher perfectly unintelligible to the sergeant; but though he could make nothing of the mysterious characters, Delves thought his leader might be able to unravel them, and he therefore put the books carefully into his pouch. Only a few pieces of gold were found in Lord Wilmot's purse; so that he must have disposed of the large sum of money which he had obtained that morning from Zachary Trangmar. But of this the sergeant knew nothing, and consequently made no inquiries on the subject.

Just as the search was completed, Colonel Maunsel was seen tottering down the principal staircase, which communicated with the entrance-hall. He was supported by old Martin Geere, and appeared greatly debilitated. But he was not allowed to descend to the hall. At a sign from Delves, two troopers planted themselves at the foot of the staircase, crossing their carabines, as an intimation to the old Cavalier that he could not pass. Thereupon, he stopped midway in the staircase, and gazed at the group below.

"Who have you there?" he exclaimed. "It is not—it cannot be the king! Some one cried out just now that his Majesty was taken, but I will not believe the evil tidings."

"Fear nothing, colonel," cried Lord Wilmot. "Our gracious monarch will never be captured by these men. He is safe from their pursuit."

"Heaven be praised!" the old Cavalier fervently ejaculated. "I cannot discern the features of him who speaks to me, but the voice is the voice of a friend."

"Inveterate malignant as thou art, there is no reason why thou shouldst remain in ignorance of the rank and title of the prisoner we have made," Delves rejoined, "and I will therefore declare them unto thee. Not many minutes since, two men rode up to thy gates with such blind precipitation, that they perceived not, till too late, that the house was in the possession of the soldiers of the Commonwealth. One of these insensate persons was speedily captured, and proved to be the Lord Wilmot, the chosen friend of thy sovereign. The other effected a retreat, but our captain hath started in pursuit of him, and will not relinquish the chase till the prey be secured. Notwithstanding his lordship's denial, I leave thee to conjecture who was likely to have been his companion."

"For Colonel Maunsel's satisfaction, and not for thine, fellow," cried Lord Wilmot, "I repeat that it is not as thou wouldst insinuate. His Majesty is far away from this place. In regard to my own inopportune visit to Ovingdean Grange, I can, at the proper season, render such explanation as will absolve Colonel Maunsel from any suspicion of complicity with me or my companion."

"I pray your lordship not to bestow a thought upon me," the old Cavalier cried. "Let these miscreants glut themselves with my blood if they will. They have robbed me of my darling boy, and I care not what else they take."

"Be comforted, my father," said Clavering; "my troubles will

soon be over. Bethink thee of the sacred cause for which I lay
down my life. That reflection will support me in my latest hour.
Let it support thee now!"

"Well said, young sir!" exclaimed Lord Wilmot, extending
his hand to him, which Clavering warmly grasped. "These are
sentiments to deprive the scaffold of all terror. But trust me," he
added, in a cheerful tone, "you will disappoint your bloodthirsty
captors. You are reserved for better days."

"Mayhap your lordship also calculates upon escaping the punishment due to your treasonable offences against the Commonwealth?"
jeered Delves.

"I calculate upon enjoying the fruits of my fidelity to a gracious
lord and master," Lord Wilmot replied, "as well as of my unceas-
ing efforts to free his kingdom from the bloodthirsty and rebellious fanatics by whom it is overrun. Look well to thy charge,
sirrah, for, by my faith, thou shalt have some trouble to hold me."

As these bold words were uttered, his lordship's eye rested upon
John Habergeon, and he read in the old trooper's looks that any
attempt he might make for his own liberation would be effectively
seconded by him.

Upon one person, for whose benefit the captive nobleman's observations were chiefly uttered, they produced a cheering effect. Hope
was suddenly reawakened in Colonel Maunsel's breast, and he
roused himself from the state of almost atony into which he had
sunk. Things did not look now quite so desperate as they had
done. He began to conceive projects for his son's deliverance, and
even debated with himself the possibility of stirring up his household to an attack upon the Ironsides.

But Delves did not allow him much time for reflection. Though
regarding Lord Wilmot's speech as mere bravado — Cavalier's
rodomontade, he styled it—the sergeant thought that the prisoners
had given their tongues license enough. A stop must be put to
the further expression of their sentiments. Sternly ordering them
to keep silence, he signified in a peremptory tone to Colonel Maunsel
that he must retire to his own chamber. The command roused
the old Cavalier's ire, and he seemed by no means inclined to obey

it; but his son besought him by his looks to yield compliance, and, after a little hesitation, he remounted the staircase much more firmly than he had come down it, and disappeared.

Three wearisome hours passed by, and Stelfax had not returned. During the whole of this time the prisoners were detained in the entrance-hall. Not a word was exchanged between Lord Wilmot and Clavering that did not reach the ears of Delves, who stood close beside them. The sergeant, however, began to find this lengthened attendance irksome, and his men, moreover, looked as if a little change would be agreeable.

Preparations were, therefore, made for the removal of the prisoners to the church. Delves had sixteen men under his command, three of the troopers, as already intimated, having gone with Stelfax in pursuit of the fugitive Cavalier. Half of the force at his disposal the sergeant decided upon taking with him to the church, deeming that number ample guard for the prisoners: the other half should stay at the Grange to keep watch over the malignant colonel and his household. But before carrying his plan into execution, he repaired to the buttery, and causing a couple of baskets to be filled with provisions and wine, despatched Moppett and Crundy—under a guard—with these stores to the church; and, on their return, he took out his prisoners, and placing himself at the head of the escort, moved towards the sacred edifice.

Torches to light the troop were carried by old Ticehurst, the gardener, and Nut Springett, who had been pressed into the service; and the flare of the flambeaux was reflected upon the steel caps, corslets, and carabines of the Ironsides. In the midst of the guard, by whom they were closely surrounded, marched the prisoners. The torchlight flashed upon gate and wall, upon overhanging tree and thick hedge-row as the little party advanced—Delves keeping a wary look-out lest any attack should be attempted.

Though all the Roundhead soldiers were religious fanatics, not one of them had the slightest scruple in turning the sacred pile they were approaching into a strong-room for their prisoners, and a barrack for themselves. No feeling of irreverence crossed them

as the church-door was unlocked, and the sergeant marched into
the little nave with as much unconcern as if he had been entering a stable.   Old Ticehurst and Springett were dismissed at the
church-door, their services being no longer required; but the
torches were brought into the building, and set up in such a
position that their flame illuminated the whole of the interior.
Very strange the place looked by this lurid light—as much like a
sepulchre as a church.

The sergeant's first business was to secure his prisoners.   Finding all as he had left it, he put them inside the tower, informing
them with a grin that they saw their place of lodging for the night.
Lord Wilmot glanced at the bare walls and the cold flagged floor,
and shuddered involuntarily, but made no remonstrance, and Clavering was equally silent.   But John Habergeon did not display
any such self-restraint, but loudly remonstrated with the sergeant, and in the end succeeded in obtaining from him an oaken
bench, a flask of wine, a loaf of bread with some cold viands, and
a small lighted lamp.   The strong oak door of the tower was left
ajar, in order that the movements of the prisoners might be observed; and close to this door a trooper—it was Helpless Henly—
was posted.

The prisoners disposed of, the gaolers prepared to enjoy themselves.   The church-door was locked inside to prevent all chance
of sudden intrusion; benches were drawn together, on one of which
the contents of the baskets were placed; and Delves, who declared
he was sore hungered, set his comrades the example by making a
vigorous attack upon a goose-pie, which, in addition to being very
savoury, was strongly provocative of thirst, compelling the sergeant
to make frequent application to the wine-flask.

Indeed, it would almost seem as if those who stocked the baskets
had sought out the most powerful incentives to drinking.   Besides
the goose-pie before mentioned, there was the best part of a salted
chine of beef, together with three or four powdered neats' tongues.
These relishing viands soon produced the intended effect upon those
who partook of them, and flask after flask was quickly emptied.

But the thirst of the Ironsides seemed to increase instead of diminishing, and Tola Fell asked leave of the sergeant to procure a fresh supply of wine from the Grange. Delves, however, who could not fail to perceive that a certain impression had been already produced by the copious draughts which his comrades had swallowed, peremptorily refused—a decision which naturally occasioned some grumbling—but good humour was at once restored by the accidental discovery by Besadaiah Eavestaff of a couple of large stone bottles of strong waters, snugly packed at the bottom of a basket, which had been hitherto unaccountably overlooked. Loud shouts were raised by the troopers as these bottles were brought forth. In vain Delves, who began to be seriously apprehensive of the consequences, enjoined the men to abstain from further intemperance. His authority was set at nought. The bottles were passed from hand to hand, and as one of them neared the sergeant, he found the odour so irresistible that he could not pass the vessel without taking toll of its contents. The strong waters quickly unloosed the tongues of the troopers; they began to laugh and talk loudly, to sing and shout, comporting themselves as boisterously as wassailers at a tavern. They gave themselves up to enjoyment, and in order to set themselves completely at ease, unbuckled their belts, and took off their bandoleers, corslets, and steel caps, and in the end disembarrassed themselves of their scarlet jerkins. Stretching themselves luxuriously upon the benches, they lighted their pipes, and soon filled the church with the fumes of tobacco. After a while, their potations began to tell. Half of them dropped asleep, and Helpless Henly, who had drunk rather more than his comrades, was obliged to lean against the wall for support, looking the picture of inebriety. Delves was greatly enraged at the insubordination of his men. Finding it vain to rouse Helpless Henly to a sense of duty, he pushed him aside, and took his place. The drunken fellow reeled forward, and, stumbling over a bench, lay stretched upon the flags, whence he was unable to rise. At the noise caused by the fall of the huge Ironside, both Lord Wilmot and Clavering, who had been seated on the bench, started to their feet, and the former advanced to the door to see what was the matter, but, being instantly noticed by Delves, he was ordered back. But the glance had been enough to disclose to his lordship the inebriate condition of the troopers, and he whispered to his companions that he thought an attempt to escape would soon be practicable. The only person, as it seemed to him, capable of offering effectual resistance was Delves. If he were overcome, the rest might be easily mastered. Having heard what Lord Wilmot said, John Habergeon crept stealthily to the door, and, after reconnoitring the scene before him for a short time, told his companions to hold themselves in readiness for a sudden outburst.

"The grand point," he said, "is to prevent, if possible, these rascals from using their fire-arms, or the alarm will be given to their comrades at the Grange. When the attack is made, let me go out first, and I will engage to disarm the sergeant. With the rest we must take our chance."

II.

THE CHASE OF THE CAVALIER.

LEAVING the desecrated church for a while, we will now follow Stelfax and his men in their chase after the fugitive Cavalier.

On gaining the brow of the hill which the flying horseman had crossed, the Roundhead leader looked around in vain for the object of his quest, and came to a momentary halt. The position he and his men had attained was a most commanding one, being, in fact, the south-eastern boundary of the existing race-course. To those unfamiliar with the locality, it may be proper to mention that the Brighton race-course—one of the most beautifully situated in England—forms a wide semicircular sweep over the gently undulating ridges of a very extensive down. The large arc described by this noble hill embraces part of Kemp Town, and constitutes a worthy background to Brighton itself. At present the race-hill retains much of its original character; but encroachments are being constantly made upon the springy turf so dear to the pedestrian and the horseman. At the time, however, of our story the eminence was wholly uncultivated and unenclosed. Magnificent was the view which it offered to Stelfax and his followers. The sea was dyed with the gorgeous hues of the sun, which had just sank beneath the waves. Towards the west the whole line of coast was visible, from the little fishing town of Brightelmstone, with its small ruinous castle or block-house standing close to the shore; Shoreham, with its harbour, in which a few vessels were

moored; and, farther on, Worthing, and the narrow neck of land
beyond it jutting out far into the sea. In this direction, also, the
Isle of Wight could now be distinctly seen, rising proudly out of
the glowing waters. Exactly opposite the Roundhead leader—
though to reach it he would have had to cross a lower intermediate
hill—stood one of those ancient encampments found on many commanding points of the downs, and denominated the White Hawk.
Hard by this antique camp stood a fire-beacon. Other camp-crowned
hills were also visible from the spot where Stelfax stood—namely,
Ditchling, which, moreover, possessed a beacon; Hollingsbury,
Wolstonbury, and Chanctonbury, the latter constituting a landmark from its clump of fir-trees.

The view Stelfax beheld, though sufficiently striking, differed
materially from that which would now be offered to a spectator
stationed on the same spot. No modern race-stand towered before
the stern soldier of the Commonwealth as he cast his eye on the
opposite hill—no lines of white railings marked out the course reserved for struggling steeds—no mighty structures reared on the
southern slopes of the declivity met his ken—no stately terraces
built on the high cliffs overlooking the sea awakened his admiration, or proclaimed the vicinity of a large and well-built town.
Nothing of this kind did the Roundhead behold. In the valley
immediately beneath him were a barn and sheepfold. At the
point called the Black Rock, near the coast, a small farm-house,
with two or three cottages adjoining it, could be distinguished.
These were the only habitations in sight. An air of solitude per-
vaded the hill. A single figure, darkly defined against the still
radiant western sky, and dilated to gigantic proportions, could be
perceived on the verge of the Roman encampment near the fire-
beacon. None else was in sight, save an old grey-coated shepherd, who, crook in hand, and attended by his dog, was driving a
flock of loudly-bleating sheep down the steep escarpment towards
the fold in the valley.

A few seconds sufficed to place all we have taken so long to
describe before the quick-sighted Ironside leader. He looked
right and left, but could discern no trace of the fugitive, and yet

he ought to be in view. The dark figure near the White Hawk camp could not possibly be him. The spot wasoo far off to have been reached. But Stelfax did not pause long in reflection. Dashing down the hill-side towards the shepherd, he fiercely demanded whether he had seen a horseman pass by, and in which direction he had ridden.

"Oh yes, I seed him," the old shepherd replied; "he were going at a desperate pace for sure, and well-nigh trampled down some of my sheep as he rode through the flock."

"But which way did he take?" Stelfax furiously demanded. "And mark me, thou hoary knave! I read deceit in thine eye. Attempt to mislead me, and I will return and shoot thee down with as little scruple as I would the cur at thy heels."

"I have no thought to deceive you, honoured captain," the old man replied, in a voice quavering with terror. "The person you be searching after rode off by yon patch of gorse." Pointing, as he spoke, with his crook towards ʰᵊ acclivity on the north-west.

Stelfax tarried not a moment longer, but galloped off with his men in the direction indicated by the shepherd. The brow of the hill was covered so thickly with furze that it was impossible to pursue a straightforward course over it, and the Ironsides had to deviate a little to the left in order to avoid the impediment. They soon, however, crossed the summit, and then fresh valleys opened on either side. New downs, too, rose before them, varying little in aspect or character from those which they had just traversed. Though the summits still glowed with the reflected radiance of the sky, the coombs looked dull and sombre; but there was no positive obscurity, and as Stelfax plunged his gaze into the hollows, he failed in discovering the object of his quest. On either hand the valleys were wide and extensive, and the sides of the hills bare, and destitute of covert sufficient to screen the fugitive from observation. The valley on the left, which ran in a northerly direction—the course apparently taken by the fugitive—was so broad and open, that, had the flying horseman gone that way, he must have been at once distinguished. But neither on the right or on the left could he be seen. If he had ascended the opposite downs, he must necessarily be in view. But he was not there. These considerations led Stelfax to the conclusion that he must have found some place of concealment, and his suspicions were instantly directed to a small holt or thicket growing near the foot of the opposite hill, which would offer convenient shelter. Satisfied with the correctness of his supposition, the Roundhead leader at once gave directions to his men to separate, and approach the wood in such manner as would enable them most completely to invest it. The injunctions were promptly obeyed, Stelfax himself moving off a little to the left, and then mounting the hill-side, so as to bring himself close to the top of the holt, which straggled slantingly up the acclivity. These precautionary measures taken, entrance was simultaneously made into the thicket at four different points. The timber of which the holt was composed consisted almost entirely of ash, hazel, and oaks. None of the trees had attained any great size, and being planted closely together—much too closely to allow free growth—while brambles and thorns likewise abounded in the thicket, it was in places almost impervious. The crashing of branches proclaimed the advance of the Ironsides, and more than one pheasant was disturbed by them. But as yet the fugitive had not been detected. All at once Stelfax, who had pushed on more expeditiously than his men, descried the horseman hidden in the depths of the grove. Unable to repress a shout of exultation at the sight, he called to the Cavalier to surrender, but the latter replied by firing a pistol at him: the thickly intervening trees rendering it impossible that aim could be taken, the ball lodged in the trunk of an adjoining oak. The Cavalier then turned and endeavoured to make good his retreat, while Stelfax pressed vigorously after him, shouting to his men to intercept him. But it soon appeared that the fugitive was quite as active as his pursuers, and understood rather better than they did how to make his way through a tangled thicket. He dexterously slipped through the trees, while the fiery haste and impetuosity of Stelfax only tended to his own disadvantage. The Roundhead leader made one or two ineffectual dashes at the Cavalier, but the other easily avoided him, and, guided by the noise made by the advancing troopers,

he likewise managed to keep out of their way. This adroit mode
of proceeding soon increased the distance between Stelfax and himself, and enabled him to obtain a considerable start ere the Roundhead leader and his men could extricate themselves from the holt
and give chase.

Both pursued and pursuers now went along at a headlong pace.
For some little time the Cavalier kept in the valley, and crossed
the rough and ill-kept road leading to Lewes. At that time there
was no direct road from the metropolis to Brightelmstone, and
only the deep-rutted cart-road just mentioned between the latter
place and Lewes. The whole district being perfectly open and
unenclosed—not a hedge or fence existing, save in the neighbourhood of some sequestered homestead—there was nothing to check
the progress either of the fugitive or those on his track.

On—on they went—now traversing a winding valley, now
mounting a hill—anon descending to another dell—crossing it, and
making a new ascent. All this without in the slightest degree
relaxing speed. The Cavalier seemed in no wise troubled about
his pursuers, feeling confident, apparently, that he should leave
them behind in the end. Hitherto not a single individual had
been encountered. The downs seemed wholly deserted.

The Cavalier had now gained the summit of the hill on which
the ancient encampment called Hollingsbury Castle may be traced,
and as his pursuers were not more than half way up the hill,
he drew in the rein near the old earthwork, to breathe his panting
steed for a moment. Seeing him pause thus, Stelfax and his
men hurried on; but ere they could get within pistol-shot, he
speeded off down the smooth turf of the declivity, as if making
for the pretty little village of Preston, the church of which could
be discerned in the valley, about half a mile off, embosomed in
trees. But the fugitive, it soon became manifest, had no intention of entering the village. He soon struck off on the right,
and keeping on the slopes of the hill until he had passed Patcham
and its hanging wood, crossed the valley now traversed by the
railway, and ascended the opposite hill. Probably, he had conjectured that the Ironsides, finding their efforts to come up with

him fruitless, would desist from further pursuit—but in this supposition he was deceived. Stelfax was not the man to be baffled. As long as their horses would carry them, he and his troopers would follow—and though their steeds were not so swift as that of the Cavalier, they were stronger, and capable of greater endurance. So not many minutes elapsed ere they were on the top of the down and galloping after him.

With the evident intention of disembarrassing himself of them, the fugitive now led them into all sorts of difficult places, and practised every possible manœuvre to shake them off. In vain. They still held on; while the stratagems essayed by the Cavalier had more than once well-nigh led to his capture.

It was after a mischance of this kind, in which an attempt to double had been dexterously checked by Stelfax, that he suddenly changed his plan, and once more set off straight-a-head with great swiftness.

They were now upon the chain of downs that terminates on the north in the lofty and steep escarpment closely adjoining the extraordinary trench popularly known as the Devil's Dyke. It was towards the steepest part of this dangerous declivity that the Cavalier now rode. Perfectly acquainted with the country, as the result proved, he knew whither he was going, and was prepared for the hazardous feat he had to perform. Not so his pursuers. This precipitous escarpment, which stands like a great natural bulwark at the south of the broad Weald of Sussex— the whole of that immense and beautiful tract being discernible at one glance from it—slopes suddenly and abruptly down, without the slightest interruption to the valley, the perilous nature of the descent being materially increased by the slippery condition of the turf, which offers, at dry seasons especially, a very insecure footing. A single false step would send the luckless wight who made it sliding to the foot of the escarpment in double-quick time. On the brow of this lofty hill are the remains of an encampment, with a wide ditch and a rampart surrounding it of nearly a mile in circumference. Adjacent to this camp, and dividing it from the lower range of downs, is the Dyke.

Skirting the brink of this remarkable chasm, the Cavalier rode on, and passing through a breach in the outworks of the camp, made for that portion of the rampart which overlooks the steepest part of the declivity. He paused not for a moment, but ere reaching the verge of the rampart, cast a glance of defiance at his pursuers. Stelfax, at that instant, was passing through the breach on the south side of the camp. Unaware of the perilous nature of the feat about to be attempted, he saw the Cavalier spring from the edge of the rampart, and plunge down the descent beyond it. Intending to follow him, the Roundhead officer rode on, but as he neared the brink of the declivity, and its precipitous and dangerous character became fully revealed to him, he recoiled, and drew in the rein with such force that he almost pulled back his steed upon its haunches. Just in time! In another instant he would have leaped the rampart, and must have rolled from top to bottom of the sharp descent. Cautiously approaching the edge of the declivity, to his infinite astonishment and vexation he beheld the bold horseman rapidly descending the steep escarpment, apparently with perfect ease and security. The rider seemed to trust himself entirely to his horse, not attempting to direct him, but leaving him to take his own way. All he did was to lean back as much as he could in the saddle to avoid sliding out of it on to the horse's shoulder. In this way he had accomplished nearly half the descent.

The sight stung Stelfax to the quick. His prey he now felt would escape him. If the fugitive should reach the bottom in safety, his escape was inevitable. Long before the valley could be gained by any secure descent, he would be far out of harm's way, and Stelfax, fearless and venturesome as he was, did not like to essay this perilous descent, not deeming his horse sufficiently sure-footed to accomplish it. There was but one way of arresting the fugitive. Stelfax took a pistol from his holster, and fired. His mark had not been the Cavalier, but his steed. The ball lodged in the gallant animal's brain. Instantly quitting the almost sliding posture he had assumed, he sprang with a slight bound in the air, and then dropped. The Cavalier had managed to disengage himself from the saddle, but fell in the attempt, and could not recover his footing. He and his slaughtered steed rolled together to the bottom of the declivity, where both lay motionless.

"We have Abijam now—dead or alive," cried Stelfax to his men, who by this time had come up. "Mattathias and Enoch go ye down to the valley by yon safe though circuitous route on the left, while Nathan Guestling and I will find our way down on the right. Lose no time—though there is little fear that our prey will escape us now. He hath not stirred since he fell, and I fear me is killed outright."

III.

OF THE GUESTS AT THE POYNINGS' ARMS.

On reaching the valley, Stelfax, closely followed by Nathan Guestling, rode towards the spot where the luckless Cavalier was lying. Hitherto, he had not moved; but when the Roundheads drew near, he began to exhibit some symptoms of animation, and made an effort to regain his feet. The exertion, however, was too much for him, and he sank back with a groan.

Flinging himself from his horse, and giving the bridle to Guestling, Stelfax bent over the prostrate Cavalier, and carefully studied his features. The result of this examination was by no means satisfactory. The person under his scrutiny was some ten years older than Charles Stuart, though his slight figure and swarthy complexion, fine black eyes, and long dark locks, had given him a general resemblance to the youthful monarch. On closer inspection, however, the likeness vanished, and the stranger's lineaments were found to be different in many points from those of the king. Stelfax gave vent to his disappointment in a loud and angry exclamation, and called out to the two other troopers, who rode up at the moment, that it was not Abijam after all. Hearing what passed, the prostrate Cavalier raised himself upon his elbow, and cried, "So you took me for the king—ha! No wonder you gave me so hot a chase Learn to your confusion that his Majesty is safe from pursuit, and never likely to fall into rebellious hands."

"So your friend, Lord Wilmot, affirmed, sir," rejoined Stelfax: "but I attached little credit to his assertion, and I attach no more to yours. You are my prisoner. Under what name and title do you surrender?"

"It is my pleasure to guard my incognito as long as I can," the Cavalier replied. "I must therefore decline to furnish you with my name. As to title, I have none."

"You are too modest, methinks, sir," Stelfax cried. "Remain unknown, if you will, for the present. If you are not treated with the consideration due to your rank, you have only yourself to blame."

"I have no rank whatever, I repeat," the Cavalier replied. "I am but a simple gentleman—and a very poor gentleman into the bargain—thanks to the fines and confiscations of your State Council. Will one of your men lend a hand to lift me up?"

"I will do as much for you myself, sir," Stelfax replied, helping him to his feet. "I hope you are not much hurt?"

"No bones are broken, I think," said the other; "but I am a good deal shaken. You gave me rather an awkward tumble down the hill—but I should not heed that if my horse had been spared," glancing, as the words were uttered, with great commiseration at the body of the poor animal lying stark beside him. "He was a gallant steed! I shall never get such another."

"A brave horse, in sooth!" exclaimed Stelfax. "I felt sorry to despatch him—but I must have shot him or you. You may, however, console yourself for the loss by reflecting that you will never more, in all likelihood, require his services."

"That is but cold comfort," the other rejoined. "However, we Cavaliers are not accustomed to despair, even at the foot of the scaffold. I hope to give you another run as good as the one you have just enjoyed—with this difference only, that on the next occasion you may be left in the lurch."

"Many a fox-chase has been less exciting, no doubt," said Stelfax, entering into the jest. "But you must now submit to be searched by my men, sir. I regret that the measure cannot be dispensed with—but my orders are strict. All letters and papers must be sent to head-quarters—and perhaps I may learn at the same time whom I have the honour of addressing."

Due precautions against a contingency like the present must have been taken by the Cavalier, since only a few unimportant articles were found upon him, and nothing whatever to afford a clue to his identity. Seeing the prisoner look very faint, and scarcely able to stand, though he uttered no complaint, Stelfax caused him to be lifted on to the croup of Nathan Guestling's horse, and secured by a broad belt passed round his own waist and that of the stalwart trooper in front. He then directed Mattathias and Enoch to ride one on either side of the captive, to prevent the possibility of escape, and set off for a hamlet, close at hand, where he made sure of obtaining restoratives for the luckless Royalist. The place for which the Roundhead captain was bound was Poynings, one of the prettiest and most picturesque villages amidst the South Downs, and then remarkable for its fine old manor-house appertaining to the baronial family that took its name from the place, as well as for its antique church, which latter still exists.

Night was now coming on apace, but the sky was clear, and the light of the heavenly bodies dispelled the darkness. The hour of eight was tolled out as the little troop entered Poynings. The trampling of the horses quickly roused the villagers, and brought them to the doors of their cottages to see the soldiers pass, and great anxiety was evinced to obtain a glimpse of the malignant prisoner. But no near approach to him was permitted by the guard, and the curiosity of the spectators remained unsatisfied.

A decent hostelry was soon found near the church, and here Stelfax alighted, and caused his prisoner, who was unable to dismount without assistance, to be lifted from the trooper's horse and carried inside. This service was rendered by the landlord, who announced himself to the Roundhead leader as Simon Piddinghoe, of the Poynings' Arms, at the honourable captain's service. The Cavalier was supported by the assiduous host into a large, comfortable-looking house-place, with a wood fire blazing upon the hearth—deep ingle-nooks on either side of the chimney—and a couple of cozy benches

with high backs calculated to keep off all draught advancing far
into the room, with a long and strong oak table between them. On
these high-backed benches some nine or ten guests were seated,
smoking and quaffing the stout amber ale, the mulled sack, and
other liquors for which the Poynings' Arms was famed.

The company consisted, as it turned out, of the village schoolmaster, Master Cisbury Oldfirle, who was accounted a man of parts
and erudition, and who, at all events, considered himself such—two
or three other inhabitants of the village of the better class—and a
brace of sturdy farmers from the neighbourhood, who were discussing their evening pint, or quart, as it might be, before going home
to their dames. Besides these, there were some other guests—non-
descript individuals, whose precise position in society Simon Piddinghoe himself would have found it difficult to assign, and who
might be disbanded Royalist soldiers, gentlemen out-at-elbows from
drink or play, bankrupt tradesmen from London, or what you
please. Shabby roysterers like these often took up their quarters
in country hostels at the time—carefully selecting houses where
good liquor and a good bowling-green were to be found; and notwithstanding their tarnished lace cloaks, threadbare doublets, and
slouched Spanish hats, they were heartily welcomed by mine host
—so long as they had wherewithal to pay the shot. To these personages the arrival of the Ironsides seemed to afford anything but
satisfaction, though they endeavoured to put a good face upon
their vexation, and rose with the rest of the company to salute the
Roundhead captain on his entrance. All arose but one—a fierce,
swash-buckling fellow, with a long rapier at his side, who was afterwards addressed by the host as Captain Goldspur. With a muttered oath, this personage pulled his slouched hat over his beetle-
brows, shifted himself in his seat, and turned his back upon Stelfax.
As the captive Cavalier was brought into the room, and the light
of the fire illumined his features, Simon Piddinghoe gave a slight
start of recognition; but a pressure of his arm by the prisoner
cautioned him to hold his tongue.

By Stelfax's directions the luckless gentleman was accommodated
with an easy-chair near the fire, and a glass of strong water being
administered to him by the host, he speedily began to revive.

Meantime, the company had resumed their seats, though the questionable individuals we have described were evidently ill at ease, and Captain Goldspur, who puffed away furiously at his pipe, looked askance at Stelfax from beneath his heavy brews. But if he or his companions meditated any attack upon the Roundhead leader, the formidable appearance of the latter served to restrain them. Neither was Stelfax unsupported. His three men had entered the room and seated themselves at the further end of the benches, ready to obey their captain's slightest behest.

However conversation might have gone on before the arrival of the Ironsides, it flagged now—the only person who maintained his character for loquacity being Cisbury Oldfirle. He talked on with his wonted volubility. Undismayed by Stelfax's stern looks, he entered into conversation with him, and gave him many particulars concerning the ancient family of Poynings, to which the other listened with some degree of attention, and then inquired whether the worshipful captain had heard the legend of the Devil's Dyke, and finding—as might be expected—that he had not, volunteered to relate it to him—premising that he could not entirely vouch for its authenticity. Having been supplied by the assiduous host with a pottle of admirably brewed sack, Stelfax felt disposed to accord the talkative pedagogue his attention, and listened with more patience than might have been expected to the weird, and somewhat extravagant, legend which will be found narrated—almost in Master Oldfirle's own language—in the next chapter.

IV.

𝔗𝔥𝔢 𝔏𝔢𝔤𝔢𝔫𝔡 𝔬𝔣 𝔱𝔥𝔢 𝔇𝔢𝔟𝔦𝔩'𝔰 𝔇𝔶𝔨𝔢.

AS RELATED BY MASTER CISBURY OLDFIRLE, SCHOOLMASTER, OF POYNINGS.

THE wondrous event I am about to detail happened in the
time of the good Saint Cuthman of Steyning, in this county—a
holy man, who from his extraordinary piety and austerity was be-
lieved to be endowed with supernatural power. Many miracles
are attributed to him, some of which occurred long before his
canonisation. While yet a boy, and employed in tending his father's
sheep on the downs, in order to pursue his devotional exercises
undisturbed, he was wont to trace a large circle round the flock with
his crook, beyond which none of them could stray, neither could
any enemy approach them. Moreover, the good saint could punish
the scoffer, as well as bless and sustain the lowly and the well-doer.
Derided by certain blasphemous haymakers for carrying his palsied
mother in a barrow—no better means of conveyance being at hand
at the time—he brought down a heavy shower upon their heads,
rendering their labour of no account; and thenceforward, whenever
grass was cut and dried within that meadow, rain would fall upon
it, and turn it to litter. Such was holy Cuthman—a man, you will
perceive, whom it was necessary to treat with the respect due to his
exalted virtues.

At a later period of the saint's life, when his aged mother had gone from him, when he had built a wooden church with his own hands at Steyning—wherein, in the fulness of time, he was interred —and when his reputation for sanctity and austerity had greatly increased, causing him to be equally reverenced and dreaded— dreaded, I mean, by evil-doers, to whom he was especially obnoxious —the holy man walked forth one afternoon, in early autumn, wholly unattended, across the downs; his purpose being to visit a recluse, named Sister Ursula, who dwelt in a solitary cell on the summit of a hill adjoining Poynings, and whom he had been told was sick, and desirous of being shriven by him. Now Saint Cuth- man had his staff in his hand, without which he never journeyed abroad, and he walked on until he reached the eminence for which he was bound. On the brow of this hill in former times the heathen invaders of the land had made a camp, vestiges of which may still be discerned. But it was not with these memorials of a bygone and benighted people that Saint Cuthman concerned himself. If he thought about the framers of those mighty earthworks at all, it was with thanksgiving that they had been swept away, and had given place to a generation to whom the purer and brighter light of the Gospel was vouchsafed.

Thus communing with himself it may be, holy Cuthman reached the northern boundary of the rampart surrounding the old Roman camp, and cast his eyes over the vast Weald of Sussex, displayed before him like a map. The contemplation of this fair and fertile district filled his soul with gladness; but what chiefly rejoiced him was to note how the edifices reared for worship had multiplied since he first looked upon the extensive plain. He strove to count the numerous churches scattered about, but soon gave up the attempt—he might as well have tried to number the trees. But the difficulty he experienced increased his satisfaction, inasmuch as it proved to him that true religion had taken deep root in the land. And he gave glory and praise ac- cordingly, where glory and praise are due.

Scarcely were his audibly-uttered thanksgivings ended, when he became aware that some one stood nigh him, and turning his head, he beheld a tall man of singularly swarthy complexion,

haughty mien, and eyes that seemed to burn like coals of fire.
The habiliments of this mysterious and sinister-looking personage
were of blood-red hue, and though their richness and the egret
in his velvet cap betokened princely rank, he bore the implements
of a common labourer—namely, a pickaxe and a shovel. No sound
had proclaimed the stranger's approach, and his appearance was as
sudden and startling as if he had risen from the earth. As Saint
Cuthman regarded him with the aversion inspired by the sight of
a venomous and deadly snake, yet wholly without fear, he knew
that he was in the presence of the Author of Ill.

"Comest thou to tempt me, accursed one?" the holy man sternly
demanded. "If so, learn that I am proof against thy wiles. Depart from me, or I will summon good spirits that shall cast thee
hence."

"Thou canst not do so," the inauspicious-looking stranger replied, laughing derisively. "I am master here. Altars have been
reared to strange gods upon this hill, and sacrifices made to them;
—nay, I myself have been worshipped as Dis, and the blood of
black bulls has been poured out upon the ground in mine honour.
Therefore, the hill is mine, and thou thyself art an intruder upon it,
and deservest to be cast down headlong into the plain. Yet will I
spare thee——"

"Thou darest not so much as injure a hair of my head, Sa-
thanas," interrupted the Saint, in a menacing voice, and raising
his staff as he spoke. "Approach! and lightnings shall blast thee."

"I tell thee I have no design to harm thee," returned the Fiend,
with a look that showed he would willingly have rent the holy
man in pieces. "But give heed to what I am about to say.
Vainly hast thou essayed to count the churches in the Sussex
Weald, and thou hast glorified Heaven because of the number of
the worshippers gathered within those fanes. Now mark me, thou
servant of God! Thou hast taken a farewell look of that plain, so
thickly studded with structures pleasing in thy sight, but an
abomination to me. Before to-morrow morn, that vast district—
far as thine eye can stretch—even to the foot of yon distant Surrey
hills—the whole Weald of Sussex, with its many churches, its

churchmen, and its congregations, shall be whelmed beneath the sea."

"Thou mockest me," returned Saint Cuthman, contemptuously; "but I know thee to be the Father of Lies."

"Disbelieve me, if I fail in my task—not till then," said the Fiend. "With the implements which I hold in my hand I will cut such a dyke through this hill, and through the hills lying between it and Hove, as shall let in the waters of the deep, so that all dwelling within yonder plain shall be drowned by them."

"And thinkest thou thy evil work will be permitted?" cried the Saint, shaking his head.

"Thou, at least, canst not prevent it," rejoined the Fiend, with a bitter laugh. "I will take my chance of other hindrance."

The holy man appeared for a moment troubled, but his confidence was presently restored.

"Thou deceivest thyself," he said. "The task thou proposest to execute is beyond thy power."

"Beyond *my* power!" exclaimed the Demon. "It is a trifle in comparison with what I can achieve. I have had a hand in many wonderful works, some of which are recognised as mine, though I have not got credit for a tithe of those I have performed. Devil's bridges are common enough, methinks, in mountainous gorges— devil's towers are by no means rare in old castles. Most of the camps upon these downs were planned and executed by me—the very rampart upon which we stand being partly my work. The first Cæsar has got the credit of many of my performances, and he is welcome to it. He is not the only man who has worn laurels belonging by right to others. Saint as thou art, it is meet thou give the devil his due. Do so, and thou must needs praise his industry."

"Thy industry in evil-doing is unquestionable," rejoined the Saint. "But good work is out of thy power. Thou darest not affirm that thou hast had any hand in the erection of temples and holy piles."

"Ask thy compeers, Saint Dunstan and Saint Augustine—they will tell thee differently. But I disdain to boast. I have certainly had no hand in thy ugly little wooden church at Steyning."

"And thy present feat is to be performed before to-morrow, thou sayest?" demanded the Saint, highly offended at this un-called-for allusion to his own favourite structure.

"Between sunset and sunrise, most saintly sir."

"That is but a short time for so mighty a task," said the holy man, in an incredulous tone. "Bethink thee a September night is not a long night?"

"The shortest night is long enough for me," the Fiend replied. "If the dawn comes and finds my work incomplete, thou shalt be at liberty to deride me."

"I shall never treat thee otherwise than with scorn," the Saint rejoined. "But thou hast said it, and I hold thee to thy word. Between sunset and sunrise thy task must be done. If thou failest—from whatever cause—thy evil scheme shall be for ever abandoned."

"Be it so! I am content," the Fiend rejoined. "But I shall not fail," he added, with a fearful laugh "Come hither at sunset, and thou wilt see me commence my work. Thou mayst tarry nigh me, if thou wilt, till it be done."

"Heaven forfend that it should be done!" ejaculated the Saint, casting his eyes upwards.

When he looked up again towards the spot where the Evil One had stood, he could no more perceive him.

"No!" exclaimed the good Saint, allowing his gaze to wander over the smiling and far-stretching Weald, "I cannot believe that I am taking farewell of this lovely plain. I cannot for an instant believe that its destruction will be permitted. Its people have not sinned, but have incurred the hatred of the Arch-Fiend solely because of their piety and zeal. It shall be my business to defeat his hateful design."

The holy man turned away, and quitting the camp, proceeded in an easterly direction over the hill, until he came to a small stone structure, standing near a grey old thorn-tree, on an acclivity covered with gorse and heather. The occupant of this solitary cell belonged to a priory of Benedictine nuns, situated at Leominsters near Arundel, and attached to the Abbey of Almenesches, in Normandy. Sister Ursula Braose had retired to this lonesome spot in order to pass the whole of her time in devotion, and had acquired a reputation for sanctity and asceticism scarcely inferior to that of holy Cuthman himself. She was a daughter of the noble house of Braose of Bramber Castle. Once a week the purveyor of the priory at Leominster brought her a scanty supply of provisions (for the poor soul needed but little), and it was from him that Saint Cuthman had heard of her illness, and of her desire to be shriven by him.

He found the recluse occupied in her devotions. She was kneeling before an ivory crucifix fastened against the wall of her cell, and was so absorbed as to be entirely unconscious of the Saint's approach. He did not make his presence known to her till she had done. Sister Ursula Braose had once been remarkable for beauty, but years, the austere life she had led, and the frequent and severe penances she had undergone, had obliterated all traces of loveliness from her features. She was old and wrinkled now; her hair white as snow, and her fingers thin as those of a skeleton. She was clothed in a loose black robe, with a cincture of cord round her waist. Reverentially saluting the holy man, she prayed him to be seated upon a stool, which, with another small seat hewn out of stone, a stone table, and a straw pallet, formed the entire furniture of her cell. An iron lamp hung by a chain from the roof. On the table were placed a missal written on vellum, an hour-glass, and a small taper.

After inquiring as to her ailments, and expressing his satisfaction that she felt somewhat better, Saint Cuthman said, " Are you still fasting, sister? I know you are wont only to break bread and drink water after the hour of vespers."

" Since yestere'en, nothing has passed my lips, holy father," the recluse replied.

" It is well," said the Saint. " The prohibition I am about to lay upon you—painful to any other, unaccustomed to severe mortification of the flesh—will by you be scarcely accounted a penance. I enjoin you to refrain from all refreshment of the body, whether by food or rest, until to-morrow morning. Think you, you can promise compliance with the order?"

"Do I think it, holy father?" Sister Ursula cried. "If Heaven will spare me so long, I am sure of it. I was in hopes," she added, almost with a look of disappointment, "that you were about to enjoin me some severe discipline, such as my sinfulness merits, and I pray you to add sharp flagellations, or other wholesome correction of the flesh, to your mandate."

"Nay," rejoined the Saint, smiling at the recluse's zeal; "the scourge is unneeded. You have no heavy offence, I am well assured, on your conscience. But keep strict vigil throughout the night, and suffer not sleep to weigh down your eyelids for a moment, or you may be exposed to temptation and danger. The Arch-Fiend himself will be abroad."

"I will spend the livelong night in prayer," said Sister Ursula, trembling.

"Fear nothing," returned the Saint; "the Prince of Darkness has other business on hand, and will not trouble you. He will be engaged in a terrible work, but, with Heaven's aid, good sister, yours shall be the hand to confound him."

"Mine!" exclaimed the recluse, seeking by her looks for an explanation from the holy man.

"When the sun hath gone down," rejoined Saint Cuthman, "which will be about the seventh hour, turn this hour-glass, and let the sand run out six times—six times, do you mark, good sister? That will bring you to the first hour after midnight. Kneel then before yon crucifix and pray fervently, that the dark designs of him who took our Saviour to the top of the high mountain, and showed him all the kingdoms of the world in a moment, may be defeated. Next, light this taper, which I will presently consecrate; set it within the bars of that little grated window looking towards the east, and pray that its glimmer may be as the first grey light of dawn. Again, I say, do you mark me, sister?"

"Not a word uttered by you, holy father, but hath sunk deep in my breast," she replied. "Your instructions shall be scrupulously obeyed."

"Nothing evil shall cross this threshold during the night," pursued the Saint. "I will guard it as, in the days of my youth,

I guarded my father's flocks on the hills. Light not your lamp but only the taper, as I have bidden you; and stir not forth on any threat or summons, for such will only be a snare to injure you; and let not your heart quail because of the frightful sounds you may hear. Though the earth should quake beneath your feet, and this solid hill tremble to its foundations, yet shall not a stone of your cell be removed, neither shall any harm befal you."

The Saint then took up the taper, and blessed it in these terms: "*Domine Jesu Christi, fili Dei vivi, benedic candelam istam supplicationibus nostris : infunde ei, Domine, per virtutem sanctæ crucis benedictionem cælestem ; ut quibuscumque locis accensa, sive posita fuerit, discedant principes tenebrarum, et contremiscant, et fugiunt pavidi cum omnibus ministris suis ab habitationibus illis : nec præsumant amplius inquietare, aut molestare servientes tibi omnipotenti Deo.*"

After going through certain other ceremonials, which it is needless to describe, the Saint sat down, and addressing Sister Ursula, declared his readiness to shrive her.

The recluse then knelt down before him, and inclining her head so as to conceal her features, said she had one secret within her breast which she had never revealed to her confessor—one sin upon her soul, of which she had never been able to repent.

After duly reproving her, the Saint told her to make clean her breast by confession, declaring she would then be able to repent.

Thus exhorted, Sister Ursula replied, in accents half suffocated by irrepressible emotion: "My secret is, that I loved you—you, holy father—when I was young: my unrepented sin is, that I have never been able to banish that love from my heart."

"Alas! sister," rejoined the holy man, trembling in spite of himself, "we have been equally unhappy. In days, long gone by, I could not behold unmoved the charms of the fair and noble Lady Ursula Braose. But I conquered the passion, and repented that I had ever indulged it. Thou must do likewise. The struggle may be hard, but strength will be given thee for it. Hast thou aught more to confess?"

And the poor recluse, who shed abundance of tears, replying

in the negative, the Saint gave her absolution, saying that the penance he had already enjoined was sufficient, and that ere the morrow her breast would be free from its load. Struck by her looks, which were those of one not long for this world, he told her that if her sickness should prove mortal, dirges and trentals should be said for the repose of her soul.

The recluse thanked him, and after a while became composed and even cheerful.

Saint Cuthman tarried in the cell, discoursing with her upon the glorious prospects of futurity, and carefully avoiding any reference to the past, until, from the door of the little structure, which opened toward the west, he beheld the sun sink into the sea. Telling the good sister that a thousand lives depended upon her vigilance, he gave her his benediction and departed, never more to behold her alive.

As he took his way towards the north-eastern boundary of the ancient encampment, a noise resembling thunder smote his ear, and the ground shook so violently beneath his feet that he could scarcely stand, but reeled to and fro, as if his brain—his! whose lips no drink stronger than water had ever passed—had been assailed by the fumes of wine. Nevertheless, he went on, and, after a while, reached the lofty headland overlooking Poynings.

Here, as he expected, he beheld the Arch-Fiend at work. The infernal excavator had already made a great breach into the down, and enormous fragments of chalk and flint-stones rolled down with a terrific crash, like that caused by an avalanche amidst the Alps. Every stroke of his terrible pickaxe shook the hill to its centre. No one, who was not sustained by supernatural power, could have stood firmly upon the quaking headland. But Saint Cuthman, planting his staff upon the ground, remained unmoved—the only human witness of the astounding scene. The Fiend's proportions had now become colossal, and he looked like one of that giant race whom poets of heathendom tell us warred against Jove. His garb was suited to his task, and resembled that of a miner. His brawny and hirsute arms were bared to the shoulder, and the curled goat's-horns were visible on his uncovered head. His implements had become enormous as himself, and the broadest and heaviest anchor-fluke ever forged was as nought to the curved iron head of his pick-axe.   Each stroke plunged fathom-deep into the ground, and tore up huge boulder-like masses of chalk, the smallest of which might have loaded a wain. The Fiend worked away with might and main, and the concussion produced by his tremendous strokes was incessant and terrible, echoing far over the Weald like the rattling of a dreadful thunderstorm.

But the sand ran out, and Sister Ursula turned her glass for the first time.

Suddenly, the Fiend stopped, and clapped his hand to his side, as if in pain—" A sharp stitch !" quoth he. " My side tingles as if pricked by a thousand pins. The sensation is by no means pleasant—but 'twill soon pass !" Then perceiving the Saint watching him, he called out derisively—" Aha! art thou there, thou saintly man? What thinkest thou now of the chance of escape for thy friends in the Weald? Thou art a judge of such matters, I doubt not. Is my Dyke broad enough and profound enough, thinkest thou—or shall I widen it and deepen it yet more?" And the chasm resounded with his mocking laughter.

" Thou art but a slovenly workman, after all," remarked Saint Cuthman. " The sides of thy Dyke are rough and uneven, and want levelling. A mortal labourer would be shrewdly reprimanded if he left them in such an untidy condition."

· " No mortal labourer could make such a trench," cried the Fiend. " However, it shall never be said that I am a slovenly workman."

Whereupon he seized his spade, and proceeded to level the banks of the Dyke, carefully removing all roughness and irregularity.

" Will that satisfy thy precise notions?" he called out, when he had done.

" I cannot deny that it looks better," returned the holy man, glad to think that another hour had passed—for a soft touch falling upon his brow made him aware that, at this moment, Sister Ursula had turned the hour-glass for the second time.

A sharp sudden pain smote the Fiend, and made him roar out

lustily, "Another stitch, and worse than the first! But it shall not hinder my task."

Again he fell to work. Again, the hill was shaken to its base. Again, mighty masses of chalk were hurled into the valley, crushing everything upon which they descended. Again, the strokes of the pickaxe echoed throughout the Weald.

It was now dark. But the fiery breath of the Demon sufficed to light him in his task. He toiled away with right good will, for the Devil can work hard enough, I promise you, if the task be to his mind. All at once he suspended his labour. The hour-glass had been turned for the third time.

"What is the matter with thee?" demanded the Saint.

"I know not," replied the writhing Fiend. "A sudden attack of cramp in the arms and legs, I fancy. I must have caught cold on these windy downs. I will do a little lighter work till the fit passes off." Upon this, he took up the shovel and began to trim the sides of the Dyke as before.

While he was thus engaged, the further end of the chasm closed up, so that when he took up the pickaxe once more he had all his work to do again. This caused him to snort and roar like a mad bull, and so much flame and smoke issued from his mouth and nostrils, that the bottom of the Dyke resembled the bed of a volcano.

Sister Ursula then turned the glass for the fourth time. Here-upon, an enormous mass of breccia, or gold-stone, as the common folk call it, which the Fiend had dislodged, rolled down upon his foot, and crushed it. This so enraged him, that he sent the frag-ment of gold-stone whizzing over the hills to Hove. What with rubbing his bruised foot, and roaring, a quarter of an hour elapsed before he could resume his work.

The fifth turning of the glass gave him such pains in the back, that for some minutes he was completely disabled.

"An attack of lumbago," he cried. "I seem liable to all mortal ailments to-night."

"Thou hadst better desist," said the Saint. "The next attack may cripple thee for all time."

"I am all right again," shouted the Demon. "It was but a

passing seizure, like those that have gone before it. Thou shalt now see what I can do."

And he began to ply his pickaxe with greater energy than ever; toiling on without intermission, filling the chasm with flame from his fiery nostrils, and producing the effect of a continuous thunderstorm over the Weald. Thus he wrought on, I say, uninterruptedly, for the space of another hour.

Sister Ursula then turned the glass for the last time.

The Fiend was suddenly checked—but not this time by pains in the limbs, or prostration of strength. He had struck the pickaxe so deeply into the chalk that he could not remove it. He strained every nerve to pluck it forth, but it continued firmly embedded, and the helve, which was thick as the mainmast of a ship, and of toughest oak, broke in his grasp.

While he was roaring like an infuriated lion with rage and mortification, Saint Cuthman called out to him to come forth.

"Wherefore should I come forth?" the Fiend cried. "Thou thinkest I am baffled; but thou art mistaken. I will dig out my axe-head presently, and my shovel will furnish me with a new handle."

"Cease, if thou canst, for a short space, to breathe forth flame and smoke; and look towards the east," cried the Saint.

"There is a glimmer of light in the sky in that quarter!" exclaimed the Demon, holding his breath; "but dawn cannot be come already."

"The streak of light grows rapidly wider and brighter," said the Saint. "The shades of night are fleeing fast away. The larks are beginning to rise and carol forth their matin hymns on the downs. The rooks are cawing amid the trees of the park beneath us. The cattle are lowing in the meads—and hark! dost thou not hear the cocks crowing in the adjacent village of Poynings?"

"Cocks crowing at Poynings!" yelled the Fiend. "It must be the dawn. But the sun shall not behold my discomfiture."

"Hide thy head in darkness, accursed being!" exclaimed the Saint, raising his staff. "Hence with thee! and return not to this hill. The dwellers within the Sussex Weald are saved from thy malice, and may henceforth worship without fear. Get thee hence, I say."

Abashed by the awful looks of the Saint, the Demon fled. Howling with rage, like a wild beast robbed of its prey, he ran to the northern boundary of the rampart surrounding the camp, where the marks of his gigantic feet may still be seen indelibly impressed on the sod. Then springing off, and unfolding his sable pinions, he soared over the Weald, alighting on Leith Hill.

Just as he took flight, Sister Ursula's taper went out. Instant darkness fell upon the hill, and Night resumed her former sway. The village cocks ceased crowing, the larks paused in their songs and dropped to the ground like stones, the rooks returned to roost, and the lowing herds became silent.

Saint Cuthman had to make a considerable circuit to reach Sister Ursula's cell, a deep gulf having been placed between it and the headland on which he had taken his stand. On arriving at the little structure he found that the recluse's troubles were over. Her loving heart had for ever ceased to beat. Her failing strength had sufficed to turn the hour-glass for the last time, and just as the consecrated taper expired, she passed away. In death, she still retained the attitude of prayer—her clasped hands being raised heavenwards.

"*Suspice Domine, preces nostras pro animâ famulæ tuæ; ut si quæ ei maculæ de terrenis contagiis adhæserunt, remissionis tuæ misericordia deleantur!*" ejaculated the holy man. "She could not have had a better ending! May my own be like it! She shall have sepulture in my mother's grave at Steyning. And masses and trentals, according to my promise, shall be said for the repose of her soul. Peace be with her!" And he went on his way.

Thus was the Demon banished by Saint Cuthman from that hill overlooking the fair Sussex Weald, and the people of the plain ever after prayed in peace. But the Devil's handiwork—the unfinished Dyke—exists to this day. Though I never heard that his pickaxe has been found.

V.

HOW STELFAX TOOK THE CAVALIER TO THE GRANGE; AND WHAT HAPPENED BY THE WAY.

SOME few interruptions were offered to the schoolmaster's narration both by Stelfax and his men; and when it came to an end, the Roundhead leader observed that it was a monkish and superstitious legend, fit only for old wives and children, and that for his own part he did not believe in the pretended miracles of Saint Cuthman, or those of any other Romish saint in the calendar. On this observation being made, Captain Goldspur got up, and looking as if he would no longer remain in the company of a person who expressed such heterodox opinions, he was marching out of the room, when, at a sign from Stelfax, two of the troopers caught hold of him, and forced him back to his seat. In doing this, they deprived him of his long rapier, which Stelfax consigned to the host, bidding him put it aside for the present. In an authoritative tone the Roundhead leader then informed the company that none of them must leave the house until after his departure with the prisoner— a piece of good news to Simon Piddinghoe, who ventured to express a hope that the worshipful captain would prolong his stay to as late an hour as possible. Stelfax, indeed, seemed in no hurry to depart. His seat by the fireside was very comfortable, and the mulled sack super-excellent—so remarkably good, indeed, that, having finished his pottle during the progress of the schoolmaster's legend, he ordered the host to brew a second.

By this time, the prisoner had shaken off in a great measure the effects of his fall. Of a reckless turn, like most Cavaliers, he either felt—or feigned to feel—indifferent to his present position. His chair was next that of Stelfax, and hearing the praises bestowed by the latter upon the sack, he begged to be allowed a measure for himself—and the favour was unhesitatingly granted. After the failure of his attempt to march off, Captain Goldspur's audacity seemed to forsake him, and withdrawing as far as he could from the presence of the hateful Stelfax, he lapsed into gloomy silence. His companions were equally taciturn and moody. But the rest of the company took no umbrage at their detention, appearing rather pleased by the excuse it offered them for making a night of it. Whether Stelfax sat long to vex Goldspur and his sullen comrades—or whether, as is more probable, he felt disposed to rest and enjoy himself after a hard day's work—certain it is that eleven o'clock had struck ere he rose to depart. The reckoning was then paid—rather to Simon Piddinghoe's surprise, for the soldiers of the Republic were not notorious for scrupulously discharging their scores; the horses were brought out; the prisoner was placed on the crupper behind Nathan Guestling, and strapped to that stout trooper as he had previously been. All these arrangements made, Stelfax mounted, and after partaking of a stirrup-cup proffered by the host, put himself at the head of the little troop, and rode out of Poynings.

Notwithstanding the Roundhead leader's injunctions to the contrary, one person had contrived to slip out of the house unobserved. When the host returned to his guests to tell them they were now free to depart if they were so minded, he remarked that Captain Goldspur was gone, and had taken his rapier with him. Upon which he muttered, "There will be mischief, I fear.—And who, think you, yon red-coated knaves have got as a prisoner, my worthy masters?" he added.

"Nay, I know not," the schoolmaster rejoined. "Who should it be?"

"No other than Colonel George Gunter of Racton," the host replied; "as worthy a gentleman as any in the county, and as staunch a partisan as ever breathed of the — of——You know whom I mean."

"Was that Colonel Gunter of Racton?" cried a personage in a tarnished lace cloak and dilapidated Spanish hat. "Would I had known it."

"Why, what wouldst thou have done, Master Jervoise Rumboldsdyke?" demanded the inquisitive schoolmaster.

"No matter," the other rejoined. "It may not yet be too late. Tell me the way taken by those cursed troopers," he added to the host.

"They rode towards Patcham," Simon Piddinghoe replied. "No doubt they are bound for Lewes, where the detachment is quartered."

"To Lewes!" exclaimed Rumboldsdyke. "To Lewes, then, let us hie. Here is thy reckoning, mine host." And flinging a double-crown upon the table he rushed out of the house, followed by his comrades.

It was a clear starlight night, and by no means dark. Stelfax kept a little in advance of his men, but did not urge his horse beyond a walk. Their road lay partly along a valley, partly over a lower range of downs. After a while, they reached Patcham, and were passing the thick hanging wood on the hill-side, when a pistol—for such the fire-arm seemed to be from its report—was discharged at Stelfax. The bullet struck the Roundhead leader's gorget, but did him no injury. He instantly turned, and dashing to the edge of the wood, called, in a voice of thunder, upon his dastardly assailant to show himself, and come forth if he dared. But no answer was returned to the summons, neither could any lurking assassin be detected. Deeming search useless at such an hour, Stelfax set off again; but he now mended his pace, and being under no apprehension of losing his way, he rode over the silent and solitary downs in the direction of Ovingdean, where he arrived without further molestation of any kind, and deposited his prisoner at the Grange.

VI.

BY WHAT MEANS THE PRISONERS ESCAPED FROM THE CHURCH.

WE must now return to the church, and see what the disorderly
rout left within it were about. It was past midnight. The torches
were still blazing, but the thick vapour that rose from their flames,
combined with the tobacco-smoke, filled the whole body of the
fabric, and so obscured its more distant portions, that the arched
screen separating the chancel from the nave could scarcely be discerned. The light, struggling through this vapour, only imperfectly
revealed the figures of the Ironsides stretched upon the benches,
some of them, as we have said, asleep, and the rest in a drowsy
state, half-stupified with drink. All their boisterous merriment
had long since ceased, and nothing was heard but the heavy
breathing of the slumbering topers. All at once, a slight noise
reached the ears of the sergeant, and looking in the direction
whence it proceeded, he thought he discerned a dark figure in the
pulpit. After steadily regarding the object for a few moments,
during which it continued perfectly motionless, a superstitious terror
took possession of Delves, and he began to think it was the Enemy
of Mankind standing before him in person. Rousing up Besadaiah Eavestaff, who was near to him, he directed his attention to
the mysterious figure, and asked him, in accents that betrayed his
alarm, what he thought of it?

"It is the Evil One," Besadaiah rejoined, rubbing his eyes.

"But how comes he here, in yonder pulpit, and in the garb of a minister of the Church? I am not afraid—I will address him."

With this he got up, and supporting himself with his carabine, staggered towards the pulpit.

"Aha!" he exclaimed, as he drew near, "I have it now, ser geant. Whom dost thou think his Satanic Majesty turns out to be? No other than Master Increase Micklegift, the Independent minister, whom we ejected from the neighbouring mansion by our captain's commands. How comes he here? Doth he take up his abode altogether within this church?"

"If it be indeed Master Micklegift, and not an evil spirit in his form," Delves rejoined, "question him thyself."

"He shall not need to do so," cried Micklegift, for it was he. "I have placed myself here to see how you who profess to be soldiers fighting for the cause of religion and truth would comport yourselves, and I find that ye are as riotous and intemperate as the scoffers, brawlers, and tipplers whom ye profess to reprobate. Are ye not ashamed to be wallowing in drunkenness when ye should watch and pray? Call ye yourselves good soldiers of the Republic? You are said to be the favoured host of our great Joshua, Cromwell; but is it by conduct like this that you have earned his regard? Hardly so, methinks! If you must needs turn this tabernacle into a place of duresse for your prisoners, why should you thus defile it? For your profaneness and irreverence ye ought to be driven forth with stripes, and if a judgment should fall upon your heads ye will richly have merited it."

"Peace!" exclaimed Besadaiah; "I will hear no more from thee."

"Nay, there is reason in what the good man saith," cried Delves. "We deserve his rebukes. It must be owned that our conduct this night hath not been in accordance either with our principles or our duty."

"Our captain mislikes this man, and suspects him of being in league with the malignants," cried Besadaiah. "By his own showing he hath been playing the spy upon us. Let him come down from that pulpit, and free us at once from his presence, or I will send a bullet through his brain."

"Thou darest not lift thy hand against me, thou sacrilegious ruffian," thundered Micklegift. "My purpose is to hold forth unto thee and to thy comrades, and to strive to awaken ye all to a sense of your sinfulness."

"It will be labour thrown away, worthy sir," said Delves, "so I pray you forbear. With what intent you have come hither, and hidden yourself away until this moment, is best known to your secret heart. But such conduct is questionable, and seems to justify our captain's doubts as to your sincerity to the cause. I have prisoners in charge here, as you are aware—prisoners for whose security I am responsible. I cannot tell but you may have some design to give them aid, and must therefore enjoin you to quit the church without delay."

"What if I refuse to go?" rejoined Micklegift. "What if, in my turn, I command thee and thy sacrilegious crew to depart from the tabernacle which ye have profaned?"

"You will do well not to provoke me further," Besadaiah cried, in a menacing voice, and levelling his musket at the Independent minister as he spoke. "Come down, I say, at once, and quit the church—or that pulpit shall be thy coffin."

"Put down thy weapon, Besadaiah, and harm not the man," interposed Delves. "Though his conduct be suspicious, he may have no ill intent. Hearken unto me, Master Micklegift, and compel me not to have recourse to harsh measures with thee. Thou canst not stay here."

"The church is mine, and nothing but force shall make me quit it," cried Micklegift, vehemently.

"I grieve to hear you say so," the sergeant rejoined. "I desire not to use violence, but your obstinacy will leave me no other alternative."

"Better let me put an end to the discussion, sergeant," growled Besadaiah, again raising his carabine.

"Not in that way, I tell thee," Delves rejoined. "For the last time, I say unto thee, Master Micklegift, wilt thou depart peaceably, or must I put thee forth?"

"I will not leave mine own church at thine, or at any man's

bidding," the Independent minister rejoined; "and I counsel thee not to attempt to use force against me, or thou wilt rue it. Lay but a finger upon me, and I will render thine arm powerless."

"Tut! tut! this is idle vaunting!" the sergeant exclaimed. "Since thou wilt not be advised, thou must take the consequences."

"No; it is thou who must take the consequences, sergeant. I have warned thee," Micklegift rejoined, raising his hands.

"Aid me to put him forth, Besadaiah," said Delves, "for I perceive he is disposed to offer resistance. But take heed thou doest him no injury."

Rearing his carabine against the door of a pew, he marched towards the pulpit. Besadaiah also laid down his musket, and followed him. But scarcely had the foremost of the two Ironsides set foot on the pulpit-steps, when Micklegift clapped his hands together, and called out with a loud voice, "Arise!—it is time!"

At the signal, for such it proved, two persons suddenly sprang up behind the troopers, and in an instant possessed themselves of the carabines which had been so imprudently abandoned. These personages, it soon appeared, were no other than the Saxbys, father and son, who had contrived to secrete themselves until this moment within the chancel. Levelling the guns at the Roundhead soldiers, Ninian and his father threatened to shoot them if they stirred a step. It was now Micklegift's turn to triumph. Not only had his signal summoned the Saxbys from their hiding-place, but at the same moment the prisoners burst forth from the interior of the tower, and so unexpectedly, that ere the drunken and drowsy troopers could recover from their surprise and seize their arms, they were deprived of them by their assailants. Aided by circumstances, the stratagem completely succeeded. All the fire-arms were secured by the Royalists. Helpless Henly was so overcome by the liquor he had swallowed, that he could not raise himself from the ground; and two others were in nearly the like state. The Royalists now numbered five, but as they had obtained possession of all the muskets and pistols belonging to the troop, it followed that they were completely masters of the position. Without much difficulty, the newly liberated prisoners succeeded in driving such of the Ironsides as were capable of offering re-sistance into the tower which they themselves had so recently occupied, and locked the door upon them. This done, they turned their attention to Delves and Besadaiah, over whom the two Saxbys still kept guard, with levelled muskets. On coming up, John Habergeon at once rushed in and grappled with the sergeant, while Ninian and his father laid hold of Besadaiah. A coil of rope which had been brought in by the troopers was soon found by Micklegift, who by this time had descended from the pulpit, and with it Delves and his comrade were bound hand and foot, and handkerchiefs tied over their mouths. Though the trouble seemed needless, similar precautions were taken with Helpless Henly and the two other equally inert troopers; and only one of them stirred and opened his eyes while the cords were being fastened round his wrists.

The Royalists next transformed themselves into the semblance of Republican soldiers, by putting on the habiliments and accou-trements of their enemies, equipping themselves in the scarlet doublets, tassets, breastplates, headpieces, and bandoleers of the Ironsides, buckling on their swords, and appropriating their cara-bines and pistols. These operations were conducted as expe-ditiously as possible, for the troopers shut up within the tower had begun to vociferate loudly, and make as much noise as they could, in the hope of giving the alarm; and though the thick walls of the chamber in which they were enclosed greatly dead-ened the clamour, still the Royalists did not know whether it might not be heard at the Grange. So the utmost despatch was used. And no sooner was their task accomplished, than the newly released prisoners, with their deliverers, Micklegift and the two Saxbys, quitted the church, locking the door upon their foes.

On issuing from the church, Micklegift quitted the party, and hastened to the parsonage, to make preparations for instant flight. For some time Ovingdean would be no safe place for him. The Royalists agreed to keep together for the present, unless circumstances should require them to separate. Command of the little party naturally devolved upon Lord Wilmot, and his first instructions were to proceed to the stables, and help themselves to the troopers' horses.

By this time the moon had risen, but her lustre was frequently obscured by passing clouds. Not being familiar with the locality, Lord Wilmot placed himself under the guidance of Ninian Saxby, who now led the way to the stables. As the young falconer marched along in this unaccustomed guise of steel cap and breastplate, he almost lost the sense of his own identity, and while eyeing his accoutrements with secret satisfaction, flattered himself that he made a very smart soldier, and only regretted that Patty Whinchat could not behold him.

The party were crossing the valley a little to the south of the Grange, when the sound of their footsteps attracted the attention of the patrol at the door of the mansion. The sentinel immediately advanced to the gate, and challenged them.

"Who are ye that go there?" he demanded.

"Friends!" responded John Habergeon, in the true puritanical snuffle.

"Advance, friends, and give the countersign," rejoined the sentinel.

"Maccabæus and his company," John replied, having luckily overheard the watchword whispered by the sergeant to his men.

"Pass on, then," cried the trooper. "Yet stay!—whither go ye?"

"To the stables, by order of Sergeant Delves."

"Good!—but what means the clamour within the church?"

"It is caused by the malignant prisoners, who like not their lodging," John replied, with a laugh, which was echoed by the trooper.

"Is that all?" he said. "I feared something might have gone wrong."

"Hath aught been heard of our captain?" demanded Lord Wilmot, disguising his voice as well as he was able.

"He returned half an hour ago with the prisoner," replied the sentinel.

" Did you hear that?" Lord Wilmot observed in a low voice to Clavering. "Colonel Gunter is taken. He must be rescued at any cost."

" Do you go back to the church after seeing to the horses, or are some of us to take your place?" inquired the sentinel.

" We will return presently and ascertain the captain's pleasure," returned Lord Wilmot.

Upon this the Royalists moved on, and the sentinel went back to his post.

In another minute the party reached the stables. Opening the door, Ninian quickly roused up a couple of grooms who were lying asleep on a pile of straw. A lighted horn lantern was hanging by a pulley overhead. At first the grooms took the whole party for Republican soldiers, and seemed reluctant to get up, but when Ninian made himself known, they quickly bestirred themselves. Each stall had a couple of horses within it; but though the stables were large, there was not accommodation for so many, and several of the troopers' steeds had been placed in the cow-house. It was in the latter place that Lord Wilmot found his own charger. Having selected such horses as they thought would best suit them —keeping one for Colonel Gunter, in case they should succeed in liberating him—they turned all the others loose in the farm-yard, hiding away the saddles and bridles.

But just as the party issued forth from the stables with their newly acquired steeds, an alarming sound reached their ears.

The bell of the church began to toll.

How it could be rung by the imprisoned Ironsides, the Royalists could not conjecture, for they had seen no bell-rope; but so it was. The bell went on tolling, and with momentarily increasing rapidity and loudness.

At this sound, the sentinel posted outside the Grange gave the alarm. In another minute the door of the mansion was thrown open, and, a light streaming forth, showed the soldiers rushing out.

Though somewhat taken by surprise, Lord Wilmot and his party promptly prepared to act.

BOOK VII.

—◆—

CAPTAIN TATTERSALL OF THE *SWIFTSURE*.

P

I.

HOW SERGEANT DELVES WAS REPRIMANDED BY HIS LEADER

WEARIED by his long ride, and by his exertions throughout the day, Stelfax, on his return to Ovingdean Grange with the prisoner, retired to the chamber he had appropriated, and merely taking off the more cumbrous parts of his accoutrements, flung himself on the couch. He was buried in profound slumber, when the knocking of the butt-end of a carabine at the door roused him, causing him to spring up instantly and seize his arms. Clapping his steel cap on his head, but without tarrying to buckle on his corslet and leg-pieces, he marched to the door, and, unfastening it, found Mattathias outside, who acquainted him with the strange ringing of the church bell. Indeed, the sound could be plainly distinguished where they were, though the room was at the back of the house.

Stelfax was not so much alarmed as his subordinate, for it did not occur to him as possible that Delves could be the dupe of a stratagem. Something, however, was wrong, and must be promptly rectified. He therefore hurried down stairs, with the intention of repairing to the church, but, on gaining the entrance-hall, found it invaded by a tumultuous assemblage of the household, who had flocked thither on hearing the bell toll, and two or three minutes were spent in their dispersion. But this being accomplished, he left a small guard in the hall, as well to watch over the prisoner, who was confined in a little room adjacent to the library, as to keep the household in order, and then went forth with the rest of his troop.

Meanwhile, a trumpet had more than once been sounded outside to recal the men supposed to be gone to the stables; but no notice was taken of the summons. When informed of this circumstance, Stelfax was exceedingly wroth, and despatched Nathan Guestling to the stables, commanding the instant return of the offenders. A further interruption to his progress occurred at the gate. A posse of villagers, only partially attired, and armed with such weapons as came readiest to hand, was here congregated, anxious to learn the cause of the disturbance. Distrusting these hinds, Stelfax peremptorily ordered them to return to their dwellings, threatening to fire upon them if they hesitated to comply. Intimidated by the menace, the poor fellows retired, while the Ironside captain and his men pursued their way to the church. The torches having been left burning by the fugitive Royalists when they quitted their temporary prison, the light of the flambeaux was dimly distinguishable through the windows as Stelfax passed through the churchyard; but nothing, as yet, had occurred to rouse his suspicions. His surprise and rage, however, may be conceived when his thundering knock at the church door, which he found locked, remained unanswered. Violently shaking the door, he endeavoured by main strength to burst it open, and, aided by his men, he speedily accomplished his object. A scene then lay before him so startling and extraordinary, that he could scarcely believe in its reality.

His astonishment and stupefaction, however, soon gave way to fury. Snatching a torch, he threw its light upon the prostrate forms of Delves and Besadaiah, and then commanded that the handkerchiefs should be taken from their mouths, but that the cords with which they were bound should not be unloosed.

"How is this, sergeant?" he demanded in a severe voice, as the order was obeyed. "How comes it that I find thee thus?"

Delves gave utterance to a groan, but made no other reply.

"How hast thou fulfilled thine office?" continued Stelfax, with increased severity. "Where are the captives committed to thy charge?"

SERGEANT DELVES REPRIMANDED

p. 213

"Gone, captain—all gone!" groaned Delves, in a tone of deep contrition. "They have escaped from me. I will not attempt to extenuate my conduct. I have been guilty of gross neglect."

"Soh! thou dost confess it!—ha!" exclaimed Stelfax, with concentrated fury. "Negligent and disobedient dog, thou deservest that I should pistol thee without grace allowed for prayer."

"Despatch me, captain, without pity," the sergeant rejoined. "I deserve to die. You cannot be more angered with me than I am with myself. Were I to live a hundred years, instead of only so many seconds, I should never regain my own good opinion. To think that I, who have been signalled out for public commendation by the Lord General himself—who have been deemed worthy of your confidence, captain—who prided myself upon strictness of discipline, and blind obedience to the orders of my superior—that I should have failed on all points!—it is too much—it is more than I can bear. Place your pistol at my head, and finish me."

"No," rejoined Stelfax; "I will not forestal the provost-marshal's office. Grievously am I disappointed in thee, O Deodatus Delves! —shamefully hast thou betrayed thy trust! But how came the matter to pass? It passeth my comprehension to understand how thou and thy comrades could be overcome and bound by so few. Ye would almost seem to have proffered your limbs to the fetters of the enemy."

"Our prisoners had a subtle demon to aid them, captain," replied Delves. "Strong waters were treacherously introduced with the provisions from the house, and robbed the men of their senses, so that they were no longer under my control. I say not this in my own defence, but in explanation. The truth will appear upon inquiry, if I be brought before a court-martial."

"Why didst thou not snatch the mischievous drink from the besotted fools?" demanded Stelfax.

"Alack, captain, all my efforts were unavailing. They resisted, and would not be bidden. But this was only part of a scheme, which I believe to have been devised by the Independent minister, Increase Micklegift. Men were hidden within the church, who came forth suddenly to aid in liberating the captives."

"All this shows how culpably negligent hath been thy conduct," said Stelfax. "A notable example will be made of thee."

"Reproach me no more, captain," cried Delves. "Your words are not needed to sharpen the stings of my own conscience. Oh. if I be not discarded from the service, no departure from duty shall ever again be laid to my charge."

"Misconduct like thine cannot be lightly passed over, I tell thee," returned Stelfax, somewhat appeased, though not choosing to let it appear that he was so. "Thou hast suffered a prisoner of great importance to escape from thee. Thou wert made responsible—body for body—for the security of the Lord Wilmot, who was committed to thy charge. How wilt thou answer for his evasion?"

"Even as you yourself have said, captain, with mine own body," the sergeant returned.

"Go to! dolt. Think'st thou thy worthless carcase, or those of all thy mutinous comrades, will weigh with the Lord General against the head of this malignant nobleman? A great prize has been lost through thy negligence. I have hunted down Lord Wilmot's companion, and brought him back captive, and thou mayst guess how it would have gladdened our general to receive the twain from my hands. Thou thyself wouldst have been advanced in his favour. I make little account of young Maunsel and the others, but the Lord Wilmot is a great loss."

"But may he not be recaptured?" said Delves. "Release me from these bonds, and I will not rest till I bring him back to you, dead or alive. Fear nothing! I have no desire to escape punishment, but am wishful to repair the mischief I have done."

"Be it so, then," said Stelfax, after a moment's reflection. "I will give thee a chance of redeeming thy errors. Untie those cords, and set him free," he added, to the men near him.

The order was instantly obeyed, and the like grace was accorded to Besadaiah, who humbled himself, as the sergeant had done, promising better conduct in future.

Long before this, the troopers shut up in the tower had been let out, but they kept aloof, as long as they could, from their in-

censed leader. How the church bell had been rung was then ex
plained. One of their number, aided by his comrades, who lifted
him on their shoulders, after the manner practised by profes-
sional tumblers, had contrived to catch hold of the bell-rope,
which had been tied up at a point supposed to be out of reach.
The bell was then tolled without difficulty. The Ironside leader's
anger being by this time considerably abated, he contented himself
with sharply reprimanding all the minor culprits. But the state
in which Helpless Henly and the two other drunken troopers
were found did not admit of their conduct being passed over so
lightly. Causing the bandages to be removed from their mouths,
but not suffering the cords with which they were bound to be taken
off, their leader left them in this state to sleep off the effects of
their drunken revel. While mustering the men, it suddenly occurred to him to inquire from Delves whom he had sent to the
stables.

"I have sent no one," the sergeant replied. "If any have gone
thither, it must be the cunning malignants who carried off our
weapons and accoutrements."

"Thou art right!" exclaimed Stelfax. "Fool that I was, not
to perceive this sooner! These men were seen and challenged by
the sentinel, who took them for comrades because they were accoutred like us, and gave the watchword. Let us to the stables at
once—though I fear the birds are flown. In that case we must
scour the country for them."

Upon which he rushed out of the church, followed by his men.

II.

IN WHAT MANNER COLONEL GUNTER WAS LIBERATED.

No notice, as we have shown, was taken by Lord Wilmot and the little party under his command of the trumpeter's summons; but as it was almost certain that a messenger would speedily be sent to order their return, preparations were made for his reception. For this purpose, John Habergeon and the elder Saxby dismounted and entered the stable; and as soon as Nathan Guestling arrived there, the door was closed upon him, and, being seized by these two powerful men, he was thrown down, bound hand and foot with a halter, and almost stifled with a horse-cloth wrapped round his face.

This task accomplished, the pair issued from the stables, and found that, in the interim, Lord Wilmot had sent the horses, in charge of the grooms, to a particular spot at the back of the garden indicated by Ninian. Stelfax had been seen to go to the church with a party of men, and the house being left comparatively undefended, his lordship apprehended little resistance, and ordered his party to set forward at once.

As they approached the mansion, the sentinel called out to them, " How now, comrades! Are ye come at last? Wherefore did ye not answer the recal? Did ye not hear the alarm-bell rung from the church?"

"Question us not—we are in haste," Lord Wilmot hastily replied, pressing on with the others. " Come with us inside, and thou shalt hear that which will surprise thee."

" What hath happened?" demanded the man, preceding them into the house. But scarcely had he crossed the threshold than the Royalists closed round him and disarmed him.

" Utter but a cry," said Lord Wilmot, clapping a pistol close to his head, " and it will be thy last. Thou art wholly in our power. But do as I bid thee, and thy life shall be spared. Dost heed me, knave?"

The man made no reply, but did not attempt to give the alarm.

At the moment when the Royalists thus gained admittance to the hall it was empty. On a table at one side a lamp was burning, but Ninian quickly extinguished it, and plunged the place in darkness. Just as this was accomplished, the door of a room adjoining the library was opened, and a harsh voice demanded who was there.

" Do thou answer," said Lord Wilmot to the sentinel, still holding the mouth of the pistol to his head.

" 'Tis I—Gabriel Flint," responded the sentinel.

" Ha! what dost thou there, Gabriel?" inquired the other.

" Speak as I enjoin thee," muttered Lord Wilmot, breathing a few words in his ear.

" The captain hath sent a file of men for the prisoner," said Flint.

" Ay, bring him forth without delay," added John Habergeon, in a snuffling, puritanical voice. " We are to take him to his friends at the church."

" Ye shall have him, and welcome," replied the other. " But tell me, comrade, what was the meaning of that ringing of the church bell?"

" 'Twas a mere trick of the prisoners," responded John; " they had barricaded the door of the tower wherein they were confined, and I suppose contrived to clamber up the walls and reach the bell-rope. The noise is checked now."

" Ay, our captain would soon put a stop to such vagaries, I'll warrant him," responded the trooper. " Come forth, prisoner," he added.

"Whither would ye take me?" demanded Colonel Gunter, as he approached the door of the room.

"To your friends," replied the trooper, in a jeering tone. "They are anxious for your company."

"They are," Lord Wilmot answered. "Be quick!"

Colonel Gunter fancied he recognised the voice, and accelerated his movements.

"Here is the prisoner," said the trooper, pushing the colonel forth—"take him! But the lamp has gone out, I perceive. I will bring a light instantly."

"It is needless," John Habergeon replied. "We care not to behold the Amalekite's features. We will take thy word that it is the right man."

While this brief colloquy occurred, Lord Wilmot grasped the colonel's arm, and made his presence known to him in a whisper.

"You here, my good lord, and in that garb?" exclaimed Colonel Gunter, in a low tone.

"Hush!" cried Lord Wilmot. "We are all friends—except this rascal, whose brains I will blow out if he ventures to utter a word. Move on with the prisoner!—to the church!" he added, aloud.

"Not so fast, comrades!—not so fast! A word with you ere you depart!" cried the trooper, appearing at the door with a light.

All chance of concealment was then at an end.

"Ha! what is this?" cried the trooper. "Malignants in the garb of soldiers of the Republic. Where are ye, comrades? Treason!—help!—succour!"

As he spoke, he discharged his pistol at the retreating Royalists. The ball passed within an inch of Lord Wilmot's head, but fortunately missed him.

John Habergeon and Ninian Saxby fired at the trooper in return, but as the latter had instantly retreated into the room, no damage was done him. Prohibiting any continuance of the conflict, Lord Wilmot ordered his party to move on. He still kept hold of the sentinel, intending to release him at the door. But, ere the Royalists could pass forth, they were again delayed in

an unexpected manner. The discharge of fire-arms operated as a
signal to another set of persons who had been secretly meditating
an attack upon the Roundheads, and who now found that their
design had been anticipated. From the passage leading to the
buttery and kitchen flocked some half-dozen or more of the household, headed by Giles Moppett and Crundy, and armed with
partisans and bills. At the same time, Colonel Maunsel, sword in
hand, appeared at the head of the staircase, closely attended by
Martin Geere, with a musket over his shoulder, while a few paces
behind them were Mr. Beard and Dulcia, with Patty Whinchat.

It will now be proper to explain how all these persons chanced
to appear with so much suddenness. As may be supposed, on
that eventful night none of the inmates of the Grange retired
to rest; and consequently they were all aware that Stelfax had returned with a new prisoner. Though entertaining no hope whatever of accomplishing his son's and Lord Wilmot's deliverance from
their enemies, Colonel Maunsel did not entirely despair of setting
free the captive last brought in. Who this personage might be the
old Cavalier was entirely ignorant. All the household were firmly
persuaded it was the king; and though Colonel Maunsel, who
had received an assurance to the contrary from Lord Wilmot,
did not share in their belief, still he felt certain the individual
must be a Royalist of distinction—and, in all probability, a friend.
An effort must, therefore, be made for his liberation. Through the
agency of Martin Geere and Giles Moppett, who were employed
by the colonel in preparation for this project, the whole of the
household were secretly armed, and commanded to hold themselves
in readiness, in case the attempt could be made with any prospect
of success. So long as the Ironsides maintained an imposing
force, and, indeed, outnumbered the colonel's retainers, any such
attempt would have been fraught with the greatest risk; but when
Stelfax set off for the church, taking half a dozen men with him,
and leaving but a slender guard of three or four behind—of which
Colonel Maunsel was made aware by Moppett—then it seemed to
the old Cavalier that the right moment had arrived. But Moppett
had a plan of his own for rendering the matter quite certain

With the aid of his fellow-servants, he undertook to secure
three of the Ironsides in the cellar, whither he knew they were
about to go, and besought his master to wait till he could carry
the plan into effect. Though anxious for the onset, Colonel
Maunsel agreed to the delay—or rather, allowed himself to be
persuaded by Mr. Beard to adopt this prudent course. The
good clergyman and his daughter had remained with the colonel
to a late hour, and finding it was his intention to watch throughout
the night, Mr. Beard desired permission to keep him company, and
of course the request could not be refused. Dulcia was unwilling
to leave her father—and Patty did not like to quit her young
mistress—so they all remained in an upper room, which Colonel
Maunsel had chosen for himself when driven from his own chamber by Stelfax. Within this room the colonel was pacing to
and fro, supported by Martin Geere, scarcely able to control his
impatience, and eagerly expecting Moppett's appearance, when
the report of a pistol, almost instantly followed by two other shots,
suddenly smote his ears. Drawing his sword, he hastened, without
support, along the corridor to the head of the stairs, followed somewhat more cautiously by the others.

Patty Whinchat had snatched up a taper before quitting the
room, and others of the household, when issuing from the buttery
and kitchen, had brought lamps with them, so there was now light
enough to reveal the disguised Royalists near the door. Deceived
by their accoutrements, the old Cavalier took them for Parliamentary soldiers, and naturally concluded they were marching off
with the prisoner. But his blood was now up, and although Mr.
Beard besought him not to interfere and so jeopardise his own
safety, he shouted out to the supposed Roundheads to set free their
prisoner instantly. Then turning to his household, he vociferated,

"Upon them, my men!—upon them!—strike hard, and fear
not!—I will be down with you on the instant, and will show
you how such crop-eared curs ought to be dealt with. Upon them
I say! Wherefore do you hesitate?"

"They do well to hesitate in attacking friends and supporters of
the good cause, Colonel Maunsel," cried Lord Wilmot.

"Royalists in the garb of rebels!" exclaimed the old Cavalier

"Ay, Royalists!" cried Clavering. "If you do not recognise Lord Wilmot, surely my voice cannot be strange to you?"

"Methinks your honour will recognise mine?" John Habergeon called out.

"And mine also, I am assured?" Ninian added.

"I know you all now," cried the colonel, who had been for a moment speechless with astonishment. "Come to my arms, my dear boy, that I may embrace thee once more!" he added, hurrying down the staircase in a delirium of joy, while Clavering sprang forward to meet him. "Art thou indeed free?" he cried, catching the young man in his arms, and folding him to his breast.

"Free as yourself, father," Clavering rejoined. "We have left those caitiff Roundheads in our places in the church."

"Amazement!" exclaimed the colonel. "This passes all my comprehension."

"Your honour would be still more amazed if you could hear how it has been accomplished," John Habergeon remarked; "but there is not time to tell it now."

While this was going on, the trooper who had kept guard over Colonel Gunter had been attacked by a strong body of the household, and was now dragged forth by them in triumph, with his arms pinioned with his own belt. Seeing this, Lord Wilmot consigned the sentinel to Moppett and Crundy, bidding them take both rascals away, and shoot them if they thought proper.

"Nay, we will not put them to death," said Moppett, "but we will clap them with their comrades in the cellar." And both prisoners were haled away.

"I must perforce tear your son from your embraces, Colonel Maunsel," said Lord Wilmot. "We shall have the Ironsides back from the church, and then all our trouble will be lost. We came here to liberate a brother Royalist—Colonel Gunter of Racton," he added, in a low voice, to the old Cavalier.

"Ha!" exclaimed Colonel Maunsel, warmly grasping the hand of the newly-liberated prisoner. "I knew him not, but was about to make an effort for his liberation. However, you have got the start of me."

"Nevertheless, I thank you as heartily, Colonel Maunsel, as if

you had been first to help me," said Colonel Gunter. And he
then added, in a low tone, "We came to consult with you
about procuring a vessel, either at Newhaven or Shoreham, to
convey his Majesty to France."

"A word, ere I answer you!" exclaimed the old Cavalier, eagerly.
"You can assure me, I trust, that his Majesty is in safety?"

"We have every reason to believe so," replied Gunter. "Lord
Wilmot left him at Boscobel in the care of loyal liegemen, who will
guard him with their life—as you would guard him, colonel. But
how think you? Can a vessel be procured?"

"I doubt it not," said the old Cavalier. "There is a skipper of
Shoreham, named Nicholas Tattersall, who is master of a fast-sailing
brig, called the *Swiftsure*. I know him to be an honest fellow,
who may be trusted in such an enterprise; but, unluckily, he is
away at present—at Plymouth, I believe—and his return is uncertain."

"Nicholas Tattersall! I shall not forget the name, colonel," replied Gunter. "If his Majesty should not otherwise be provided,
Tattersall shall be our man."

"If we ourselves do not depart at once we shall have small
chance of lending his Majesty further aid," said Lord Wilmot.
"Will you not go with us, Colonel Maunsel? If you stay, you
will have to brook the rage—perhaps the vengeance—of that disappointed and savage Ironside captain."

"I fear him not," replied the old Cavalier. "I will not quit my
house, unless forced from it."

Despite the hurry and confusion of the moment, it will not be
supposed that Clavering—aware of her presence—would fail to
seek out Dulcia. When his father became engaged with Colonel
Gunter he instantly took advantage of the opportunity offered him
to fly to her. The poor damsel needed his support. The sudden
revulsion of feeling she experienced was too much for her. Her
lover's fate had appeared to her to be sealed. Escape for him from
the clutches of Stelfax seemed impossible. Yet at the very moment
when such an occurrence was least expected, he stood before her—
free! Yes, free! The garb in which he was arrayed told how he

had escaped. But explanation was unneeded. Enough for her he was out of the power of his relentless captor, who had pronounced that his doom would be death. After gazing at him for a short space intently, through eyes streaming with tears, she gave utterance to a wild, irrepressible cry of delight, which had yet something thrilling and painful about it, and sank upon his shoulder. Mr. Beard, who was standing beside his daughter, watching her with great anxiety, would have removed her, but Clavering besought him to forbear.

"Leave her with me for a moment, good sir," he said. "My time is short. Heaven only knows when we shall meet again!"

"Place yourself wholly in the hands of Providence, my dear young friend," the clergyman rejoined. "After this display of His mercy manifested towards you, you can never doubt His ability to aid you, if He be so minded. Resign yourself, henceforth, to His will and guidance."

"My heart is full to overflowing with gratitude to the Great Disposer of Events," said Clavering; "but He would not have us remain inactive. As He prompts, we must obey. If I might counsel you, I would urge you to fly for a season with Dulcia from this dwelling, and seek a more secure asylum elsewhere."

"Whither should I go?" Mr. Beard replied. "There is no place of security for me and for my child. No, I will not voluntarily quit the house that has sheltered me so long. I will not desert the patron who has so long befriended me, and who has need of my ministry and assistance. And my child will tarry with me."

"To the last, father," Dulcia cried, raising her head. "My place is near your side, and I will never abandon it."

"I would not have you do so!" exclaimed Clavering. "But it drives me almost to distraction to think what may happen when that fierce Republican officer returns. I cannot—will not leave you."

"You must—you must, dear Clavering," said Dulcia. "Fly with your friends, and think not of us, or think that we are under the protection of a watchful Providence. Your staying here would not add to our security, and would lead to your own certain recapture. Go!—go with my father's blessing, and my own heartfelt wishes for your preservation. Stay not a moment longer. Pray Heaven you have not stayed too long already!"

This latter exclamation was caused by a movement of alarm among the Royalists. A noise was heard outside, announcing the return of Stelfax and his men.

"They are upon us!" exclaimed Lord Wilmot. "Secure the door, and extinguish the lights."

The latter order was instantly obeyed, and the first part of the directions was attended to with equal promptitude by John Habergeon and Ninian, who, flying to the door, bolted and barred it.

Before proceeding further, we may mention that Ninian had found Patty's presence as irresistible as that of Dulcia proved to his young master. Marching up to her in military fashion, but with rather more swagger in his gait than was consistent with his Roundhead accoutrements, he tried to catch her in his arms. Patty either did not recognise him at first in his disguise, or pretended not to do so, for she screamed slightly, and checked his attempted familiarity by a sound box on the ear. However, an explanation quickly ensued, and she was congratulating him on his escape, when the alarm of Stelfax's return was given as above narrated, and the young falconer suddenly recalled to sterner duties.

The door, which was of oak and of considerable strength, possessing, moreover, ponderous bolts and bars, was only just barricaded in time. The next moment it was forcibly tried, and the voice of Stelfax was heard furiously demanding admittance. The windows in front of the old mansion were deeply embayed, and projected far beyond the walls. They were built of stone, with massive upright posts and transverse bars; and the divisions between the bars were secured by iron stanchions, so that, although only curtains were drawn inside, no danger of unlicensed entrance into the house was to be apprehended. Finding the door solid enough to resist all his efforts to burst it open, Stelfax turned his attention to the windows lighting the hall, and

which were at no great height from the ground. But here, again,
he was disappointed, as was shown by his exclamations, which,
being uttered in a loud key, were quite audible to those inside.

"They are here," cried the Ironside captain. "I am well
assured of it. What ho! within," he vociferated. "I summon you
to surrender in the name of the Republic. Ye will be put to death
if you resist."

"Away with you up-stairs!" cried Colonel Maunsel to Mr.
Beard and the women. "Get out of harm's way as quickly as
you can. We shall have hot work presently. Take care of yourselves, and find some shelter," he added to the others. "They are
about to fire upon us."

Thus cautioned, such members of the household as were left in the
hall beat a hasty retreat into the passage leading to the buttery;
Dulcia and Patty skipped up the great staircase, followed more
leisurely by Mr. Beard, who deemed it inconsistent with his calling
to display haste even at a moment of danger; while the others
stepped quickly into the banqueting-room, the door of which
was open. The next moment a loud explosion was heard. A
volley of shot was poured against one of the windows, shivering
the beautiful stained glass within it, while several of the bullets
struck against the foot of the grand staircase. Luckily, no further
damage was done.

"Now make for your horses with all possible despatch," cried
Colonel Maunsel to Lord Wilmot and the others. "These knaves
will go to the back of the house next, and try to cut off your retreat."

"On my soul, I am half inclined to stay and give them battle,"
Lord Wilmot said. "We are equal to them in numbers, I think,
without counting your servants."

"My servants must not be counted, my lord," the old Cavalier
replied. "They would go for nothing in a conflict of this kind.
But, however disposed you may be for an engagement with the
rascals, I would beg of you to depart. You owe it to his Majesty
to care for your own safety."

"That is true," Lord Wilmot replied "And it decides me to

shun an encounter with them, if it can be helped. But will you
not go with us?"

"No, my lord," Colonel Maunsel replied, firmly. "My place is
here. To your horses as fast as you can! Heaven grant these
Roundheads reach not the back of the house ere you get out.
Ninian will show you the way. If you have no other place of
refuge, go to the Star at Alfriston, where you are certain to find
shelter. John Habergeon knows the house well. Adieu, my dear
lord!—and adieu to all!"

On this the Royalists hurried across the hall, and, guided by
Ninian, tracked the passage leading to the buttery, and made for the
outlet at the rear of the house. Clavering lingered behind for a
moment to receive his father's blessing, and then speeded after the
others.

A walled enclosure, possessing two or three outlets leading to
different parts of the premises, protected the back part of the mansion. The nearest way to the spot where the horses were stationed
lay through the farm-yard, but if this course had been taken, the
fugitive Royalists must at once have encountered the enemy, and
Ninian therefore led them by a roundabout course through the
garden, with which one of the doors in the yard communicated.

We have stated that Clavering was the last to come forth, and
ere he stepped into the yard, all the others had crossed it and
passed into the garden, with the single exception of John Habergeon. The old trooper waited for his young master, and it was
well he did so. While Clavering was hurrying towards the outlet
which John held open for him, urging him to look quick, for the
red-coats were at hand (as was, indeed, evident by the noise), a
door on the opposite side of the yard was burst open, and in rushed
Stelfax and his men. Though the place was obscure, the light of
the moon betrayed Clavering to his foes, and the infuriated Roundhead leader made a bound towards him like that of a tiger.

But he was balked of his prey, just when he fancied he had it
in his grasp. Clavering succeeded in passing through the door,
which was clapped to in the face of his pursuer by John Habergeon. The door could be bolted on the inner side, but on the
outer, or garden side, there was only an iron handle connected

with the latch. Seizing this handle, John urged his young master
to fly, telling him he could hold the door for a minute or two, and
then should be able to take care of himself. The old trooper's tone
of determination was not to be mistaken, so Clavering flew across
the garden in the direction taken by the other fugitives.

Meantime, Stelfax tugged with all his might against the door,
but John maintained it firmly against him, until, hearing the other
prepare to fire at him through the boards, he deemed it prudent to
let go, and decamped just in time to avoid the lodgement of a
bullet in his body. Speeding with the swiftness of lightning
across the grass-plot, he tried to gain the screen of the yew-tree
avenue. But ere he got half way to it, the Ironsides were out and
after him. Several shots were fired at him, and one or two of them
must have checked his career, if he had not been provided with
steel cap and back-piece, both of which were bullet-proof. As it
was, he got off unscathed, and, passing through a gate, reached the
little thicket at the back of the garden.

The report of the fire-arms had alarmed his friends; all of whom,
Clavering included, had reached their horses, and were already in
the saddle. Guessing what had happened, and fearing John might
be shot or captured, yet anxious to lend him aid, they rode
towards the garden gate, and had the satisfaction to see him issue
from it unhurt. The old trooper shouted for joy at the sight of
his friends, and in another instant was on the back of the steed,
the bridle of which was held for him by Ninian. Hardly was this
accomplished, when Stelfax and his men appeared.

On beholding the foe, Lord Wilmot drew his sword, and calling
upon his companions to follow him, charged the Roundheads, resolved to hew them down. But the Ironside leader did not care
to abide the attack. His own pistols and the carabines of his men
had been discharged, and time had not been allowed them to re-
load. He therefore gave the word to retreat into the garden, and
the command was promptly obeyed. Satisfied with this success,
and not caring to continue the struggle, the Royalists contented
themselves with a loud triumphant shout that made the holt ring
again, and rode off

III.

THE NIGHT RIDE TO NEWHAVEN—THE BRIG AND THE FRIGATE.

LORD WILMOT determined to act upon Colonel Maunsel's sug‑
gestion, and seek an asylum at the Star at Alfriston; and both
Colonel Gunter and Clavering approved of the plan. John Haber‑
geon undertook to get them secretly into the house. To reach
Alfriston, they must proceed by Newhaven; for, although the
former village lay a few miles to the south-east of the little sea‑
port at the mouth of the Ouse, the river had to be crossed, and
this could only be accomplished either by the ferry at Newhaven
or the bridge at Lewes. Towards Newhaven, therefore, they
directed their course.

The night was clear and calm, and a crescent moon hung like
a lamp in the deep starlit vault. It was about the second hour
after midnight, and had any one seen the troop careering over the
downs at that lonesome time, they might have been judged to be
bent on some dark design. But to newly-escaped captives, as they
all were, the sense of freedom was inexpressibly delightful. It
being a principle with the Cavaliers to banish care, and make the
most of the passing moment, they all appeared in good spirits.
The fineness of the night, the fresh air, and the pleasant and
wholesome exercise so exhilarated them, that Lord Wilmot and
Colonel Gunter soon became quite cheerful, and even Clavering
shook off his misgivings.

Pursuing their way, in the first instance, along the undulating ridge of the hill trending towards the coast, they passed an ancient barrow, and a fire-beacon contiguous to it, which latter occupied the site of the present windmill, until they came to the Newhaven road, skirting which, and keeping on the turf, they descended the gentle declivity dipping into Rottingdean.

And here we may, parenthetically, remark, that no more delightful ride or walk can be found in any part of the kingdom than is to be had by following the line of coast between Brighton and Newhaven. Fine turf, which need never be quitted, is to be found the whole way. A little to the west of Rottingdean the cliffs form a natural terrace carpeted with sod as smooth as velvet, redolent of wild thyme and other fragrant herbs, and commanding splendid sea-views; but, indeed, nearly the same thing may be said of eight miles out of the nine. The elasticity of the turf, and the freshness of the breeze, make exercise taken under such circumstances a delightful recreation.

Rottingdean, a village of some antiquity, was then nearly as large as it is at the present time. A few little tenements, occupied by fishermen, were built near the shore, but the better sort of habitations lay further up the valley, near the church. Three or four broad-bottomed boats were hauled up, high and dry, on the shingly beach, but there were no other evidences of any maritime calling on the part of the inhabitants. The whole village seemed fast asleep. Not a dog barked as the Royalists rode past the cottages, and mounted the opposite hill.

At that time the Sussex roads were accounted among the worst in England, and as the best were bad enough, their condition may be surmised. The ascents were excessively steep, and the descents proportionately dangerous. The ruts were tremendous; and in bad weather, or after the breaking up of a frost, the chalky mud was so thick, slab, and tenacious, that carts and other vehicles often stuck fast in it, and could with difficulty be extricated. The coast road nigh which our Royalists rode was as indifferent as any in the county, but the turf on either side of it was exquisite—fine as a well-kept bowling-green.

On gaining the brow of the hill on the further side of Rotting·
dean, Lord Wilmot allowed his gaze to range over the sea, a
wide expanse of which here lay before him. A pleasant breeze was
blowing from the south-east. In the deep stillness of the night the
waves could be distinctly heard dashing upon the shore, and
rattling amongst the shingles. The beams of the moon fell in a
line of quivering light athwart the waves, tipping their edges with
silver, and within this line a small brig could be discerned, shaping
her course towards the south, as if about to cross the Channel. As
he watched this little vessel cleaving her way through the glittering waters, Lord Wilmot could not help exclaiming aloud, "Yon
brig seems bound for the opposite shore. Would that the object
of our greatest solicitude were on board her!"

"In that case, we might say that all our anxiety was ended,"
cried Colonel Gunter.

"Not so," said Clavering, "for if I mistake not, there is a frigate
cruising out yonder, opposite Newhaven, which will speedily compel
the little sloop to haul to, so that if his Majesty were on board of
the latter vessel he would inevitably be captured."

"By Heaven, you are right!" exclaimed Lord Wilmot. "Rebels
swarm upon the waters as they do on the land. These shores
are so jealously watched, that escape seems barely possible. See! a
gun is fired by the frigate as a signal to the brig to stay her course."

As he spoke, a flash was visible from the side of the more distant
vessel, followed soon afterwards by a loud report. The sloop
instantly lowered her sails in obedience to the summons to stay,
and floated listlessly upon the waves.

"I hope no Royalist is on board that little bark," exclaimed
Colonel Gunter. "If so, he will soon be in the hands of the enemy,
for see! a boat is lowered from the frigate."

The Royalists paused to look on. In another minute the boat
was manned, and propelled with lusty strokes by a dozen well-armed
seamen, accompanied by an officer seated in the stern.

"There they go, in evident expectation of making a prize," cried
Lord Wilmot. "Let us hope the rascals may be disappointed.
But as we can render no assistance to the good cause, but may

jeopardise our own safety by needless delay, we had best move on."

"We have here a proof of the great hazard his Majesty will incur by attempting this means of escape," Clavering observed to Lord Wilmot. "Does not the incident excite your lordship's apprehensions?"

"The risk will be great, undoubtedly," Lord Wilmot replied; "but it must be run. The king is exposed to greater perils on shore. A fast-sailing sloop and a good captain are what we need; and these requisites are to be found, according to your father, in the *Swiftsure*, commanded by Captain Nicholas Tattersall, of Shoreham."

"I know Captain Tattersall. He is a good seaman, and a trusty fellow," exclaimed Clavering.

"Unluckily, he is absent just now," Lord Wilmot replied; "but if circumstances compel us to wait, we will have recourse to him."

Having mounted two or three eminences, and descended into as many hollows, the party now reached a flat upland covered with gorse and brambles, and soon afterwards the road, instead of continuing along the summits of the cliffs, turned off on the left in a rapid descent towards Newhaven, which was only about a mile distant. From this point, had there been light enough, the greater part of the Lewes levels, with the noble downs beyond them, would have been visible, but the distant landscape was buried in obscurity, increased by vapours arising from the broad swampy tract below. About half a mile off, on a headland overlooking the quay of Newhaven, and known as the Castle Hill, stood another fire-beacon. Riding rapidly down the hill, and passing the old church, amidst its trees, on the right, the fugitives dashed through the town to the ferry.

Though of no great width, the Ouse has a channel of considerable depth, and the tide, which runs up higher than Lewes, being confined within narrow banks, rises with great rapidity, and ebbs with equal speed. At the present day the river is crossed by a drawbridge, but at the time of our story the only means of transit was by the ferry in question. When the cavalcade reached the bank, they easily discovered the large flat-bottomed, punt-shaped boat, used for the conveyance of men and cattle across the stream, with its huge oars and poles inside it.   But it was chained fast to a post on the hard, and no ferryman was there to set it free or undertake its conduct across the river.   Our Royalists, however, were not men to be easily checked.   With the aid of a stone, John Habergeon soon broke off the staple that held the chain, and he and Eustace Saxby undertook to perform the part of ferrymen. Three of the horses—all that the boat would hold at a time securely—were embarked; and these, with the three Cavaliers, having been transported to the other side, the self-constituted boatmen returned for the rest of the horses, which had been left in charge of Ninian.   These also, together with the young falconer, were safely ferried across the Ouse.   This done, and horses and men being landed, the boat was turned adrift, and borne rapidly by the ebbing current towards the sea, John Habergeon observing, with a laugh, "If those rascally Roundheads should pursue us, they will be brought to a stop here, for there is not another ferry-boat or a bridge betwixt Newhaven and Lewes."

On leaving Newhaven, the fugitives took a northerly course, and for some time followed the road leading from Seaford to Denton and Tarring Neville.   They were now skirting a disused channel of the Ouse, and could hear the hollow cry of the bittern booming across the marshy levels.   Enveloped in the mists arising from this fenny region, they could scarcely see a yard before them, and had to proceed with some caution, until, after passing through Denton, they struck across the uplands on the right, and soon got clear of the fogs.   They then made their way, regardless of all impediments, to Alfriston, where they arrived long before any of the inhabitants of the village were stirring, and proceeded forthwith towards the place of refuge recommended by Colonel Maunsel.

IV.

THE STAR AT ALFRISTON.

THE Star at Alfriston, happily still existing, is one of the best specimens to be met with of an ancient English hostelry. Dating back as far as the early part of the sixteenth century, this curious old building was originally designed as a resting-place for pilgrims and mendicant friars, and was meant, moreover, to afford sanctuary to such as claimed ecclesiastical protection. The woodwork of the ancient hostelry is enriched with quaint and grotesque carvings, all of which are imbued with mediæval character and spirit. On either side of the wide-arched portal are saintly figures, and under the windows of the door may be seen two snakes with tails entwined. At the corner of the structure is a large carved lion, and over it two apes sustaining a mace crowned. Near the sign-post there used to be a dog, and beside it a bacchanalian figure with bottle and glass—but these, and doubtless many other equally curious memorials of the past, are gone. Within, there are other traces of antiquity. On the main beam of the principal room is a shield, inscribed with the sacred characters I. H. S.

How it came to pass at a period like that in which our Tale is laid, when all ecclesiastical ornaments were mutilated or destroyed by bigots and fanatics, that such decorations as were possessed by the old hostelry of Alfriston should have been spared, we pretend not to determine. Such must have been the case, since they are still preserved. Perhaps the inhabitants of the village were less bigoted than their neighbours, or they may have respected the idolatrous carvings of the inn out of regard for the worthy host. Honest Stephen Buxted brewed such good ale, sold such good wine, and trimmed his sails so dexterously, that he found favour with both factions. Secretly, however, his inclinations were for the Royalists, by whom, as we have intimated, he was trusted; many fugitive Cavaliers having at various times found refuge beneath his roof.

Dawn was just breaking as the little cavalcade entered Alfriston. Slackening their pace, they rode through the village as quietly as they could, being anxious not to disturb the slumbers of the inhabitants. The fine old cruciform church, with its lofty spire, round which the jackdaws were already wheeling, making the welkin ring with their cawing, reared itself before them. But neither on this ancient structure, nor on the mutilated stone-cross standing in the centre of the street, did the Royalists bestow much attention. Their object being to gain secret admittance to the hostelry, they did not halt before the front door, but turned down a lane at the side of the house, and at once proceeded to the stables. Here John Habergeon, in fulfilment of his promise, quickly managed to knock up the ostler, who, as soon as he recognised him, came forth and helped to convey their steeds to the stalls.

While this was going on, Stephen Buxted made his appearance at the back door of the hostelry, anxious to know what guests had thus unexpectedly arrived, but being completely in dishabille, having only just sprung out of bed, he did not care to venture forth in the chilly air. Seeing a Republican soldier, as he supposed, issue from the stable, honest Stephen was about to beat a hasty retreat, and shut the door after him, when Clavering—for he it was who had come forth—arrested him by calling out, in the Cavaliers' shibboleth, that he was a friend of Cæsar.

"A friend of Cæsar in the accoutrements of a rebel!" muttered Buxted. "Seek not to impose upon me, good master," he added, aloud. "Be you whom you may, you cannot enter the house at this untimely hour. You must tarry for an hour or two within the stable, and make shift with clean straw for a bed."

So saying, he was again about to retire, when Clavering once more arrested him, by calling out, "Do you not know me, Buxted?"

"The voice sounds familiar!" cried the host, pausing. "Surely it cannot be Master Clavering Maunsel, of Ovingdean Grange?"

"You have guessed aright, Buxted," the young man replied, advancing towards him, so as to afford the host a better view of his features; and he then added, in a lower voice, "I and some friends have. come to take shelter with you, and if you can accommodate us, it is possible we may remain with you for a few days—perhaps a week."

"You and your friends shall be welcome, good Master Clavering," the host replied. "I trust all is well with your honoured father. I need scarcely say that the son of.Colonel Maunsel shall have the best entertainment my poor house affords."

"Any entertainment will suffice for me, Buxted," Clavering rejoined; "but there is one with me whose high rank demands more than ordinary care."

"High rank, said you, Master Clavering?" cried the host. "Surely, it is not our gracious master in person? Oh! if it should be, he shall be welcome to all Stephen Buxted possesses!"

"I know your loyalty and devotion, my worthy host," Clavering replied. "But this is not the king. I would it were! he could not be in better hands than yours. But if your sovereign will not lodge with you, you will have one of his Majesty's trustiest advisers as your guest. And who knows but ere long you may have the king himself beneath your roof!"

"It would, indeed, delight me to have an opportunity of testifying my loyalty!" cried Buxted. "But bid your friends come in at once, and do not remain out there in the yard. I hope your entrance into the village may not have been observed, for we have many curious gossips in Alfriston, though they are, for the most part, well affected towards the king. I will say that for them."

"So far as I can judge, our arrival has been wholly unnoticed," said Clavering. "We did not encounter a soul in the street, and no one that I observed looked forth at us. But I will now go and fetch my friends."

"And I will be with them in a moment," the host replied. "I

will but go up-stairs and put on a few clothes, that I may attend
upon them more decorously."

With this he disappeared, while Clavering crossed over to the
stables, and presently returned with the rest of the party, all
of whom entered the house. As our young friend knew his way to
the parlour, he did not wait for the host to conduct him thither, but
ushered Lord Wilmot and Colonel Gunter into the room, where in
another minute they were joined by the host, who by this time had
managed to put on his doublet and hose. To honest Buxted's
inquiries as to what he could bring them, his guests replied that
what they needed most was rest. Accordingly, he led them at
once to sleeping apartments, of which there were, luckily, several
unoccupied in the house, and he undertook to hide their martial
accoutrements, so soon as they should have taken them off. Ere
long the whole party, having placed their heads upon the pillow,
lost the recollection of their perils and fatigue.

For nearly a week did Clavering and Colonel Gunter, with two
out of the three followers belonging to the former—namely, John
Habergeon and the elder Saxby—remain at the Star. During
this time they ran many risks of discovery, strict search being
made for them throughout the whole district by the Ironsides; but
such were the precautions taken by Buxted, and so great the vigilance and fidelity of his household, that, though on one occasion a
party of troopers actually came to the house and remained there
more than an hour, subjecting the host and hostess and all their
servants to sharp interrogatories, they failed to detect their prey.

On the second night, Lord Wilmot took leave of his friends, and
set out for Trent House, in Somersetshire—the residence of Colonel
Wyndham, a distinguished Royalist—where he expected to obtain
tidings of the fugitive monarch. His lordship was attended by
Ninian Saxby, who was to be the bearer of intelligence as soon as
there should be any to communicate. All such letters were to be
addressed with the greatest privacy to Colonel Gunter's residence,
Racton, near Chichester, whither he and Clavering intended shortly
to proceed.

Endeavours were made by the two Cavaliers left behind at

Alfriston to engage a vessel for the king's service, and with this object many secret visits were paid to Newhaven by John Habergeon and Eustace Saxby—it not being deemed prudent that the principals should be seen—but without much prospect of success.

At the expiration of a week the two Cavaliers began to tire of the inactive life they were leading. Clavering's wound had nearly healed, and he had quite recovered the use of his arm, so that he was now fit for any service. They therefore resolved to quit their present asylum, and proceed to Racton. But the Ironsides being still as much on the alert as ever, it behoved them to be exceedingly cautious in their movements. Disguises were therefore procured for them by Stephen Buxted, of such kind as would be most likely to elude suspicion; but, for greater security, they started on their journey soon after midnight, and on foot.

We shall find them at a halting-place on their way ere long; but, meanwhile, we may mention that Eustace Saxby had left them to pay a stealthy visit to Ovingdean Grange, and ascertain how matters were going on there; and that John Habergeon was to make a last attempt on that very night to hire a vessel at Newhaven, the result of which he had undertaken to communicate to Clavering and Colonel Gunter in a manner hereafter to be described.

V.

HOW MR. BEARD AND DULCIA WERE TAKEN AS HOSTAGES FOR COLONEL
MAUNSEL.

IT will now be necessary to go back to the night on which the
Royalists made their escape from Stelfax, in order to see how that
officer comported himself after the loss of his prey. He returned
to the house breathing vengeance against all those who had aided
the prisoners in their flight—foremost amongst whom was Colonel
Maunsel. The execution, however, of his vindictive schemes
was deferred till the morrow, his chief desire at present being, if
possible, to recapture the fugitives. But, as the Royalists had fore-
seen, great delay was experienced in catching the horses, and even
when this point was achieved, for some time the bridles and saddles
could not be found. But although nearly an hour was thus wasted,
the infuriated Republican officer would not relinquish the design of
pursuit. Submission to defeat was intolerable to him, and so long
as a chance remained of retrieving his discomfiture, he was resolved
not to throw it away. In less than an hour, then, after the departure
of the fugitives, he started in pursuit, at the head of some seven or
eight men. Delves was left behind, with orders to watch over the
house, and though he pleaded hard to be allowed to accompany his
leader, permission was not granted him. Stelfax had noted the
course taken in the first instance by the fugitives, and galloping to
Rottingdean, ascertained from a fisherman, who had heard the caval-

cade pass his cottage, that they had gone on towards Newhaven. To the latter place, therefore, Stelfax rode with all possible despatch, but his mortification and rage were boundless, when, on arriving at the ferry, he found that the Royalists had got across, and that the boat was turned adrift. Further pursuit was, therefore, out of the question, as he was well aware there was no means of crossing the Ouse nearer than the bridge at Lewes.

After a brief debate with himself, Stelfax, unable to brook the idea of returning empty-handed, sent back his men to Ovingdean, and rode on alone by the western side of the levels, through Rodmill and Kingston to Lewes; proceeding at once to the castle, where the detachment under his command was quartered. His first business was to call out one-and-twenty men, whom he divided into three parties, assigning to each a separate district—thus one party was instructed to make a perquisition of the coast, from Seaford to Eastbourne; another the mid country, comprehending Bedding-ham, the Firle range of downs, Alciston, Selmeston, and Hailsham; and a third Mount Caburn, Glynde, Laughton, and Ringmer. The men were, in short, to scour the whole country to the south-east of Lewes, making a circuit of fifteen or twenty miles, or more if needed, and not to return without bringing the fugitives with them. It had been Stelfax's intention to take the command of one of these parties, but he began to find that fatigue had made some inroads even upon his iron frame, and that if he did not allow him-self repose he might break down. Contenting himself, therefore, with giving such precise instructions to the men as he fancied must ensure the accomplishment of his purpose, he flung himself upon his hard soldier's couch, and became presently oblivious of his cares.

His instructions were carefully obeyed. The whole district he had indicated was traversed by his men; but without effect. No traces of the fugitives could be detected. Whither they had gone after leaving Newhaven was a mystery that could not be solved—no one appearing to have seen them. Even when the pursuers were really on the right scent, they remained at fault. A visit, as we have already mentioned, was paid to the Star at Alfriston; but though the whole of the fugitives were at that time in the hostelry, they were

so well concealed that not the slightest suspicion of their propinquity
was entertained by the Ironsides. In anticipation of a visit of the
kind, the horses brought off by the Royalists had been removed
to an out-of-the-way shed at some distance from the inn. Luckily,
no one in the village had witnessed the arrival of the fugitives,
so betrayal was impossible, except by the ostler, and there was
no fear of him. From Alfriston the troopers went on to Wilming-
ton, where of course they did not learn much. But besides miss-
ing the objects of their quest, all three parties were more than
once duped by false intelligence. Notwithstanding their disappointment, the search was continued throughout the day, and
it was only at nightfall that the three divisions returned to Lewes,
and faced their wrathful leader. Their failure was a heavy blow
to Stelfax. He had delayed his return to Ovingdean till night,
hoping to go back in triumph. But shame, and the sense of discomfiture, detained him till the next day, when, determined to make
an imposing appearance, he rode thither at the head of fifty men.

By this time, owing to the exertions of the sergeant, discipline
had been completely restored among the men left under his charge.
Helpless Henly and the two others, who had been guilty of insubordination and drunkenness, were still under arrest. Delves was
therefore able to give a satisfactory account of himself to his leader.
But it was not equally satisfactory to Stelfax to learn that Colonel
Maunsel was dangerously ill, and entirely confined to his bed. The
vexations and anxieties undergone by the old Cavalier had proved
too much for him. On the day after his son's escape with the other
Royalists, he was unable to leave his couch, and his enfeebled condition greatly alarmed those in attendance upon him. No improve-
ment had taken place in his health, but rather the reverse, when
Stelfax arrived at the Grange.

Without making any remark on the information he had received,
but determined to judge for himself, the Ironside leader marched
at once to the room in which the colonel was lying, and found him
supported by pillows, and looking the picture of death. Mr. Beard
and Dulcia were seated by the couch, and the former had a Bible
on his knee. Both arose as Stelfax entered, and the old Cavalier
made an effort to raise himself.

For a moment not a word was said. The stern Republican officer folded his arms upon his breast, and gazed steadfastly, but not without a slight touch of compassion in his glance, at the invalided but still noble-looking gentleman before him. At length he said,

"I have come to carry you a prisoner to Lewes, Colonel Maunsel. Are you ready to go?"

"You must prepare a litter for my transport," the old Cavalier replied, feebly. "I cannot move a limb."

"Surely, sir," cried Mr. Beard to Stelfax, "if you have any touch of humanity in your composition you will not attempt to move the colonel in this state. He will never reach Lewes alive."

Dulcia cast a supplicating look at the Roundhead leader, but did not speak.

"Waste not your time in idle entreaties, my good friend," observed Colonel Maunsel, feebly. "I know the ruthless and inflexible character of this man too well to suppose him accessible to the common dictates of humanity. Take me, sir," he continued, sternly. "Bid your soldiers bear me, living, to the grave."

"Remove him at your proper peril, sir," exclaimed Mr. Beard. "I warn you again that he is dangerously ill. If he dies by the way, his death will lie at your door."

"Such an occurrence, were it to take place, would not trouble me much," Stelfax rejoined. "But I have no personal animosity to Colonel Maunsel, who, though an inveterate malignant, is a brave man, and I should be loth to abridge the little life left him. I will, therefore, consent to leave him undisturbed if a hostage be given me for his surrender in the event of recovery."

"What hostage do you require, sir?" demanded Mr. Beard, quickly. "I am of little account, as compared with my honoured patron. Yet, peradventure, I may suffice."

"Not alone, sir," Stelfax replied. "I must have your daughter as well."

"Accede not to the proposition, my good friend," Colonel Maunsel observed, faintly. "Above all, place not Dulcia in this man's power. Let him take me. What are a few hours more of wretched existence to a sufferer like myself? Better—far better! they were ended!"

"It must not be so, father," Dulcia interposed. "Since hostages are required, who so fitting as we, who owe all to our generous protector?"

"You are right, my child," said Mr. Beard. "The course we ought to pursue is manifest. We will go."

"I will not consent to this," cried Colonel Maunsel. "Dulcia may be taken to the Castle, and placed in its dungeons, or in the martyr-cells beneath the White Hart, which have of late, as I understand, been put to their former use. Such barbarity shall never be practised if I can hinder it."

"I have no design to place either Mr. Beard or his daughter in actual durance, unless compelled, Colonel Maunsel," replied Stelfax. "All I require is to have them in safe custody. They may choose a lodging where they will in Lewes."

"Promise me that, on your honour as a soldier, and I am content," rejoined the old Cavalier. "If I am ever able to leave this couch, I will deliver myself up to you, and then their immediate release must follow. Meantime, I consider myself your prisoner on parole."

"Enough, sir," rejoined Stelfax. "You have the promise you require from me."

The old Cavalier then addressed himself to Mr. Beard, and looking anxiously at him, said,

"Use my name with Master Zachary Trangmar of the Priory House, and I doubt not he will provide you and Dulcia with a lodging."

"What! the old usurer of Mock-Beggar Hall!" exclaimed Stelfax. "I know him. He has rooms enow, and to spare; but I doubt if much furniture will be found within them."

"There will be sufficient for us if we obtain shelter," replied the good clergyman, fearing lest some fresh difficulty should be thrown in the way of an arrangement which he thought beneficial to his patron. "My daughter and myself will but make a few needful preparations, and we shall then be ready to attend you."

Patty Whinchat here emerged from the corner into which she had retreated on the entrance of the Ironside captain, and besought his permission to accompany her young mistress, which was readily accorded her. Telling Mr. Beard that he should set forth in half an hour, Stelfax bowed a stiff adieu to the old Cavalier, and, quitting the room, strode down the grand staircase to the entrance-hall, where he found Delves awaiting orders.

Meantime, the good clergyman and his daughter bade fare-well—it might be, from the sad state in which they left him, an eternal valediction—to their kindly patron; Mr. Beard invoking blessings on the worthy gentleman's head, and praying Heaven to spare him; and Dulcia, who was drowned in tears, bending to receive the colonel's benediction. This parting over, their place was supplied by Martin Geere, whose devotion to his master left no doubt that the old Cavalier would be carefully tended by him.

In allowing Colonel Maunsel to remain at his own house a prisoner on parole, and taking Mr. Beard and his daughter a. hostages for the old Cavalier's surrender in case of recovery, Stelfax was influenced by other motives than those which he allowed to appear. Under such an arrangement, Clavering Maunsel and his friends were not unlikely, he judged, to pay a secret visit to the Grange, and might—were due vigilance observed—be recaptured; while, by withdrawing Dulcia from her present asylum, he would have her altogether in his power. Not wishing to alarm her and Mr. Beard too much in the first instance, he had proposed a lodging in the town, and was well pleased when the colonel mentioned old Zachary Trangmar, in whom he felt sure a ready instrument would be found. Such were some of the motives that influenced him; but he might have others, for his designs were dark and inscrutable. But while abandoning Ovingdean Grange, Stelfax deemed it necessary that careful watch should be kept over the house, and no one appeared to him—for reasons which he scarcely liked to acknowledge to himself—to be so well qualified for the office of a spy as the person who had recently out-manœuvred him—namely, Increase Micklegift. But where was he to be found? Little expecting friendly overtures from the man he had injured, but dreading his vengeance, the Independent minister had fled. Stelfax questioned Delves about Micklegift, and the sergeant replied that there was in the village an elder named Morefruit Stone, who he thought might be able to communicate with the fugitive minister. Stelfax immediately caught at the suggestion, and said:

"Hie thee to Stone at once, and say unto him, that if he hath any means of communicating with Micklegift, he may inform him that I bear him no malice for what he hath done to me and to my men, but desire to do him a friendly service, and to that end request him to come over to me without delay to the castle at Lewes. Lest he suspect that, perchance, there may be a design to ensnare him, give him a solemn assurance of safety. About thine errand at once!"

Delves departed, and soon afterwards returned with the information that he had seen Stone, and had reason to believe he had succeeded in his object.

During the whole time that Stelfax remained at the Grange, the troop by whom he was attended were not permitted to dismount, but remained drawn up before the gates of the mansion, where, with their fine horses and polished accoutrements, they made a gallant show. The whole village turned out to look at them; and though the household at the Grange were in great terror of a second visitation, which might prove worse than the first—bad as that had been—their curiosity at last got the better of their fears, and they went forth to enjoy the spectacle. Greatly were Moppett, Crundy, and the rest rejoiced to learn that the unwelcome guests whom they had been obliged to entertain and serve for two mortal days and nights, and whose insults and ill-usage they had endured for that seemingly interminable period, were to be withdrawn. But their joy was somewhat damped by learning that good Mr. Beard and his daughter were to be taken away from them. However, since there was no help for it, they must needs submit. All they could do was to pray for the speedy return of the worthy pastor and Mistress Dulcia. It was a great matter that the colonel himself—as they feared he might have been—was not to be taken from them.

At the appointed time the poor clergyman and his daughter, followed by Patty carrying a cloak-bag and some other trifling matters required by her young mistress, descended into the hall. By Stelfax's directions horses had been brought round for them from the stables, and though Dulcia would have willingly declined his help, the Ironside captain gallantly assisted her to mount her palfrey. Mr. Beard was accommodated with a strong, steady-going pad-nag, and Patty was placed on a pillion behind him. While this was going on, Delves and the troopers who had been quartered at the Grange joined their comrades. Helpless Henly and the two others who were still under arrest were deprived of their arms and guarded, looking much abashed at their ignominious position.

All being in readiness, Stelfax sprang into the saddle, and gave the word to start. The walls and gables of the old mansion then rang with the inspiriting clangour as the trumpeters sounded a march, and the troop rode slowly out of the village, and mounted the hill on the right, greatly to the relief of the inmates of the Grange, who felt as if a heavy nightmare were taken off their breasts. Most of the cottagers, however, followed the soldiers to the summit of the eminence, and stationed themselves near the ancient barrow to watch the progress of the cavalcade over the downs. The day was fine, and the polished casques and corslets of the warriors gleamed brightly in the sunshine, the long array of martial-looking figures constituting a striking spectacle.

No incident deserving mention marked the ride to Lewes. It was a melancholy journey to Dulcia, and not all Stelfax's efforts, who rode beside her, and who was officious in his attentions, could draw her into conversation. Mr. Beard was equally sad. Patty, however, whose spirits were ever of the lightest, was amused by the novelty of the situation, and thought it a fine thing to have so many stalwart-looking troopers riding beside her; some of whom could not help casting furtive glances at the pretty handmaiden.

On arriving at Lewes, Stelfax conducted his prisoners at once to Mock-Beggar Hall. At first old Zachary Trangmar peremptorily refused to receive them, alleging the want of suitable accommodation, but the Ironside captain overruled his objections, and used such arguments with him, that, in the end, though with great reluctance, the old usurer assented. Eventually, therefore, Mr. Beard and his daughter, with her attendant, were admitted, and took possession of a suite of dismantled rooms, none of which contained an article of furniture. However, their wants in this respect were partially supplied, in the course of the evening, by Skrow Antram and the old couple whom we have described as living with Zachary in the capacity of servants.

VI.

THE SHEPHERDS ON MOUNT CABURN.

SOVRAN in beauty is Mount Caburn. Fairest of Sussex hills. Firle Ridge, with its beacon-crowned headland, frowning from the opposite side of the wide gorge, like a rival potentate, may be a more striking object—the long and precipitous escarpment of Kingston Hill, rising on the westerly side of the Lewes levels, is imposing—Mount Harry, with its historical recollections, at the back of the old town, has charms of its own—Ditchling is loftier— Wolstonbury and Chanctonbury have each special and peculiar points of attraction; but if we were called upon to indicate the hill which unites the greatest beauty of form with the rarest advantages of situation, we should unhesitatingly mention Mount Caburn.

Magnificent is the prospect it commands. Look where you will the eye is delighted. Towards the west lies the broad alluvial plain, known as the Lewes Levels, through which the meandering and deep-channelled Ouse works its way towards its embouchure at Newhaven. Here, where the narrow and tortuous river is itself unseen, its course may be detected by the craft it bears along; for here, not unfrequently, as has been sung of the same spot.

the sail
Majestic moves along the sedgy vale.

Here, at the present day, may be seen the swift locomotive shooting along its iron path towards the coast. At the opposite side of
this wide plain—once the bed of an inland sea or marine lake
—stand the lofty and precipitous escarpments, just mentioned,
of Kingston Hill. Turn but a little to the north, and lo! the
ancient town of Lewes rises before you with its lordly castle and
old priory ruins, backed by Mount Harry. Yon bold and picturesque headland in front is Firle Beacon. It would almost seem
as if some diluvian convulsion had torn these hills asunder.
Through the wide ravine or valley, by which they are separated,
now runs a branch of the railway, which may be followed, if you
list, for miles in a south-easterly direction. Tracking the line of
coast, you discern Pevensey Castle and Battle Abbey. Close at
hand is pleasant and picturesque Beddingham, with its antique
and square-towered church; and nearer yet, at the base of the hill,
delightfully-situated Glynde, with the old Elizabethan mansion
and well-timbered park adjoining it. But turn again towards
the east and north-east, and let your gaze wander over the vast
district. The view is almost unbounded—a splendid panorama,
scarcely to be surpassed for variety and extent. Numberless hamlets
with their churches, mansions surrounded by parks, detached farm-
houses and homesteads may be discerned in this wide-spread plain,
while in certain parts of it the countless hedge-rows, interspersed
with taller timber, give it the appearance of an immense garden.

But it is not merely from the splendid prospect it enjoys, from
the smoothness and beauty of its outline, from its gentle undulations, graceful slopes, deep dells and hollowed coombs, that Mount
Caburn merits distinction. In addition to other attractions, it
possesses the most perfect specimen of an ancient entrenchment
to be met with on the Sussex Downs. The strength of this encampment shows the estimation in which the position it occupies
was held. Circular in form, with double trenches, the outer of
which is broad and deep, while the inner platform rises to a considerable height, the old defensive earthwork looks almost as fresh
as when first constructed. Two centuries have, no doubt, wrought
many and great changes in this part of Sussex; have multiplied

its inhabitants, reclaimed and cultivated its wastes, digged sluices in its marshy levels, and, above all, carried railways through its plains, its devious valleys, and along its coast. But the general aspect of the country is the same. Above all, Mount Caburn is unchanged. In the middle of the seventeenth century this majestic hill looked as smooth and beautiful as it does in our own day.

The shades of night had scarcely fled from the summit of Mount Caburn, when two shepherds—such, at least, their garb proclaimed them—emerged from the inner trench of the encampment, and mounting upon the elevated platform withinside, gazed towards the beacon-crowned headland of Firle. The habiliments of these per sonages, as we have said, exactly resembled those of the swains accustomed to tend the flocks on the downs. Each of them wore a long-skirted loose coat of grey serge, stout hobnailed boots, brown leathern gaiters, and a broad-brimmed felt hat, being furthermore provided with a crook. But no dog followed them, and if you could have looked beneath those grey serge coats, you would have found that the pacific-looking swains had pistols and short hunting-swords stuck in their belts. Moreover, if you had peered beneath the hats pulled down over their brows, you would have seen at once they were not the simple rustics they professed to be. Both of them might be termed young men, though one of them had the advan-tage of his companion in this respect by some years, and both might be accounted handsome. The younger of the two, indeed, was singularly good-looking. But as there is no need to make a mystery of the matter, we may state at once that they were Cavalier acquaintances, though the reader might have failed to recognise them as such, inasmuch as the outward distinctions of the party to which they belonged were gone. Long scented locks and peaked beards had vanished, and given place to close-cropped heads and smooth-shaven chins. Metamorphosed, however, as they were, the two per-sons were no other than Colonel Gunter and Clavering Maunsel.

Night had but recently fled, and the sun had not yet risen to gladden the hills and gild them with his beams. Mists lay in the marshy levels on the right, and a thin curtain of vapour shrouded Beddingham, concealing all of the village except the square tower of its church. Mists also hung over Glynde Place, and the woods adjoining it. But the summits of the downs, though grey-looking and somewhat sombre, were wholly free from fog; an 1 a ruddy glow in the east announced the speedy advent of the sun. The gaze of the Cavaliers was turned towards the elevated ridge on the further side of the valley, but though both strained their eyes in this direction for some minutes, they could not descry the object they sought. Neither spoke, but each continued to look eagerly towards the Firle heights. Each moment the sky had been growing brighter and redder, as if the east were all a-flame, when suddenly the god of day himself appeared, and, ere long, the hills glowed with his splendour. It was at this juncture that the object which our two Cavaliers had sought for so eagerly became visible. It was a shepherd like themselves, a tall man clothed in a long-skirted loose great-coat, with a crook in his hand.

"He is there! I see him! It is John Habergeon!" exclaimed Clavering. "We shall now learn whether he has succeeded in engaging the vessel."

"He has failed," cried Colonel Gunter. "See you not he holds the crook horizontally above his head, as was agreed should be the signal in that event."

"I fear it is so," Clavering replied. "But give me your crook, and I will make the matter sure."

As he spoke, he placed the two staves crosswise, and held them aloft.

In answer to the signal, the individual on the opposite hill instantly dropped his crook, and extended his long arms horizontally from his body.

"There is now no doubt whatever of failure," Clavering observed, in a tone of disappointment. "A vessel is not to be procured for the king at Newhaven. We must seek for means of transport across the Channel elsewhere."

"Stay! he has more to communicate," Colonel Gunter exclaimed. "He has fixed a white kerchief like a small banner to the hook of his staff, and hoists it aloft."

"That is the signal of danger," rejoined Clavering. And look! he waves the kerchief thrice. The danger is urgent. He himself is making off. We must fly."

"Ay, let us to Racton at once," Colonel Gunter returned. "Nothing more is to be done here. If we are lucky enough to reach my house, we can rest in security, and hatch fresh schemes for his Majesty's deliverance."

On this, they crossed the encampment, and plunged into the devious and secluded dell on the right.

They reached Racton, after many hairbreadth 'scapes, on the evening of the following day. Nearly a fortnight elapsed before John Habergeon was able to join his young master, and he then brought word that Colonel Maunsel had been dangerously ill—in fact, at the point of death—but was now better. Immediately on his recovery, the colonel had gone over to Lewes to surrender himself to Stelfax, and procure the liberation of Mr. Beard and Dulcia, who had been taken as hostages for him by the Republican officer. This the colonel had accomplished, and he had furthermore obtained permission, on account of his infirmities, to continue a prisoner on parole at his own dwelling. Such was the sum of the intelligence brought by the old trooper from Ovingdean Grange; and it was far better than could have been anticipated. Information of Lord Wilmot's movements, and of those of his royal master, was furnished by the faithful and active emissary, Ninian Saxby, who passed constantly to and fro between the Cavaliers in various disguises. Many changes of plan took place, but at last it was definitively settled that the king should embark at Shoreham, and Colonel Gunter received orders to hire Captain Tattersall's brig, the *Swiftsure*.

VII.

OUR story must now be advanced about a week beyond the foregoing date, which will bring us to the 13th of October, 1651. On the afternoon of this day, two well-mounted horsemen, followed at a respectful distance by a servant likewise on horseback, rode from Bramber towards Shoreham. To judge from their attire, both horsemen must be Roundheads. They wore neither laced cloaks nor laced bands. Their garments were sad-coloured, and destitute of all embroidery, and their hats tall and steeple-crowned, and lacking feathers. Moreover, their locks were cropped close to the head. Their servant, a tall, powerful-looking man, well-stricken in years, was habited as became a follower of such puritanical-looking masters. But though the horsemen were dressed like Roundheads, their deportment, when not in the presence of witnesses, would have led to a very different conclusion, and any one who could have listened to their discourse would soon have learnt that they belonged to the opposite faction. Once more we have to announce our friends Colonel Gunter and Clavering Maunsel in a new disguise, though it will be scarcely necessary, we think, to state that their tall old serving-man was John Habergeon.

From its advantageous situation near the mouth of the Adur, Shoreham soon became one of the principal harbours on the Sussex coast. At the time of our Tale it was much frequented, and several sloops, with other vessels of larger tonnage, were now to be seen in the haven. At low water, the embouchure of the Adur, which is of some width, is characterised by large, glistening banks of mud, but as the channel at this time happened to be full, it presented the appearance of a broad and goodly river. The ancient church, with the habitations near it, which could be seen on the near banks of the river, was that of Old Shoreham; but it was towards New Shoreham and its haven that our friends bent their course. Here, as at the older seaport, there is a church of great antiquity and beauty; and after passing this noble structure—not without bestowing upon it a glance of admiration—the disguised Cavaliers proceeded to the Dolphin, an inn built on the edge of the quay, much frequented by seafaring people, and then tenanted by one Absolom Bridger. Dismounting, and giving their horses to John Habergeon, by whom they were taken to the stables, the two friends entered the house, and after ordering some oysters and a bottle of sack, and desiring to be shown into a private room, Colonel Gunter inquired of the host whether he knew Captain Tattersall, of the *Swiftsure*.

"Know him! I have known Nick Tattersall since he was a boy!" exclaimed Bridger; "and a better seaman or an honester fellow doesn't exist."

"Thou speakest warmly of him, friend Absolom," replied Colonel Gunter, thinking it necessary to support his puritanical character; "but is he in your harbour of Shoreham at present?"

"He was here this very morning," Bridger replied, "by the same token that he discussed a cup of sack with an egg in it. He has but newly returned from Plymouth, and will soon make a trip to Poole, in Dorsetshire."

"So I have heard," replied Colonel Gunter. "I have a commission to give him, and would gladly speak with him, if he can be found."

"Found he can easily be, I will answer for it," Bridger replied. "I will fetch him to you anon, and you shall have the oysters and sack without delay."

Not many minutes after the host's disappearance, the door was suddenly opened, and a tall man, clad in a plainly-cut black cloak and Geneva band, and wearing a lofty steeple-crowned hat, peered inquisitively into the room. His eye rested upon Clavering, who at once recognised him, and was about to address him, when the other raised his finger to his lips in token of silence, hastily retreated, and closed the door.

"Who is that mysterious personage?" Colonel Gunter inquired, not altogether liking the intrusion. "I hope he is not an enemy—he evidently knows you."

"I ought to regard him as a friend, seeing that he once rendered me a most important service," Clavering replied. "But I confess I distrust him, and am sorry to see him here. It is Increase Micklegift, who, when our worthy Mr. Beard was deprived of his living at Ovingdean, succeeded to the church. He is an Independent minister. Ever since he assisted Lord Wilmot and myself, with the others, to escape from the church, he has never dared, so I learn from John Habergeon, to show himself at the rectory or in the village. I am surprised to find him here."

"I am sorry he recognised you," Colonel Gunter replied, somewhat thoughtfully; "for though he may not suspect our errand, he may be troublesome to us."

"I do not think any danger is to be apprehended from him," Clavering replied. "He is in as much jeopardy as we ourselves are, and if he were to fall into Stelfax's hands little clemency would be shown him."

"Granting that his conduct has compromised him with the Roundheads," observed Colonel Gunter, "do you not see, my good young friend, that he is the more likely to be anxious to purchase his safety, which he might easily do if he knew our design. He could make his own terms with Stelfax."

"True," rejoined Clavering, uneasily "I see the danger. But I trust it may be averted. Ah! here comes our host. We will question him on the subject."

As he spoke, Master Bridger entered with the oysters and a flask of wine, and as he was placing them on the table, Clavering said:

"Tell me, worthy host, who was the tall man who looked into the room just now? He had the air of a preacher of the gospel."

"And such he is," Bridger replied. "I dare not mention his name, for he is in some trouble with the authorities. It may be that he mistook the door, for he occupies the adjoining chamber."

"What! he is in the next room!" exclaimed Colonel Gunter, glancing significantly at Clavering. "Bring clean pipes, Absolom, and a paper of thy best Spanish tobacco."

"Anon, anon! worshipful sirs. I have done your bidding as regards Captain Tattersall. A messenger has been despatched for him."

"Show him in on his arrival," said Colonel Gunter.

"You shall not have long to wait, then," answered Bridger with a laugh. "I hear his lusty voice outside. Walk in, Captain Tattersall—walk in," he added, opening the door. "These are the gentlemen who desire to speak with you."

The shipmaster who was thus introduced seemed a very good specimen of his class, and his looks by no means belied the favourable description of him given by the host. Apparently, he was turned forty, but his features were so brown and weather-beaten that it was difficult to determine his age precisely. Squarely built, and somewhat under the middle size, he had a broad, good-humoured, honest-looking physiognomy, by no means destitute of shrewdness, and seemed every inch a seaman. He was rather roughly attired, his apparel consisting of a Guernsey shirt, a loose jacket of stout blue cloth, ample galligaskins, or slops of brown flannel, nether hose of the same colour, and square-toed shoes. On his head he had a cap, originally bright scarlet, though now somewhat weather-stained; but this he doffed on entering the room.

"This is Captain Nicholas Tattersall, worthy sirs," said Bridger, slapping the skipper familiarly on the back as he spoke; "as honest a shipmaster—I will say it to his face—as ever sailed."

"A truce to compliments, friend Absolom," said Tattersall, bluntly—his voice was deep and hoarse, as might be expected from such a broad-chested personage. "You know I like them not. Your servant, gentlemen," he added to the others. "You desire to speak to me, as I understand?"

"We do," Colonel Gunter replied. "Pray be seated, Captain Tattersall. Happy to make your acquaintance, sir. Bring another glass, Absolom. Will it please you to taste this sack, captain?"

"The captain prefers brandy, worthy sir," hastily interposed Bridger. "I have a runlet of rare old Nantz, given me by a French skipper, which I keep for his special drinking."

"Bring the brandy at once, then," said Colonel Gunter, "and take care we be not interrupted."

Upon this the host departed, but almost immediately reappeared with a very promising-looking square-shaped bottle, the contents of which having been tasted by Tattersall, were pronounced by him to be of the right sort. Having thus attended to all the requirements of his guests, Bridger left them and closed the door. As he went forth, Clavering satisfied himself that no eavesdropper was without. Pipes were next lighted, and glasses filled. After a few preliminary whiffs, Tattersall said,

"Now, gentlemen, what may be your business with me?" adding, with rather a droll expression of countenance, "Nothing against the Republic, I hope?"

"Oh no—nothing treasonable," Colonel Gunter replied, with a laugh. "Take another glass of brandy, captain, and then we'll enter upon the business."

"Much obliged, but I've had enough for the present," Tattersall rejoined, dryly. "Come, masters, speak out! You needn't be palavering with me. Something's in the wind, I can see plainly enough. What is it? You make believe to be Roundheads, but I know on which side your swords would be drawn if it came to a fight."

"And on which side, in your apprehension, would it be, Captain Tattersall?" demanded Clavering.

"On the king's, Master Clavering Maunsel," the skipper replied, with a wink. "Lord bless me! though you have cropped your locks, and put on the raiments of the sanctified, do you think I don't know you? Here's your father's health, young sir," he proceeded, filling his glass from the square-shaped bottle, "and somebody else's," he added, in a whisper. "We understand each other now, gentlemen, I fancy."

"We very soon shall do so," replied Colonel Gunter, with a laugh. "You are right in all your surmises, Captain Tattersall. I am a loyalist as well as my young friend Clavering Maunsel. Our business with you may be told in a word. We want you to convey two friends of ours—two particular friends—privily across the Channel."

"Two particular friends, eh!" cried Tattersall. "Oh yes! I *do* understand," he added, with a wink. "Very intimate friends, no doubt. Why not call them relations—near relations—such as fathers, or brothers, or uncles?"

"You mistake me, captain," rejoined Colonel Gunter. "The gentlemen in question are relatives neither of Mr. Clavering Maunsel nor of myself. They are merely friends. They are not even fugitive Cavaliers; but having been engaged in a fatal duel, desire to get out of the way till the affair has blown over."

"That's the plain English of it, eh?" exclaimed the skipper, somewhat incredulously. "I see you're not inclined to trust me. Quite right to be cautious. But I thought young Mr. Maunsel knew me too well to doubt me."

"I have the most perfect confidence in you, Captain Tattersall," said Clavering, "but——"

"But you daren't commit your friends," supplied the skipper. "I understand. Well, I've no objection to take these unlucky duellists across the Channel, if you make it worth my while. What do you offer for the job?"

"Fifty golden caroluses," replied Colonel Gunter.

"Humph! I might have been content with that sum if they had been political offenders—good men, with a price set upon their heads—but simple fugitives from justice must pay double."

"Well, we won't haggle about the payment," rejoined Gunter. "Let it be a bargain. Say a hundred caroluses."

"Fifty as earnest, or I won't engage," cried Tattersall.

"Here they are!" replied Colonel Gunter, tossing him a bag of gold, which had originally come out of Zachary Trangmar's chest. "Count them at your leisure."

"That's the way to do business," said Tattersall, laughing, as he took the bag. "But mark me!" he added, with a slight change of tone. "I make one condition. I must see the gentlemen before I agree to take them."

"But you *have* agreed! you are partly paid!" Colonel Gunter exclaimed, somewhat sharply.

"The money shall be refunded, of course, if I can't fulfil my engagement," replied Tattersall, coolly. "But as I have just said, I must see the gentlemen. Seamen have strange fancies, and I mayn't like their looks."

"I am sure you will, Tattersall," remarked Clavering, laughing. "Colonel Gunter need not be uneasy as to your stipulation."

"Is this Colonel Gunter?" cried the skipper, eyeing the person named. "I was not aware of it. Your humble servant, colonel."

"Sir, I am yours," replied Gunter, returning his bow. "Well, then, if the countenances of my friends please you, they are to have a passage? Is it so?"

Tattersall nodded assent, but did not remove the pipe from his mouth.

"When can you start?" pursued Gunter.

"The wind is sou'-west, and not favourable for crossing the Channel," the skipper replied; "and I must get in my cargo, for it won't do to let my men into the scheme. My next trip is fixed for Poole, and I must ostensibly hold to the arrangement. But I may be ready in a couple of days, or three at the outside, if that will do."

"It must do, captain," replied Gunter. "But don't lose any time. My friends are very anxious to be off. You will never forgive yourself if anything should happen—to one of them in particular—in consequence of the delay."

"Shan't I?" exclaimed Tattersall, with a knowing look; "then the 'one in particular' must be of vast interest to me. However, I won't make any further inquiries, since you are not disposed to satisfy me. Where and when shall we meet again?"

Colonel Gunter consulted Clavering by a look.

"Let the meeting take place at my father's house, at Ovingdean Grange, on the evening of the day after to-morrow," said young Maunsel.

"Good," replied the skipper. "I know the Grange well. I often go to Rottingdean. I shall be glad to see your worthy father, Colonel Maunsel, for whom I have a high respect. I was sorry to hear he had got into some trouble of late. I was told he had been taken to Lewes Castle."

"Your information is not exactly correct, captain," Clavering replied. "Our chaplain, Mr. Beard, the deprived pastor of Ovingdean, and his daughter, were taken in his stead, my father being nearly at death's door when the Ironside leader, Stelfax, came to make him a prisoner. On his recovery, about a week ago, the colonel went to Lewes to surrender himself and obtain the release of his hostages, and met with better treatment than he anticipated: not only did he procure the liberation of Mr. Beard and his daughter, but he was allowed to remain a prisoner on parole at Ovingdean, where all three now are."

"I am glad to hear it," said Tattersall. "If all goes well, on the afternoon of the day after to-morrow—that is to say on Wednesday, it being now Monday—about five o'clock, I will be at Ovingdean Grange. If anything should prevent my coming, I will send. But your friends may hold themselves prepared to start. I will get all ready—if I can."

"You clog your promises with so many doubts, captain," observed Colonel Gunter, "that you also must make me fear their fulfilment. However, I will hope for the best. At five o'clock on Wednesday next I shall expect to see you at Ovingdean Grange, and my friends must then abide your scrutiny."

"And if Captain Tattersall, when he does see them, be not delighted to lend them aid, he is not the man I take him for," said Clavering.

"Well, we shall see," replied the skipper, rising. "Since time presses, I will go and see about getting in my cargo at once."

"Stay, Tattersall," cried Clavering, filling the skipper's glass.

"One toast ereyou go; I'm sure you won't refuse it: May the king enjoy his own again!"

"May the king enjoy his own again!" cried the skipper, emptying the glass; "and," he added, significantly, "if I can help him to it, I will. What was that noise? I thought I heard some one suddenly start up in the next room."

"Very likely," replied Clavering. "The room is occupied by an Independent minister, lately of Ovingdean. But he couldn't overhear us."

"I hope not," replied Tattersall. "I hate the Independents. Adieu, gentlemen. On Wednesday, at five."

"Till then adieu, captain," said Gunter. "And harkye, don't mention a word that has passed to your wife—if you happen to possess one."

"No fear of my blabbing, colonel," replied Tattersall. And he quitted the room.

Clavering went out immediately after him, and found that the door of the adjoining room was open, and the apartment vacant. Micklegift, if he had been there, was gone.

The two gentlemen did not remain much longer at the Dolphin, but paid their reckoning and called for their horses, which were soon brought out by John Habergeon. They then rode through Old Shoreham, and kept along the Bramber road, on the banks of the Arun, until they reached the bridge.

Here they dismissed John Habergeon, who was directed by Clavering to pay a secret visit that night to Ovingdean Grange, and acquaint his father that all had been satisfactorily arranged, and that he and his friends might be expected on Wednesday afternoon. Charged with this message, of the importance of which, insignificant as it sounded, he was well aware, the old trooper rode up the acclivities on the right of the valley, and soon disappeared.

Having crossed the bridge, the two gentlemen pursued the high road to Chichester, and reached Racton late in the day, without misadventure.

BOOK VIII.

CHARLES THE SECOND AT OVINGDEAN GRANGE

I.

THE PAPER BULLET.

On their return to Racton that night, Colonel Gunter and his guest partook of supper, and were still seated over a flask of excellent Bordeaux, when a confidential servant entered, and informed his master that the messenger had just arrived, and craved admittance.

The colonel looked surprised, but bade the man show the messenger in without delay. Whereupon the servant withdrew, and presently afterwards reappeared with Ninian Saxby.

The young falconer had doffed the gay and becoming habiliments in which he appeared during the time of his service with Colonel Maunsel, and was now very soberly clad in a tight-fitting jerkin of black cloth, a long black cloak without plait or ornament, funnel-topped boots armed with large spurs, a small plain band, and a steeple-crowned hat. By his side he wore a long tuck—a weapon proper to the fanatical party to which he was now supposed to belong. His brown curling locks, once his ornament and pride, no longer offended the severe eye of the zealot. Shears, remorseless as those of Atropos, had cropped them off close to his head; rendering him, in Cavalier parlance, "a prick-eared cur." But the merry eye, laughing features, and careless bearing of the young man somewhat belied his puritanical attire; though, no doubt, he could assume a more sedate look and deportment when occasion required.

Colonel Gunter waited till the servant had retired, and then asked Ninian whence he came?

"From Hambledon, in Hampshire," was the answer.

"Where does the king lodge to-night?" demanded Colonel Gunter. "Tarries he still at Hele House, near Amesbury, where my worthy cousin Hyde has been fortunate enough to afford him an asylum?"

"No, your honour," Ninian replied. "His Majesty quitted Hele House this morning, after remaining there for three or four days, and came on to Hambledon, on his way into Sussex. He and the noble Lord Wilmot will pass the night at the house of worshipful Master Symons, who, as I believe, married your honour's sister; though, as far as I can guess, the lady only, and not her husband, will be made acquainted with the rank of her guests."

"And quite right too," cried Colonel Gunter, with a laugh. "Tom Symons, though a worthy fellow, is too fond of the bottle to be trusted in a matter of such vital consequence. But my sister, though I say it, is a woman in a thousand, and entire reliance may be placed upon her judgment and discretion. But hast thou nothing for me?"

"This little ball, your honour, which I should have swallowed if I had fallen into the hands of the Philistines," Ninian replied.

So saying, he produced a small paper bullet, and handed it with the points of his fingers to Colonel Gunter, who, having unfolded the tightly-compressed sheet of tissue paper, and carefully smoothed its creases, soon made himself master of the contents of the letter, which then became apparent. This done, he crushed the despatch in his hand, and tossed it into the wood fire blazing cheerily on the hearth, where it was instantly consumed.

"Lord Wilmot writes that his Majesty is eager to embark," the colonel observed to Clavering, "and fully calculating upon our success in hiring Tattersall's brig, proposes to go on board to-morrow night. His lordship assigns no reason for thus advancing the hour of departure; but the king may, perhaps, have taken alarm at some movement of the enemy, or it may only be a natural anxiety on his Majesty's part to get out of harm's way. Was aught said on the subject to thee, Ninian?"

" His lordship told me that the king desires most ardently to embark to-morrow night," replied Ninian, " or early in the morning, as his Majesty entertains the notion that the moment will be propitious for his escape, and that, if deferred, ill consequences may ensue."

" But how are we to carry out the king's wishes?" cried Gunter. " We have arranged with Tattersall for Wednesday night, not Wednesday morning, and it will be scarcely possible, I fear, to prevail upon the stubborn skipper to set sail earlier. Besides, the rascal stipulated for an interview with his two passengers before he would agree to convey them across the Channel."

" True," replied Clavering; " but Tattersall is a loyal fellow, and I believe him to be only desirous of satisfying himself that it is the king who is to sail with him. Had he been trusted, in my opinion he would not have made the stipulation; but you did not deem such a course prudent."

" I judged it better not to tell him too much," replied Gunter. " Not that I believe for a moment that the reward offered by the Council of State would tempt him to betray the king. He is too loyal and honest for such a detestable act. But when the penalties of high treason stare him in the face—when loss of life and confiscation of property may follow his complicity in a scheme like the present —I feel unwilling to alarm him, lest he may decline altogether."

" I have no fear of him," cried Clavering. " Animated by the same spirit of loyalty as ourselves, he will run all risks to save his sovereign. Should we hesitate if placed in a similar situation? Would the fear of death affright us? Assuredly not. We should rather rejoice in the opportunity afforded of proving our loyalty and devotion. Such I firmly believe to be Tattersall's sentiments. But come what may, he must be ready to take his Majesty and Lord Wilmot on board to-morrow night, and to set sail on the following day."

" I will engage that Captain Tattersall shall be ready, if your honours choose to confide in me," said Ninian.

" Thou!" exclaimed both his auditors.

"Yes, I," the young falconer replied; "and that without further compromising his Majesty than has been done at present. I will ride over to Shoreham to-night, see Captain Tattersall early in the morning, and make all straight with him. The *Swiftsure* shall be ready to receive her royal passenger at midnight to-morrow, and to sail ere daybreak."

"Accomplish this, and thou wilt earn a title to thy sovereign's gratitude," said Colonel Gunter. "In any case, thou mayst rest assured of a good reward from me."

"And from me also," said Clavering. "Hark thee, Ninian, so soon as thou hast arranged matters with Tattersall, ride on to the Grange, and acquaint my father with the change of plans. John Habergeon will have led him to expect us on Wednesday afternoon."

"Your commands shall be obeyed," replied Ninian, turning to depart.

"Stay!" exclaimed Colonel Gunter; "thou hast not yet told us where we are to meet Lord Wilmot and his Majesty to-morrow morning."

"I thought his lordship's letter might have mentioned the place of rendezvous," replied Ninian. "At five o'clock in the morning, the king and his escort will leave Mr. Symons's house, near Hambledon, and your honour and Captain Clavering are to meet them, an hour later, in the central avenue of Stanstead Forest."

"It is well," said Colonel Gunter. "We must be astir betimes, Clavering. And now, Ninian, I will not detain thee longer than shall enable thee to drink a bumper of canary to his Majesty's prosperous voyage across the Channel."

So saying, he filled a goblet with wine, and gave it to the young falconer, who did justice to the pledge proposed to him. Colonel Gunter then inquired from Ninian whether his horse was fully equal to the journey he had to perform, and being answered in the affirmative, he bade the young man good night, enjoining him to act with the utmost caution, since much now depended upon him.

Ninian, with much earnestness, and more modesty than he usually exhibited, replied that he felt the full responsibility of the task he had undertaken, and would discharge it to the best of his ability. He then took his departure, and in less than a quarter of an hour started for Shoreham.

Not long afterwards the two Cavaliers, having to rise early, with the prospect of a hard day's work to follow, retired to rest.

II.

FIVE o'clock had not struck next morning, when Colonel Gunter entered Clavering's chamber, and found his guest not only awake, but fully attired and prepared for the journey. So blithe were the young man's looks, that Colonel Gunter could not help commenting upon them, and said, " I am glad to see you look so cheerful, my young friend. It shows that you calculate on success, and I doubt not your anticipations will be realised."

" Ere many hours have flown, his Majesty, I hope, will have quitted these ungrateful shores," said Clavering; " and I feel assured that although he is now driven hence by the malice of rebels and fanatics, he will return to his kingdom in triumph."

" Amen!" replied Colonel Gunter. " Like myself, I see you are well armed—pistols in your belt and rapier by your side. I trust we shall have no occasion to use our weapons. But the king shall never fall into the hands of the rebels while we have breath to defend him. And now, since you are ready, let us set forth at once."

" With all my heart," replied Clavering: " I am impatient to greet his Majesty on the day which I trust will be that of his happy deliverance."

None of the household were astir at this early hour except the confidential servant who had waited upon his master on the previous evening. This attentive personage had prepared a slight repast for them, and set it out in the library, but neither of the gentlemen cared to partake of it, nor would they be prevailed upon to fortify their stomachs against the morning air by a glass of strong waters, at the butler's recommendation. Proceeding at once to the stables, they mounted their steeds, which they found in readiness, and rode off.

Racton, Colonel Gunter's residence, it has already been mentioned, was about four miles to the north-west of Chichester, and though a house of no great size or pretension, was very pleasantly situated at a short distance from Stanstead Park, then belonging to Lord Lumley. This park, with the stately mansion in the midst of it, now lay before our friends; they did not, however, enter it, but skirting the moss-grown palings by which it was surrounded, shaped their course towards the forest, which lay further to the west. As the sun had not yet appeared to enliven nature with his kindling beams, and dispel the mists of night, which still hung heavy over the woods and the landscape, the atmosphere felt excessively cold, causing the two gentlemen to draw their ample cloaks somewhat more tightly round them. It was now, it must be borne in mind, the middle of October, and the foliage was dyed with the glowing tints bestowed by the later days of autumn. Heavy dews hung on the leaves, and the ferns, briars, and gorse growing on the roadside were plentifully charged with moisture.

The horses snorted frequently and loudly as their riders walked them along, and the breath from the animals' nostrils arose like steam. The rabbits on the sandy banks scudded off to their holes on the approach of the horsemen. The pheasant ran along the ground, thickly strewn with brown leaves, and gained the shelter of the copse. The blackbird started from the holly-bush, and the cries of the jay, the mellow notes of the wood-pigeon, and the chatter of the magpie resounded from the thicket. Ere long the two Cavaliers gained the forest, which was of considerable extent, and boasted some noble timber, being especially rich, like most large woods in this part of Sussex, in beech-trees Passing a grove of these magnifi-

cent trees, crowning a sandy eminence from which their mighty
roots protruded, our friends began to descend a long sweeping
glade, broken here and there by scattered trees—ancient oaks
with gnarled trunks and giant arms, towering elms, or venerable
thorns. In a ferny brake on the right was couched a herd of
deer, and as the two horsemen neared them, these graceful denizens
of the forest started up from their bed, and tripped across the
glade. A little further on, the deep secluded character of the forest
in some measure disappeared, though the scene lost nothing of its
picturesqueness and sylvan beauty.

By this time the sun had begun to o'er-top the trees on the
east, and to light up the groves on the western side of the glade,
chequering the open sward with shadows, though the opposite side
was still buried in gloom. Riding quickly on, the two Cavaliers
speedily reached the central avenue in the forest—a wide alley two
miles in length, and skirted by noble trees—and they had no
sooner entered it than they descried a little cavalcade advancing
from the opposite direction, though still about a mile off.

"Yonder comes the king!" exclaimed Colonel Gunter. "We
are not a minute too soon, after all. Forward! my young friend
—forward!" And as he spoke he urged on his steed, while
Clavering likewise quickened his pace.

The cavalcade descried by our friends consisted of four persons,
all well mounted, and all plainly attired in sad-coloured garments
—long black cloaks, square-toed boots drawn above the knee, and
hats with tall conical crowns and broad penthouse brims. They
might have been taken for demure and fanatical Republicans. The
two gentlemen in advance were Colonel Robert Philips, of Monta-
cute House, in Somersetshire, a devoted Royalist, and Captain
Thomas Gunter, our worthy colonel's kinsman. Of the pair who
came behind, he who rode on the left was Lord Wilmot; but it is
the individual on the right who claims our chief attention.

Tall of stature, and, so far as could be judged in his unbecoming
attire, strongly and well proportioned, this personage possessed features which could scarcely be termed handsome. And yet, though
the countenance might be somewhat harsh, the eyes were so large,

quick, and expressive, so full of fire and intelligence, of malice and, it might be, merriment, that it was difficult to say that he was ill-looking. The owner of that remarkable physiognomy used himself to describe it as ugly, but it may be doubted whether any one else concurred with him in opinion. The features, though large, and perhaps a little coarse, were by no means heavy, but susceptible of the most captivating, vivacious, and humorous expression. Drollery, indeed, and good humour might be said to characterise the face, though there was a strong touch of sarcasm about the mouth. The complexion of the person under consideration was singularly swarthy, his eyebrows thick and black, and the little that could be seen of his close-cropped hair, of the same raven hue. Such was the fugitive monarch, Charles Stuart, as he appeared to the two Cavaliers when they rode forward to salute him.

As our friends came within a bow-shot of the king, he ordered a halt, and stood still to await their approach — his attendants drawing back so as to leave his Majesty in front. On seeing the little cortége halt in this manner, the two Cavaliers slackened their pace, approaching the royal wanderer as ceremoniously and with as profound respect as if he had been surrounded by a large retinue, and aided and accompanied by all the pomp and show of princely state. When within a short distance of the king, they both drew up, and, uncovering, bowed to the saddle-bow. Charles returned their salutation with the dignity and grace peculiar to him. His whole deportment was changed, and notwithstanding his sorry attire, he now looked every inch a king. Nothing could be more affable and condescending than his manner, while the air of majesty which he ceased not to retain, heightened the effect of his gracious demeanour.

"Well met, gentlemen!" he cried. "A good morning to both of you. Delighted to see you. Approach, Mr. Clavering Maunsel. We have not seen you since the night after Worcester's luckless engagement, when, at great personal risk, you delivered us from imminent capture by the rebels. Approach, brave young sir, that we may tender our thanks for the service, which, rest assured, will never be obliterated from our memory."

At this intimation, Clavering sprang from his steed, and giving the bridle to Colonel Gunter, stepped forward, and bending the knee reverentially before the young monarch, kissed the hand which the latter extended towards him.

"Rise, sir," said Charles. "We are greatly beholden to you, but you must content yourself with bare thanks for the present, our fallen estate not permitting us the means of adequately rewarding services like yours. But a day may come, and then they shall not be forgotten. And now, what tidings do you bring of your worthy father?—he is well, I trust? And the valiant old trooper who fought with him at Edge Hill and Naseby, and whom he sent with you to Worcester—how is he named?—let me see—oh! John Habergeon—how fares it with the tough old fellow? I trust no prick-eared fanatic has shortened his days? We shall put Colonel Maunsel's loyalty and hospitality to the proof, for we propose to pass a few hours with him at Ovingdean Grange before proceeding to Shoreham. The visit, we trust, can be made without risk? But these questions, and others which we design to put to you, can be answered more leisurely as we ride along. So mount, young sir, and take a place beside us."

And while Clavering hastened to obey his Majesty's behest, Charles accorded an equally gracious reception to Colonel Gunter; with this difference only, that he allowed the latter to perform the ceremony of kissing hands without quitting the saddle.

The cavalcade was now once more in motion, and proceeding at a trot along the avenue. Colonel Philips and Captain Gunter rode in advance as before, while the rear was brought up by Colonel Gunter and Lord Wilmot, the king and Clavering occupying the centre. After a little preliminary discourse, Charles broached the subject of greatest interest to himself, and inquired, with an anxiety which he did not attempt to conceal, whether Tattersall's vessel was engaged, and ready to sail that night, or early in the morning?

"The brig is secured, as I trust, sire," Clavering replied; "but arrangements were made for to-morrow night, not for the morning. However, I do not believe that the earlier hour will make much difference to Captain Tattersall; and our faithful messenger Ninian Saxby, has already been despatched to him to expedite matters."

"Tattersall *must* start before daybreak to-morrow morning," said Charles. "I am superstitious enough to attach great importance to the arrangement, and feel persuaded that delay will be fraught with danger."

"Heaven forfend!" exclaimed Clavering. "I would we had been sooner aware of your Majesty's wishes in this particular."

"That could not easily be," replied the king. "Till yesterday I was indifferent to the matter, but now I am bent upon it."

"Far be it from me to attempt to shake your Majesty's resolution," said Clavering. "You would not, I am sure, feel so strong a conviction without cause. And perhaps this acceleration of your plans may save you from some secret danger."

As he spoke, his thoughts involuntarily reverted to Micklegift, but he did not think it needful to mention his misgivings to the king. "I had previously prepared my father for the honour and gratification he might expect in a visit from your Majesty to-morrow; but his impatience will be so great that he will be far better pleased that it should occur to-day."

"I hope we shall take him by surprise," said the king. "I do not desire him to make any preparations. I must be received by him, not as the king, but as plain William Jackson. Besides, if by any accident the expected visit of to-morrow should have reached the enemy, and bring them to the house, they will be a day too late."

"True," replied Clavering, thoughtfully. "All things considered, I am not sorry that your Majesty has advanced the hour of your departure."

At this juncture an opening in the trees displayed a fine view of the country, the prospect being terminated by Portsmouth, with its shipping, and the Isle of Wight.

The king stopped to gaze at the scene, and his little escort halted likewise. After looking for a few moments at the distant arsenal, with its forts, docks, and storehouses, he exclaimed, in tones of some emotion, not unmingled with bitterness,

"Oh, that yon noble arsenal, with its fortifications and stores, and the powerful fleet in its harbour, were mine! I should not need more to regain my kingdom. But all have fallen from me except you, my faithful followers, and a few others, and I ought, therefore, to estimate your loyalty at its true value."

After a brief pause he continued, in a voice of deep emotion, "Now that the hour is almost come when I must exile myself from my country, and seek shelter on a foreign shore, I shrink from the effort, and almost prefer death to a flight, which has something cowardly and dishonourable about it—unworthy of the descendant of a royal line, and himself a king."

"View not your withdrawal in that light, my gracious liege," said Clavering. "There is nothing unworthy in your meditated flight. On the contrary, it is a course of action dictated by prudence. If a chance remained of regaining your kingdom, I and your faithful liegemen would urge you to stay. But the moment is unpropitious, and you do wisely to withdraw till this terrible tempest now passing over the land shall have exhausted its fury. Leave your misguided and ungrateful subjects for a while to the care of the usurper Cromwell—they will soon be heartily sick of him, and eager to recal you."

"What you say is true—perfectly true," replied Charles; "I must go. Yet it is hard to fly from a kingdom, even when it is mine no longer."

"Your kingdom is not lost, my liege," cried Clavering. "You design not to abdicate."

"Never!" exclaimed Charles. "I will sooner mount my murdered father's scaffold than do so."

"Then I am right in saying your kingdom is not lost, sire. A king is not the less a king because he can only rally round him a few faithful followers. Our spirit in time will animate others, and will catch and spread till the whole land is on fire. Treason and rebellion will be burned out, and your subjects eager to herald your return."

"I trust it may be so," replied the king. "Have any tidings been heard of the Earl of Derby? A court-martial hath sat upon him, as I am informed, by virtue of a commission from the arch-traitor Cromwell, and it hath, in violation of all laws of honourable warfare, since quarter was promised the earl on surrender, condemned him to death by the headsman. But his lordship hath since petitioned Cromwell, as I am told, for a remission of his sentence—with what result?—can any of ye tell me, gentlemen?"

There was a profound silence. And Clavering and Colonel Gunter, on whom Charles fixed inquiring glances, cast down their eyes.

"Your silence shows me that the petition has been ineffectual," continued the king. "Not content with shedding the best blood of England, the murderous villain would pour out more. He would spare none of you if ye fell into his hands. O my valiant and chivalrous Derby, thou soul of honour and loyalty, and art thou to perish thus! When and where is the shameful deed to be done?"

"To-morrow at noon, at Bolton, in Lancashire, as I am informed, my liege," replied Clavering, to whom the question seemed to be addressed.

"To-morrow at noon—ha!" exclaimed Charles, sadly. "Then one of the best and bravest spirits in England will wing its flight to purer spheres! Prepare yourselves to be astonished, gentlemen, by what I am about to relate. As I live and stand before you," he added, in a tone of so much solemnity that it struck awe in his hearers, "I have been warned that Derby would die at the time you have mentioned."

"May I venture to ask your Majesty how you received the warning?" said Clavering.

"From the earl himself," replied Charles. "You all stare and look incredulous. But it is so, unless I have conjured up a phantom from mine own imagination. I saw him the night before last at midnight—I saw him again last night. Nay, methought I beheld his shadowy figure, not long ago, in this very forest."

"Here! in this forest, sire?" exclaimed Clavering.

"Moving amidst the trees by my side," replied Charles. "I

beheld him quite plainly, though I mentioned not the circumstance."

"And the apparition, if such it may be called, came to warn
your Majesty, you say?" cried Clavering.

"The earl, or a spirit in his likeness, warned me," replied the
king, "that his execution would take place to-morrow—the truth
of which sad intelligence you yourself have just confirmed—and
the semblance of my gallant Derby added, that if I quitted not
England before his head was laid upon the block, I should share
the same fate as my martyred father. Hence my anxiety to set
sail at daybreak to-morrow will be intelligible to you."

"Your haste and inquietude are now perfectly intelligible, sire,"
replied Clavering.

"The circumstance is strange, and inexplicable even to myself,"
said Charles. "But it is best to accept such matters as they come,
without seeking to examine them too closely. It may be a delu-
sion, or it may be real, I cannot say which; but I shall act as if the
warning had been given me by my beloved Derby in person. But
I shall grow sad if I suffer my thoughts to dwell longer on this
theme. Let us on!"

With this, he put his steed once more in motion, and the little
cavalcade proceeded in the same order and at the same pace as before.
By pursuing the avenue to its full extent, the king would have been
brought nearer Stanstead House than his conductors judged prudent.
They therefore turned off on the left, and soon came to a more open
part of the forest, where the timber, being scattered, attained larger
growth. Here they encountered a woodman, with a hatchet over his
shoulder, accompanied by a lad, and both stood still to gaze at the
cavalcade; but on recognising Colonel Gunter, who was known to
him, the forester doffed his fur cap and went his way. Further
on, they met a couple of huntsmen in Lord Lumley's livery, and
these men likewise testified surprise on beholding the party. But
again Colonel Gunter's presence prevented interruption.

After quitting the forest and skirting Stanstead Park, the royal
party pursued their way through a lovely and well-wooded district, until they came to the foot of an eminence called Bow Hill,

and entered the narrow and picturesque vale denominated Kingly Bottom—so called from a battle between the inhabitants of Chichester and the Danes—and Charles failed not to notice the group of venerable yew-trees—venerable in *his* days, though still extant, with the trifle of two centuries added to their age—that adorn the valley. After this, they passed Stoke Down, bestowing a passing observation on the curious circular hollows indented in the sod.

From the acclivities over which the travellers next rode the ancient and picturesque city of Chichester could be seen on the level land near the sea, the tall spire and pinnacles of its noble cathedral, the adjacent bell-tower, and the quaint old octagonal market-cross, erected in the fifteenth century, all rising above the crumbling walls still surrounding the city. As Charles looked towards this fine old cathedral, he could not help deploring to his companions the damage it had sustained at the hands of the sacrilegious Republican soldiers.

Avoiding Chichester, the king and his company pursued their way along the beautiful and well-wooded slopes of the Goodwood downs. If the journey had been unattended with risk, it would have been delightful; but beset by peril as he was, on all sides, Charles did not lose his sense of enjoyment. The constant presence of danger had made him well-nigh indifferent to it. Constitutionally brave, almost reckless, he was assailed by no idle apprehensions. The chief maxim in his philosophy was to make the most of the passing moment, and not to let the chances of future misfortune damp present enjoyment.

The fineness of the weather contributed materially to the pleasure of the ride. It was an exquisite morning, and the day promised to continue equally beautiful throughout. The trees were clothed with the glowing livery of later autumn, and as the whole district was well and variously wooded, there was every variety of shade in the foliage still left, from bright yellow to deepest red. Corn was then, as now, extensively grown in the broad and fertile fields in the flat land nearer the sea, but the crops had been gathered, and the fields were for the most part covered with stubble. The prospect offered to the king, as he looked towards the coast, was varied and extensive. On the left, the ancient mansion of Halnaker, now in ruins, but at that time presenting a goodly specimen of the Tudor era of architecture, seemed to invite him to halt; and Colonel Gunter informed his Majesty that over the buttery hatch in this old house were scrolls hospitably entreating visitors to " come in and drink," assuring them they would be " les bien-venus."   Notwithstanding these inducements to tarry, Charles rode on, galloping along the fine avenue of chesnut-trees, the fallen leaves of which now thickly strewed the ground.

Halnaker was soon left behind, and ere long the somewhat devious course of the royal party led them through the exquisite grove of beech-trees skirting Slindon Park, the remarkable beauty of the timber eliciting the warm admiration of the king, who would fain have loitered to admire it at his leisure

III.

AN ENCOUNTER WITH THE GOVERNOR OF ARUNDEL CASTLE.

THE proud-looking castle of Arundel was now visible, magnificently situated on the terrace of a hill, surrounded by noble woods, above which towered the ancient central keep. From the spot where the royal party surveyed it, about two miles off, the stately edifice looked the picture of feudal grandeur, but a nearer approach showed how grievously it had been injured. At the outbreak of the Great Rebellion, Arundel Castle fell into the hands of the Parliamentary forces, but surrendered to Lord Hopton in 1643. It did not, however, remain long in the possession of the Royalists, being retaken within two months, after a siege of seventeen days, by Sir William Waller, when a thousand prisoners were made by the victorious party. The castle was then plundered and partly destroyed, and great ravages committed in the ancient and beautiful church of Saint Nicholas, contiguous to it. At the time of our story it was occupied as a garrison by the Parliamentary troops, the command of the castle, with the title of governor, having been very recently accorded to Colonel Morley, a Republican officer of great strictness and severity. Though the interior of the ancient and stately fabric was mutilated and destroyed, though the carved tombs and monuments, stone pulpit, arches, altars, delicate tracery, and exquisite architectural ornaments of the church were defaced, though much of the fine timber growing near the fortress was remorselessly hewn down, the defences of the castle were still maintained, and it was even then looked upon as a place of considerable strength.

"I was with Lord Hopton when he took yon fortress in '43," observed Colonel Gunter to the king. "The rascals surrendered on the first summons, and saved us the trouble of a siege. But it cost Waller seventeen days of good hard work to get it back again. The rogues have done as much mischief as they can both to castle and church. We must, perforce, pass through the town, as we shall to cross the Arun by the bridge."

Charles made no objection, and the party rode on until they reached the hill on which the proud fortress is planted. They were mounting the ascent somewhat leisurely, when the merry notes of a hunting-horn greeted their ears, and the next moment a company of well-nigh a dozen horsemen, with a pack of hounds, appeared at the top of the hill. From the buff coats, boots, and other habiliments worn by these horsemen, it was evident that they were troopers from the castle going forth to indulge in the pastime of hunting, but though for the convenience of the chase they had laid aside their swords, carabines, and heavy steel accoutrements, they had still bandoleers over their shoulders, and pistols in their holsters. In this troop one person was a little in advance of the others, and it was evident from the superiority of his attire, as well as from the deference shown him, that he was higher in station than his companions. The individual in question was no other than the newly-appointed governor of Arundel Castle. Colonel Morley was a tall, raw-boned personage, with broad cheeks and flat nose, and the truculence of his looks was not diminished by a long pair of starched moustaches, which projected, like the whiskers of a tiger, from his face. Colonel Gunter instantly recognised him, and informing the king who was coming towards them, asked if his Majesty preferred to turn aside?

"On no account," replied Charles. "That would excite instant suspicion. Colonel Morley has seen us. Go boldly on."

The two parties now rapidly approached each other. The Royalists displayed great nerve, and did not flinch from the encounter. Colonel Morley eyed the troop advancing towards him sharply and suspiciously. He allowed them to approach quite close without question, but just as they were about to pass he called out to them, in an authoritative tone, to stay.

"Who are ye?" he demanded. "And whither go ye?"

"We are from Chichester, worshipful sir, of which city I am mayor," replied Colonel Gunter, "on our way to Steyning, to attend the marriage of a cousin of mine, a very comely damsel, who is to be wedded this day to an elder of that town."

The governor took little notice of the reply, but looking fixedly at the king, said:

"Who art thou, friend? Thy face seems familiar to me."

"Very like it may be, worshipful sir, if you have ever visited Chichester," replied Charles, without betraying the slightest confusion. "I am an alderman and maltster of the city, by name William Jackson. You have heard of me, I doubt not?"

"I cannot say that I have, but then I have recently arrived here," replied the governor of the castle, to whom the answers appeared satisfactory. "Pass on your way, Mr. Mayor, and you, good master alderman, and take my best wishes for the happiness of the bride, especially if she be as comely as ye represent her. And harkye, one of my men shall go with you, and see you safely through the town, or, peradventure, ye may be hindered. Go with them, Corporal Gird-the-Loins Grimbald."

The pretended mayor of Chichester thanked the governor of Arundel Castle for his courtesy, after which the Royalist party, attended by Corporal Grimbald, a very grim-looking corporal indeed, set off in one direction, while Colonel Morley, winding his horn to call the hounds together, rode off in another, followed by the troopers. The royal party soon afterwards entered Arundel, and it was fortunate that they had the grim-visaged corporal with them, for the town proved to be full of soldiers. Many of these glanced inquisitively at the travellers, but, seeing Grimbald, concluded all must be right. A nearer inspection of the castle showed the extent of the damage done to it by the Parliamentary soldiers. Sentinels fully accoutred, and armed with carabines, were posted at the gates of the fortress, and within the base-court could be seen other men drawn up, and going through their exercise. Our party, however, pushed on, and made for the bridge, where Corporal Gird-the-Loins Grimbald quitted them.

IV.

THE BLACKSMITH OF ANGMERING.

HAVING crossed the narrow but rushing Arun, the travellers now pursued their way along a winding lane, bordered in many places by fine trees, and enjoying glimpses of delicious woodland scenery. As they approached Angmering, it was discovered that the king's horse had lost a shoe. At first, it was feared that the loss could not be remedied at any place nearer than Steyning, but luckily a little smithy was found on the skirts of Angmering Park, while a small wayside inn, very pleasantly situated in the midst of some fine elm-trees, offered them the refreshment they so much needed, both for themselves and their steeds. Since quitting Stanstead Forest they had now ridden upwards of twenty miles, the king and those with him having previously ridden ten miles from Hambledon. All the party were as hungry as hunters. Charles declared he felt absolutely voracious, and directed Colonel Gunter to order the best breakfast that could be provided at the little inn, while he himself got his horse shod.

The blacksmith, a shrewd-looking fellow, lifted up the horse's feet deliberately, and then, with rather a singular look, remarked,

"Why, master, how comes this? Your horse has but three shoes left, and all three were put on in different counties; and one in Worcestershire."

"You are right, friend," replied Charles, laughing. "This horse was ridden at the fight at Worcester. I bought him from a disbanded Cavalier."

"Well, he shall have an honest Roundhead shoe this time, I can promise you, master," cried the blacksmith, plying his bellows, and soon afterwards placing a glowing shoe on the anvil. "I should like to belabour all Royalists in this fashion," he added, as he struck the heated iron.

"What! would you serve Charles Stuart himself so?" demanded Charles.

"Ay, marry, him worse than any other," replied the blacksmith, with a blow that made the anvil ring. "I heard say at Arundel that the Young Man has been taken, and I hope it be true."

"Well, one thing is quite certain, thou wouldst never lend him a hand to escape," observed Charles.

"No, nor a shoe, nor a nail," replied the smith. "I'd lame his horse, if he brought him to me."

"Well, don't lame mine, friend, I prithee," said Charles. "Take him to the stable, and see him well fed when thou hast done. I must in to breakfast."

The blacksmith promising compliance, Charles entered the little inn, where he found his companions seated at a table, with a goodly loaf of bread, a half-consumed cheese, and a lump of butter before them, together with two capacious jugs filled with ale, and drinking-horns. They did not rise, of course, on his Majesty's appearance, but he took the place reserved for him between Clavering and Lord Wilmot. Charles was scarcely seated when a large dish of fried ham and eggs was placed upon the table by a comely-looking damsel. A second supply was ordered to be prepared, and the king and his hungry followers did ample justice to the repast.

Having pretty nearly cleared the board and quite emptied both jugs of their contents, the party arose, and called for the reckoning, which was moderate enough, as may be supposed. Colonel Gunter defrayed it, while the others went forth to look after their steeds. The blacksmith had charge of the king's horse, and in return for the half-crown which Charles bestowed upon him, wished the young monarch a prosperous journey, adding,

"And that's more than I would wish Charles Stuart. But talking of the Young Man, master, what manner of man is he?"

"A marvellous proper man," replied the king; "about a foot taller than myself, very broad across the shoulders, fair-haired——"

"Nay, that can't be!" exclaimed the blacksmith, "for I have heard tell that he is as dark as a gipsy. I should say he was more like your honour."

"How now, sirrah! hast thou the impudence to tell me to my face that I am like Charles Stuart?" cried the king, with affected wrath. "I have half a mind to chastise thee."

"Nay, I meant no offence," replied the smith. "The devil, they say, is not so black as he's painted, and a man may be swart as a gipsy and yet handsome for all that. Handsome is that handsome does, and your honour having paid me handsomely, I wish you a prosperous journey. Good luck attend you wherever you go!" So saying, he retired into his smithy.

By this time all the party having mounted, they again set forth on their way.

V.

ANGMERING PARK, through a portion of which the royal party now rode, possessed many points of great beauty, and boasted much noble timber. In especial, there was a fine grove of oaks, old as the Druids, and tenanted at that time by a colony of herons; the birds, or their progeny, having since migrated to Parham. Charles cast a passing glance at the long-legged, long-necked birds congregated on the higher branches of the trees, and listened for a moment to their harsh cries. Quitting Angmering Park, and approaching Clapham Wood through a beautiful sylvan district, the party now obtained a fine view of Highdown Hill, on the summit of which, in later years, has been placed the Miller's Tomb.

From Clapham Wood the travellers made their way towards Findon, proceeding along the valley at the base of Cissbury Hill, a noble down, boasting, like so many of its neighbouring eminences, a large encampment, and commanding extensive views both of sea and land. Mounting the western slope of down in order to enjoy the prospect, the troop presently came to some circular hollows similar to those which they had previously passed at Stoke Down.

In one of these cavities a little hut had been constructed. On a wooden bench in front of the lowly habitation sat a venerable figure, which irresistibly attracted the king's attention, and arrested his progress. The personage seemed to be of an age almost patriarchal, to judge from his hoary locks and long silvery beard. Originally he must have been of lofty stature, but his frame was bent by the weight of years, and his limbs shrunken. His head was uncovered, and his brow and features ploughed deeply with wrinkles. His garb was that of a common shepherd of the downs. At his feet lay a dog, whose appearance was almost as antiquated as that of his master. On the bench near this patriarch of the hills sat a little girl, who was reading the Bible to him.

Perceiving from the king's looks that he desired to know something concerning this venerable personage, Colonel Gunter informed his Majesty that the name of the shepherd was Oswald Barcombe. He was what in popular parlance was called a "wise man," and had had plenty of time to acquire wisdom, for his life had extended far beyond the limits ordinarily allotted to man. For some time—almost beyond the memory of the existing generation—he had inhabited that hollow, and had scooped out a cave in the chalk, with which the hut communicated.

These particulars, combined with the old shepherd's venerable and patriarchal appearance, interested Charles so much that he alighted, and committing his horse to Clavering, advanced alone towards the cavity in the midst of which the old man was seated. Perceiving the stranger approach, the little girl left off reading, and pulled the old man by the sleeve to make him aware that some one was at hand. Thus admonished, the patriarch raised his head, and fixed his dim, almost sightless orbs on the king.

"Who art thou that seekest the dwelling of old Oswald Barcombe?" he demanded.

"A wanderer, without home or name," replied the king. "A price is set upon my head, and I am flying from a country which I can no more call mine own. Yet, looking upon thee, old man, I could not pass thy dwelling without craving thy blessing."

"Thou shalt have my blessing and welcome, my son," replied the venerable shepherd; "and I trust it may profit thee."

"Tell me thy age, I prithee, father?" said the king. "Thou must have seen many years."

"Many, many years, my son. A hundred and ten, as far as I can reckon. It may be a year more, or a year less, for I have well-nigh lost the count. Many changes have I seen as well as years. When I was a lad, bluff Harry the Eighth ruled the land, and I lived through the reigns of all his children. They were a royal race, those Tudors. The Stuarts came next, and I saw them both out, father and son, though good King Charles might have been on the throne now, if his enemies had not done him to death."

"Thou sayest truly, old man," replied Charles. "'Twas a deed of which a terrible account will be required of the parricides hereafter, should they even escape earthly punishment. But I honour thee for thy courage, old friend. Few men there are—whatever their secret sentiments may be—bold enough, now-a-days, to couple the epithet 'good' with the name of Charles the First."

"But Charles the First *was* a good king, and I will maintain it," replied Oswald. "I am too old to be a Republican. Go into the cave, my child, and tarry there till I call thee forth. I have a word to say in private to this stranger."

And as the girl departed on the old man's behest, Charles inquired, with some curiosity, if the little maid was his granddaughter.

"She belongs to the fourth generation," replied the old shepherd. "Edith is my great-grandson's daughter. But now that she is gone, I will speak to thee plainly. Thou hast intimated to me that thou art a fugitive Royalist. I cannot give thee shelter, but I can offer thee sympathy. I love not the present state of things. Night and day do I pray for the young king's safety, and for his restoration to the throne of his ancestors. In all likelihood I am the oldest man in the land, and Heaven will listen to me."

"Say'st thou so, father?" cried Charles; "then the king might trust his life to thee?"

"Is the king on these hills?" demanded the old shepherd, trembling.

"He stands before thee!" exclaimed Charles. "Nay, he kneels to thee—implores thy blessing. Thou wilt not withhold it, father?"

Mastering his astonishment by a marvellous effort, with a dignity which nothing but extreme age could impart, and with an expression of countenance almost sublime, the patriarch spread his arms over the head of the kneeling monarch, and in a tone of the utmost solemnity and fervour pronounced a benediction upon him.

"I feel that this blessing from one who, like thyself, has out-lived all earthly passions, will indeed profit me," said Charles, rising. "I am compelled to fly from my kingdom, but I shall return to it ere long, and trust to find thee living."

"Not so, sire," replied old Oswald; "my sand is nearly run. You will reascend the throne—of that I am well assured—but ere that happy event occurs, the old shepherd of Cissbury Hill will be laid in the grave already digged for him in this hollow. But while life remains he will not cease to pray for your restoration. Yet take counsel from me, sire," the old man continued, in a slightly troubled tone. "I dream dreams, and behold visions. I have watched the stars on many a night from this hill-top, and have learnt strange lore from the heavenly bodies. To-day you are in safety, but be not found within this rebellious land to-morrow."

"I design not to be so," replied the king. "Fare thee well, father!" And he extended his hand to the patriarch, who pressed it reverently to his lips. "Give this to little Edith," added Charles, placing a piece of gold in the old man's palm. "Once more, farewell!"

He then ran quickly up the side of the little hollow, mounted his horse, and rode off, remaining silent and abstracted for some time, much to the disappointment of his escort, who were curious to learn what had passed between him and the old shepherd of Cissbury Hill.

VI

WHAT HAPPENED AT THE WHITE HORSE AT STEYNING.

LEAVING Findon to the left, the travellers next crossed the range of hills, of which the lofty headland known as Chanctonbury Ring is the termination on the north-west, and descended upon Steyning. It had been their intention to push on to Bramber, but on entering the town they accidentally learnt that a troop of horse had just ridden off in that direction, so they judged it best to make a brief halt lest they should overtake them. Riding into the yard of the White Horse, they dismounted, and ordered their horses to be taken to the stables. There were a good many persons in the yard at the time, and amongst them were two individuals, who, despite their threadbare apparel, gave themselves great airs, strutted about like well-clad gallants, pounding the earth with their heavy-heeled boots, and making their long rapiers clatter against the stones. These two personages, who were no other than the redoubted Captain Goldspur and his friend Jervoise Rumboldsdyke, had watched the arrival of the party with some curiosity, and as Charles was about to enter the house, the captain strode up to him, and said, in a low, significant tone, " Art thou a friend to Cæsar?"   And then, without waiting for a reply, he exclaimed, " Why, zounds! can it be?—it is—it is Cæsar himself!"

"Be silent, sir!—I charge you on your allegiance," said Charles, authoritatively.

"I am dumb, sire," replied Goldspur, respectfully. "But I pray your Majesty to believe that my sword, my life, are at your disposal."

Rumboldsdyke coming up at the moment, his friend whispered a word to him, which instantly produced a magical effect upon the ruffling blade, whose demeanour became as respectful as that of Goldspur.

"This is Master Jervoise Rumboldsdyke, an it please your Majesty," said Goldspur, in a low tone. "Like myself, he hath lost his fortune in your service. But what matters that? We would lose fifty fortunes—if we had them—in such a cause—and our lives into the bargain. Would we not, Rumboldsdyke?"

"Ay, that would we!" exclaimed the other ruffler.

Charles would have gladly dispensed both with the presence and professions of such suspicious adherents, but fearing some indiscretion on their part, he deemed it best to keep them in sight, and therefore invited them to enter the house, and drink a bottle of canary with him—an invitation which, as may be supposed, they gratefully accepted.

Charles found Colonel Gunter waiting for him just within the doorway, and the latter looked surprised and somewhat uneasy at perceiving his Majesty attended by the two threadbare Cavaliers. A glance from the king, however, reassured him, and on looking more narrowly at the persons with him, he remembered to have seen them amongst the guests at the Poynings' Arms on the night when he was taken there by Stelfax, after his descent of the declivity near the Devil's Dyke. Goldspur, however, sought to set him completely at ease by stepping up to him, and saying in his ear,

"It is all right, Colonel Gunter. We are both friends to Cæsar—both men of honesty and mettle. Do you not remember the night at the Poynings' Arms, when that rascally Ironside captain brought you a prisoner there? Do you not recollect Captain Goldspur and his friend Jervoise Rumboldsdyke? I made an effort for your liberation. A shot was fired from Patcham Wood: 'twas I who sent the bullet at the accursed Stelfax!"

"Enough! enough! Captain Goldspur. I remember you perfectly," replied Gunter, hastily. "But come into this private
room. We shall be more at our ease there."

So saying, he led the way into a parlour looking towards the
back of the house. Charles had already preceded him, and having
hastily apprised the others of the addition they might expect to
their party, they were prepared for the appearance of the two
rufflers. Glasses and a couple of flasks of canary had already been
placed on the table, so there was no present occasion to summon
the host; and Gunter, having closed the door in order to prevent
intrusion, proceeded to introduce the new comers, whom he described as men who would not stick at a trifle to serve their
friends.

The introduction over, Lord Wilmot, in a haughty tone, thus
addressed them:

"Harkye, Captain Goldspur, and you, Master Rumboldsdyke—
since such are the names you choose to go by——"

"'Go by'—was that the word?" interrupted Goldspur, indignantly. "They are as much our names, my lord, as Henry Wilmot,
Baron Wilmot in England, and Viscount Wilmot in Ireland, is
your own."

"Oddsfish, my lord!" exclaimed Charles, laughing, "you are
known to these gentlemen, it seems, as well as we ourselves appear
to be."

"It were needless to remind his lordship where we have had the
honour of meeting him," observed Goldspur. "But if he desires
it, I will mention——"

"Nay, it is needless to enter into particulars," cried Lord
Wilmot. "I fancy I have seen your faces before, but not under
very creditable circumstances."

"Your lordship does not mean to cast any reflections upon our
honour, I trust?" said Goldspur, frowning, and laying his hand
upon the hilt of his blade.

"Oh, not in the least, captain," said Lord Wilmot, calmly. "I
have no doubt you are both men of honour, according to your own
acceptation of the term. But I was about to observe, when you

first interrupted me, that you have chosen to force your company upon us——"

"Force, my lord!" cried Goldspur, indignantly. "Neither Master Rumboldsdyke nor myself desire to force our company upon any man. We sought only to offer our swords and our lives to our gracious master. We yield to no man living—not even to yourself, Lord Wilmot—in devotion to the king, and we are ready to approve it. We may have tarnished cloaks and threadbare jerkins, but we have loyal hearts in our breasts."

"I believe you, gentlemen—I believe you," replied the king. "Wilmot, thou art wrong in doubting these good fellows."

"I hope I am," replied his lordship; "but I must be permitted to observe, that if I perceive the slightest indication of treachery on their part, I shall not hesitate to shoot both of them through the head."

"If his Majesty is satisfied with our professions we are content," said Goldspur.

"And so I am," replied the king—"though it will be needful to keep a wary eye upon them," he muttered to himself. "Sit down, gentlemen. Stand not upon ceremony with me, but fill your glasses to the brim."

"Mine shall be emptied to a pledge that I drink daily," quoth Goldspur. "May the king enjoy his own again, and that right speedily!"

"I echo the sentiment!" added Rumboldsdyke.

"I thank you both for this display of your loyalty and attachment," said Charles; "but I must pray you to be prudent, and make no further demonstration of your zeal. We are bound to Bramber, and perhaps to Brightelmstone. Is there any danger on the way?"

"A troop of horse has just gone on to Shoreham, sire," said Goldspur. "But they will have passed through Bramber before you get there."

"Can you tell us aught of Stelfax, Captain Goldspur?" inquired Clavering.

"The detested dog is still at Lewes," replied the other, "and is constantly occupied in scouring the country, and searching houses for fugitive Cavaliers. It is not for me to inquire into his Majesty's plans, but if they are such as to require the service of scouts upon the motions of the enemy, so as to give timely notice of danger, I and Master Rumboldsdyke will be ready to perform the office, and we have companions who will lend us aid."

"May it not be advisable to employ these men as scouts?" said Charles, in a low tone to Clavering.

"I think so, most undoubtedly," the young man replied. "Hark ye, Captain Goldspur," he continued aloud, "his Majesty thinks well of your proposal. You and your friend, I presume, are provided with horses. Ride to Lewes, or the neighbourhood, with all possible despatch. Station your scouts about Southover, and about the western side of the town, and if any sudden movements are made this evening by Stelfax, or the Ironsides, give us immediate warning at my father's residence, Ovingdean Grange. You know the way to it, I make no doubt, across the downs."

"It will not be the first time that I and Master Rumboldsdyke have visited Ovingdean Grange," replied Goldspur. "We have recently become acquainted with your worthy father, Colonel Maunsel."

"Indeed!" exclaimed Clavering, in surprise.

"And I may add," pursued Goldspur, "we have served him in the capacity we are about to serve his Majesty; we have acted as his scouts upon the detested Stelfax. Nay, more, we have watched over Mock-Beggar Hall, where worthy Master Beard and his daughter, the lovely Mistress Dulcia, were lodged during their stay at Lewes, and we escorted them back to the Grange."

"What you tell me, captain, satisfies me that you may indeed be trusted," said Clavering.

"Why, it seems we have stumbled on the very men we needed," observed Charles. "But who is this lovely Mistress Dulcia Beard they have guarded?"

"The daughter of my father's chaplain. Your Majesty will be‑ hold her at Ovingdean Grange," replied Clavering.

And shall find her, no doubt, well worthy our regard," replied the king, noticing the young man's heightened colour.

"Have we your Majesty's commands to set forward to Lewes on this service?" demanded Goldspur.

"You have, sir," replied Charles. "And we pray you to lose no time by the way. If there should be danger, you will not fail to make it known to Colonel Maunsel, at Ovingdean Grange.'

"On that your Majesty may rely. We now humbly take our leave." On this the twain made a profound obeisance and departed.

"And your Majesty is of opinion that these fellows may be trusted?" observed Lord Wilmot, as soon as they were gone.

"I am convinced of it," replied Charles. "I have not the slightest misgiving as to their fidelity. Nay, I think it very lucky we encountered them."

"I hope it may turn out as you anticipate," said Lord Wilmot; "but I am not without fears to the contrary."

"Thou art always full of apprehension, Wilmot," said the king. "I never allow fears to disturb me. Give me another glass of canary. Here is to fair Mistress Dulcia Beard!" he added, with a smile at Clavering. "You must tell me more about her as we ride on."

Charles and his companions remained for about a quarter of an hour longer in the parlour. They then summoned the host, paid their shot, and called for their horses. As the street near the inn seemed to be rather full of people, and some one amongst them might possibly recognise the royal fugitive, it was agreed that his Majesty's horse should be led to the outskirts of the town, on the road to Bramber, where he could join them.

Accordingly, while the others were engaged with the ostler, Charles slipped away, and proceeding along the street in which stands the curious old gabled house called the Brotherhood Hall, even then used as a grammar school, soon reached the antique church, built on the site of the still older wooden fabric constructed by Saint Cuthman, of whom mention has been made in an earlier portion of our Tale.

Having lingered near this old pile for a few minutes, without bestowing many thoughts, we fear, upon good Saint Cuthman, Charles set off again, and marching at a quick pace was presently out of the town, and at the spot where his attendants were waiting for him. Here he mounted his horse, and the troop set off for Bramber, the woody mound upon which the ruins of the old Norman castle are situated rising majestically before them at the distance of less than a mile.

VII.

DITCHLING BEACON.

The royal wanderer, now approaching the ancient stronghold of
the Braoses, had neither leisure nor inclination to mount the woody
sides of the eminence and examine the shattered fragment of its
keep, supposed to have been demolished by gunpowder, but was
fain to content himself with such view as the road afforded of the
picturesque ruins of the castle, and the venerable church of Saint
Nicholas nestling under its grey and crumbling walls. Charles,
however, was much amused by the diminutive size and quaint
architecture of the habitations composing the little village of Bramber, many of which were so low that a tall man could look in at their
upper windows. Several of these curious old houses, which were
built towards the latter end of the sixteenth century, are still left,
and a very good notion of an English village in Shakspeare's time
may be formed by a visit to Bramber. The king's advance-guard
ascertained, greatly to their satisfaction, that the troop of Republican soldiers had gone on to Shoreham; and as Charles crossed the
little bridge over the Adur, he could see the long line of red coats,
distinguishable by their glittering casques and corslets, passing on
the left bank of the river on their way thither. Under ordinary circumstances the royal party would have taken the same route;
but even if they had intended it, the hostile force in advance would

have deterred them from proceeding in that direction. They now proposed to continue their journey along a little-frequented road, leading from the defile o' the Adur to Poynings, and running at the foot of the precipitous range of downs overlooking the Weald of Sussex.

Here it was that Colonel Gunter, and his kinsman the captain, took leave of the king for a while, and struck off along the uplands on the east bank of the Adur, in the direction of Shoreham, it being the colonel's intention to seek an interview with Captain Tattersall, and ensure, at any cost, the skipper's departure before daybreak. The colonel set out on his expedition, full of confidence that he should be at Ovingdean Grange almost as soon as the king himself, and should bring his Majesty word that all had been satisfactorily settled. While, therefore, Charles and his now diminished escort rode in one direction, Colonel Gunter and his kinsman set off in another; the latter shaping their course towards Shoreham, but keeping on the acclivities, in order to avoid the soldiers.

Meanwhile, Charles and his party, who were now under the guidance of Clavering, crossed the spur of a down extending into the mighty fissure through which the Adur finds its way to the sea, and then took their way along the foot of the lofty escarpment to the picturesque village of Poynings, which we have visited on a former occasion. On the road to Poynings the king failed not to question Clavering as to the state of his feelings in respect to Dulcia Beard, and having ascertained, beyond a doubt, that the young man's affections were irrevocably fixed upon the damsel, he promised to exert all his influence with Colonel Maunsel to induce him to assent to the match.

"And I will lose no time about it," added the good-natured monarch. "I will attack the old gentleman on the subject immediately on my arrival at the Grange."

At Poynings the king did not fail to admire the beautiful old church, and the ancient manor-house amidst its woods; neither did he neglect to take a deep draught of Simon Piddinghoe's stout March ale, a black jack, filled to the brim with the excellent beverage, being brought to the door of the hostel by the officious landlord, at Clavering's directions. Neither did his Majesty escape without a brief chat with the talkative schoolmaster, Cisbury Oldfirle, who came forth with his pipe in one hand and a jug of ale in the other, to have a word with the strangers, and who, thinking that the king looked the most good-humoured person of the party, took the liberty of addressing him. The record of their conversation, however, has not been preserved.

Quitting Poynings, the royal party rode off, and proceeded at a rapid trot along a pleasant shady lane bordered by trees, whose branches often overhung it, until they came to the foot of Wolstonbury Hill, one of the most beautiful of the South Downs, which rose smoothly and gently before them, as if inviting them to ascend to the encampment upon its brow. They did, indeed, mount so far upon the velvet sward of the hill as enabled them to survey the surrounding district. From the elevated point they had now reached they overlooked Danny Park, which then contained, and still boasts, many magnificent oaks, and other fine timber. Embosomed in the midst of these woods stood an ancient Elizabethan mansion—yet maintained in all its integrity. Further on, at the outskirts of the park, could be discerned the pretty little hamlet of Hurstpierrepoint, with its church, then a very secluded village indeed, but now, owing to the convenience of railways, the natural beauty of the spot, and the predilection of the inhabitants of Brighton for it, promising to become a considerable place. For a few minutes Charles suffered his gaze to wander over this fair sylvan scene, and then gave the word to his attendants to proceed.

Hereupon Clavering, on whom, as we have said, the conduct of the troop now devolved, descended to the plain, and still keeping at the foot of the downs, crossed that part of the country now traversed by the railway, and pushed on till he came nearly to the foot of the lofty eminence on which Ditchling Beacon is situated.

Here the travellers climbed the downs, and soon gained the summit of this majestic hill—the loftiest point amid the South Downs. Within a short distance of the beacon the king halted, in order to enjoy the magnificent prospect. Almost the whole of

Sussex now lay before him, and after gazing at the vast panorama for some minutes in silence, he observed, with a sigh, deep almost as that heaved by the Moorish king when looking back on his lost Granada,

"When shall I gaze upon this splendid prospect again? when shall I call this fair country mine? Heaven only knows!"

"The day will come, doubt it not, sire," exclaimed Clavering, "and I hope to bring you again to Ditchling Beacon, and remind you of my words! But now let us on. We are nearly at our journey's end."

"And you are impatient, no doubt, that I should settle the business with your father," replied Charles, with a sudden change of manner. "Don't be uneasy. Fair Mistress Dulcia shall be yours!"

They now set forward at a quick trot, shaping their course in a south-easterly direction across the downs, and made such good progress, that in less than half an hour they had gained the northern extremity of the White Hawk Hill, and were within a mile of their destination. No sooner had they reached this point, than a man started from out a patch of gorse amidst which he had been lying, and ran towards them. It was Ninian Saxby.

"Is all right?" demanded the king. "May we safely approach the Grange?"

"With perfect safety, my liege," replied Ninian, doffing his cap. "No danger whatever is to be apprehended, and the colonel is out of measure delighted at the honour intended him."

The little cavalcade was now once more in motion, and rode on till they came to the ancient barrow at the summit of the hill, at the rear of the mansion, where they found another person stationed. This was Eustace Saxby, and he corroborated his son's information that all was right.

Here the **party** dismounted, and committing their horses to the two men, who were to take them round the back of the holt to the stables, **they** descended the hill, the king walking by the side of Clavering.

In the course of their descent of the hill they had to pass a small cottage, somewhat retired from the road, and shaded by an elm-tree. This cottage, which stood opposite the north garden-wall of the Grange, belonged to Morefruit Stone, the Puritan. Within it, at this moment, were two other persons besides old Morefruit and his daughter, who had witnessed, with great surprise, and even consternation, the arrival of the royal party on the hill-top. Keeping themselves carefully out of sight, these individuals watched Clavering and his royal companion as they descended the hill together, and on beholding the king, who accidentally made a pause near the cottage, one of the spies—evidently from his garb an officer in the Republican army—exclaimed, in a stern, wrathful tone to the other,

"It is he! it is Charles Stuart himself! He has come before his time. Thou hast deceived me, or hast given him warning."

"I have not deceived thee, Captain Stelfax," rejoined Micklegift; "neither am I to blame if Charles Stuart has advanced the hour of his arrival."

"But he finds me wholly unprepared?" cried Stelfax, in a tone of fierce disappointment. "I shall lose him, unless he tarries for the night in the dwelling of this old Amalekite. My men are all at Lewes. What is to be done? I shall be balked of my prey."

"There is yet a means of accomplishing his capture, if thou darest attempt it, single-handed," replied Micklegift.

"What is there I dare not do?" rejoined Stelfax. "Show me thy plan."

"It is this," answered Micklegift. "I will introduce thee secretly to the house—into the sleeping-chamber of the old Amalekite. We shall not be noticed, for all the household will be occupied with the arrival of this company. Peradventure thou mayst be able to seize the Young Man."

"I will seize him, or slay him, and take my chance for the rest," rejoined Stelfax, in a determined voice. "Look forth, I prithee," he added to Morefruit Stone, "and see if they be gone."

"No one is in sight," replied the elder, looking forth.

"Stay thou within thy cottage," said Stelfax. "We may need thee anon. Make good thy words," he added to Micklegift, "and conduct me to Colonel Maunsel's chamber."

On this they quitted the cottage together, and taking a few steps up the hill, reached a door in the wall, which Micklegift unlocked. They then went into the garden.

VIII.

OF THE KING'S RECEPTION AT THE GRANGE.

ON approaching the front of the mansion, Clavering besought the king's permission to step forward, and receiving it, hastened to ring the bell at the gate, and thus announce to his father the arrival of his royal guest.

Immediately on the summons, which he had for some time been impatiently awaiting, Colonel Maunsel appeared at the open doorway, at the head of his retainers, all of whom were clad in their richest liveries, as if for some high festivity. Never did the old Cavalier appear to greater advantage than on this occasion. He was attired in a rich court suit of black velvet, with rapier and plumed Spanish hat to correspond, and being roused to unwonted energy by the strong excitement of the moment, he moved with all his former grace and stateliness. Close behind him came Mr. Beard and Dulcia, the former in a plain suit of black, and the latter attired with great neatness and simplicity, but without any pretension to show or elegance. Such, however, was the effect of her charms of person and manner, and so little did she require the aid of dress and ornament, that Charles, when he beheld her, was quite electrified by her surpassing beauty, and thought he had never seen court dame so lovely as this country damsel, whose sole decoration was a few flowers placed amidst her fair clustering tresses. With the object of it before him, he ceased to wonder at Clavering's passion.

Behind Colonel Maunsel, in the entrance-hall, appeared all the retainers that could be mustered for the occasion—all, as we have just intimated, in gala attire. None of these, it may be proper to state, had any positive knowledge of the exalted rank of the guest whom their master was about to welcome, though most of them suspected the truth. But though, as we are aware, the whole of the colonel's household were staunch Royalists, and might have been entrusted with the secret without fear of the consequences, the only one amongst them absolutely confided in was old Martin Geere. Greatly elated, and anxious to maintain his master's importance, the old serving-man now assumed a consequential manner and dignified deportment quite unlike his ordinary bearing. He was provided with a wand to marshal the household, and enable him to act as sort of usher in the approaching ceremony.

At the precise moment when the old Cavalier appeared at the doorway, attended as we have described, Charles entered the gate of the mansion, Clavering respectfully retiring as the monarch advanced, and Lord Wilmot and Colonel Philips holding back, so that the king might be left alone. Notwithstanding the disguise adopted by the royal wanderer, and the change effected in his general appearance, Colonel Maunsel instantly recognised him, and, taking off his hat, advanced slowly and with great dignity, but with the most profound respect, to meet him and give him welcome. If Charles had come there in the plenitude of his power, in gorgeous apparel, and attended by a brilliant bevy of courtiers, instead of as a proscribed fugitive, and scantily attended, Colonel Maunsel could not have shown him greater reverence. It was with great difficulty that he prevented himself from bending the knee to the young king, and it was only, indeed, a gesture from Charles that restrained him. Contenting himself, therefore, with making a profound obeisance, he said, with a look that conveyed all he did not dare to utter, "Welcome, sir! thrice welcome to Ovingdean Grange. My poor dwelling is honoured indeed by the presence of such a guest."

"I thank you most heartily for your welcome, Colonel Maunsel," replied Charles. "But it is far more than I merit. I have no other claim upon your attention save this—and it is much, I own," he added, with some significance—"that you were warmly attached to my father."

"No man more so, sir," replied the old Cavalier, emphatically—"no man more so. But pardon me if I say that your claims upon me are equal to those of your much-honoured, much-lamented sire."

"You are pleased to say so, colonel," observed the king, "and I thank you for the assurance. But a truce to claims real or imaginary! Allow me to see the interior of your mansion, which, if it corresponds with the outside, must be well worth inspection."

"'Tis a comfortable old house, quite sufficient for a plain country gentleman like myself, sir," replied the colonel; " and if I am able to keep it up I shall be quite content. But the fines and confiscations of the rogues in power have well-nigh ruined me."

" Ay, ay, we are alike in misfortune. Colonel Maunsel," observed the king. "You have lost much—I have lost all. But better days, I trust, are in store for both of us."

"I trust so, sir," the old Cavalier replied. "But now, I pray you, deign to enter my humble dwelling. And you, too, gentlemen," he added, saluting the others. "Clavering, I am right glad to see thee, boy. Thy turn will come anon. Meantime, welcome thy father's guests, and show them in."

So saying, and respectfully retiring before the king, taking especial care not to turn his back upon his Majesty, the old Cavalier moved towards the house His master's gestures were imitated by Martin Geere, but so unsuccessfully, that, in retreating somewhat too hastily, he came in contact with the steps, and tumbled backwards, amidst the titters of the rest of the serving-men. Charles would willingly have dispensed with so much ceremony, but aware of the punctilious character of his host, he did not like to put a stop to it. In this way he was ushered into the house, and compelled to take precedence of the others, who held back until he had entered.

x

No sooner had Charles set foot in the entrance-hall, than the colonel once more gave him a hearty welcome to Ovingdean Grange, to which the king made a suitable reply. Mr. Beard then received the honour of a presentation, and his Majesty expressing a hope that he might be speedily restored to the living of which he had been deprived, he replied with humility,

"I do not despair, sir. *Vincit qui patitur.*"

"And this, I suppose, is your daughter, Mr. Beard?" inquired the king, determined to put his promise to Clavering into immediate execution, and looking with such undisguised admiration at Dulcia as summoned the roses to her cheek. "On my faith, fair damsel," he continued, "I have heard Clavering Maunsel speak of you—and in rapturous terms, I promise you—but, as I live, his description did not do you justice."

"I must pray you, sir, to spare the maiden's blushes," interposed Colonel Maunsel. "She is simple and home-bred, and unaccustomed to compliments."

"Egad! colonel, you mistake," cried the monarch; "I never spoke with greater sincerity in my life. Your son did not say half so much of fair Mistress Dulcia as she deserves. She is lovely enough to grace the proudest hall in England—ay, a palace, if there be a palace left in the country. If I had been in Clavering's place I should have fallen in love to a dead certainty; and if—as perhaps might be the case—the fair Dulcia had not proved altogether insensible to my suit, I should have asked my father's consent," he added, to the colonel.

This speech, as may be imagined, greatly embarrassed one person to whom it referred, but the king seemed wholly to disregard her confusion.

"And what should you have answered, colonel, if such a question had been put to you?" pursued Charles.

"'Faith, sir, I can't say—I have not given the matter consideration," replied the old Cavalier.

"Then do so," rejoined the king; "and decide before I leave, for I have made up my mind that it shall be a match."

"You must have other and more important affairs to think of, I should fancy, sir," remarked Colonel Maunsel, "than to trouble yourself, at a time like the present, about the loves of a foolish boy and girl. If there should be any fondness between them—of which I am ignorant—they must wait."

"Very prudent and proper," rejoined the king. "Let them wait if you desire it, my good colonel, but not too long—not too long. There! we may consider the matter as settled," he added, with a glance at Clavering.

"Upon my word, sir," cried the colonel, "you are very peremptory—and as prompt as peremptory. You have only been here a few minutes, and yet have made up a marriage, whether the parties chiefly concerned like it or not."

"Oddsfish! colonel," exclaimed Charles, "I have taken care to satisfy myself on that score. Your consent alone is wanted, for good Mr. Beard's, I can see, is given already."

"Nay, if I thought the happiness of the young folks was at stake," replied the colonel, "I should not withhold my consent, you may depend, sir."

"I knew it!—I knew it!" cried Charles, triumphantly. "Bravo! bravissimo! Clavering, I congratulate you. You will soon have the prettiest wife in Sussex, and my only regret is that I cannot be present at the wedding. And now, colonel, before doing anything else, I would fain refresh myself with a little cold water, and get rid of the dust and heat of the journey."

"I will instantly attend you to a chamber, sir, where all is in readiness," said the old Cavalier.

"On no account, colonel," cried the king. "I will not permit it. You overwhelm me by your kindness. You have other guests to attend to besides myself. Clavering will show me the way—that is, if he can quit the side of his intended. Come, confess!" he added, playfully, as he approached the young couple. "Have I not done you both a good turn?"

"In good truth you have, sir," replied Clavering. "I will answer for Dulcia," he added, as the blushing damsel turned away to hide her confusion.

x 2

"Up-stairs at once, and away!" cried Charles, "or we shall have the old gentleman retract his promise."

Urged on by the king, who seemed determined to prevent any further display of etiquette, Clavering ran up the grand staircase, while Charles followed with equal celerity, much to the discomposure of Colonel Maunsel, who thought that his son ought to have observed more ceremony.

On being ushered into the colonel's sleeping-chamber, the king threw himself into an elbow-chair and indulged in a hearty laugh. Clavering, meanwhile, anxious to escape from the raillery in which it was evident that the mirthful young monarch was disposed to indulge at his expense, proceeded towards the inner chamber to ascertain that all the necessaries for the king's toilette were ready, and finding that no change of linen had been placed there, he begged leave to retire in order to repair the omission. Charles nodded in token of assent, and Clavering, with a profound obeisance, quitted the room, leaving his Majesty still laughing heartily at the thoughts that tickled his fancy.

By-and-by a gentle tap was heard at the door, and, in reply to Charles's summons to come in, Patty Whinchat entered, carrying with much care a fine linen shirt with laced ruffles, and a laced band of snowy whiteness placed upon it. Curtseying to the king, she tripped into the inner room and deposited the linen on the bed.

Her errand performed, Patty returned, and dropping another curtsey to the king, observed,

"Captain Clavering bade me say, sir, that if you have occasion for any change of apparel, you will find all you require in the wardrobe."

"Captain Clavering is very obliging," replied Charles, glancing admiringly at her. "How art thou called, child, and what office dost fill in the house?"

"I am named Patty Whinchat, an please you, sir," she replied; "and am handmaiden to Mistress Dulcia Beard."

"Oddsfish, Patty!" exclaimed the king, "thy good looks rival those of thy mistress. Ye are both so pretty, that if I were asked which to take I should be fairly perplexed in the choice."

"But you are not asked to take either of us, sir," Patty rejoined. "My mistress has got a lover, and I——"

"More than one, I'll be sworn!" interrupted the king, "or the serving-men have no taste. However, there'll be no great harm in robbing your favoured and fortunate swain, whoever he may be, of a kiss"—suiting the action to the word. "You have plenty to spare, both for him and me."

"You are mistaken, sir," replied Patty; "I shouldn't have half enow for Ninian Saxby, if I let him take as many as he wants. But don't detain me, sir, I pray of you. I mustn't stay here another minute. I'm wanted down stairs. Somebody is below, I'm told," she added, mysteriously, "and I'm dying to have a peep at him."

"And who may this 'somebody' be whom thou art so curious to behold, child?" inquired Charles.

"The servants will have it the king is here," rejoined Patty; "but they've said the same thing so often before that I don't exactly believe them."

"What sort of person is the king, child?" said Charles. "Should you know him if you beheld him?"

"Know him!" exclaimed Patty. "To be sure! the very instant I clapped eyes upon him."

"But what is he like? Remarkably handsome, eh?"

"Handsome! quite the contrary! He's remarkably plain—harsh features, and very dark. Mercy on us! if it should——"

"Why, what's the matter, child?"

"If it should be the king whom I've been talking to all the time!" she exclaimed, trembling.

"If it were the king, I'll answer for it he would be the last person to be offended with so pretty a lass as thyself," said Charles, reassuring her with another kiss. "But hie thee down stairs, and thou mayst possibly find out some one who will better answer to thy notions of what a monarch ought to be than myself."

Patty then curtseyed and moved towards the door, but she could not help casting another look at the king ere she quitted the room, exclaiming,

"Oh, if it should be his Majesty, I shall never get over it!"

Much diverted by the incident, Charles went into the inner room, and before proceeding to disrobe himself, placed his rapier and the brace of pocket-pistols, which he usually carried with him, on a table set near the arras curtain hung between the two rooms. His ablutions performed, he next exchanged his travel-soiled under-garments for the fair linen provided by Patty, humming the while some snatches of a then popular French romance.

"Egad!" he exclaimed, taking up the doublet he had just laid aside, "this is a very comfortable old house, and I should have been quite as well lodged here as at Trent—and well cared for, more-over, by the pretty little Phillis who has just left me. For many reasons I am glad I came here, though Wilmot would fain have dis-suaded me from doing so on the score of danger! Pshaw! no danger is to be apprehended—at all events, not to-day—and to-morrow his enemies will look in vain for Charles Stuart. Hang these Puri-tanical garments," he added, throwing down the jerkin in disgust, "I abominate them. Let us see what this wardrobe contains. A doublet of Clavering's might suit me." With this he opened the door of the wardrobe, and taking out a handsome suit of black taffeta, exclaimed, "Oddsfish! these are the very things."

With this, he proceeded to array himself in the new-found ap-parel, which fitted him to admiration, and was adjusting his laced band before a mirror set in a frame of black oak, when the arras, curtain was suddenly drawn aside, and two men, whose appear-ance and looks left him no doubt of their intentions, stepped from behind it.

IX.

HOW THE KING WAS SHUT UP IN THE HIDING PLACE.

IT is scarcely necessary to say that the menacing intruders who surprised Charles at his toilette were Stelfax and Micklegift. The Ironside leader's first act was to possess himself of the pistols and rapier, which the king had incautiously laid upon the table, and deliver them to his companion.

"Ha! betrayed!" exclaimed Charles, springing towards the table in search of his arms, and perceiving to his dismay that they were gone.

Even in this extremity he did not lose his self-possession, but eyed his foes resolutely and even haughtily.

"What makes you here?" he sternly demanded.

"I am here to arrest thee, Charles Stuart, in the name of the Parliament of England, and by order of his Excellency the Lord General Cromwell. Surrender thyself my prisoner—rescue or no rescue—or I will shoot thee through the head."

"Beware ere thou liftest thine hand against the Lord's anointed!" exclaimed Charles, with a look and gesture so full of majesty that it inspired awe in both his hearers, and the Ironside captain involuntarily lowered the pistol which he had levelled at the king.

Charles instantly perceived the slight advantage he had gained, and sought to profit by it. If he could only gain time, he thought, assistance might arrive. He glanced around to see if there was a hand-bell within reach, a whistle, or any other means of giving the alarm. But nothing presented itself.

"For the second time, I ask thee, Charles Stuart," said Stelfax, "dost thou yield thyself a prisoner, or wilt thou compel me to lay violent hands upon thy person?"

"Off, villains!" exclaimed the king, retreating a few paces. "Touch me at your peril. I will resist to the death."

"Be ruled by my counsel, O insensate young man!" exclaimed Micklegift. "Resistance is useless, and will bring instant destruction upon thee. Yield thee to what cannot be averted, and submit patiently to the decrees of Heaven."

"Heaven hath never decreed that I shall perish by such base hands as those of thy comrade!" cried the king.

"Better for thee thou shouldst die by my hands than by those of the headsman, like thy tyrannous father," retorted Stelfax. "For the last time, I ask thee, dost thou yield thyself a prisoner?"

Charles seemed to have taken a sudden resolution.

"Since it cannot be helped, I yield," he said; "but I couple my surrender with no promise. Keep guard over me as best ye may, I will escape if I can."

Stelfax made no reply, but signed to the monarch to come forth into the outer room. Charles obeyed, and marched towards his captors with great dignity and unshaken firmness, secretly wondering what they meant to do with him. He was not long kept in suspense.

They were now in the centre of the chamber, and Stelfax directed his companion to open the door of the hiding-place. "Thou know'st the secret spring," he said—"touch it, I prithee. I will not quit the prisoner, even for a moment."

Micklegift did as he was enjoined, pressed his hand upon the little knob that moved the pillar, and the aperture was disclosed.

"Enter that hiding-place, Charles Stuart," said Stelfax, sternly, to the king. "It was contrived for thy fugitive followers, and may therefore serve thy turn. 'Tis in vain to dispute my authority. I am thy master now, by right of the sword," he added, presenting his rapier's point at the king's breast, "and will be obeyed. Enter, I command thee!"

Charles had no alternative but compliance. A struggle, under such disadvantageous circumstances, must have cost him his life.

"Plague take 'em!" he muttered, as he went into the hiding-place. "What the deuce can they all be about down stairs, to allow me to be trapped in this manner? Will no one come to the rescue?"

But as rescue came not, he went in.

Stelfax quickly followed, but, ere he passed quite through the aperture, he called out to Micklegift:

"Hie thee back as quickly as thou canst to Morefruit Stone's cottage. Despatch him with all haste to Lewes for my men. Then return to this chamber, and if nought has happened in the interval, tap thrice against these boards. I shall know thy signal, and will come forth. The Lord hath delivered Abijam into my hands at last, and he shall never quit them with life!"

So saying, he closed the door of the hiding-place.

Micklegift then passed through a small door in the inner chamber, partially concealed by arras, through which he and Stelfax had obtained admittance. This outlet communicated with a back staircase, which the Independent minister hastily descended. At the foot of the staircase was a postern, which let him out into the garden

X.

THE PURITAN'S DAUGHTER.

NOT many minutes after the king's immurement in the hiding-place, Clavering tapped at the chamber door, and receiving no answer, though he repeated the application yet more loudly, ventured to enter the apartment. Pausing for a moment in the outer chamber, and coughing slightly to announce his presence, he went on, and was both surprised and alarmed not to perceive the king. Remarking, however, that his Majesty had changed his attire, and that the small door communicating with the back staircase was left partly open, he concluded Charles must have discovered that means of exit, and had probably found his way to the garden. Notwithstanding this conviction, however, he could not shake off a strong feeling of uneasiness, and resolving to satisfy himself without delay, quickly descended the winding staircase and reached the postern at its foot, which he found unlocked. The latter circumstance convinced him that he was right in his conjecture, and he now felt certain of finding his Majesty in the garden. But though he visited every walk, alley, and labyrinth, he was unsuccessful, and all his alarm returned, and with additional force. One hope alone sustained him. The king—though this appeared highly improbable —might have strayed into the orchard, or the holt beyond it. To the orchard he flew at once, and had scarcely opened the gate leading to it when he encountered old Ticehurst, the gardener, and

Nut Springett. In answer to his inquiries, Ticehurst stated that about five minutes ago he had seen a tall, dark man, answering to the description of the person Captain Clavering was inquiring about, issue from the postern, and pass out at the gate in the north wall near Morefruit Stone's cottage. Still more perplexed, but thinking this must be the king, though he was wholly unable to account for such imprudence on his Majesty's part, Clavering hurried off in the direction taken by the person whom the gardeners had seen, and passed through the gate referred to by them. Not fifty yards off, and shaded by a fine elm-tree, stood Morefruit Stone's cottage. Great was his surprise, on entering it, to find Increase Micklegift in the hands of John Habergeon and Ninian Saxby. The only person in the cottage, besides the Independent minister and his captors, was Morefruit Stone's daughter, Temperance, a comely damsel, to whom Ninian had once paid considerable attention. Instantly divining that treachery had been practised by Micklegift, Clavering drew his sword, and placing its point at the other's throat, demanded, in a terrible voice,

"What hast thou done with him? Where is he?"

"Harm me, and thou shalt never learn," replied the Independent minister, composedly.

"Let us take him to the house at once, captain, and examine him there," said John Habergeon. "He has important revelations to make. I warrant we will find means of making him speak."

"Try!" rejoined Micklegift, with a look of cold contempt.

"Ay, we will try, and to some purpose, presently, I warrant thee," rejoined John. "We will question thee with the thumb-screw and the scourge, after Captain Stelfax's fashion."

"How came you to find the villain here?" inquired Clavering.

"We received our information from pretty Temperance Stone," said Ninian, with a grateful look at the damsel in question; "and I shall not soon forget the service she has done us."

"Woe to her! for she hath betrayed her father and her father's friend," said Micklegift, sternly. "Her love for this vain youth shall never prosper."

"That is more than you can answer for, rascal," replied Ninian

"Where is her father?" demanded Clavering.

"He hath escaped from the hands of these Philistines," said Micklegift, with a look of triumph, "and will yet bring the enemy upon you."

"Be not alarmed, sir," replied John Habergeon. "He hath started for Lewes, but he cannot have gone far. Eustace Saxby is upon his track. Besides, there are others on the look-out, whose vigilance he will find it difficult to elude."

"I have not told all I know," said Temperance; "but since I am provoked, I will withhold nothing." And she then proceeded to relate to Clavering that Micklegift and Stelfax were concealed in her father's cottage as he had passed on his way with the other gentlemen to the house. That one of the party had been recognised by the two men, who declared it was the Young Man. That Stelfax then declared that at all hazards he would obtain admission to the house and accomplish his arrest, and Micklegift agreed to accompany him, telling him he knew a way by which they could obtain secret admission to the colonel's sleeping-chamber.

"The colonel's sleeping-chamber, damsel—art sure he mentioned that room?" demanded John Habergeon. "If so, they must have gained admission by the postern opening from the back stairs into the garden."

"They did so," replied Clavering. "But how came the door open?"

A scornful smile lighted up Micklegift's sallow features.

"He hath a master-key, no doubt," replied Temperance, "for he unlocked the garden-gate, and they went in together. Feeling sure some great mischief was afoot, I made an excuse to quit the cottage, and hastened in search of Ninian, whom I found with his father and John Habergeon, and told him what had happened, and they all three came back with me."

"We saw Micklegift from a distance enter the cottage," said Ninian, "and pounced upon him before he was aware. And here we have him safe enough, as you see, to answer for his offences."

"But where is Stelfax?" exclaimed Clavering. "Where is——"

"The Young Man Charles Stuart thou wouldst say," supplied Micklegift. "Neither of them wilt thou find till it be too late."

"Villain, I will force thee to disclose where the king is!" cried Clavering, with a look of distraction—"I will tear the secret from thy breast."

"Hold, your honour!" exclaimed John. "I think I have discovered it. Where was the king last seen?"

"I left him alone to attire himself in my father's sleeping-chamber," replied Clavering.

"Then, depend upon it he is shut up in the hiding-place, and Stelfax is there with him," cried John.

"A shrewd guess!" exclaimed Clavering. "I can see from this rascal's looks that thou art in the right. Bring him along! We must not lose a moment in setting our royal master free."

"Hold yet a moment, and listen to me," said Micklegift. "I will not deny that you have hit upon the truth, for it is vain to attempt further concealment. But ye cannot liberate Charles Stuart without my aid. Stelfax will slay his prisoner rather than yield him to you. Such I know to be his purpose, and ye are acquainted with his determined character. Promise to do me no injury, and I will avert this direful catastrophe, which will otherwise inevitably ensue."

Clavering reflected for a moment, and then replied, "I give thee the promise thou requirest. Bring him along."

"Nay, there will be no need to use force," said Micklegift. "I will go peaceably enough."

"You must come with us too, fair mistress," said Ninian to Temperance. "We cannot leave you behind."

"I have no desire to be left," replied the blushing maiden, displaying great readiness to accompany him.

The whole party then quitted the cottage. Micklegift marched between John and Ninian, who, notwithstanding their captive's promise to go quietly, thought it right to keep firm hold of him. In this manner they crossed the garden and proceeded to the little postern.

XI.

IN WHICH THE TABLES ARE TURNED UPON STELFAX.

A PRISONER in a narrow cell, with an inexorable gaoler close beside him, and ready to slay him if he attempted escape, Charles did not lose his confidence. Deliverance he felt sure would come. His absence must be ere long discovered by the inmates of the house, and then search would be made for him, and it was scarcely probable that this hiding-place, of which he himself had heard Clavering speak, would remain unvisited. Still, great risk might be incurred at the moment when his liberation should be attempted, and he tried to consider what ought to be done at that hazardous conjuncture. Leaning against the wall of the cell, he assumed a perfectly indifferent air, and began to hum snatches of French ditties, as he had previously done while making his toilette. This show of gaiety and unconcern was so annoying to Stelfax, that he at last sternly rebuked him for his unseemly levity.

"Would you prefer that I should join you in a hymn, captain?" said Charles. "Lead on, and I will accompany you."

"Trouble me not, thou vain young man, but keep silence," rejoined Stelfax, sternly.

The careless monarch was not, however, to be checked, but went on humming his songs in spite of his moody gaoler. In this manner nearly half an hour passed away. Charles then began to find the confinement irksome, and asked, with some impatience, how long he was to be kept there? Stelfax made no reply, but the next moment the attention of both was caught by a slight sound —a tap against the piece of wood screening the entrance to the recess. Charles started, but controlled himself by a great effort. Was relief come? Or was it the aid expected by Stelfax?

The Ironside captain likewise listened attentively, and not without anxiety. The tap was repeated; and again, after a pause, for the third time. There could be no doubt now. It was Micklegift.

Sternly enjoining the king to follow him, Stelfax moved forward.

At this moment the secret spring was touched, the door of the recess flew open, and the voice of the Independent minister was heard to call out, " It is I, Increase Micklegift. Come forth without fear."

Addressing another stern injunction to the king to follow him, Stelfax drew a pistol from his belt, and grasping his bared sword in his left hand, to be ready for instant service if required, stepped out into the room.

Micklegift was standing in the middle of the chamber, almost opposite the fireplace, and, on seeing Stelfax, signed to him to follow him to the inner room, moving quickly in that direction himself.

" Stay!" vociferated Stelfax, angrily. " Whither goest thou? I may need thy aid with the prisoner."

Glancing backwards as he spoke, to ascertain whether Charles was following, he caught sight of two men lurking within the angle of the chimney-piece, ready to spring upon him.

" Ah! treacherous dog, thou hast played me false!" he vociferated. " But thou shalt not escape punishment!" With which words he fired his pistol at the Independent minister, and with fatal effect. Micklegift uttered a cry, staggered, and fell backwards. " Neither shalt thou escape!" he continued, turning to attack the king, who at this moment appeared at the entrance of the recess; but ere he could execute his purpose, or indeed turn completely round, John Habergeon had thrown himself upon him, and, aided by Ninian, succeeded in disarming him.

Charles himself was close at hand, but did not interfere in the struggle, seeing his assistance was wholly unneeded. Clavering had also sprung, sword in hand, from behind a piece of furniture; but ere he could reach the scene of action the seizure of the redoubted Ironside leader was accomplished, and all that was left for the young man to do was to congratulate his Majesty on his deliverance.

But there were others, as it presently appeared, who were equally anxious to express their feelings of satisfaction. The arras curtain was drawn aside, and from the inner room issued a number of persons, who had been anxiously awaiting the result of Micklegift's device, which, though successful as far as the king's safety was concerned, had proved disastrous to himself. No one, however, troubled himself about the luckless Independent minister for the moment. He was left to lie where he had fallen. All the attention was directed towards the king. The party now flocking towards him, which consisted of Colonel Maunsel, Lord Wilmot, Colonel Philips, with Mr. Beard and his daughter, together with old Martin Geere, were enthusiastic in their demonstrations of joy. Concealment was no longer possible, neither was it attempted. Charles was now recognised by all as their sovereign. Bending the knee before the monarch, Colonel Maunsel took the hand which his Majesty graciously extended towards him, and gave utterance to his unbounded feelings of delight, while the rest, completely carried away by enthusiasm, made the roof echo with their loyal shouts of " God save King Charles!"

Much touched by this exhibition of their loyalty, Charles, as soon as he could obtain silence, thanked them for their zeal, in accents betraying the depth of his emotion, and attesting his sincerity.

But another matter now claimed the king's attention. One of his enemies was gone to his account, but the more dangerous of the two was left, to expiate his offences with his life. Charles prepared to pass judgment upon him.

Disarmed, with his elbows tightly pinioned to his side by a sword-belt, having a guard on either hand ready to stab him or shoot him if he attempted resistance—which, indeed, in his present state, was well-nigh impossible—the Ironside captain, who refused to move at John Habergeon's bidding, was forcibly dragged before the king.

Meanwhile, Charles having seated himself in a richly-carved oak chair, high-backed, and provided with a cushion of Utrecht velvet, placed his foot on a stool covered with the same material, which was set before him with the most profound respect by old Martin Geere. At the same time the company stationed themselves on either side of the chair occupied by his Majesty, thus giving the group some slight resemblance to a gathering round the throne. On the right of the king, and close to the royal chair, stood Colonel Maunsel, leaning on his drawn sword. On the same side were Lord Wilmot and Colonel Philips. On the left stood Clavering, with his rapier bared, and held with its point to the ground. Near to Clavering were Dulcia and Mr. Beard. At some little distance, near the inner room, was a group, consisting of Giles Moppett, Elias Crundy, and others of the household, together with Patty Whinchat and Temperance Stone. When Stelfax was brought before the king, John Habergeon would fain have compelled him to make an obeisance, but the stubborn Republican refused, and, drawing himself up, said, "I will not bow the head to the son of the tyrant."

"Let him be," said Charles. "It is too late to teach him manners. What hast thou to say, fellow," he continued, addressing the prisoner, "why I should not order thee to instant execution?"

"Nothing," replied Stelfax, resolutely. "I am prepared to die. A soldier of the Lord would scorn to ask life from the son of Rehoboam."

"Thy life is justly forfeited," said the king. "Thou hast compassed my destruction, and hast lifted thy sacrilegious hand against the Lord's anointed; but it was not Heaven's will that I should thus perish."

"It may be thou art reserved to be a scourge to the land like thy father," said Stelfax; "but if there are any left of my mind, thy reign will be short, and thy end bloody."

"I pray your Majesty give no further hearing to the rebellious villain," said John Habergeon. "Let us take him forth, and deal with him as his crimes deserve. We will first strike off the hand which he hath impiously raised against your sacred person."

Ere Charles could give his consent to the solicitation, Dulcia stepped forward, and threw herself at his feet. In this supplicating posture she lifted up her hands, and said, in accents of the most earnest entreaty, "Beseech your Majesty, cut not off the man's life thus suddenly. Give him time for repentance."

"He is a soldier, lady," replied the king, gravely, "and, as such, should be prepared to die. We see no reason why delay should be granted him. He would have given none to ourself. Yet he shall have time for prayer. See that it be so, good fellow," he added to John Habergeon.

"I will go with him, and strive to bring him to repentance, said Mr. Beard.

"I do not desire thy presence," said Stelfax, sternly. "I can make up my account with Heaven without thy aid. Yon hypocritical traitor, whom I have despatched before me," he added, looking towards the body of Micklegift, "hath disgusted me with all who profess the sacred calling."

"What! hast thou no repentance for the bloody deed thou hast done?" demanded the clergyman.

"Wherefore should I repent?" rejoined Stelfax. "The man was justly slain. He had betrayed me."

"There thou art wrong," remarked John Habergeon. "Micklegift was a captive in our hands, and we compelled him to lure thee forth, in order to prevent harm being done by thee to his Majesty."

"And well was it for Charles Stuart that ye employed the device," remarked Stelfax. "If that bullet had not been wasted on the fool Micklegift, it would have been lodged in your king's brain. Well was it also for Charles Stuart that he came to this house ere I was prepared for him. Had he tarried till to-morrow, his escape had been impossible."

CHARLES II. AT OVINGDEAN GRANGE

p. 322

"My warning, you see, was not in vain," observed the king to Clavering.

Again Dulcia interceded for Stelfax, imploring his Majesty not to doom him to instant death.

"You seem to have an interest more than ordinary in this man, young lady," said Charles. "Whence arises it? Speak frankly, if you desire to serve him."

"I owe him some gratitude, my liege," replied Dulcia, "inasmuch as he respected me when I was in his power. While detained as a prisoner with my father at Lewes, Captain Stelfax sought to win my love, but by honourable means alone, and finding at length that his suit was hopeless, he generously—nay, I must use the word, sire—he generously set my father and myself at liberty.'

"This is true, my gracious liege," said Mr. Beard. "As my daughter hath stated, we were both in his hands for nigh three weeks, and were treated by him with much respect—nay, with kindness."

"I am bound also to add my testimony to that already given, that the man showed me much personal consideration, and detained me not when I surrendered myself to him at Lewes," said Colonel Maunsel.

"Oddsfish!" exclaimed the good-natured monarch, "the knave seems to have some better qualities than might be expected. And so you intercede for him, eh, fair mistress?"

"Earnestly—most earnestly," cried Dulcia.

"And you too, worthy sir?" continued the king, turning to Mr. Beard.

"As earnestly as my child, sire," the good clergyman replied.

"And what says Colonel Maunsel?" cried Charles, looking at the old Cavalier.

"Nay, my liege, I know not what to say," rejoined the colonel, with a look of perplexity. "I do not like to beg the man's life, after what hath happened——"

"Tut! tut!" exclaimed the king. "Whatever faults may be imputed to him, it shall never be said that Charles Stuart was wanting in magnanimity. I forgive the fellow his attempt upon my life. Nay, it is my pleasure that he be set free."

"Set free!" exclaimed Stelfax, in surprise.

"Ay, but not till it can be done with safety," said the king. "Of that Colonel Maunsel will judge."

"Colonel Maunsel will exercise his own discretion in the matter," said Stelfax; "but henceforth your Majesty—for I must needs style you so—will have no enemy in me. My lips shall be sealed to all I have seen and heard this day. I am not a man to make professions, but thus much I will promise Colonel Maunsel in return for his generosity, that he shall not, if I can help it, be called to account for sheltering his proscribed sovereign. To that I plight my word."

"And you will keep your word, I am certain, Captain Stelfax," rejoined the king. "Unbind him," he added to John Habergeon.

But as the old trooper hesitated to obey the king's command, and was on the point of remonstrating with his Majesty on the apparent imprudence of the step, Dulcia, who had already risen, sprang towards the prisoner, and with her own hands undid his bonds.

"We are now quits, Captain Stelfax," she said.

"I owe my life to you, maiden," replied the other, in a voice of deep emotion. "Would it could be devoted to your service!—but I know this cannot be. May you be happy!"

Dulcia did not trust herself to reply, but went hastily back to Clavering, who had looked on in speechless astonishment.

"Take Captain Stelfax below," said Colonel Maunsel to John Habergeon, "and see that he wants nothing. Circumstances, as you will readily apprehend, sir," he added to the Ironside leader, "will not permit me to requite your former civility to myself by allowing you to depart as a prisoner on parole, but your comforts shall be attended to."

"I cannot expect better treatment," replied Stelfax. "The best wish I can offer to your Majesty is that you may soon see the other side of the Channel."

With an obeisance to the king he then retired, John Habergeon and Ninian marching on either side of him.

"There is some good about that rough Republican," observed the king, when he was gone.

"Your Majesty seems to think so," observed Lord Wilmot. "After your magnanimous treatment of him, I do not wonder he was converted, and only marvel he did not swear fidelity on the spot."

"Oddsfish! my lord, you overrate my conduct. I had taken the sting from the hornet, why crush the creature? Besides, I owed the fellow something, for he might have despatched me when I was alone with him in yon hiding-place. But the matter is well over, and without harm to any one except that miserable Independent minister, who seems to have deserved his fate."

"I fear he did, sire," replied Colonel Maunsel. "And since all has ended so fortunately, I will pray your Majesty to adjourn to the banqueting-room, where a trifling collation awaits you. As things have turned out, it is lucky that the chief part of the dishes composing the repast are cold, otherwise the cook's labour might have been thrown away."

"To the banqueting-chamber, then, at once," exclaimed the king, gaily. "'Fore George! colonel, I promise to do justice to your feast, whether the meats be hot or cold. My confinement in yon lurking-hole has given me a wondrous appetite. Your hand, fair mistress."

Blushing with pleasure at the honour conferred upon her, Dulcia gave her hand to his Majesty, who led her down the grand staircase, and through the entrance-hall into the dining-room, where the tables were groaning beneath the weight of a sumptuous repast.

All the guests had very speedily assembled, and a place was assigned to each by Colonel Maunsel—Charles, however, insisting upon Dulcia sitting near him, though he good-naturedly intimated to Clavering that he might occupy the chair on the damsel's other side. The repast was abundant and excellent, and the best wines in the colonel's cellar, as might naturally be expected, were produced on the occasion, old Martin Geere taking care that the glasses were kept constantly filled. The party were still seated at table, though the appetites of most of the guests were satisfied, when Colonel Gunter, and his kinsman, Captain Gunter, were announced, and the two gentlemen entered the room. They had just arrived from Shoreham, and brought the welcome intelligence that Captain Tattersall had got in his cargo, and was quite ready to sail the next morning before daybreak.

"The rascal, however, still sticks to his terms," said Colonel Gunter, "and insists upon seeing his passengers before he will agree to take them. But it is only a whim, I am certain. There will be no real difficulty with him."

"But why did you not bring him here?" cried the king.

"For the best of all reasons, my liege," replied Gunter; "because he would not come. But he has appointed to meet you this evening at the George at Brightelmstone; and though I am very reluctant to disturb your enjoyment, and withdraw you from further participation of Colonel Maunsel's hospitality, yet I think it will be best and wisest to repair to Brightelmstone without delay."

"You summon me from a most delightful entertainment," said the king. "However, sit down for a moment, man, and do you also take a chair, Captain Gunter. Let all glasses be charged—my own, you see, is full to the brim. I will not depart without drinking the health of our host, and I hope it may not be long ere I shall visit him again—though in other sort than the present—at Ovingdean Grange."

The old Cavalier was quite overwhelmed by the gracious words of his royal master, and vainly endeavoured to express his deep sense of gratitude. Charles, however, took him kindly by the hand, and said,

"Not another word, colonel—not another word. I know what you would say. Do not forget your promise to me to make these two young people happy. Take my word for it, your son could not have made a better choice. I must now bid you adieu! Brief as my visit has been, it has comprehended incident enough to serve me for a much longer interval, and I might have remained a week in some other places and not have had half so much excitement. My adventures at Ovingdean Grange are a worthy finish to my six weeks' wanderings."

The king then rose, and all the company rose likewise. Finding it was his Majesty's wish to depart immediately, notwithstanding his disappointment at losing his royal guest, and his desire to detain him, Colonel Maunsel did not offer any opposition, but ordered the horses to be brought round without delay. While his injunctions were being fulfilled, the king repaired to the colonel's chamber, and resumed the travelling habiliments which he had temporarily laid aside. Equipped as he had been on his arrival, he then descended to the entrance-hall, where all were assembled to witness his departure, the household crowding round him, and reiterating their expressions of loyalty and devotion as he came down the staircase. Foremost amongst them was Patty Whinchat, who was fortunate enough to obtain a valedictory word and smile from his Majesty. Temperance Stone was also amongst the throng, and from that moment adjured her Republican notions, and became a staunch Royalist. Bowing repeatedly to the assemblage, and addressing a few parting civilities to Dulcia and Mr. Beard, Charles went forth with his host, who would insist upon holding the stirrup for him as he mounted, and who invoked Heaven's blessings on his Majesty's head, as the king bade him a kindly farewell.

Accompanied by an escort, consisting of Clavering Maunsel and Lord Wilmot, Colonel Philips and the two Gunters, and followed by John Habergeon and Ninian Saxby, the king rode slowly up the valley, and then mounted the eminence on the left.

On gaining the brow of the hill, he paused for a moment to take a last look of the old house amidst its trees, and then rode round the sweeping heights of White Hawk Hill in the direction of Brightelmstone.

BOOK IX.

BRIGHTELMSTONE IN 1651.

I.

A GLANCE AT BRIGHTELMSTONE IN THE NINETEENTH CENTURY.

LITTLE did Charles the Second foresee, when halting on the evening in question with his escort on the smooth and pleasant slopes of the hill now laid out as the Queen's Park, that on the site of the obscure fishing-village towards which he gazed, would arise, some two centuries later, one of the fairest and most magnificent cities ever built on the margin of the sea, since the time when Pompeii the Beautiful was destroyed by the fiery ashes of Vesuvius. Little did he think that the bare and solitary cliffs above which he stood would be covered with lines of stately terraces, comprising mansions many of which would rival in size and splendour the most princely habitations of the London of his own day. Little did he think that in that wide hollow, now known as the Steyne, through the midst of which an open brook found its way to the sea, where stunted trees distorted by the gales, and mean scattered habitations surrounded by patches of ill-kept gardens, and tenanted by fishermen and other seafaring folk, could alone be distinguished —little did he think that in this dreary hollow one of the most refined of his successors, and one whose Sybaritic tastes were in many respects akin to his own, would construct a palace of Oriental splendour. Little did he foresee that, in the lapse of time, this remote and almost unknown fishing-village on the Sussex coast should become, by agencies of which he could not dream, and which, if described, he might not have credited, so connected with the great metropolis itself, as to form almost its marine suburb. Little did he foresee these wondrous and inconceivable changes. And if a vision of the Brighton of the Nineteenth Century could have been revealed to him, he might have thought he had been suddenly transported to some other and more favoured portion f the globe. What two centuries more may do for this superb marine city we are not bold enough to speculate. But if the changes should be as great as those which have occurred since Charles the Second gazed upon the little parent village on the evening of the 14th of October, 1651, Brighton will have become a marvellous city indeed.

But since there was no magician in the young king's escort to raise up for him a vision of the future splendid city, nor any astrologer to foretel its grandeur, Charles saw only that which was exhibited to the ordinary eye of humanity. And the picture, it must be owned, was one that did not excite any extraordinary interest in his breast; neither might it merit any special description, except that there may be some persons not indisposed to learn what the Queen of English watering-places was like two centuries ago.

Immediately below the gentle declivity where Charles was stationed, and almost on the spot now occupied by Royal Crescent, stood three windmills, not very far apart from each other. These windmills, with a solitary farm-house and barn, together with a few scattered cottages, were the only buildings discernible on the eastern cliff. The village of Brightelmstone actually stood on the western side of the Steyne, where the older part of the town is still to be found. Here, on a gentle declivity of the hill, on the summit of which stood the ancient church of Saint Nicholas, then far removed from every other habitation, and serving as a landmark to the mariner, was collected together a considerable number of houses, few of them of any size or pretension, and for the most part constructed of glazed bricks mingled with flints, in order to resist the weather, and having shingle roofs.

Like most old Sussex towns—as, for example, Chichester and Lewes—Brightelmstone was so closely and compactly built that it might be described as a great block of houses, intersected by alleys or lanes so extremely narrow as scarcely to allow tw persons meeting in them to pass each other, and known in th dialect of the place as "twittens." But perhaps the most curious feature of the old town, all traces of which have long since been swept away by the encroachments of the sea, was then to be found below the cliff. Here was built a long street of little tenements, stretching from the Steyne for more than a quarter of a mile along the shore in the direction of Hove. These tenements were exclusively inhabited by fishermen and boatmen, a bold and hardy, though somewhat troublesome, race, who claimed to themselves certain privileges and immunities, and were uncommonly tenacious, and, indeed, pugnacious, in the maintenance of their supposed rights. The Brightelmstone fishermen formed a distinct class from the rest of the townsfolk, and were constantly at loggerheads with the latter. On the edge of the cliff, and towering above these humble dwellings, which it threatened to crush by its fall (and such an accident did eventually occur), stood, at the date of our story, an ancient castle, or block-house of stone, constructed by Henry VIII., about the year 1539, for the defence of the coast. The town of Brightelmstone, as we have stated, was chiefly concentrated on the side of the hill, and did not extend beyond West-street, whither we shall presently repair. From this point to the neighbouring village of Hove there only intervened a few cottages and a single farm-house, and these at wide intervals.

Noting much that we have described—namely, the old church, the cluster of houses on the hill-side, and the block-house—Charles suffered his gaze to stray towards Shoreham, where he could just descry the masts of the vessels within the harbour, and wondered whether any that he saw belonged to the *Swiftsure*.

Satisfied with his survey, Charles put his horse in motion, and the whole party rode on, taking their way down the declivity, which is now occupied by a dense mass of habitations, but which was then merely the green slope of a down—its smoothness being nere and there broken by a patch of gorse or a venerable hawthorn. Sheep were fed, and the shepherd trod on the thymy turf then covering the descent where now runs the crowded thoroughfare of Saint James's-street. At the foot of the hill grew a small straggling holt, and the stunted trees composing it looked like well-worn brooms, so distorted were they by the strong south-westerly gales blowing along the valley.

On the verge of this thicket a halt was made, and it was then arranged that the king should proceed, under the guidance of Colonel Gunter only, to the George Inn, in West-street. Lord Wilmot was to join them there after a while; but it was not deemed prudent that the others should appear at the inn—at all events, not until a much later hour. Meanwhile, they undertook to act as scouts about the town, under the direction of Clavering Maunsel.

These arrangements made, the king and Colonel Gunter dismounted, and leaving their steeds with the others, crossed a bridge over the little brook running through the valley, and immediately afterwards entered the town. Their object being to elude observation, they walked quickly, Colonel Gunter, as acquainted with the place, keeping slightly ahead of the monarch. After proceeding to a short distance up North-street, they plunged into a narrow alley on the left, and having tracked a series of " twittens," without encountering any material check in their progress, except such as was offered by a fat fishwoman, who compelled them both to seek temporary refuge in an open doorway while she passed by, they issued forth in West-street—if street a few scattered houses ought to be called—at the lower end of which, within a hundred yards of the sea, stood the hostel of which they were in search.

II.

THE GEORGE AT BRIGHTELMSTONE.

THE George Inn, which still exists, though, since the event we are about to relate it has very properly altered its designation, and is now known as the King's Head, was a comfortable house, noted for good liquor and for the civility of the host, whose name was of good augury to the guest, being no other than Bonfellow Smith.

The hostel, which stood on the west side of the straggling street, was detached from the adjacent habitations, and was further separated from the dwelling on its northerly side by a large yard. It was a commodious, well-built structure, with bay-windows, projecting porch with carved posts and lintel, gable roof covered with shingle, and large chimneys of the true Sussex build, and wore altogether a not uninviting aspect. Such, at least, was the impression produced upon Charles as he followed his conductor into the house.

Master Bonfellow Smith, host of the George, had nothing of the Puritan in his appearance or deportment. He was all smiles and civility—indeed, his manner might almost be termed obsequious—while it was abundantly manifest from his rotund person, rosy gills, and double chin, that he was by no means accustomed to mortify the flesh. Originally, he had filled the office of groom of the chamber in the royal establishment at Whitehall, and was

then a great man—a very great man. But times had changed
Rebellion and revolution were in the ascendant; the royal household was broken up and dispersed; and our groom of the chamber
retired in disgust to his native village of Brightelmstone, and
eventually became landlord of the comfortable hostel where we find
him. Master Bonfellow Smith was lucky enough to possess a wife
who proved of infinite use to him in his business. Like her husband,
she had filled a subordinate situation in the royal household at
Whitehall, having been tire-maiden to one of the queen's gentle-
women, and, like him, she could not forget her former importance;
but being a person of great prudence, she accommodated herself
to existing circumstances, and did not allow her recollections of
bygone grandeur to interfere with the discharge of her duties
as a landlady. Mrs. Smith was some years younger than her
spouse; and had been accounted very pretty by pages and other
gallants at Whitehall. She was still a comely woman, though on
rather a large scale. It was by this worthy couple that Charles
was welcomed on entering the inn.

Bowing obsequiously to his guests, on hearing that they meant
to take supper, and expected two or three friends to join them at
it, the host directed his wife to bring lights—it was now growing
rapidly dusk—and ushered the gentlemen into a roomy chamber on
the right, which looked very snug and comfortable, inasmuch as a
cheerful fire was burning on the hearth. The apartment was
wainscoted with black oak, and well provided with elbow-chairs of
the same material. A solid oak table stood in the centre of the
floor, and a bow-window at the side looked into the inn yard.

Buxom Mrs. Smith followed close upon the king's heels with
the lights, and was about to set them down upon the table, when
Charles turned and looked her full in the face. Her features
seemed familiar to him, though he could not call to mind under
what circumstances he had previously beheld them. But if the
king's memory was at fault, Mrs. Smith's was not. She instantly
recognised the young monarch in his disguise, uttered a faint
scream, and began to gasp and shake so violently that the candles
threatened to fall from her hold.

" 'Oons! Joan—what the plague ails the woman?" exclaimed Bonfellow Smith, staring at her in surprise. " What's the matter, I say?"

" I do—o—on't know—I ca—a—n't speak," she stammered, as Charles signed to her to keep silence.

" Don't know—and can't speak!" echoed Smith. " 'Sbud! this is something new. You can use your tongue pretty freely in an ordinary way. Set down the candles and leave the room."

" Allow me to help you, my good mistress," said the king, taking the candles from her, and placing them on the table.

" I beg your honour's pardon," exclaimed Smith, in an apologetic tone. " I can't think what has come to my wife. I never saw her in such a way before. Don't stand staring there, Joan, I tell 'ee."

" Never mind your wife, my good man," said Charles. " She'll be all right presently. Draw the window-curtain, for we don't care to be overlooked—and then we'll talk about supper. Compose yourself, if possible, my good Joan," he added, in a whisper, " or you will rouse your husband's suspicions."

" Oh! your Majesty needn't fear him," she rejoined, in the same tone. " You haven't a more loyal subject than Smith. He would lay down his life for you. Here, hubby! hubby!" she cried aloud, " come this way! Look at this gentleman, and you'll no longer wonder at my excitement. Don't you know him?" she added, seizing his hand.

" Know him! Gadzooks! I should think I did!" exclaimed Smith, now almost as much excited as his wife. " I should know that face amid a thousand. Oh dear! oh dear! that the like of this should ever have come to pass!"

" Down on your knees, hubby—down on your knees!" cried Mrs. Smith. " Render your homage to his Majesty—swear fidelity to him!"

" I swear to be faithful, my gracious liege," cried Bonfellow Smith, as he and his wife prostrated themselves before Charles. " Command me as you please!—take all I possess—my house, my goods, my chattels, my wife—everything."

"Nay, I won't rob you of your wife, my good fellow," replied
Charles, laughing. "I accept your assurances of fidelity, satisfied
that I may rely upon them, and hoping most sincerely that they
may not be put to the test during my brief stay under your roof.
Accident, or rather, I ought to say, a kind Providence, has again
thrown me amongst friends, who will, I am firmly persuaded, watch
over my security. To show the entire confidence I repose in you
both, I will unhesitatingly inform you that, early to-morrow morning, I am about to embark at Shoreham for France, and I will tarry
with you till the latest moment. The captain of the vessel will be
here presently, and I expect some other friends. You must give us
a good supper—look well after me—take care there are no unlicensed intruders—you understand?—and some day I will requite
your devotion."

"All shall be done as your Majesty desires," said Smith.

"And I'll see to the supper, your Majesty," added Mrs. Smith.

"Enough, my good friends," rejoined Charles. "Rise both of you.
As to you, Joan," he continued, drawing her towards him, "your
husband will not be jealous, I am sure, if I venture to press those
tempting lips."

"Oh! take as many kisses as you please, sire! Your Majesty is
heartily welcome!" cried Smith.

"It is not the first 'time I have kissed your dame, my good host,"
said Charles, laughing.

"Not the first time by a score, an please your Majesty!" replied
the hostess, dropping a grateful curtsey. "I have often told Smith
how the merry young prince used to chase me along the corridor.
Ah! those were happy times!"

"Nouns! wife, the good times will come back, thou mayst rest
assured," cried Smith. "The king will enjoy his own again, and
then, 'sbodikins! I shall be a lord, and thou wilt be a lady, Joan!
thou wilt be a lady! Which nobody can deny! which nobody can
deny!" And he sang and capered about the room in so droll
a manner, that both Charles and Colonel Gunter were ready to die
with laughing.

"It's now my turn to call you to your senses, hubby," cried Mrs.

Smith, forcibly restraining him. "Don't you hear some one calling you outside?"

"Gadzooks! so I do," rejoined Smith, pausing. "Coming, sir—coming! You'll be a lady, my duck. Which nobody can deny!"

"It is the voice of a friend," replied Charles. "You may admit him."

"Will it please you to step in here, sir?" cried Smith. "Nouns! wife, if it isn't Lord Wilmot!" he added, as his lordship entered the room. "Only to think that the George should be thus honoured! Henceforth the house shall be called the King's Head."

"Better wait till the king is safe upon the throne," replied his prudent spouse, in a whisper. "It won't do to offend the round-headed Commonwealth knaves."

"You are right, my dear—you are always right. Which nobody can deny!" he replied, in the same tone.

"You will rejoice to find, my lord, that I have again fallen amongst friends," said Charles to Lord Wilmot. "These good folks are old acquaintances, and belonged to the king my father's household at Whitehall."

"I congratulate you on your good fortune, my liege," replied his lordship. "Nay, I think I remember them. That should be Bonfellow Smith, and, unless I am greatly mistaken, this must be pretty Joan Awbray, my lady's own tirewoman."

"Your lordship is right in both instances," said the host. "But the somewhile Joan Awbray is now Mrs. Bonfellow Smith, at your lordship's service."

After his lordship had passed a few compliments upon Mrs. Smith's improved appearance, and expressed his satisfaction at seeing her husband again, Charles gave the worthy couple a good-natured hint to withdraw, and they both left the room, re-newing their protestations of devotion, and promising that all needful precautions should be taken for his Majesty's security.

They had not been gone more than five minutes when heavy footsteps were heard outside, and a hoarse voice was heard inquiring if Master William Jackson was in the house.

"There he is! that's Captain Tattersall," cried Colonel Gunter, flying to the door. "This way, captain," he added. "Here we are! here's Mr. Jackson."

On this summons Tattersall entered the room. His apparel was pretty nearly the same as that in which he appeared on a former occasion, except that he now wore a pair of heavy boots. He brought with him a great bundle of seamen's attire, of which the host, who had followed him into the room, hastened to relieve him.

"Ay, ay, put those traps down, mine host," cried the skipper; "or, harkye, you had best convey them to some chamber above stairs. Mayhap they'll be wanted by-and-by. Good e'en to you, gentlemen—good e'en to you," he added, bowing to the company. While doing so, he fixed a scrutinising look upon the two strangers, and appeared particularly struck by the king's appearance.

"Glad to see you, Captain Tattersall," cried Colonel Gunter, clapping him on the shoulder. "You are as punctual as the clock. This is my friend, Mr. Barlow, captain," indicating Lord Wilmot, "and this is Mr. William Jackson," he added, pointing to the king.

"Barlow and Jackson, eh!" exclaimed the skipper, placing his finger on the side of his nose. "Two very good travelling names, though Smith might be better."

"My name is Smith, I beg to observe, Captain Tattersall," remarked the host—"Bonfellow Smith. Which nobody *can* deny!"

"True, I had forgotten that," replied Tattersall, laughing.

"Bring pipes, Spanish tobacco, ale and brandy—Nantz, d'ye mark, host," cried Colonel Gunter.

"Your honour shall be served in a trice," replied Smith, disappearing.

"Pray be seated, Captain Tattersall—pray be seated," said Charles. "There will be no difficulty about our passage, I suppose, captain? You are very particular, I hear. But I hope our looks satisfy you."

"Your looks are very much in your favour with me, Mr. Jackson," the skipper replied, significantly, "though they mightn't please every other shipmaster equally well. But I think I have seen you before, sir."

"Indeed!" exclaimed the king. "Where, and when, captain? I don't recollect the occasion."

"Possibly not, sir," returned the skipper. "But I have good reason to remember it. It was in the year 1648—three years ago, Heaven save the mark—that the royal fleet, under the command of his Royal Highness Prince Charles, suddenly appeared off this coast, and captured several sloops, fishing-vessels, and other craft—my brig, the *Swiftsure*, being amongst the number."

"And you were made prisoner?" cried the king.

"I was made prisoner," replied the skipper, "and with several of my fellow shipmasters was brought before the young prince. And what do you think his Royal Highness did?"

"Nay, I can't tell," replied the king. "Treated you like rebels, it may be?—ordered you all to be handcuffed and placed below the hatches?"

"Nothing of the sort," rejoined Tattersall. "The only punishment he inflicted upon us was to make each of us toss off a glass of brandy to his royal father's health, and then—bless his noble heart!—he set us all free."

"Oddsfish! that's rather like him, I must say," observed Charles. "He has been doing foolish things all his life—eh, Barlow?"

"Perfectly true, Mr. Jackson," replied the other.

"But I don't look upon this as a foolish thing," said Tattersall. "Leastways, his clemency wasn't thrown away upon me, for I vowed then, that if ever opportunity offered, I'd show my gratitude, and I'll be as good as my word."

"Delighted to hear you say so, Captain Tattersall," observed the king. "The feeling is very creditable to you. But I don't see how I am connected with the circumstance you have related."

"We are friends of Cæsar, I believe?" said Tattersall.

"All friends of Cæsar, captain," replied the host, bringing in a bottle of brandy and glasses, while his wife followed with pipes and tobacco. "Mrs. Bonfellow Smith is Cæsar's particular friend. Which nobody can deny!"

"He always was fond of the lasses," said Tattersall, laughing. "Give me a glass of brandy, sirrah host. As I told you just now, I drank to the late king's health by command of the noble prince, his son."

"But that was upon compulsion," observed Charles, "and must have gone against the grain."

"It went no more against the grain than the pledge I am about to drink now," rejoined the skipper. "Here's to the noble young prince who gave me freedom, and by the act bound me to him by ties of everlasting gratitude! Here's to him who ought to wear the crown of England, only rogues have dispossessed him of it. Here's to my royal master—for I acknowledge no other, except the Master above!—and may he soon be out of the reach of his enemies, and it shan't be Nick Tattersall's fault if he be not so." So saying, he drained the glass to the last drop.

"Oddsfish! Tattersall," cried the king, "you were represented to me as a half-Republican, but I find you a thorough-going Royalist."

"Whatever flag I may be obliged to hoist, my true colours are the king's colours, and those I wear next my heart," replied Tattersall. "And now to cut matters short, since all's settled, I'll make bold to tell your Majesty what I think had best be done. You may have noticed that I brought a bundle of seamen's clothes with me. Let me recommend your Majesty, and your fellow-passenger that is to be, to rig yourselves out in the gear. You will find a suit apiece, so that in case of any unexpected hindrance —as you have no passes, and might be stopped—you can go on board as part of my crew. The brig will slip her moorings, and get out of the harbour two hours after midnight, and will lie off shore in waiting for us. I've got a boat to take us to her. I don't anticipate any difficulty, but it's best to be on the safe side."

"I quite agree with you, Tattersall," replied Charles. "You have shown great forethought. I ought to have introduced Lord Wilmot to you. (Tattersall bowed.) His lordship and I will at once proceed to change our attire. Colonel Gunter will attend to your wants in the interim, and ere you have smoked your first pipe we will be back with you, fully equipped in the habiliments you have so thoughtfully provided for us."

So saying, his Majesty and Lord Wilmot quitted the room, preceded by the hostess, bearing a light.

III.

"AND now, Captain Tattersall," said Gunter, as soon as they were alone, "we'll settle our accounts, if you please. Here's the other half of the passage-money—fifty caroluses."

"Well, a bargain's a bargain, colonel," replied the skipper, bestowing the bag of gold in his jacket; "but if you had only spoken plainly at first, and told me who wanted a passage with me, I would have placed my vessel at his Majesty's disposal."

"You can't blame me for acting cautiously in a case of such importance, captain," Gunter replied. "And pardon me for saying that I didn't know you so well as I do now. Besides, you richly deserve all you've got, and more, and I trust this matter will be the making of you."

"I hope to Heaven it may, colonel!" replied Tattersall. "How-somever, as I said before, if I save his Majesty it'll be reward enough for me. I'll have it written on my tombstone. 'Here lies Nick Tattersall, who faithfully preserved his king.' Moreover, if I accomplish this voyage securely, I'll change the name of my ship, and call her the *Royal Escape.*"

"An excellent name," said Gunter, filling a pipe with tobacco and lighting it, while the skipper followed his example: "and I hope your brig will earn a title to it. The wind is favourable, eh?"

"Ay, the wind is nor'-east, and if it holds where it is—and I feel pretty sure it will—we shall have a quick run across to Fécamp, near Havre-de-Grace, in Normandy, for that's the port I mean to make for."

"Fécamp, eh? I fancied you would have tried for Dieppe. But the port matters not, provided you land his Majesty safely in France—that's the main point. I hope you won't fall in with any cruisers."

"I hope we shan't," rejoined the skipper, puffing away at his pipe, "but I ain't much afeard of 'em. The *Swiftsure* 'll show 'em a light pair of heels; and if they do overhaul us, they'll take the king and his lordship for part o' the crew. What I should least like to meet would be one of them rattlin' Ostend privateers, which, ever since the war broke out betwixt France and Spain, have been hoverin' about the French coast, on the look-out for prizes. I shouldn't like to meet one o' them ugly customers, for they might plunder us, and set us ashore in England."

"'Sdeath! that would be a mishap indeed!" exclaimed Gunter. "But let us hope for the best. Heaven, that has preserved the king through so many dangers, won't desert him at the last. But what's that?" he added, as exclamations and laughter, proceeding from the hostess, were heard outside.

"I shouldn't wonder if two of my crew have arrived, colonel," replied Tattersall, with a wink. "I've been expectin' 'em. Ay, here they come!" he cried, as the door was thrown open by the hostess, who was laughing immoderately, and two rollicking individuals, with the gait, gestures, looks, and attire of seamen of the period—that is to say, blue jackets and brown slops, Guernsey shirts and red caps, like the skipper himself—rolled, rather than walked, into the room.

"Why, they're enough to deceive a body to one's very face!" exclaimed Mrs. Smith, holding up her hands in admiration. "If I didn't know better, I should take 'em for real sailors."

"Real sailors!" cried Charles, chucking her under the chin; 'so we be, my pretty hostess—reg'lar jack-tars, I can promise ye. I say, capt'n, put in a word for us, will ye? How long have my messmate Tom Barlow and I sailed wi' ye i' the *Swiftsure?*"

"Ever since 1648, Will Jackson," replied Tattersall, emitting a long puff of tobacco. "But sit down, my lads—sit down. Take a glass of grog, and smoke a pipe. Don't mind me—I'm not partic'lar when ashore. This gentleman, I dare say, won't mind ye."

"Not in the least," replied Gunter. "Sit down, my lads, I beg of you. These are two stout fellows, capt'n, especially Tom Barlow."

"Ay, he's big enough in all conscience," said Tattersall, remarking that Lord Wilmot's breadth of shoulder and athletic proportions seemed materially increased by his change of costume; "but they're both able-bodied rascals. Harkye, hostess, give 'em each a glass of brandy, and fill a pipe for Will Jackson with this prime Spanish tobacco. He's too bashful to help himself."

"Shiver my timbers, but she shall do nothing of the sort!" cried the king. "She shan't turn her pretty fingers into tobacco-stoppers. A hand like this was never made for such work." And he pressed it gallantly to his lips.

"'Oons, Will, I was wrong, it seems, in callin' thee bashful," observed Tattersall, laughing. "Thou seem'st free and easy enough now, I must say."

"Well, I declare if it ben't just like a play!" exclaimed Mrs. Smith, delighted.

"I hope our comedy mayn't take a serious turn!" exclaimed Colonel Gunter, uneasily. "What's that?" he added, as the tramping of horses, accompanied by the clattering of arms, was heard in the inn-yard. Cautiously lifting the edge of the curtain, he peeped forth, and immediately afterwards cried out in alarm, "The Ironsides are upon us! Half a dozen or more of them are in the yard —and some are dismounting. We shall have them here in a moment."

"Lord preserve us! What'll become of the king?" cried the hostess, almost sinking with fright.

"Peace, Joan!" said Charles. "My safety will depend a good deal upon your composure."

All had started to their feet except the young monarch, who completely maintained his self-possession.

"Sit down all of you," he said. "Do you, Wilmot, feign to

be drunk—sleepily drunk, d'ye understand? Gunter, you must play the Puritan—you can act the part to the life, if you choose. I shall be as drunk as Wilmot—but wide awake."

At this moment Bonfellow Smith rushed into the room exclaiming, distractedly,

" The troopers are here! the troopers are here! What's to be done?"

" Be quiet!" rejoined his wife. " Go and see what they are about! We are all prepared for them."

Overcoming his fright as well as he could, Smith left the room, and presently after ominous sounds were heard without, announcing that sentinels were being posted at the doors of the hostel with orders to shoot any one who might attempt to escape. A stern voice was then heard in the passage, holding a brief colloquy with the host, after which the door was thrown open, and a sergeant of Ironsides, in full accoutrements, with pistols in belt and drawn sword in hand, strode into the room, followed by three others, armed with carabines. Poor Bonfellow Smith did not venture further than the doorway, where he stood a terrified spectator of the scene, his naturally rosy countenance having become as white as his own apron.

Meanwhile, a great change had taken place in the appearance of three of the personages at the table. Lord Wilmot appeared to be fast asleep, with his head upon the board, and Charles, to judge from his looks, was completely overcome by liquor. Never was the appearance of a drunken man better simulated than by the king—head hanging down—eyes half shut, and stupid in expression—limbs wholly unequal to their office, since their owner could apparently neither rise from his chair nor guide the pipe to his lips. Colonel Gunter had put on a black skull-cap and spectacles, and smoothed down his bands. By elongating his features, he managed to give them a decidedly Puritanical expression.

Delves (for he was the sergeant of Ironsides in question) marched towards the group at the table. Colonel Gunter and Tattersall rose at his approach, but the other two remained as we have described them, except that Charles apparently made an effort to get up, and failing totally, seemed to maintain his balance in the chair with difficulty. Delves, though regarding him at first with suspicion, could evidently make nothing of him, but turning his attention to Lord Wilmot, seized him by the shoulder, and shook him lustily. Thus roused, his lordship looked up for a moment with the vacant stare of an intoxicated man, and then laid his head down again.

"Who are these drunken fellows?" demanded Delves of Tattersall.

"Two of my crew," replied the skipper, "and both, I am sorry to say, the worse for liquor, as you can scarce fail to perceive."

"It is only too apparent," replied the sergeant, with a look of infinite disgust. "How art thou named, friend?" he added to the skipper. "Thy calling I can pretty well guess at."

"I have no reason to be ashamed either of my name or calling," replied Tattersall, bluffly. "I am Nicholas Tattersall, captain of the *Swiftsure*, now lying in Shoreham harbour. My papers are all regular, if you desire to look at them," he added, producing a packet from his breast.

"No, I care not to see them," replied Delves. "I am satisfied with what you tell me. But mark me, Nicholas Tattersall. Certain intelligence has reached me that the Young Man Charles Stuart is in this neighbourhood, and is seeking to obtain passage in some vessel across the Channel. Take heed thou aidest him not, or thou wilt be hanged as a traitor."

"Hanged, quotha!—hang our captain!" hiccupped Charles. "Not while Will Jackson can lift an arm (hiccup). If any man touches our capt'n (hiccup), I'll smash him like this pipe," breaking the pipe to pieces upon the table.

"You ought to put these two drunkards in irons, and give them a round dozen apiece in the morning," said Delves, angrily.

"I must take a lesson from your service," rejoined Tattersall. "You are strict enough, I make no doubt. Yet methinks I have heard of some delinquencies on the part of the troopers at Ovingdean Grange."

"That will never occur again," said Delves, somewhat abashed. "But there is one person here whom I have not yet questioned.

Thy name and station?" he added to Colonel Gunter. "Take care thou dost not equivocate."

"I had best not equivocate with you, sergeant, that I can see plainly enough," replied Gunter. "My name is Seek-the-Fold Stray-Not Lamb—Four-Year-Old South-Down Mutton, the profane are wont to call me in derision. I am a Muggletonian, and hold forth at the conventicle in Ship-street. If thou doubtest me, sergeant, appeal to the host."

"Thou art mocking me, I suspect, friend," said Delves, sternly.

"He hath spoken falsely, sergeant," said Nathan Guestling, who was one of the troopers standing behind. "He hath already been a prisoner in our hands. It is the man whom our captain chased across the downs on that unlucky night, and brought back a prisoner to Ovingdean. Pluck the spectacles from off his nose, and the cap from off his head, and thou wilt instantly recognise him. I knew him at once."

"Thou art right, Nathan!—it is he!" exclaimed Delves. "I am glad we shall not go away empty-handed. Thou art my prisoner," he added to Colonel Gunter; "come forth, or my men will fire upon thee."

"Nay, I will come peaceably," replied Gunter, stepping forward.

Nathan Guestling and Besadaiah (for the latter also was present) placed themselves one on either side of the prisoner, and in this manner he was led out of the room. But just as he was going forth he whispered to the landlord that he felt certain of a rescue, and would be back again ere long. Shortly afterwards, a trampling in the inn-yard announced the departure of the troopers, and the host came in to say they were gone—though the satisfactory intelligence was somewhat damped by the thought that Colonel Gunter had been carried off a captive.

IV.

CONTAINING PARTICULARS OF THE CONFLICT ON KINGSTON HILL, AND OF
THE EMBARKATION AT SHOREHAM.

CHARLES would have been greatly troubled by the loss of his
faithful adherent, had he not felt almost certain that Gunter would
be rescued by Clavering and the other Royalists hovering about the
town, and that he should see him again before he started for
Shoreham. Lord Wilmot was also of the same opinion. Whatever
Tattersall might secretly think of the chances in the colonel's
favour, he kept his sentiments to himself, and continued to puff
away at his pipe; but the host and hostess were loud in their expressions of delight at his Majesty's providential escape.

"I owe my safety entirely to Captain Tattersall," observed
Charles. "Had he not brought these disguises with him, Lord
Wilmot and I should have been infallibly detected."

"It was lucky I thought of them," replied Tattersall, quietly.

Shortly after this, a very nice little supper was placed on the
table by the hostess, to which both the monarch and his companions
did ample justice. A glass or two of choice canary, poured out
for him by Mrs. Smith, quickly dispelled the king's gloom, and
before the repast was over he had regained his customary spirits,
and was laughing and talking as merrily as ever. As soon as the
table was cleared, pipes and tobacco were again introduced. A jug
of cold water and a bottle of right Nantz were placed near Captain

Tattersall, but Charles and Lord Wilmot confined their potations to canary. As it was now getting late, and all the other guests in the house had long since left, the inn doors were locked, and the servants, who were no longer required, were sent to bed. By his Majesty's special invitation, the host and hostess joined the party in the parlour, and it was ever afterwards a subject of infinite gratulation to them that they had been allowed to sit down in his Majesty's presence. Captain Tattersall, who was of a jovial turn, did his best to amuse the company—sang nautical ballads, and related droll incidents in his own career, at which the king laughed heartily.

In this way time passed quickly away. It had now struck one o'clock. Nothing had been heard of Clavering Maunsel and his party, and Charles almost began to despair of seeing Colonel Gunter again.

"In another hour your Majesty will be thinking of starting, I presume?" observed Tattersall.

"True," replied Charles, looking at the clock; "I did not think it was so late. But I hope our friends will be here before then."

"They are here now, or I am much mistaken," cried Lord Wilmot, starting up, as the sound of horses' feet was heard in the inn-yard.

"Look out, and make sure that the Ironsides have not returned," said Charles.

His lordship obeyed, and after cautiously peering through the window-curtain, declared it was Clavering Maunsel and the others. "And I am almost certain Gunter is with them," added his lordship.

"Now Heaven be thanked!" exclaimed Charles. "That is good news indeed!"

At this moment, a cautious knocking was heard at the yard door.

"Admit them straight, my good host," cried the king. And Smith flew to execute his Majesty's commands.

Immediately afterwards quick footsteps were heard in the passage, and Colonel Gunter and Clavering entered the room. They were

followed in another moment by Colonel Philips and Captain Gunter,
and three other persons, who remained in the background.

"I am as good as my word, you see, my gracious liege," said
Colonel Gunter. "I promised to be back before your Majesty
left, and here I am."

"And delighted I am to see you again," replied the king. "But
how did you manage to escape from those rascally Ironsides?"

"My friends rescued me, as I felt sure they would," rejoined
Gunter, pointing to Clavering and the others; "but they had hard
work to do it."

"So it would seem," replied Charles, noticing that the young
man and those near him bore marks of a recent and severe conflict. "Tell me how it chanced?"

"Your Majesty has some enemies the less," replied Clavering.
"But you have lost one faithful subject," he added, gravely.

"How?" exclaimed Charles, glancing at the group in the background. "I discover not stout John Habergeou. Is he gone?"

"Ay, my liege," Clavering replied. "He died like a brave and
loyal man, sword in hand, smiting the enemies of his king. Thus
it fell out: I and those with me were aware of the visit of the
Ironsides to this inn, for we were scouting about the town;
but we did not think it prudent to attack them, lest the townsfolk
should come to their aid. Ensconced where we could observe
them, we saw them issue forth with a single prisoner—your
Majesty we feared it might be. But be it whom it might, we
resolved upon a rescue. I ought to mention, that we had been
joined by three recruits, two of whom are here present, and who
rendered us good service. The Ironsides left Brightelmstone,
and rode across the downs in the direction of Lewes. We followed, but did not come up with them until they reached Kingston Hill. We then shouted loudly to them to stop, and they drew
up and awaited our approach. Sword in hand we charged them
—your name, my liege, forming our battle-cry. So furious was
our assault that it proved irresistible. The shock scattered them,
and a hand-to-hand conflict ensued—such a conflict as, since the
days of the old Romans, I verily believe that hill hath never seen.

The turf is reddened with the blood of your enemies, sire. We were triumphant. Half a dozen Ironsides now lie stark upon Kingston Hill. Amongst them, alas! is John Habergeon. But he sold his life dearly. Three of our foemen—their sergeant Delves being among the number—fell by his hand. Give me a glass of wine, my good hostess. I am somewhat faint."

"That task be mine," cried Charles, filling a glass for him. "You have gained a glorious victory, but I would it had not been purchased by the death of John Habergeon."

"He died as he would have wished to die—with your Majesty's name upon his lips," rejoined Clavering.

Charles was silent for a moment, and then said: "A brave fellow is gone, but he has left good men behind him. I am glad to see that Ninian Saxby has escaped unhurt——"

"Not altogether unhurt, an please your Majesty," replied Ninian, stepping forward. "I have received a few sharp cuts, but nothing to signify. I gave the Roundheaded rogues as good as they brought, —and better!"

"I doubt it not," said Charles, smiling. "Thou art a brave lad. But what do I see? Surely these are the gentlemen whom I met at Steyning?"

"Your Majesty is in the right," replied Goldspur, coming forward and making an obeisance. "I and my friend Jervoise Rumboldsdyke have been anxious to approve our loyalty, and at length we have found occasion for doing so. Mr. Clavering Maunsel will declare whether we have comported ourselves well or not."

"Both gentlemen behaved with great bravery, sire," said Clavering.

"I am glad to hear it," said the king. "I only wish I could reward you according to your deserts. But my exchequer is pretty much in the same state as your own."

"Our exchequer is better furnished than your Majesty supposes," rejoined Goldspur; "that is, it will be so to-morrow," he added, correcting himself. "A rascally porter, named Skrow Antram, who served old Zachary Trangmar, the rich usurer of Lewes, joined us this evening, and was shot in the fight on Kingston Hill. With his dying breath he confessed to me and my friend

Rumboldsdyke that he had robbed the old usurer his master, and told us where he had hidden the gold. To-morrow we shall visit old Zachary, and make a bargain with him for the discovery of the treasure. The old usurer must come down handsomely, for his porter had purloined a good round sum."

"Well resolved," replied Charles. "I am sure you will not make yourselves accomplices of the rogue Antram, and sully your honour as Cavaliers by appropriating the treasure. And now, Captain Tattersall, there is no need to tarry longer here. Let us to Shoreham. These gentlemen will go with us, and constitute my escort."

"I am at your Majesty's disposal," replied the skipper.

"Farewell, then, my worthy host and hostess," said Charles. "Rest assured I shall often think of the eventful night I have spent at the George at Brightelmstone."

"I shall venture to remind your Majesty of it one of these days," said Smith.

"You shall not need, my good fellow; nor you, my buxom Joan. Harkye, gentlemen, he amongst you who has the stoutest horse must give Captain Tattersall a seat behind him."

"Then I will take him," said Colonel Philips, "for I am well mounted."

"Give me thy purse, Wilmot," said the king. And on receiving it, he took forth five gold pieces, and placed them in the hostess's hands. "There is for the reckoning, bonny Joan. One kiss at parting, and then adieu!"

Charles then left the room, and was attended to the yard by both host and hostess, neither of whom would leave him till he took his departure. Honest Smith prayed that every blessing might attend his Majesty, coupled with a hope that the George might speedily be again honoured by his presence. Mrs. Smith's sobs prevented her from saying anything. At length all the party were mounted, Captain Tattersall being accommodated with a seat behind Colonel Philips. The king then gave the word to start, and bade adieu to the host and hostess, giving his hand to the latter, who bathed it with her tears, while pressing it to her lips.

The cavalcade being then put in motion, took the road along the coast through Hove. It was a fine, clear, starlight night, with the wind blowing freshly from the north-east. In little more than half an hour the troop approached Shoreham, no mis-adventure or hindrance of any kind having occurred to them. Captain Tattersall now directed the king's attention to a vessel which could just be distinguished lying out at sea, at about a quarter of a mile's distance, and informed him it was the *Swift-sure*.

A halt was then called. Charles dismounted, and bade adieu to his followers, thanking them all warmly for their services, and saying something kindly to each. His last words were reserved for Clavering Maunsel. Bidding the young man remember him to his father, he added, "And fail not to commend me to good Mr. Beard and fair Mistress Dulcia. Ere long, I hope to hear of your union with the object of your wishes."

By this time Lord Wilmot and Captain Tattersall had dis-mounted. The skipper then walked on in advance, leaving the king and his lordship to follow. After crossing a heavy bank of shingle, they reached the edge of a little creek divided by an outer bank from the sea. Tattersall then gave a low whistle, in reply to which the sound of oars was heard, and a boat was seen advancing from under the shade of the opposite bank. This boat, which was manned by a couple of stout-looking seamen, soon touched the strand. The king and Lord Wilmot leaped into it, and were quickly followed by Tattersall, who seated himself in the stern. The men then plying their oars briskly, the boat was soon out of the creek, and cleaving its way through the sea.

In ten minutes more they were beside the *Swiftsure*. Charles sprang up the vessel's side as actively as any seaman could have per-formed the feat, and was followed by the two others, while the boat pulled off again to shore. The king then looked towards the group of horsemen, whom he could dimly discern on the beach, and a joyful shout reached his ears.

The brig then stood out to sea, and Charles was safely landed on the morning of the following day at Fecamp.

L'Envoy.

THE king's recommendation was not neglected. Ere the year was out, Clavering was made happy with the hand of the fair Dulcia, and had no reason to repent his choice.

Charles, we need scarcely say, had to wait nine years for the Restoration, and long before that auspicious event, Colonel Maunsel was gathered to his fathers. But good Mr. Beard lived to be reinstated in his living, and again officiated in the little village church. He took for the text of the first sermon preached by him on resuming his duties, these verses from the 129th Psalm: "*The plowers plowed upon my back; they made long their furrows.— The Lord is righteous: he hath cut asunder the cords of the wicked.*"

Clavering and Dulcia continued to reside at Ovingdean Grange to the close of their days, which extended in both instances into another century. Though the Maunsel family is now extinct in the direct line, worthy representatives are left—both at Rottingdean and Lewes—of the good old stock of the BEARDS. And we may add, that the old house at Ovingdean still belongs to a branch of the same family.

Stelfax, at that time a colonel in the Guards, and in high favour with Monk, formed part of the royal escort from Blackheath, on the glorious 29th of May, 1660, when the king made his triumphal entry into London. Charles particularly distinguished him, and good-humouredly observed, "Have you forgotten the half-hour we spent together in the hiding-place at Ovingdean, colonel?"

"I have forgotten all, except your Majesty's generosity," replied Stelfax, bending to the saddle-bow. He was already, we may perceive, a courtier.

Ninian Saxby became the fortunate possessor of Patty Whinchat, and was blessed with a numerous progeny. After his father's death he filled the post of ostreger to Clavering, who grew passionately fond of all country sports. Some of Ninian's descendants, we believe, may be found in the neighbourhood of Ovingdean to this day.

The body of stout old John Habergeon was removed from Kingston Hill, and buried in the village churchyard. Peace be with him!

Captain Tattersall received a considerable sum for his services. Moreover, a pension of a hundred a year was settled upon him and his descendants; and he was likewise presented with a handsome ring by the grateful monarch. Would you know more of the worthy skipper's virtues, go seek his monument in the old parish churchyard at Brighton! There you may read the following epitaph:

> Within this marble monument doth lie
> Approved faith, honour, and loyalty.
> In this cold clay he now has ta'en his station,
> That once preserved the church, the crown, and nation.
> When Charles the great was nothing but a breath,
> This valiant soul stept between him and death.
> Usurpers' threats and tyrant rebels' frown
> Could not affright his virtue to the Crown;
> Which glorious act of his for church and state
> Eight princes in one day did gratulate;
> Professing all to him in debt to be,
> As all the world are to his memory.

Bonfellow Smith had gone the way of all flesh before that most festive time, when—to the infinite satisfaction of all landlords—universal England drunk did get—

> For joy that Charles, her monarch, was restored.

But his still buxom widow at once took down the old sign of the George, and set up in its place King Charles the Second's Head.

If Clavering's services were not more fully requited, it was his own fault rather than that of his sovereign. Charles endeavoured to persuade him to quit his seclusion and come to court, offering him knighthood. But he was too happy at Ovingdean Grange to leave it, and respectfully declined the honour. By this time he had become, what he continued to remain to the last

A fishing, hawking, hunting. Country Gentleman

THE END.